VICE GRIP

Vice Grip

A NOVEL

BY
Michael J. V. Thomas

ZONE PRESS
Denton, Texas

Vice Grip

A Novel

Copyright 2003 by Michael J. V. Thomas. All rights reserved.

No part of this book may be reproduced or transmitted in any form or by any means, graphic, electronic, or mechanical, including photocopying, recording, taping, or by any information storage retrieval system, without the permission in writing from the publisher.

Zone Press
an imprint of Rogers Publishing and Consulting, Inc.

For information address:
PO Box 474
Nocona, Texas 76255
940-825-3855
info@zonepress.com

Although some characters and events in this book are based on fact, this is a work of fiction.

Printed in the United States of America
ISBN: 0-9727488-3-0

Dedication

This book is dedicated to my consultant, editor, and proofreader. She remains unnamed by choice because of the slight sleaze and explicitness of the manuscript that was in no way her idea. Actual writing is often fun, easy and simple. Her job was not.

Ode To A Vice

From a mélange of roving, waving nasty sows,
Streets swollen with steamers, tankers, filthy cows,
To glory hole booths that rock and thump,
And simpering faggots that pat your rump,
Out to NorthPark to watch 'em whack,
There goes your partner on a fat one's back.
Looking at a porno mag…glared at by Felton,
Havin' a drink with a hooker…at the Hilton,
Don't forget Jackson Street, the pimps, and fairies at the parks.
The glory of fighting a hustler for your pistol in the dark,
But you've learned to work vice with the best.
You've trod on the seamiest side and passed the test.

By TAL

VICE GRIP

CHAPTER 1

The parking lot could accommodate two hundred cars; it surrounded the store on three sides. Adjacent to the rear outer wall of the business, a dilapidated wooden fence separated it from a run-down, rent-by-the-hour motel. The new metal building was nothing more than a large square barn one hundred feet on a side with fifteen-foot-high walls. Inside, a thin layer of insulation was held against the ceiling with chicken wire. Drains were strategically placed in the bare concrete floor so that the entire place could be hosed down when necessary.

The store was divided into three large rooms. Books, magazines, videos, and gadgets encircled the center sales counter and cashier platform. To the left was a theater with seating for at least seventy-five. On the right was an arcade area with fifty booths.

The "In Use" sign above one of the Istanbull Adult Bookstore's arcade booths lit up as Wade Thompson inserted his first quarter. As the timed segment of a pornographic movie flickered onto the stained screen a foot in front of him, he eased open the door and left it ajar. Arcade etiquette dictates that brief eye contact be made prior to entering an occupied booth, and moments before, a sixty-year-old man had given Wade a hungry gaze. Those seeking anonymous man-to-man activity observe this arcade aisle rule of silence to weed out anyone desiring frivolous conversation, instead of serious sex.

As Wade had anticipated, the gap in the thin plywood door soon widened, and the old man squeezed into the booth facing Wade. With two men inside an unventilated three-and-a-half-foot square enclosure, the stench of the old man's "cum breath" became overpowering, and Wade began taking very shallow breaths.

Mistaking Wade's breathing pattern to indicate interest, the old guy brushed Wade's crotch area with one hand, and pushed the door shut with his other. He slithered his back down the booth's wall stopping with his wrinkled face inches from Wade's zipper.

"Anything I can do to please you?" he asked.

Wade pushed the door open, extricated himself, and said, "No, I was just here to watch the movie." Disappointment spread across the old man's face as he rose from his crouched position, and left the booth.

Wade began planning the arrest. One in which no one would get hurt. Creative and experienced vice cops often make safe arrests without alerting anyone in the immediate area that they are working the place. The technique is never mastered; it just works better on some occasions than on others.

Most people tend to stereotype men who frequent adult bookstores as effeminate, docile creatures. Some are. Many are married, or are single bisexuals. A surprising number of these are influential in the business world and community, and highly-educated professionals are well represented among bookstore goers. Wade had personally arrested more than a few teachers, counselors, doctors, dentists, lawyers, and ministers for public lewdness. Men suffering severe, untreated mental disorders were common among the clientele.

When confronted and arrested for performing some vile act on another male, many men see their lifestyle, family position, and reputation crumble before them. Therefore, their immediate reaction is, at best, unpredictable. They may violently resist, attempting to escape. The vice terms 'riding one around the parking lot', and 'there goes your partner on a fat one's back', make humorous reference to very serious and dangerous situations that can arise when a vice detective attempts to arrest a suspect who can become an adrenaline-charged physical powerhouse in an instant.

Wade began his search for his partner, John Forsky. He knew that by prolonging this arrest, he ran the chance of getting beat on the case if his suspect left the premises. He was betting on this schlongmonger hanging around for a while.

Efficiency comes into play here. Including driving time, it may take a pair of detectives two hours or longer to process one prisoner after a simple arrest. Under normal circumstances, handling two prisoners took about the same amount of time.

Forsky sat on the back row in the theater. A man in his late fifties sat next to him, reached into his lap, and "honked" his genitals. "Had your battery charged lately?" he asked.

"I am fully charged, and have no need for your mechanical services," said Forsky. Dejected defendant #2 left to seek greener pastures in the arcade. Twenty seconds later, Forsky and Wade located one another, and worked out an arrest strategy.

"Got one, John?" Wade asked.

"Yeah, real fat guy, about three hundred pounds, brown hair and beige windbreaker. He should be in the arcade now."

"I got an old skinny one," Wade said. "Gray-headed, white shirt, dark slacks…let's get 'em and herd 'em to the car."

Forsky nodded in agreement. "Is yours a fighter?"

"No, he's okay. How about yours?"

"Harmless unless he falls on you." Both detectives walked into the arcade, doing their utmost to watch out for one another as each attempted to locate his respective suspect.

Wade found the old man leaning against a booth, smoking an unfiltered cigarette. He smiled as the officer approached.

"You wanna go outside? I got a van out back that'll give us some privacy," Wade said.

Lecherous grin on his wrinkled face, the man stubbed out his cigarette on the concrete floor, and said, "Lead the way, sir."

Forsky found his man headed toward the exit, and said, " If you still want to hook up that battery charger, let's go out to my van."

Fat man replied, "Sure, honey, but I hope you don't mind if I'm in a hurry. I've got to be back at work soon."

"Fine, let's go," Forsky said, forcing a grin.

Wade, with his suspect in tow, began wandering through the arcade maze, pretending to be a bit lost. Forsky made eye contact with Wade, signaling all was well, and the foursome headed out the door.

Wade and his suspect fell thirty feet behind Forsky and his man, as they left the Istanbull and walked to the back of the parking lot where the detectives' car sat. As everyone rounded the corner of the building, the detectives exchanged a glance, an acknowledgement that the time was right.

Forsky held his open badge case at the suspect's eye level, and told the man, "I'm a police officer, and you're under arrest for public lewdness."

The fat guy's ruddy complexion changed to a dead man's pallor. He swayed with the shock, became unsteady on his feet, and ended up leaning over the hood of an adjacent car, attempting to stabilize himself. Forsky feared the man might be having a heart attack, but he had seen many persons react in a similar manner over the years. No one ever had a heart attack, no one passed out, and the effects were of short duration. To Forsky's relief, the suspect stood up, and Forsky handcuffed him.

As the detective searched the prisoner, the airline employee made the statement that one in five vice suspects make in the first few moments following an arrest, "I knew you were a cop."

In simultaneous process, Wade arrested his defendant, who remained very much at ease. An indignant smirk passed over his face as he remarked, "You must be mistaken. I've never seen you before."

While it seldom works to a suspect's advantage, complete denial is worth a try. It is a tactic born of sheer desperation. There is simply not much in the way of legitimate defenses for a defendant to fall back on. Both suspects, in conclusion, pled guilty as such persons routinely did in ninety-nine percent of these cases.

Noteworthy only in the vice office of the police department, the detectives' two arrests were the first to be made in the Istanbull, the newest flagship schlong parlor in Dallas. These christening arrests on that cool, clear March day in 1997 were mere precursors for the vile events that would occur at the establishment in the years ahead. Men would continue to perform various revolting acts on fellow men at the store. To the vice cops, the fact that the fellow men held no objections to being plundered was of no consequence, since Texas law forbade such behavior in public places.

It was five p.m. when Wade and Forsky completed their paperwork. The prisoners were booked. The detectives' shift would end in an hour. Heavy afternoon traffic precluded going to any of the regular vice haunts, in particular those in the north part of town where the Istanbull and other adult bookstores were located.

When the phone on his desk rang, Wade answered, "Vice. Thompson," all the while hoping the caller would need no vice work done this late in the day.

"Wade, Jan. Are you busy?" fallen woman Jan Doxee said.

"Hi, Jan, have you got something for us?" Wade said with a get-to-the-point inflection. He was tired and in no mood for conversation, but knew that whatever information she had would be worth his effort.

"An escort service…maybe a big one. They advertise in the usual places. All the girls are under thirty. Their office is in a strip shopping center in North Dallas. They have two girls working the phones beginning at four in the afternoon," her voice raced on and on.

Wade easily appraised the situation. Jan Doxee had said

it all when she mentioned that "all the girls are under thirty". She had been scorned in an unmerciful way. The agency had refused to hire her because she was too old. She could hardly file an age discrimination suit against the illegal prostitution business, so she called Wade instead. Regardless of Jan's motives, Wade would look into it. Jan was sober, and when she was sober, she was worth listening to.

Jan Doxee had been an escort service harlot for a number of years, and had also built up a lucrative freelance business on the side. Her clientele included several wealthy, influential middle-aged men in the Dallas area. People could know the woman for years and have no inkling she was a prostitute. Jan was atypical of the breed and discreet to a fault. Few would guess the woman was well into her forties. She was attractive by any standard despite the fact she had suffered from alcoholism and depression for a long time.

The detectives and their boss, Sergeant Talbert Sanderson, became acquainted with Jan when they were working an escort service investigation from a downtown hotel room one night in 1985. Posing as an out-of-town businessman, Wade called the service and requested companionship for the evening. Following the customary lengthy waiting period, Jan Doxee arrived at the officer's room. Wade was prepared with all the right credentials, luggage, and appropriate clothes. Doxee interrogated him in a relentless manner for almost an hour to satisfy herself that Wade was not a cop. In concluding her inquiry, she asked to look at his wallet. He handed her the one he carried just for such occasions. As Doxee's slender hand with perfectly manicured nails grasped the wallet, Wade remembered the court subpoena. As he hurried from the office earlier, the subpoena had been thrust at him by the vice clerk. He had folded it three times to make it fit into the wallet.

Wade cringed as Jan unfolded it twice. Then, to his amazement, she went no further and passed the wallet and the still folded subpoena back to his outstretched hand. He had just managed to pass the most difficult "are you a cop" test ever administered to him. The woman then said all the right things necessary to make a textbook whore case. "Two fold Jan" could have easily been "Three fold Jan" and walked out the door.

Jan Doxee called Wade on occasion providing him with useful information on organized escort service operations. With rare exception, it involved a competitor or an agency that had beaten her out of money. Wade and Forsky made a number of good catches over the years based on Jan Doxee's information. She was shrewd, too shrewd, in fact, and the detectives had to be careful in dealing with her. They were aware of the volume of her business. If what she gave them was only equal to or of lesser magnitude than her own ventures, the detectives would have another undercover cop attempt to make a case on her. This scheme was called into play a few times, but the undercover officer was never able to make a case. Jan became very aware of how the game was played. Wade and Forsky never had to discuss this with her. She knew the consequences could be perilous to her career if she provided less-than-worthwhile information.

Wade interrupted Jan, "Can you get us some names? Who's running the service, the usual stuff, you know."

The woman realized she had been rattling on nonstop, and responded to Wade's cue, "I'll get all the particulars in the next few days. You and John need to get these people. They're ruthless."

"Ruthless" is a word seldom used in describing operators of escort services. They may be shady, despicable, sleazy, or obnoxious, but not ruthless. It was Jan Doxee's way of saying she was humiliated by the insult. Her vindictive manner was the only impetus necessary for her to go to work on it right away. She was a better streetwise detective than many that used the title in an official capacity. Jan had excellent sources that Wade and Forsky would never know about.

Wade glanced over at Forsky and asked, "Ever hear of a service called 'Luscious Lovelies'?"

"No, but someone has an incredible imaginative streak to come up with that one. Are they cutting in on Jan's business or did they beat her out of cash?"

"Worse. They wouldn't hire her because she's too old."

"Ooooh… I wouldn't want to be the owner of that outfit," John stated, well aware of Jan Doxee's vengeful nature.

"Yeah. Looks like she'll do everything but the paperwork on this one. Let's give her a few days to get all the details."

Sgt. Sanderson stuck his head out of his office, gaining the attention of Wade and Forsky. Both detectives were caught leaning back in their chairs, feet propped on their desktops. The policy manual clearly stated that officers "should not lean back in office chairs or place feet on desks", but the sergeant ignored his detectives' unapproved postures. "You guys come in here a minute," he said.

As both detectives squeezed into their boss's tiny office, Sanderson said, "Shut the door, John."

CHAPTER 2

Sanderson did not speak until Forsky closed the door. He had been a vice supervisor more than twenty years, and was respected by the four detectives who worked on his squad. He was fair and very considerate of others. As long as an officer was levelheaded and a hard worker, Sanderson had no concern about whether the subordinate put his feet on a desk. His head was blessed with an abundance of common sense and he relied on this gift. Far too many police supervisors lacked such wisdom and their ineptitude led to supervisory ineffectiveness. Some of these persons displayed a petty and jealous attitude toward good people managers like Tal Sanderson.

"Got a complaint and a request that vice supervision look into alleged harassment of bookstore personnel and prostitutes in the Long Boulevard area by vice detectives," said Sanderson, a look of chagrin on his face as he gazed at the memo. He continued, "I needn't mention this came from Raeburn Compton's office."

All three looked at one another with the same stare of disgust they shared every time one of these memos came from the community activist, shakedown artist, and amateur politician.

Forsky had long since tired of hearing himself repeat his standard response to the accusations, but he could think of nothing original to say. "We've got to do something about this guy. He's bonin' the whores, he hangs out in the bars and shakes down the owners, he gets free movies from the bookstores. Who knows what other stuff he's involved in. His criminality is no secret."

Raeburn Compton informally represented a part of Dallas that was vice-infested and he wanted to keep it that way. Decent people resided in the area, but they were old now. They had bought homes when it was a nice, upscale neighborhood. These persons could not afford to move. Instead, they watched property values plummet as they picked up vice trash in their yards: beer cans, used rubbers, and bloody syringes from the night before. This was not a Raeburn Compton concern, however. He had far more interest in stopping off at the Little Sweden to pick up a complimentary fetish video. His personal favorites dealt with foot or enema eroticism.

The FBI knew about Compton and had given his activities a cursory glance. Compton was powerful to a frightening degree not only within his own community but within the entire city. He was an ignorant loudmouth that had the support of a scary number of others who shared his views on the perpetuation of a deadbeat society. Criminals and want-something-for-nothing voters saw Raeburn Compton as a savior.

"I know, I know," said Sanderson, "but we've got to go through the motions again unless someone can come up with a better idea."

Thompson thought he had the better idea when he said, "Why not introduce Raeburn Compton to Charlene?"

All three smiled in unison with the shared belief that such a relationship might go a long way toward the conversion of slimy Raeburn into a righteous, civic-minded politico.

CHAPTER 3

Thompson and Forsky began a random observation of Compton for the next week. They did not find it necessary to go very far out of their way to do it, either. The detectives and the activist all spent a lot of time in the same part of town, immersing themselves in various vice activities. While Thompson and Forsky were assigned to work days, they came in for a couple of hours at night several times during the week. There was little variance in Compton's routine. Mornings were spent in his office. He ate lunch around noon. Mid-afternoon found him on Long Boulevard, making the rounds of the bookstores and beer joints. Compton went home around five and always had dinner with his wife. By seven, he had a second wind and was beckoned to the Long Boulevard area again.

One night near the end of the week, Thompson and Forsky noticed Compton's Lincoln parked in front of a room at one of the fleabag motels on Long, the Hollywood. The detectives were familiar with Compton's regular motel haunt and this was not it. Perhaps the Hollywood also provided the politician with a free room for periodic whore therapy?

"Let's wait a while and see what he's up to," Thompson said.

Frustrated, Forsky remarked, "We know what he's up to, Wade. He's in that room ravaging some street whore, but I'm curious to see who he's ravaging. We might know her."

It was after nine when the officers parked across the street from the motel. At ten, just as they were going to call it a night,

Raeburn Compton walked out of the room. His shirttail was out and he fumbled trying to get his car door unlocked and opened.

"John, he must have gotten drunk and fallen asleep. If he was with a whore she left before we got here," Thompson said.

"Wait a minute, Wade! Who's that?" Forsky remarked, the excitement in his voice mounting.

Using binoculars, both officers were staring at the diminutive figure walking from the room to Compton's car. Despite being two hundred yards away, a dim motel porch light provided just enough illumination for the detectives to determine that the girl was not a regular Long Boulevard prostitute.

Forsky said in amazement, "Looks about twelve years old to me. That old bastard has grandkids older than that!"

Thompson was also astounded as he replied, "I don't know if she's twelve, but she's pretty young. Dressed like a whore though."

Maybe five feet tall, the girl could not have weighed more than ninety pounds. She wore a black top, short black skirt, and black knee-length shiny boots.

Thompson said, "Raeburn looks drunk to me. Do you want to get a squad to stop him when he hits the street? Maybe they can DWI him."

"Let's do it, and we can get the girl ID'ed, too," Forsky added.

Thompson said, "Hold on. Looks like they're arguing or something."

The officers attempted to monitor the situation as best they could with binoculars and no soundtrack. Raeburn Compton stood on the driver's side of his car with the girl standing next to the front passenger door. After a few moments, Raeburn walked back into the room and slammed the door. The young girl walked toward the street.

Forsky said, "Well, it looks like Raeburn's going to spend

the night in the room. He told the girl to take a hike, and she's mighty pissed at the idea."

Thompson replied, "We still need to find out who she is. A girl that young has got to be a runaway."

Forsky was already strategy planning when he said, "Let's try her together. That kid couldn't be very streetwise."

"Okay, let's get her," Thompson said.

The miniature whore was about a block from the motel entrance when Thompson pulled up next to her. The girl glared at Forsky as he asked, "Are you dating?"

The little girl rattled off her menu of bodily services like a bored waitress, concluding with, "For both of you, it'll cost more."

Forsky told her, "Straight lay's fine, young lady, but twenty-five each is too much. We'll give you twenty each."

Thompson chimed in so he could also take credit for the case, "Yeah. We'll give you twenty for a straight."

"Okay," she said, with no discernible disappointment about the price reduction.

Her lack of street savvy was evident as she got in the vehicle at Thompson's invitation, voluntarily seating herself between two strange men. Both officers glanced at one another, an indication they were ready to make the arrest. Thompson had his ID and badge in his left hand outside of the girl's view. With his right hand, he grabbed the prostitute's left wrist, as Forsky took firm hold of her right wrist.

Thompson displayed the badge and ID as he told her, "We're police officers and you're under arrest, small lady, for prostitution."

The girl began crying hysterically. Thompson noticed her wrists were so tiny that they would easily slip out of handcuffs. She did not pose a threat to either detective, but they held on to her until she could compose herself. She relaxed somewhat, but the tears were still streaming.

As they relinquished their grips, Thompson asked the girl, "What's your name and how old are you?"

Thompson was most curious about her age.

In a most mature manner, the young hooker said, "My name is Tonya Johnson, and I'm fifteen. I'm a runaway."

"Where are you from, Tonya?" Forsky asked.

Tonya replied, "Oh, I live in Dallas, always have. This has happened three or four times before…me running away and getting arrested for whoring," she continued. "You can check, but I'm sure my folks reported me missing."

"How long have you been gone from home this time?" Thompson asked.

Tonya answered, "About a week, maybe."

As they were driving away from the arrest location, Thompson told the girl, "We'll take you to Youth and the people there will call your folks to pick you up."

"I don't mean any disrespect, sir, but I know how all this works from here. Like I told you, this isn't the first time for me," Tonya said.

Thompson and Forsky avoided any mention of Raeburn Compton. They were well aware that a few things needed discussing before they approached the girl regarding the man. Chances were good she did not even know him.

When they arrived at the Youth Division, the detectives did some preliminary paperwork that was only a portion of what was required for an adult prisoner. Kids were not placed in jail; usually they were released to their folks. Should they be charged with something serious, like murder, they would be held in a county juvenile detention facility.

A Youth Division detective called Tonya Johnson's parents. They agreed to pick up their daughter as soon as possible. Tonya was placed in a holding room alone.

Thompson looked at Forsky and said, "John, we may

as well approach her now about Raeburn Compton, don't you think?"

"We had better do it before her folks show up," Forsky replied, "if she does happen to know him, this might be a bit touchy, though."

The detectives went into the holding room. Tonya Johnson was seated on a wooden bench that had at least twenty coats of paint on it, no doubt to cover years of foul graffiti. She stared at the floor. In a moment, she raised her head in slow motion. She said nothing, but forced a smile. There were no chairs in the room; Thompson and Forsky leaned against a wall.

"Tonya, we're not here to counsel you. We'd like to ask you a few questions. Understand?" Thompson asked.

She replied, "Sure, but there's not much to tell. You want to know why I run away all the time, and if I have a pimp, and if I'm on drugs, that kind of stuff, right?"

"Well, yeah, that's a start," Forsky said.

Tonya spurted out her story, "I'm fifteen, I been having sex since I was twelve, and my parents are very strict. We don't get along well. They're both high school teachers. They love me, and all that, but I get tired of them and have to leave. My cousin, Wilma Washington, is a street girl and she's been one a long time. I stay with her some when I run off. I don't have no pimp, but Wilma does."

Thompson interrupted the girl to ask, "Tonya, that man you were with at the motel, right before we picked you up. Do you know him?"

"Why you want to know that?" she asked, becoming defensive for the first time.

The detectives looked at one another as they shared the same thought: she knows Raeburn Compton!

Thompson said, "Tonya, it's a felony for that man to have sex with a fifteen year-old girl, if he knows she's fifteen."

"I look a lot older than fifteen, everybody tells me that.

Some tricks think I'm twenty."

"No, you don't look older to anyone, Tonya, and they don't tell you that you do. I thought you were about twelve," Forsky said.

Thompson tried again, "You were very open and truthful when we first began talking. Now it's evident you're trying to hide the fact that you know the man from the motel. What's the deal here, anyway?"

Tonya Johnson's lack of experience as a petty criminal was showing. Much of her conscience was intact, providing an advantage for the detectives. Her bearing began to weaken.

"So what if I do know him, what's that got to do with anything?"

Forsky was becoming impatient and told the girl, "Tonya, we'll ask the questions, understand?"

A long silence ensued as Tonya stared at the floor for a second time. When she looked up, there were tears in her eyes. She gazed at the wall, and her mouth opened and closed, but nothing came out. Turning toward the officers, she asked, "Do y'all know who that man was?"

Thompson replied, "Yes, we know him."

"Okay," she said, tears drying, "I'm scared of him. I've known him for a while. My family knows him, too."

Thompson hoped she would have a lot to say about Raeburn Compton. However, it was apparent she was afraid of the man.

"How did you and your family get to know this man?"

"Like I said before, my folks teach school. In the summer when school's out, my daddy builds cabinets. He's real good at it. He has a shop behind our house. Raeburn Compton lived close to us then. He was redoing his house and he had daddy build him some cabinets. It took daddy half the summer to make what that man wanted. He used to come over all the time to watch daddy work."

The girl paused, and Forsky questioned her, "Did Raeburn Compton ever touch you in an inappropriate way during these visits? Do you understand what I'm asking?"

Indicating she felt more at ease, Tonya grinned and replied, "Yeah, I know what you're talking about. I'm a prostitute, remember? I'm just not a very smart one. That old man never touched me then, but he wanted to. I remember the way he looked at me. That's why he came over all the time. He didn't care about those cabinets. My daddy was always around, so he couldn't make a move."

"When did you say this happened?" asked Thompson.

"Two or three summers ago, I guess. My daddy would know for sure. Mr. Compton was a politician-type man then, too," she replied.

Forsky asked her, "How many times have you had sex with Raeburn Compton?"

Tonya had been prepared for the question and her answer sounded rehearsed, "Four times counting tonight. Every time I've run away in the last year, and we always go to that same motel room on Long."

"Does he pay you?" Thompson asked.

"Twenty dollars. Most of the time I get more than that from tricks, but I'm afraid to ask Raeburn for more. Really, I don't ask him for money anyway, he just gives me twenty. I hear other girls are too scared to even charge him," she said.

Through the large glass panel in the holding room, Thompson could see a couple in the front of the office speaking to the deskman on duty. They were in their early forties and well dressed. Thompson and Forsky left the holding room to meet Tonya's parents.

"Mr. and Mrs. Johnson, I'm Wade Thompson and this is John Forsky," Thompson said. Everyone shook hands and exchanged greetings.

Mrs. Johnson asked, "Is Tonya okay? She's not hurt or

anything, is she?"

Forsky's answered with assurance, "She's fine. Tonya's in need of a meal and some clean clothes, but she's fine."

"Tell you what, folks... why don't you go in that room and visit with your daughter for a few minutes. When you're through, we'd like to speak with both of you," Thompson accommodated the anxious parents.

Mrs. Johnson replied in earnest as she and her husband approached the holding room, "Officers, we'd be happy to meet with you, in fact we expect you to tell us what's been going on."

Once the couple was in the room with their daughter, Thompson asked Forsky, "How do you want to handle this, John? They know she's been whoring, but they may not know Raeburn Compton's been pounding their little girl."

"We'd have to take whatever action we could against any other suspect in a case like this. It's not like we're doing selective enforcement against Raeburn Compton. It's just that we've got Compton identified," Forsky said.

Thompson replied, "The difficult part will be getting Tonya Johnson to write an affidavit on Compton, but I think her folks will be all for it."

Forsky was unsure about the parents. "Let's just tell them what we've got and see how they react. Maybe they can influence Tonya if she balks at the idea. Here they come now."

The detectives led the parents into an unoccupied office.

When everyone was seated, Thompson said, "Your daughter was actually arrested for prostitution, but because of her age she'll only be charged as a runaway, if you can even call that a charge. She's being released to you. We understand from Tonya that you folks are familiar with the procedure."

Everyone forced a smile.

"I guess it's no secret that our daughter has some serious personal problems. We've tried to deal with this for more than a year now with no success," Mrs. Johnson said.

Forsky asked, "Have you sought professional help for Tonya?"

"As a matter of fact, we have…twice," said Mr. Johnson, a look of disappointment on his face. "Neither person we consulted was effective, and I think one of them had more problems than our daughter."

Thompson knew it was time to get to the point and said, "We have identified a man that your daughter had sex with this evening; Tonya knows him and you both know him. To prosecute this man, Tonya will have to write a detailed affidavit regarding their relationship and the several times they have had sex. She would have to be willing to testify against him in court, if necessary. Would you want to discuss this with her before we do?"

Mr. Johnson caught everyone off guard when he blurted out the question to the detectives, "Is it Raeburn Compton?"

Mrs. Johnson's head jerked up so quickly that Thompson feared she would fall from her chair. The expression on her face indicated that her husband had never mentioned his suspicions about Compton to her.

Mrs. Johnson asked her husband, "Robert, why have you never said anything about this? How could you keep it from me? She's my daughter, too, you know!"

"Dorothy, I didn't want to see you hurt any more than you already were," he replied in apology.

Thompson asked Mr. Johnson, "Can you explain to us how this suspicion of Raeburn Compton came about?"

"I did some work for him a few years ago. Tonya spent a lot of time in my shop during the summer. Compton came over and he'd just stare at her. I tried to dismiss this from my mind. I suffer from anxiety anyway. Then after the first time Tonya ran off, a good friend of mine who owns a garage on Long Boulevard told me he thought he saw Tonya out there one evening when he was closing up. He said he thought she got in a Lincoln with

Raeburn Compton. My suspicions don't do anyone much good right now, do they?" Mr. Johnson said.

"Mrs. Johnson looked at her husband and said in an angry tone, "I cannot believe you never told me any of this."

As Johnson searched for words of justification to console his wife, Thompson told the couple, "The man can be prosecuted. It all depends on what you and your daughter want to do."

As she stared a hole through Robert Johnson, Dorothy Johnson was quick with a firm response, "We will do whatever it takes and so will Tonya."

Mr. Johnson made it clear that he was more than a little reluctant to prosecute the man when he said, "Raeburn Compton's powerful in our neighborhood and all over town. He does things that aren't quite right and so do the thugs he's got working for him. He knows where we live; we can't afford any retaliation if we go through with this."

Dorothy Johnson was appalled at her husband's wormy response. "Robert, I can't believe you would want to let that old bastard get off free. Don't be afraid of that old man, think of our daughter, not just yourself!"

Mrs. Johnson looked at Thompson and Forsky and said with fierce determination, "Let me talk to my daughter alone, my sissy husband can stay right in here."

A humiliated Robert Johnson was silent. Thompson knew that this strong woman would be far more effective in persuading her daughter than he or Forsky could ever be. Forsky led her into the holding room.

Robert Johnson told Thompson, "There are issues here that my wife has given no consideration to, and, yes, I'm afraid to go through with any prosecution. I'd advise my daughter against it, too."

After only a few minutes, Mrs. Johnson stormed out of the holding room. She was visibly upset by her daughter's response. Tonya did not want to prosecute Raeburn Compton. The whole family was riled up and everyone was tired. The detectives could only hope that, given time, Dorothy Johnson could persuade her family to do what was right. The detectives walked to the elevator with the Johnson family.

As the Johnsons stepped into the elevator, Thompson told Mrs. Johnson, "Talk this over after everyone has rested. Let us know what you decide. We will do whatever we can to make this as painless as possible, if you choose to prosecute."

As an afterthought that might appeal to the family's civic-mindedness, Forsky said, "Your effort in terms of prosecution may prevent this man from doing the same thing to someone else's daughter."

Mrs. Johnson shook her head in discouragement and replied, "I'll see what I can do. Thank you both very much."

As the elevator door closed, Forsky, the pragmatist, told Thompson, the optimist, "No way we'll see Compton prosecuted for this."

"I'm not holding my breath, but I think Dorothy might be pretty persuasive. We'll see," Thompson said.

The next day, Thompson and Forsky worked their normal ten to six shift. They had been out of the office all day. When they returned after five, there was a message for either detective to call Mrs. Johnson.

Upon noticing the message, Forsky held it up and told Thompson," We're fixing to find out what the Johnsons want to do."

Thompson stood by Forsky's desk, waiting as John dialed the number.

"Mrs. Johnson, this is John Forsky. Has your family made a decision?" He waited for her response, then answered, "No, I don't understand. I know you're making a mistake, but I'm required to respect your wishes. Reluctant complainant and witnesses seldom result in successful prosecutions. Thank you for calling. If you change your minds, call me back," Forsky said as he hung up.

The detectives looked at one another and Thompson said, "I guess that's the end of that."

Forsky said, "Wade, those people are scared to death of that man. Mrs. Johnson didn't sound nearly as courageous just now as she did last night."

Thompson slumped into his desk chair. He didn't care to discuss the matter further.

CHAPTER 4

Like many detectives, Thompson and Forsky did not have an office in the true sense of the word. Every vice detective did have, however, two drawers on one side or the other of an ancient metal desk. Four desks were in the ten-by-fourteen foot squad room that was used by eight detectives on each of two shifts. In a typical twenty-four hour period, each desk had four assigned occupants, not to mention the various prostitutes, pimps, hustlers, schlongmongers, pornographers, bookies, and other forms of human sediment that might take up temporary abode before being booked into jail. During the course of a busy night shift, a dozen people might be in the tiny room at one time. The inefficient air-conditioning system in the 1910-era police headquarters building was to blame for the lingering foul odors, some of which defied identification.

Few vice cops spent much time in the office unless they had to be there. Prisoners and case-filing paperwork were the main reasons that officers would come in during a shift.

John Forsky had given more thought to locating Charles Williams than had Wade Thompson. Known by most folks as "Charlene", the female impersonator had been used as an informant by the detectives on many occasions. Charlene was always difficult to locate, unless he was in jail. Forsky had already checked into that possibility with negative results. Most prostitutes worked the same neighborhood for years, but Charlene worked all over town.

Thompson appeared at the office at exactly 10:00 A.M. For years, he had arrived early and sometimes even did a little work before it was necessary. Forsky was always early and always working. Thompson still enjoyed his job, just not as much as he once did. The only complaint he had with Forsky as a partner was when the two worked evenings, 6:00 P.M. to 2:00 A.M. every other month. If they finished with a prisoner at 1:00 A.M., Forsky would suggest going out to "snag" one more. More often than not, this meant cruising the streets within blocks of the office where male prostitutes, more commonly known as "hustlers", plied their trade until dawn. This last arrest sometimes made the night a long one. Perhaps the booty bandit was less than a good sport when arrested and preferred to fight in an escape attempt. Any injury to an officer and / or prisoner meant additional time and paperwork.

Hustlers were collectively the most dangerous of prostitutes. Opportunists, they preyed on frail, shy, and lonesome male homosexuals who had difficulty in establishing relationships by more conventional means. Such street creeps sometimes beat and robbed customers, most often forlorn victims that took hustlers home with them for the night. A characteristic hustler murder victim might be stabbed and slashed many times. Often when an offense like this occurred, it would be in a decent to affluent neighborhood. Most hustlers were drug users. They lived on the streets and had all sorts of foul diseases. Desperate, dangerous, nasty folks, these hustlers.

As Thompson sat behind a desk, he looked over at Forsky and said with no emotion, "John."

Forsky glanced at Thompson and said, "Wade," completing their morning ritualistic greeting.

Forsky wore a short-sleeved powder blue leisure suit with a mismatched maroon tie and two-tone brown and beige patent leather loafers. A wide perforated white leather belt completed the outdated ensemble.

"I see you've been to court today," said Thompson, grinning. Forsky had indeed been to court earlier that morning. He was well aware of the attention his outlandish attire brought him in a judicial setting. Should he be called upon to testify, the detective appeared to an unknowing defense attorney to be the ultimate simpleton. Forsky was an excellent witness, however. Many prosecutors and judges alike shared a hushed admiration for the detective's courtroom craftiness.

Forsky ignored Wade's dig at his attire. "One of the guys working nights saw Charlene last week down on South Lamar," he said. "Supposed to be living in a car behind one the Mexican beer joints."

Mexican illegal aliens were a favorite target for prostitutes. Wetbacks were easy to rob when they were drunk and they seldom reported anything to the police.

Thompson said, "Let's go down there now and look around. Wherever Charlene is, he'll be asleep for at least another hour or two."

Forsky was out of his chair before Thompson finished the sentence. They left headquarters and took their routine three-block trek to the city garage where most police vehicles were parked and serviced. The 1930's two-story concrete structure housed marked and unmarked police cars, undercover cars, and the police motorcycle fleet. Vice, intelligence, and narcotics kept undercover cars on the top floor, along with the department's wrecked vehicles, salvaged parts, and junk. Nothing parked on the second level could be seen from the street.

Undercover cars came from a variety of sources. Some were rented, others had been seized from criminals, and a few had been abandoned and came from the police automobile pound. Many of the derelict vehicles were dangerous to drive.

At the city garage, Thompson raised the hood of the old

Pontiac to make sure the linkage for the standard shift transmission was not stuck in place, as was often the case. Forsky got behind the wheel. The steering column ignition switch had been broken years before when an inept thief attempted to steal the former cab. Neither detective was mechanically inclined, but they had rigged up a workable solution using a switch under the dash. A wire from the switch traveled across the bottom of the dashboard then up the post that separated the windshield from the vent window on the driver's side. A beer bottle cap had been epoxied onto a spring-loaded starter button. Following some vigorous accelerator pumping, Forsky turned on the switch on with his right hand, using his left index finger to depress the bottle cap. The Pontiac started, just like it always had, and the detectives headed toward South Dallas.

South Lamar Street was on the outer edge of a blighted and crime-infested neighborhood. The businesses that remained in the area were mostly liquor stores, beer joints, and scrap metal yards. During pre-World War II days, much of South Dallas had been a wealthy Jewish community. Evidence of its original opulence remained in the form of several decaying mansions on a few area streets. Missing a wall, roof, or some other component of structural soundness, such a dwelling might still house a tenant from time to time, though not the type who had possessions or paid rent.

These ruins fascinated Wade Thompson. He very much enjoyed driving slowly through this part of town, imagining what it had been like in the 1930's and '40's. Several wealthy families had saved a few of the homes through meticulous restoration. For their efforts, historical status had been granted by the City of Dallas to a few blocks on one street.

Buildings that once housed Italian-owned grocery stores were on a number of corners. Most had crimson brick exteriors. They were tiny compared to present-day counterparts. Now they were second-hand stores or used tire shops.

Male and female prostitutes worked the South Lamar neighborhood day and night. John Forsky, ever the efficient operator, could not feature driving through the locale without making an arrest or two. Most arrests meant a court subpoena. Court appearances often meant overtime. It was quite typical for one case to be reset five or six times before a defendant would plead guilty or request a trial. Frugal Forsky tried to make a living on overtime earnings alone, and had been successful at it for years.

"Let's try to snag a couple on the way back," Forsky said.

Thompson agreed conditionally, "If you'll find a couple of docile ones."

South Dallas prostitutes sometimes behaved like hustlers when arrested. They did not handle things like arrests well. It was common to arrest one that had served one or more penitentiary terms. For many prostitutes, working South Dallas was desperation of the last resort. Forty- and fifty-year-old street whores could still find work, however. Decades of dope, jail, pimps, violence, depravity, and overall poor health takes a lot out of anyone. Many of the hookers still performed their own stunts as well, like jumping from a moving car to escape a deranged customer or suspected vice cop.

Five Hispanic bars lined a three-block stretch of South Lamar. Four of them had junked cars behind them. Thompson exited the Pontiac, and Forsky followed. They walked around, peering through windshields and opening doors of the junkers. An overpowering stench of human waste and rotting food permeated the area. The presence of used condoms and syringes added to the ambience of the typical and hazardous neighborhood scene.

"Hope there's not a dead body in any of these," Forsky remarked. Thompson had never been comfortable around corpses, despite the fact that he had seen his share. Forsky did not want to be burdened with the discovery of a stiff for a different reason. It would mean having to wait on homicide and crime scene people when he could better spend his time doing vice work.

Behind the last bar was a Chevrolet pickup from the 'fifties and a once-yellow school bus of similar vintage. The bus had been converted in a less-than-professional manner into a motorhome. A welded pipe framework extended from the rear of the vehicle to create a back porch complete with railings and a severely warped plywood awning. A recycled orange extension cord covered with black electrical tape ran from the driver's vent window to an outlet on an exterior wall of the bar.

Thompson yelled, "Charlene, are you in there?" There was no response. Forsky found a foot-long piece of heavy rebar on the ground.

"Wonder if this was a murder weapon?" Forsky commented as he picked it up and struck the side of the bus.

An enraged voice said, "Who's out there? What do you want?"

Forsky responded, "It's Forsky and Thompson. We need to talk to you, Charlene."

Charlene said, "Come on in, boys, but let me tell you I'm naked!"

As Forsky tried to open the door of the decrepit bus, Thompson drew the line at Charlene's response and said, "No, put something on, Charlene."

Charlene replied with disappointment, "Okay, I'm slipping into something. Give me a minute."

The mere thought of an unclad Charlene was something Thompson found most repulsive. After Forsky took a second to contemplate such a sight, he was in silent agreement with his partner and stood back from the bus.

Charlene opened the door and was in a big hurry to get the two vice cops inside.

"You boys get on in here. I don't want the neighbors to think I'm doing nasties before lunchtime," Charlene said.

Charlene was forty-two, but could pass for fifty-five. Just under six feet tall, he was thin with a medium-dark complexion. His facial hair was sparse and he only shaved every few days. Charlene's pronounced Adam's apple and his size twelve feet gave him away, just as they did so many other he-shes. Despite these obvious features, Charlene was very effeminate. His voice sounded like a woman's, not a man trying to sound like a woman. Charlene had at least fifty arrests for prostitution over the last twenty years, and had served pen time for murder following the stabbing death of his unfaithful drug-dealing lover.

The detectives were distracted for a moment and surprised at the interior hominess of the bus. It was clean. Before Thompson or Forsky could muster a response, Charlene asked in a suspicious way, "What do you all want, anyway? I know this ain't no social call, much as I'd like it to be."

Survival in the vice world required a shrewd and businesslike demeanor not only from the detectives' standpoint, but also from Charlene's as an informant. A less defensive posture for either side opened the door to very real and often unseen dangers, not to mention general ineffectiveness. This in no way negated having a caring attitude and compassion for fellow man. Adversaries could and should treat one another with dignity; success and productivity demanded it.

All this required delicate handling for everything to work in a smooth manner. Some cops and criminals interpret general decency to humankind as a weakness. Without knowing it, they place self-imposed limitations on their level of effectiveness. Two of the most common explanations are inexperience and a "tough guy" attitude developed from basic ignorance with an unrealized craving to remain ignorant.

Along similar lines, many civilians fail to understand an apparent harsh and uncharitable attitude that police officers exhibit toward criminals and, quite often, citizenry in general. Some cops make irreverent and cruel remarks regarding a person's unfortunate predicament. They may demonstrate a basic lack of care and concern for everyone. They want those around them, be they cops or non-cops, to make no mistake about their stance on an issue. To worsen matters, a constant display of negativism affects every aspect of their lives, which indeed must be quite miserable for them and those that must be around them.

Why, in a "helping" profession is such a despicable attitude so prevalent? A primary reason again is an exhibition of strength. It is the easy way out; any hint of weakness is masked. Having a positive attitude and treating people in a decent manner is the preferred method. However, this is a developed trait and one that many cops, criminals, and people in general, never master.

Dealing with destitute, deranged, diseased, perverted, addicted, evil, and miserable humans on a daily basis affects one. A natural emotional release for many in law enforcement work is to joke about the wretched persons and their wretched situations. While on the surface this gives all the appearances of cruel treatment, often no harm is intended and it serves to ward off depressive emotions that officers may otherwise experience. This would make them no less willing to help someone in need of assistance. In actual fact, such cops are better prepared to deal with the pains and perils of humanity.

Charlene, Forsky, and Thompson all understood and played this complicated game with infinite skill, even if their street protocol was lacking in other areas.

"Charlene, we've got a job for you," Forsky said.

Charlene's reply began with his pseudo-civic-minded anything-for-law-enforcement stance, "Be glad to help out... BUT, you got to do something with my new case. I picked it up last month."

"Straight whore case?" Thompson inquired.

Charlene answered, "Straight AND simple."

Forsky and Thompson looked at each other in agreement and Forsky said, "We'll do it, plus one."

Prostitution cases were misdemeanors. They could be dropped as a matter of routine by the district attorney's office upon recommendation by vice detectives. Worthwhile information and/or an arrest in a case more serious than the one to be dismissed were required. Forsky and Thompson usually traded two for one with Charlene. Charlene would do Raeburn Compton and provide information on another felony offense that would result in a clearance and an arrest.

Thompson asked Charlene, "You know Raeburn Compton?"

Charlene responded, "Well, sort of. He made goo-goo eyes at me a few times in the bars on Long Boulevard, but we ain't never become intimate in a social way. He knows I'd charge him just like I do any other customer. A lot of the ladies don't make him pay. Raeburn Compton thinks me and Hormonee Caruthers are real girls with all the right parts and everything."

Hormonee Caruthers' true name was Archie Caruthers, but no one except his mother called him Archie. To everyone else he had been "Hormonee" since a botched sex-change operation left some personal parts somewhat disfigured. Hormonee was less effeminate than Charlene, but some naïve tricks thought they were both women, something difficult for a vice cop to imagine.

"Just how am I supposed to do Raeburn Compton?" Charlene asked.

With the scenario well-planned in his head, Forsky instructed Charlene. "Lately, he's been in the LoRent bar every night for at least an hour or two. Get friendly with him, have a drink or two, but don't be aggressive. Let him make all the moves and suggestions. When he picks up a whore, he takes her across the street to the Downtown Uptown #3 Motel. He keeps the key to room #8. It's his room for whore dates and the motel doesn't rent it out. Next door is a storage room. We'll be in there filming through the louvers in the wall heater. Just make sure you're both naked. Stay on the bed and face the heater for a minute or two.

Now, don't take his billfold or anything else."

"Is that it, boys?" Charlene asked with obvious disgust. Charlene did not care to be told how to do something that he considered himself adept at doing.

The detectives stared at one another and tried to think of any overlooked detail.

Thompson replied, "Yeah, that's pretty much it. We start working evenings on April first, day after tomorrow. We'll do it at eight that evening, so we'll pick you up at seven-thirty. If for some reason he's not at the bar, we'll do it Friday night."

"I'll be ready," Charlene said, his voice devoid of any enthusiasm.

Charlene not only had to follow someone else's instructions, he had to do things when they wanted it done. Not at all the way Charlene preferred to work. For the most part, however, Charlene did as he was told. For the most part…

Much to Forsky's disappointment, there were no prostitutes to be found anywhere on South Lamar after the detectives left Charlene's place. The master of efficiency had planned a couple of pre-lunch arrests that were not going to materialize. Realizing this, a feeling of relief swept over Thompson. He sank back into the Pontiac's passenger seat, and stared silently out the window, his mind's eye restoring the South Lamar ruins.

CHAPTER 5

John Forsky, originally from the northeast, had been in Texas most of his life and spoke with a befitting Texas accent. At forty-seven, he had spent twenty-five years with the Dallas Police Department. Except for the mandatory three years working as a patrol cop, his entire career had been in vice. John was educated, very intelligent, and well read. He worked hard and played hard. Forsky had a long-time girl friend, but had never married. He had no use for lazy and incompetent people and felt a genuine obligation to make such persons aware of their objectionable character should they not already know it. Forsky had a reputation as being abrasive and uncaring; those who knew him well knew otherwise. No one could fault his work.

Wade Thompson, fifty, was a life-long Texan who had been with the department twenty-nine years. Twenty-six of those had been spent doing vice work. He had been married to the same wife for twenty-four years. Thompson enjoyed working, but did not thrive on it in the way Forsky did. His biggest fault, one that everyone made light of, was a fanatical attention to detail in his paperwork. He took great pleasure in filing complicated case reports, spending far too much time composing descriptive narratives and summaries. This worked to advantage for the partners, since Forsky detested paperwork of any sort. Both detectives had similar Republican/Catholic upbringings. Both were creative in their approaches to vice work. Neither was beyond raking his fingernails through wheel bearing grease and wearing filthy work clothes to make vice cases, should the situation warrant such measures.

As Forsky parked in front of a Mexican restaurant, Thompson grimaced at his pager's irritating beep. Thompson saw as a nemesis any device that functioned with a beep, bell, horn, whistle, buzzer, or alarm. The detective thought the absence of modern electronic communication contrivances would be a welcome luxury that the people of this planet may never again experience. With the exception of the fish locator on his bass boat, Forsky was in general agreement on the issue. Thompson seldom gave his pager number to anyone. After working hours, he turned the pager off and left it in a desk drawer. He refused to be a slave to a gadget, despite the fact that most of his co-workers were.

From the greasy phone outside the restaurant, Thompson called Tal Sanderson's office number. Sanderson did not page or call someone for trifling purposes.

"Vice, Sergeant Sanderson."

Thompson asked, "Tal, you need something?"

"Yeah, Wade. Have you all found Charlene yet?" Sanderson inquired.

Thompson acknowledged, "Sure did. We've got things set up for Thursday evening."

"Good, good. Can you and John be here around five-thirty? I need a rundown on this, " Sanderson said.

"We'll be there."

After lunch, Thompson and Forsky drove in the direction of the Dallas County Sheriff's Office to pick up some mug shots of several heathens who were known Raeburn Compton associates. As they were just blocks away from the county facility, traffic in all three of Trade Street's southbound lanes slowed almost to a standstill, unusual for early afternoon.

"Must be a wreck up ahead," Forsky remarked, as he tried

without success to maneuver from the middle to the faster moving inside lane. Thompson rolled down the window and craned his neck to see what the problem might be.

He exclaimed, "John, there's no wreck. It's Skunk Woman out in the street trying to wave down customers."

Skunk Woman, an infamous Dallas street prostitute, earned her street name not only from the four-inch silver stripe that ran vertically through her long black hair, but also for her personal brand of body odor.

"Might as well see if we can make a case on her," Forsky said. "She's gonna get run over or cause a wreck, if she stays out there."

Thompson replied, "It's the humanitarian thing to do for her, alright, but not for us."

The fifty-three-year-old Skunk Woman stood in the street proper, just off the curb forcing motorists to veer around her, causing the congestion. Forsky pulled the Pontiac alongside the woman, and stopped, making the traffic jam much worse. Horns were honking as the Skunk tried to open Thompson's locked door.

"You fellers looking for a date?" she asked with alcohol-bolstered confidence in her voice.

Thompson replied, "We sure are, but only with a woman that looks as good as you do."

Skunk Woman smiled, revealing dark, rotted teeth. While she was not intoxicated, she had definitely consumed her first few of the day. Thompson opened the door and stepped out, offering the middle of the seat to the old hooker. The traffic jam dissolved as Thompson closed his door, and Forsky gunned the Pontiac.

All business now, Skunk Woman said, "I'll do a half-and-half on each one of you for thirty dollars."

"No, twenty for a half-and-half," Forsky said. He preferred to haggle over price, even though he wasn't spending a dime. The cornered Skunk agreed to the terms.

"That'll be okay. Let's go someplace."

Forsky said, "Now that's twenty altogether, right? Ten dollars each."

A furious Skunk Woman replied, "Hell, no! It's twenty dollars each. I'm not running a charity. You know I'm worth it, anyhow."

Forsky attempted no more haggling. Had Thompson not been present, however, he would have persisted in getting a lower price.

Skunk began rummaging in her large purse, and retrieved cheese crackers and a tin of sardines from its depths. "You all don't mind if I eat while we ride, do you?"

After placing a sardine in her mouth, she grabbed a few crackers to munch on. The sight of the orange cracker residue mixed with the sardine slime on Skunk's fingers, the smell of the mixture, and of Skunk Woman herself, made Thompson's stomach turn. He noticed her long fingernails stored an abundance of cracker dust mixed with sardine oil from days gone by. The Skunk picked up a greasy, red shop cloth from the floorboard and wiped at her hands and the dribble on her chin.

Forsky, unable to stifle a grin, was very aware of his fastidious partner's discomfort. The grin shifted to Thompson's face, however, when Skunk tossed the empty cracker package and sardine can through Forsky's open window. Cracker crumbs flew back into Forsky's face, and sardine juice slopped into his lap.

Forsky asked, "You want to go to our hotel room? We're staying downtown."

"Fine with me," replied the elderly hooker.

The detectives often used this ploy with success. An old hotel was located across the street from the police building. When Thompson and Forsky were within a couple of blocks of the office, they pretended to be lost. Instead of parking in the hotel lot, they turned into the underground parking area for the police building.

Skunk Woman became hysterical and warned Forsky, "Don't drive in here, stupid! That's the police station. They'll lock us up!"

Forsky stopped at the bottom of the ramp to the parking area. Skunk Woman was trapped. As the officers attempted to identify themselves, she beat them to the punch, and said, "Skunk knew you all was vice all along."

Every vice cop had arrested Skunk Woman at least twice, and the office received regular complaints regarding her blatant streetwalking activity. Thompson and Forsky were embarrassed to bring the old woman in.

In the vice office, Captain Arlie Holland walked by the desk where the suspect and both detectives were seated. Arlie veered around the area and picked up his pace as he went toward his office where the odor would no longer threaten his breathing air.

Safely across the room, Holland grinned as he asked the detectives, "Who had the sardine daiquiri for lunch?"

Forsky said, "It's not very funny, Arlie. It smells a lot worse if you happen to be wearing these pants." Forsky pointed to the large greasy stain on his leisure suit slacks, as if it were a wound sustained in fierce battle.

Thompson and Forsky finished with the two primary pieces of paperwork necessary to book the prisoner into jail, but they also had to inventory the contents of the Skunk Woman's huge purse. Thompson found a clean desktop, and dumped the contents. Forsky had the fill-in-the-blank form, and Thompson began calling out the items.

"One can pork 'n' beans and weenies, one can Vienna sausages, a can of spaghetti, a tin of anchovies..."

An excited Forsky interrupted, "Anchovies? Anchovies? No one really eats those nasty little things, do they? I guess I should be thankful I didn't get a lapful of anchovy drippings, too."

Skunk Woman was silent. She feared a verbal reprisal from the momentarily deranged detective.

Thompson continued, "Got a small jar of vaseline, eight rubbers, one greasy washcloth, one bottle of merthiolate, a pocket knife, one inflatable pillow, insect repellent spray…"

Forsky interrupted again, "That's not a purse. It's a survival kit; you could stay in the wilderness for a week and have safe sex while you're there."

As they finished the inventory, Tal Sanderson walked into the office. The aroma emanating from the squad room had crept into the main outer office and into individual offices. Sanderson braved the odor, entered his office, and shut the door.

The city jail was located on the fourth and fifth floors of the police building. Except for drunks and traffic violators, prisoners were transferred down the street to the county jail within hours after their arrest, unless they made bond or a lawyer was able to secure their release sooner. The Skunk had no money for a lawyer, and could not make a bond. She had been arrested countless times for prostitution, had no family, suffered from alcoholism, and had a problem or two with her mind. Thompson often thought about such a plight being a sad situation indeed, but what else could be done for a person like this? Liberal-minded persons seeking a cause to exploit might argue that jail was cruel and harsh treatment for someone like the Skunk. Perhaps it was. She was safer in jail, however. She ate regular meals, she would not get run over by a car, her throat would not be slit by a sadistic customer, and she would not lift a lonely old man's wallet. But then, perhaps that lonely old man needed his wallet lifted as a reminder that his errant ways could stand correction. Did that make the Skunk Woman a humanitarian? No one on this earth knew the answers, though plenty of self-professed experts claimed they did. Thompson considered himself smart enough to know that he was not smart enough to provide the answers either. When he found himself thinking such thoughts, it disturbed him. He began to think about other things.

Forsky found an ancient bottle of stain remover in the jail matron's cleaning supplies. Using a rag, he rubbed some of the liquid into the dried sardine oil stain on his slacks. "Damn!" Forsky cried out as the cleaning fluid evaporated, melting the polyester and burning the skin underneath.

"John, I know you're grieving over the loss of your eighteen-year-old leisure suit, but we need to brief Tal on Raeburn Compton's planned conversion. Let's go."

The sergeant was elated.

"Just keep an eye on Charlene. Don't let him try to run the show," he said.

Forsky assured the boss that everything would be okay.

Lieutenant Oliver Pricklee passed by Sanderson's office. He paused, stuck his head in the door, and offered a feigned greeting to the sergeant and detectives, "Hi, everybody. How's the day been so far?"

"Pretty good, lieutenant," Forsky replied. Sanderson and the detectives froze in place, waiting for the lieutenant's exit. An awkward silence ensued.

"I see you are all quite busy plotting the demise of some vice miscreant, so I'll get out of your way," Pricklee said, feeling unwelcome and intimidated.

When Pricklee was out of earshot, Forsky said, "If he only knew how accurate his assessment was." All three smiled.

No one liked Pricklee and he knew it. He had been in vice only a short time, knew nothing about the work, and did not want to learn. He was there because it was a prestigious position and was often a stepping stone for a higher status job. Pricklee was an administrator. He had little concern for people. The man saw vice work as a filthy job that no supervisor of any rank would dirty his hands performing. A good vice supervisor did some vice work on occasion to familiarize himself with what his subordinates did everyday. A boss who did not, received no support or respect from the detectives and often did not last long in vice.

In a political maneuver, the vice captain had been pressured into accepting the lieutenant. Captain Holland was waiting for the right opportunity to transfer Pricklee to a job where his non-police talents could be better utilized.

In contrast to Pricklee, everyone in the Vice Division liked Arlie Holland. He had served in vice as a sergeant and a lieutenant. Holland was fair and practical-minded and would have made an excellent chief, but, sad to note, he was at the height of his career. He lacked a condescending manner in his treatment of subordinates and had always been a "one of the guys"-type supervisor. Thompson, Forsky, Sanderson, and others who had been around Holland for years still called him "Arlie". This informality irritated Pricklee, who always addressed the captain as "Captain". Besides, Holland would have interpreted it as a sign of disrespect if someone of Pricklee's lowly stature called him Arlie.

Forsky looked at Sanderson and said, "Talbert, there's one other thing we need to mention. Jan Doxee called about what may be a good-sized escort service operation. We haven't really done any work on it yet. She's trying to get the particulars on it now."

"I guess this is one of Jan's competitors?" Sanderson asked.

Forsky responded, "Not at all, Tal. She tried to go to work for them, but they told her they didn't hire old whores!"

"I can't imagine Jan taking that well," Sanderson said with a chuckle.

As Thompson left work, he knew he would be back early on Thursday evening. He preferred working the 6:00 P.M. to 2:00 A.M. shift. Night work was always more exciting, making an eight-hour shift breeze by. By the end of the month, however, he welcomed the change to work regular daytime hours. The change was most welcome after a hectic month that included many nights of "snagging just one more" with Forsky, and daytime court attendances.

CHAPTER 6

Wade Thompson had several trifling annoyances in the form of telephone messages on his desk that had come in during the day. He was selective in returning calls, but made quick response to most of them. He was curious about one message in particular. It had both his name and Forsky's on it.

According to the message, a woman by the name of Virginia Baccus called at 11:00 A.M. She would be in Dallas for several days and wanted to meet with the detectives. It was important that she furnish them with some vice-related information concerning a relative. Seldom did a telephone message contain such details unless the caller was insistent.

Forsky walked in the office. He was dressed in his evening "uniform", a greasy yellow Caterpillar cap, an old stained and tattered sleeveless khaki work shirt, matching shorts, and military combat boots that John had worn during military service in the early '70's. When he wore the cap, he always pulled it down tightly against his skull. John had been fishing all day and had come straight from the lake.

"Smells like you've been gutting fish all day and haven't even washed your hands," Thompson said as he handed the message to Forsky.

Forsky was on the defensive and remarked, "Texas fish have a pleasant fragrance compared to Russian sardines."

He stared at the message for a moment and said, "Name doesn't mean anything to me. You going to call her?"

"Yeah, I'll call her. Just wondered if you might know her," Thompson said.

Thompson called and an elderly-sounding woman answered on the first ring.

The woman said, "This is Virginia."

"Virginia, this is Wade Thompson. I just received your message. How can I help you?"

"I have some information that I believe you and John Forsky will be most interested in. I'm a regular person, not a criminal. I'm not trying to sell information or get myself out of a bind. No bad guys are chasing me or my family. I just want you to know from the beginning there's no shady angle here. You're welcome to check up on me if you so choose," Virginia Baccus stated.

"In your message it says something about a relative," Thompson said. "Who is your relative?"

She replied, "I'll discuss none of this on the phone. I'm staying at the TopTown Hotel. Are you acquainted with it?"

"Yes, do you want to meet there?"

"I would prefer meeting with you in the bar on the ground floor. I will be out this evening and will be visiting friends tomorrow, but I shall be free after about 2:00 P.M. Will that coincide with your schedule?" she inquired with a most professional demeanor.

Thompson responded, "We're working nights right now. It will have to be after 6:00 P.M. Is that okay?"

"Yes, that's fine. Be in the bar at seven and bring Mr. Forsky if he's available," she concluded.

By now, Thompson was very curious about what the stranger had to offer. Like many cops, he had developed an acute sense for the instantaneous judging of another's credibility. While only a "field test", such assessments were often accurate. He felt good about Virginia Baccus. He also hoped that the Raeburn Compton escapade would work as planned so there would be no conflict on Friday night.

Forsky asked Thompson, "What's the story?"

"I don't really know. She wouldn't give me a hint on the phone. We're supposed to meet her at the Lair tomorrow night at seven. She's staying at the TopTown. All I can say is she's intelligent, in charge, and she's not goofy."

Forsky said, "Good, I'm anxious to meet Strange Woman, but we better get the camera and all if we're gonna pick up Charlene at 7:30."

The detectives arrived at Charlene's motor home early. Charlene was ready and looked like the stereotypical he-she street whore if there ever was one. The makeup on his face was so thick it looked as if a chunk of it could fall off at any moment. His glued-on eyelashes must have been an inch long. Charlene's long blond wig had adorned the slick head of a store mannequin years before. If his tight skirt was a foot longer, it might reach his knees. A constrictive sleeveless top accented Charlene's muscular arms. Charlene always wore high-top tennis shoes for two reasons. As he had explained to Thompson and Forsky years before, no man could walk in high heel shoes as well as a real woman could. It did not matter how effeminate the man was, it was simply a physical impossibility. Secondly, street whores often get into predicaments that necessitate running. High heel shoes had to be jettisoned before anything else happened. Running barefoot through broken beer bottles and old syringes was always hazardous. Tennis shoes just made good sense, given the working conditions of a street whore, according to Charlene.

"Hi, boys, you all come on in," Charlene said with far more enthusiasm in his voice than he had two days before.

Thompson said, "You ready, Charlene?"

"Sure am, honey. Don't I look ready?" he replied, now a bit perturbed.

Forsky commented, "You look fine, Charlene, like a street

whore ought to."

"Thank you, John," a proud Charlene said. "Your taste in ladies is impeccable." Charlene continued, "You boys bring food and drink for the occasion? I smell spicy hot tamales."

Like most people who make an illegal living on the street, Charlene did not eat on a regular basis. What diet they existed on consisted entirely of fast food, soft drinks, coffee, and alcohol. They never drank water nor did they eat vegetables. Thompson and Forsky set the paper sacks containing two dozen pork tamales, hot, hot sauce, and three iced teas on a typing stand which Charlene had salvaged from a trash pile and used as a coffee table. They sat around it, and shared the tamales. Then they piled into the Pontiac and went in search of Raeburn Compton.

Shortly after 8:00 P.M., they observed Compton's Lincoln in front of the LoRent bar. The detectives were relieved to see it there; both knew this would be the night.

Thompson was nervous as he asked the he-she informant, "Any questions, Charlene?"

"No, dear. I can handle Raeburn Compton just fine," Charlene said.

Forsky gave Charlene additional instructions, "When this is over, come back to the car. It'll be parked behind the vacant gas station just down from the bar. Make sure no one follows you, alright?"

"Got it, baby. I'll see you then," Charlene said as he got out of the car.

Thompson and Forsky parked behind the old service station. Forsky had the video camera, tripod, blank videos, batteries, and other paraphernalia packed in an olive drab military laundry bag. Thompson was wearing faded jeans and a blue work shirt with "CITY OF MIAMI" across the back. The two looked as if they might be picking up cans or going through dumpsters looking for discarded treasures.

The detectives had to get into the storage room at the Uptown Downtown without being seen by the desk clerk. At night, he was the only employee and locked himself in the office. A thick Plexiglas partition provided the clerk with some protection from the neighborhood's unsavory night crawlers that might want to hijack him. There was no way the clerk would leave his safe confines at night to go to the storage room. Forsky and Thompson approached the motel parking lot. Outside lighting was minimal and the officers easily walked in the shadows to the storage room undetected. The owners of most of these run-down motels were foreigners who were able to make a decent living by resorting to drastic measures to cut their overhead. One such trick was to use only twenty-five watt bulbs for porch lights. Every third door had one, putting out a very faint glow.

Thompson found the door to the storage room unlocked. Actually, there was no doorknob to lock. The knob and its locking mechanism had no doubt been needed on a regular room door. As soon as they entered, Forsky used his flashlight to locate a roll of duct tape in the bottom of the laundry bag. He put tape over the doorknob hole before flipping on the light switch in the tiny room. There were no windows, but Thompson went outside again to make sure no light could be seen emanating from around the doorframe.

The six-by-eight-foot room was just large enough for the detectives, their equipment, and the four cases of cheap toilet paper that were stacked against the west wall. On the east wall was the backside of the wall heater assembly for room #8. Sheetrock had been removed on the storage room wall to provide clearance for the gas heating unit. The upper louvered vent area was approximately one-foot square and would provide an adequate space to film Raeburn's and Charlene's rendezvous.

Thompson moved a case of toilet paper against the door. Forsky set the tripod in place and mounted the camera. He adjusted the focus for the bed. Everything was prepared. Now they had to wait.

Thompson asked, "How long you think we'll be here, John?"

"I'll give them an hour at the most. I think they'll have two drinks and head over here," Forsky said.

Charlene sat in the rearmost booth at the LoRent facing the front door and Raeburn Compton. For a small bar, the LoRent did a good business. It was a convenient place for pimps and served as their collection point. Every so often, girls working the area would drop off their earnings to one of these street swine and have a quick drink before returning to work. A variety of drugs could be purchased day or night from the on-duty bartender. After 10:00 P.M. most any night, a dice game was in progress in the office. Many of the bar's regular customers carried guns but this was a rough and dangerous neighborhood; one never knew when some thug would attempt to steal drugs or gambling earnings. The crowd was mixed, black and white, which was unusual for a bar on Long Boulevard. It was refreshing, however, to see that racial prejudice was not an issue among the open-minded criminal element that frequented the LoRent.

Charlene winked and grinned at Raeburn Compton in a sensual, whore-like manner that only vice cops and worldly street scoundrels could appreciate. Raeburn noticed Charlene, but for a moment ignored his beckoning facial gestures. The pseudo politician was busy talking to the bartender, Curly Clements. Curly was not exactly a Long Boulevard vice lord, but he did some part-time pimping and sold dope as a service to well established bar patrons.

When Curly stepped away from Raeburn Compton to wait on a paying customer, Compton looked directly at Charlene and gave a reciprocating smile and wink. He got off the barstool and walked to Charlene's booth. Without invitation, he sat.

"Baby, I wasn't ignoring your pretty face. I was having a conversation with one of my constituents," Raeburn Compton said.

Charlene responded, "You don't fool me, Raeburn Compton, that's Curly Clements. He ain't nobody's constituent. He just a con man, an old con man, too."

"Well, he's still a citizen and a loyal supporter," Compton said, preferring the conversation go in a different direction. He wasn't about to defend Curly's good name, since Curly did not have one.

"Let me buy you a drink. I'm about empty myself," Compton said as he rattled the ice in his highball glass.

Compton yelled at Curly and ordered drinks. Charlene and most prostitutes always drank what Thompson referred to as "whore drinks" unknown to other bar clientele. A "whore drink" was some exotic brandy or cognac or a sweet mixed drink with a French-sounding name that was overpriced and quite nasty to the taste. Of course, Charlene requested a whore drink. Raeburn Compton had a more conventional gin and tonic, his third of the evening, his fifth for the day.

Charlene was anxious to get down to business. "What are your plans for the rest of the evening?"

Compton was caught off guard for an instant, but replied, "Uh...uh, I don't really have any unless you do. What have you got in mind?"

Charlene borrowed Thompson's favorite whore line when he told Raeburn Compton, "I was just looking for a little companionship if you know what I mean."

The buildup of anticipated passion made both Compton and Charlene thirsty. Compton ordered two more free drinks from Curly Clements.

Compton said, "I just happen to have a room for recreational companionship at the Uptown Downtown Motel, if you want to go over there."

"I know about your room, Raeburn. All the girls talk about such things," said Charlene, giggling.

Trying to appear modest and virile at the same time and failing miserably at both, Compton said, "I think those rumors have been exaggerated. I'm not really much of a ladies' man."

Charlene said, "Let's finish our drinks and go to this room I've heard about but never seen."

Thompson and Forsky had gotten as comfortable as the storage room surroundings allowed. Both detectives were a little nervous and impatient and neither was in the mood for much conversation.

Forsky said, "Wade, it's nine o'clock. They should be here any time now."

"I hope you're right. It's getting a bit claustrophobic in here," Thompson replied.

Charlene and Raeburn Compton finished their drinks. As they walked to the door, it became obvious to Charlene that Compton had too much to drink. He was unsteady on his feet and did not need to be driving a car, even though they would only go a short distance. Charlene had done plenty of things far more dangerous than riding a block or two with a drunk, but he was afraid to ride with Compton. The activist was in his sixties and took at least a dozen prescription drugs for various maladies on a daily basis in addition to consuming his fair share of alcohol.

When they got to Compton's car, Charlene said, "Raeburn, let me drive, honey. You look a little woozy."

Enraged with the insinuation he was drunk, Compton slapped Charlene's cheek with an open hand. Charlene, surprised and far more frightened than before, backed away but the old man made no attempt to strike him again. Charlene's cheek stung for a moment, but after the initial shock, he realized the frail slap wasn't much of a slap at all.

Compton had no remorse for his actions and told Charlene, "Get your ass in the car and don't ever tell me I'm drunk."

A scared Charlene did as he was told. He figured if things really got bad it would not require much effort to put Raeburn Compton in his place. He hoped Compton would safely park in front of the motel and not drive through it. Charlene fastened his seat belt, something he never did in anyone else's car.

Compton pulled onto the street. He looked at Charlene and said, "You probably enjoy getting slapped around by a man, don't you, baby?"

Charlene felt trapped, but wouldn't be for long. He decided to make the most of the situation and at Raeburn Compton's expense. Thompson and Forsky would understand. At least he hoped they would understand. Besides, the detectives did not tell Charlene that Compton was a bondage wacko who beat up on defenseless whores.

After they both lunged forward from Compton's generous application of the brakes in the motel parking lot, Charlene replied, but not loud enough for Compton to hear, "No, I don't enjoy being hit."

Compton's state of drunkenness was increasing as he said, "Baby, if you tell me you've been a naughty girl, I'll give you a spanking you won't forget."

"Raeburn, I been a good girl, and I don't want no spanking. Can we talk about something else now?" asked Charlene.

Compton did not answer. Charlene was thinking the old man was not just a whoremonger. He might be a dangerous sex deviate if he got hold of a young, inexperienced hooker. By the moment, Charlene was becoming more determined to do whatever he could to rectify the situation. He had forgotten about Thompson and Forsky.

"Okay, John, here they are." Thompson said in a loud whisper.

Forsky replied in a louder whisper, "Camera's rolling."

As they walked through the door of the tiny room, Charlene noticed the dingy yellow sheets on the half-made bed. The rest of the room complemented the sheets by being dirty and foul smelling.

Raeburn Compton sat on the bed, looked at Charlene who was still standing, and said, "Baby, what are you going to do for me now?" He acted as if his slap was an appreciated gesture of deranged foreplay.

Charlene bent over and licked the back of Raeburn Compton's neck in slow, pseudo-sensual motions, then whispered in his ear, "Take your clothes off. I'm going to rub your whole body down with oil before we do anything else."

As Compton disrobed, he noticed Charlene remained clothed, and asked with suspicion, "Why you not undressing?"

"Cause it adds to the mood, you know. They come off when the time's right," Charlene said.

Compton never mentioned anything about the lights being on. As a general rule, whores and tricks do not trust one another. Lights are seldom turned off during a date. Compton lay on the bed naked. Much to Charlene's amazement, he had become very docile. Charlene rubbed his body with baby oil for ten minutes. He became so relaxed, Charlene feared he would fall asleep. It was time to teach Raeburn Compton a lesson in humility and humanity.

Charlene instructed him to get up on all fours in the middle of the bed and the oil treatment would continue. "You be a man's man tonight, Raeburn," Charlene thought to himself.

Compton balked for a moment at the suggestion and asked, "You ain't going to make me meow like a cat or do some other weird shit, are you?"

"Oh no, baby, just more of the same," Charlene replied.

"Whatever you want to do, just do it," Compton said.

Thompson stared at Forsky with a puzzled look. Forsky

shrugged his shoulders. Neither could quite figure out what Charlene had in mind.

The female impostor sat alongside Compton in his four-legged pose and continued with the oil. By this time, baby oil was dripping from Raeburn Compton's body. It was in his ears and there must have been a half-cupful in his hair. The bed linens were soaked with the greasy mess. Charlene knelt behind Compton and rubbed a copious amount of oil on his buttocks and even more between his cheeks, way down between his cheeks. Compton smiled, closed his eyes, and moaned.

With one hand still rubbing Compton's body, Charlene pulled down his panties and in one powerful stroke, thrust his personal eight inches into Compton with precision accuracy.

Compton screamed, but Charlene lunged at him with full force for several more jabs. By this time, the whore had both hands in a death grip on the activist's waist, making it impossible for him to pull away. When Charlene let go and shoved Compton forward, he collapsed on the bed.

Thompson and Forsky looked at one another in disbelief. They needed to discuss what they had just witnessed, but that would have to wait.

Before Raeburn Compton could recover from the unexpected penetration, Charlene was headed for the door. The man yelled, "I'll kill your faggot ass. No punk's getting my booty!"

Charlene stood in the doorway, much aware that Compton was defenseless now as he lay on the bed a drunken, greasy swine. "Too late, Raeburn Compton. This punk's done got your greasy booty!" he said, and walked away, not bothering to close the door.

Compton began gathering his clothes, but then pushed them aside. In a drunken stupor, he fell asleep in the bed's nasty mire. Raeburn Compton would not be leaving anytime soon.

When Compton began snoring, Thompson, and Forsky packed up, left the storage room, and trekked to the car. Thompson asked his partner, "Did we just witness a rape of some sort?"

"Not in my opinion. There was no rape, or any offense of any kind, including prostitution, for that matter. Those were two consenting adults. We heard him tell Charlene to do whatever he wanted to. Charlene did just that. The fact that Charlene happens to be a man has nothing to do with it," Forsky said.

Thompson knew Forsky's opinion would be shared by any prosecuting attorney, and decided he was correct in his assessment of the act they had just witnessed and videotaped.

When Thompson opened the car door, he asked Charlene, "What happened back there?"

"It was back there, alright. Raeburn Compton's back there! I played rump ranger on that old pervert and he needed it! He slapped me around before we ever went to his room. I know you all didn't see that, but he did it. Then he said he'd spank me if I told him I been a bad girl! He a mean and violent old creature, but I know he's a sore and humble one right now!" Charlene exclaimed through the huge smile on his face.

No one had much to say as the detectives took Charlene to his motor home.

When Charlene got out of the car, less than a block from the school bus, he turned to Thompson. He hesitated for a moment, as if he had something to say but did not know how to say it.

"Raeburn Compton's not going to try to kill me now, is he?"

Thompson replied, "Are you kidding? After we talk to Raeburn and show him the tape, he won't want to get anywhere near you, Charlene."

"Maybe so, but it's his loser cronies I be worried about," Charlene said.

Thompson assured him, "You'll be okay, Charlene.

Raunchy Raeburn is not going to want anyone to know about this evening's adventure."

"I'm counting on you guys. Now how about my case? I got to do one more deal, right?"

Thompson replied, "Right. We'll get with you in a few days on that."

"Alright. I got to go clean off this nasty Compton and go out to make a living now," Charlene said, and disappeared into the night as Forsky drove away.

Forsky asked Thompson, "You want to go to the office? Tal will be waiting on us."

"Yeah, but Charlene's anal attack on Raeburn Compton may require a little explaining," Thompson worried.

"Wade, it's okay. Like I mentioned before, you got two consenting adults. The fact that both have peckers, and one wasn't aware of that, has no bearing on anything."

"I know, John. Let's just get to the office," Thompson said, weary of discussing the matter.

Sanderson sat alone in the break room watching the late evening news on TV when they arrived. No one else was in the entire office.

"Well, how'd it go?" the sergeant asked, as he used the remote to mute the television sound.

As he inserted the tape in the VCR, Forsky said, "Pretty good, considering."

"Considering what?" asked Sanderson.

"A picture ordinarily may be worth a thousand words, Tal, but in this case it's worth about a million. Just watch," said Forsky.

Sanderson did not understand what Forsky was talking about, but he had an idea he would find out shortly.

The video was of much better quality than anyone had anticipated. Despite filming through the heater vent louvers, the lighting had been adequate. As he watched, Sanderson was pleased with the results. When the video depicted Charlene greasing up Raeburn Compton's butt, Sanderson reacted just as the detectives had an hour earlier when they viewed the action live. He asked, "What's going on there?"

Thompson said, "Get ready, Tal. You're not going to believe this!"

Forsky reinforced Thompson's remark and said, "Yeah, brace yourself, Talbert!"

As Charlene was shown porking a screaming Raeburn Compton, Sanderson exploded into laughter. Thompson was becoming more relieved by the minute. He had not known Sanderson would handle it this well. The sergeant seemed taken with the scene and replayed it several times before asking, "Okay, whose idea was the little dose of butt action?"

Forsky remarked, "That was totally Charlene's idea. We knew nothing about it, but it worked out okay in the end."

Laughing again, Sanderson did his best to regain composure and replied, "In the end is right! Raeburn Compton's end, that is!"

Thompson felt an obligation to provide an explanation despite Sanderson's overwhelming approval. He said, "Raeburn Compton got drunk and slapped Charlene around. Then, Compton told Charlene he'd like to spank him. Well, Charlene decided he'd get even..."

Sanderson interrupted, "Have you guys given any thought as to when you're going to confront Compton with this damning evidence?"

Forsky replied, "We haven't really talked about it. Sometime next week, I suppose."

"Even if Raeburn Compton's spirit isn't in it, we should have a regular law and order advocate in his neighborhood after this. The old man can do more to clean up his area than a hundred cops could. Compton's biggest problem when he changes for the good will be with the bad guys he's been shaking down all this time. He won't be able to support their evil causes any longer and they'll see him as a real turncoat," Sanderson said with delight. "You guys helped out a bunch of folks tonight," he concluded.

As they put the video equipment away, Thompson said to Forsky, "I have one request for the rest of the night, John."

"And what's that?"

"Tonight's little adventure has left me exhausted. Let's get off on time just this once, okay?"

Forsky smirked, "I wouldn't confess this to just anyone, but I'm tired, too, from fishing all day. I really don't have the urge to ride a hustler around the parking lot tonight."

Thompson was astonished that Forsky would admit to being tired, regardless of the reason, but he was grateful nonetheless.

CHAPTER 7

Wade Thompson lived in an older, inner city Dallas neighborhood. He and his wife, Rose, had purchased the home more than twenty years ago. The house was now worth many times what they had paid for it. Real estate prices had skyrocketed because of the many young professionals that had to have a house in this part of town. Thompson could not understand someone paying an outrageous price just for a location. When he and his wife moved to the area, the neighborhood was filled with older people, many of whom had been there since the first homes were built in the early 1950's.

The original settlers may not have been as well educated as the later homebuyers, but they were not materialistic hedonists either. Most of the neighborhood pioneers were dead and gone. Thompson had more use for the older folks but did not realize it when they were around. He wished he had become acquainted with more of them. The current crop was as high strung as hound dogs and drove all the status symbol cars. The women had fashionable fat lips, boob jobs, fake fingernails, and hyphenated names. Men and women carried store-bought water with them at all times. These people turned on a computer to figure out what day of the week it was and had casual cell phone conversations in the grocery store. Their vocabularies must have been quite limited, though, Thompson thought, because they repeatedly used words and phrases like "soulmate", "in the loop", "pushing the envelope", and "worst case scenario". He also knew they must have been part of an evolving decadent society.

As Thompson drove through the neighborhood on his way to work Friday evening, he tried to anticipate what he and Forsky could expect from their meeting with Virginia Baccus. In the office, Forsky was doing research on the computer.

"Hi, John...who you checking on?" Thompson inquired.

Forsky replied, "Virginia Baccus, if that's her real name."

"I'll bet it is...you find anything at all?" Thompson asked.

"Her driver's license information will print out in a minute," Forsky said as he walked away from the machine.

Thompson was standing near the printer as it began to emit the irritating drone. The operator's license particulars on Baccus were coming up. With the printing in progress, Thompson noticed that the woman had a Beaumont, Texas address. The printing stopped and Thompson tore off the paper. He sat on Forsky's desk with the information in hand.

"Well, what's it say?" Forsky asked as if Thompson should have already read it aloud.

"She was born in 1920 and has a Beaumont address. And I guess you've done a criminal history," said Thompson.

With mild indignance, Forsky remarked, "Of course I ran a criminal history. She's clean, except for eight DWI's."

"Eight DWI's?" Thompson said in amazement. "How do you get eight DWI's?"

"My guess is you get stopped by the cops a lot when you're driving drunk," Forsky remarked. "The DWI arrests began in 1949 and the last one was in '92. Actually, that averages to less than one every five years." Thompson thought about Virginia Baccus being from Beaumont. He knew of several people from Beaumont but could think of none of them now. He had never been to the southeastern Texas city. Something bothered him about this woman's place of residence, but Thompson could not quite grasp whatever was causing the uncomfortable feeling.

The Lair Tavern was located on the ground floor of a very

old and historic Dallas hotel, the TopTown. Several miles from the downtown area, it was situated in what is now referred to as an 'inner city' neighborhood that was developed in the early 1900's. The TopTown was a ritzy place when it opened and had remained that way over many decades. Lots of old Dallas money remained in this exclusive section of the city. A number of wealthy Dallasites lived in the hotel. Two former Dallas mayors called the TopTown home. For the better part of a century, many decisions regarding the future of the City had been made over drinks in the Lair.

Thompson and Forsky were familiar with the bar. On an infrequent basis, they would make happy hour there, joining a number of prosecutors from the district attorney's office. Since happy hour ended at seven, they arrived early for the scheduled meeting and ordered drinks.

Thompson had always liked this bar. Despite the fact that there were always quite a few patrons present, day and night, it was quiet for a bar. Moreover, the jukebox had music selections that you could not find anywhere else in town. Sarah Vaughn, Mel Torme, Guy Mitchell, early Ray Price, and Nat King Cole: real music from a creative era.

Thompson said, "I have no idea what Virginia Baccus looks like, other than she's seventy-seven years old."

"Based on her criminal history, she'll be the only seventy-seven year old woman who staggers in," Forsky remarked with a grin.

At that moment, an unmistakable Virginia Baccus walked in and exchanged greetings with the bartender and several persons seated at and near the bar. Thompson approached her.

"You must be Mr. Thompson," the woman said as she shook Thompson's hand. "I'm Virginia and I am very pleased to make your acquaintance."

Wade led the woman to the table where he introduced her to John Forsky.

As a waiter brought the detectives drinks, Virginia Baccus

ordered a double scotch. The woman was elegantly dressed in slacks and a silk blouse. She wore a hat that would be inappropriate in a bar other than the Lair. Virginia was rather attractive for a woman almost eighty years old. However, it was apparent that she had endured cosmetic surgery on more than one occasion and on more than one part of her old body.

"May I see your identification?" she asked the detectives in a low, authoritative voice.

Forksy and Thompson complied with her request. Forksy thought her voice sounded familiar in a vague way.

"Thank you and thank you for being punctual. Too few people are on time these days," she said, "and please call me Virginia."

The woman continued, "I won't waste your time talking about meaningless things, so let's get to business. Jan Doxee is my daughter."

The instant shock made everything clearer to both detectives. Thompson remembered that Jan was from Beaumont and Forsky remembered the familiarity of the voice. It was markedly similar to Jan's.

Both detectives were slightly relieved but still very curious. Virginia Baccus paused and stared at the officers, studying their facial expressions.

Thompson caught the woman's glance and said, "Please… continue."

Ms. Baccus began her story, "Jan's entire family is in Beaumont. I have three other daughters, all of them married. We are all concerned about Jan's well being. She has had this drinking problem for a long time, but she's been getting much worse. I don't mean to sound hypocritical and I certainly have not been a good example for Jan. I've been a drunk off and on for fifty years myself. She almost never comes home, so I come to Dallas occasionally to check on her. I have been here since Sunday, this trip. I always stay in this hotel, I don't stay at Jan's apartment."

Thompson, in a worried voice, interrupted, "How do we know Jan won't walk into this room in the next minute?"

"Surely, in your naiveté you don't think I left that to chance, do you?" Baccus said, clearly irritated at the insinuation.

Thompson was also becoming a bit irritated, but with the woman's arrogance.

He remarked, "I just want to be certain she won't show up while we're here, I'm not accusing you of being simple-minded."

"I understand…rest assured Jan won't be here. She flew to Houston yesterday. Business, I suppose. She'll be back early tomorrow evening, in time to pick me up and take me to the airport," said the woman with all the answers.

Forsky, who did not particularly care for Virginia Baccus' manner either said, "Okay, Virginia, go ahead with your story."

She continued, "I know more than I want to know about Jan's business. As of earlier this week, I ran across some information you may be interested in. I was visiting at her place. Jan had gone shopping. This was Tuesday morning. I began snooping around, a bad habit of mine. She keeps business records of her shady dealings. Everything seemed to be well organized in a cardboard box in a closet in the spare bedroom. I'm ashamed to say I went through everything. She had wire transfer receipts, deposit slips, and other financial paperwork that would indicate she's been very successful at her trade. I think she's doing more than just charging men to pound her."

At first, Thompson could not believe this woman would use a slang term like "pound". After staring at her for a while, however, he figured Virginia had been around the block a time or two herself, though not as a prostitute. Despite the woman's numerous plastic surgeries, many of which had been successful, there was a resemblance between Jan and her snooty, high-mileage mother.

Thompson asked, "How much money are you talking about?"

Baccus continued, "What I noticed came to at least sixty, maybe eighty thousand dollars and these were recent transactions, since the first of the year. You gentlemen may have a better idea regarding her earnings than I do, but that seems like an awful lot of money for a hooker to be making."

"Hooker", Thompson thought. This woman has been around common people just long enough for some of their lowliness to rub off. Virginia Baccus was becoming tolerable. She had even admitted to not knowing something.

Thompson was certain Jan did well from a financial standpoint, far better than almost all escort service prostitutes. He and Forsky had filed an aggravated promotion of prostitution case against her a couple of days after her initial arrest when they first became acquainted with her. They arrested her at her apartment. Thompson looked around the place while Forsky kept her busy. She had at least ten thousand dollars in cash in a small open cardboard box on a hall closet shelf.

Most prostitutes, and pimps for that matter, like to brag about their earnings. The figures are always inflated usually about five to ten times the true number. It always amazed Thompson and Forsky that most cops, even vice cops, believed these exaggerated claims. A street pimp seldom had more than two or three girls working for him and only about forty percent of his workforce was made up of dependable earners. Rent, a junker to drive, cigarettes, liquor, drugs, fast food, and pimp and whore clothes took all the money the crew could scrape together. Most lived a day-to-day existence at best, a fact many people did not realize. A pimp might do a little extra work as a con man or minor drug peddler. When one of his girls was arrested, he seldom had the finances to secure her release. Escort service whores were better off than their street counterparts. They made a living but little else.

Jan Doxee was tight with her money. From all indications, she did not spend much of it. Her apartment was nice and in a decent part of town. While fashionable, her clothes were not expensive. Her car was several years old. A liquor bill was Jan's greatest monthly cash outlay. Thompson had no idea what she did with the rest of her income, which was a good bit more than what the detectives had assumed.

Forsky asked Virginia Baccus, "Did you find our business cards in the apartment?"

"They were in the box with the paperwork I told you about. In fact, there's a manila folder with a list of names of policemen and suspected policemen...at least that's what it looked like to me. Now, I'll admit to being nosy but my curiosity waned after looking at all that stuff. Perhaps you gentlemen can do some surreptitious skulking on your own," the woman said.

Thompson and Forsky had never heard of "surreptitious skulking" but they had done plenty of covert work. They did not have to see the files to begin investigating, but it would save a lot of work if they had access to the material.

Forsky looked at Ms. Baccus and said, "If copies of that paperwork were furnished to us by, say a concerned family member, we would be happy to look into the matter. Also, it would save us a tremendous amount of background work."

Baccus replied, "I understand. I'll make no promises at this point but I shall consider everything. You make me feel like a sort of double agent right now and it's not a comfortable feeling."

Thompson said, "Think it over and let us know."

She replied, "Okay, let me give you my contact information in Beaumont."

Baccus wrote her home telephone number and cell phone number on a napkin and handed it to Thompson. Somehow, he knew this was not the first time she written her phone number on a napkin and handed it to a strange man.

Forsky warned Virginia, "We appreciate you calling us, however, don't discuss this with anyone, including your family."

"Understood," Baccus said. "Thank you both for coming." They walked Virginia Baccus to the elevator just outside the entrance to the bar.

As the detectives walked through the lobby, Forsky said, "Well, it appears Jan has become a regular entrepreneur these days."

Thompson replied, "Yeah...now if we can find a good place to start and get this figured out."

Thompson would only admit to himself that this was a matter of considerable embarrassment. He thought he knew Jan Doxee and her vodka-clouded mind better than anyone else did. Thompson felt that she could not make a significant criminal move without his knowing about it. What unrealistic perceptions of the way things were!

Thompson continued, "I'm not going to concern myself with it tonight...let's eat and make a couple of street whores, what do you say, John?"

"Fine with me. I'm ready to do some real work for a change," Forsky said.

CHAPTER 8

After supper, the detectives cruised down Fort Worth Avenue, a very old business neighborhood west of downtown. In its day, before construction of a turnpike linking Dallas and Fort Worth in the mid-nineteen-fifties, Fort Worth Avenue was almost upscale. Nightclubs and motels dotted the street which was really a state highway. In that era, the trip from Dallas to Fort Worth was at least an hour's drive, if there was no traffic congestion. The Dallas-Fort Worth Turnpike cut travel time to thirty minutes, and the abandonment of the Fort Worth Avenue route seemed to happen overnight. The thoroughfare became only an access to Oak Cliff, another deteriorating part of Dallas.

The whore "promenade" on Fort Worth Avenue was about two miles long. There were seven run-down motels along the route. Black, white, and a few Hispanic prostitutes worked the area. Most lived in the motels and paid by the day. With its proximity to downtown, the motels also housed a few hustlers, those affluent enough to sleep under a roof. For vice cops, Fort Worth Avenue was safer to work than South Dallas, but only by a small margin.

With few exceptions, it was far easier for a lone detective to make a whore case. Most prostitutes avoided being confronted by two men. They knew cops worked in pairs. Some street girls, to their detriment, had either lost or never had the natural sense of fear for circumstances they should be fearful of. Others are inexperienced and lacking in street wisdom. Whatever the reason, some women think nothing of dealing with more than one man at a time. Such a careless attitude could prove hazardous to their very existence.

When driving along a whore promenade, the passenger detective drops down into the seat so that the street wench will only see the driver. After the driver makes eye contact with the prostitute, he goes to a nearby location out of sight of the hooker, and lets his partner out. The partner may stand at a bus stop or walk along the sidewalk, anything to avoid being conspicuous. After the other detective picks up the girl and makes the case, he can pull alongside his partner, and both make the arrest.

Should the pickings look good in a particular area, the detectives will swap places and attempt to make an additional case. This is contingent, of course, on the first prisoner being cooperative.

If there were several girls to choose from, John Forsky would zero in on the one he considered to offer the greatest challenge. Thompson's rule of thumb dictated the opposite approach. When tallying arrest totals and the accompanying paperwork, easy cases on ugly prostitutes counted the same as difficult cases on pretty girls, and they did not take as long to make.

Forsky saw a tall, slender girl about twenty-five standing on a corner under a street light. She did not wave or smile as he drove by. In fact, she hardly glanced at him. He looked around the rest of the area and observed eight other girls out. All were regulars and at least three of them knew the detective. He sped up, and hoped none would get a good look at him. Forsky backtracked to the first one, and pulled alongside the curb. She was on the passenger side; the window was lowered. The girl did not approach the car which was unusual. The prostitute preferred to have any conversation from right where she stood, thirty feet away.

Forsky had his greasy cap pulled down on his head as far as possible in order to make his ears stand out more. He had smeared some theatrical tooth black on his front teeth to make them appear rotten. Thompson and Forsky used lots of tooth black. They had found it the single best prop for street work, and it could be applied in an instant.

Forsky squinted through his glasses and put a strong nasal inflection in his voice as he asked, "Are you dating?"

The girl replied, "Yeah, what do you want?"

"Straight lay, no weird stuff," the detective answered for what seemed like the millionth time.

She answered, "Okay. A straight'll cost you thirty."

"I've only got twenty-five," Forsky the chiseler countered. "That okay?"

She agreed with a sigh, "Yeah."

From a technical standpoint, Forsky had a case, and a very easy one at that, so he asked, "We gonna do this long distance, or you wanna get in the car so we can go someplace?"

She said nothing, walked to the car, and got in. It was obvious she was new to the area when she asked, "You know a good place?"

This one played into Forsky's hand with every utterance. The officer assured her he had the perfect spot in mind as he drove around the block where Thompson was walking on the sidewalk. Forsky pushed to find out just how naïve the young woman was. He said, "See this guy walking? Ask him what time it is."

As Forsky pulled alongside Thompson and stopped, both officers had their badges and ID's displayed before the girl could say anything.

Thompson told her, "We're police officers. Put both hands on the dash and don't move."

He opened the passenger door as Forsky slapped a handcuff on her left wrist and bent her forward so that Thompson could get the other cuff on her right wrist.

Her mouth agape, the prostitute looked at Forsky through tears and asked, "If I had asked you if you were a cop, would you have told me?"

"Nope, not until you were arrested," Forsky replied.

Thompson made a cursory inspection of the girl's purse, making sure there were no weapons or dope in it. He got in the car and Forsky drove to the darkened entrance of a cemetery where he and his prisoner would sit on a pipe railing and wait while Thompson took the car and tried to snag one.

Thompson drove to the far end of Fort Worth Avenue where the last and largest motel was located. On a sidewalk just west of the structure was a prostitute. She was about thirty, five-foot-six, and two hundred fifty pounds. Her short skirt, several sizes too small, accented her huge anatomy as did the "EAT SHIT" T-shirt she wore. Thompson had seen the woman once before, but had never talked to her.

The vice detectives had an informal monthly award that was won by the officer hauling in the grossest specimen of Dallas whoredom. To submit an entry for "Steamer of the Month", an extra photograph was made at the time of booking. It was posted in the office on the "Wall of Shame". Captain Arlie Holland was the official judge of entries. This woman would not only be a contender, she was a guaranteed winner for Thompson.

The detective pulled alongside the woman. He appeared to be nervous and timid, saying nothing at first.

With a malt liquor in one hand, the big street whore asked Thompson, "What are you looking for, little feller?" She laughed a fat man's hearty laugh, causing the flesh under her skirt and T-shirt to shake like violently disturbed Jell-O.

At least she's in a good mood, Thompson thought to himself, hoping she wasn't a fighter.

He said, "How about sexual intercourse?" The term usually caught prostitutes off guard and was effective because no one, including vice cops, used such proper jargon.

Fat Woman replied, "Baby, if you want to call it that, it's fine with me, but a straight fuck'll cost you twenty and don't make no jokes about me getting on top. I wouldn't do that to you, sugar.

Neighborhood bushes are included in the twenty-dollar price, but if you want a room, that's ten dollars more."

"Okay, let's find some neighborhood bushes," Thompson suggested.

He was anxious to show Forsky his "Steamer" candidate, that is, if she could get in the car. Fat Woman twisted, turned, and groaned as she tried to get comfortable in the front seat. On the third attempt, she was able to close the door, which pressed against her huge body like plastic wrap on a ham sandwich.

She rubbed Thompson's right leg and said, "Okay, Cutie. Let's find us a place."

Thompson smiled at her, but remained intimidated by her size.

As Thompson was driving toward Forsky's location, Fat Woman asked, "You ain't no cop now, are you?"

"Oh, no," Thompson said, pretending to be frightened by the implication. "I'm a bookkeeper."

The detective drove in front of the cemetery. He hoped she wouldn't say that she became violent around cops and sat on them. As Thompson stopped, Forsky hurried to the passenger door. Fat Woman knew the whole story as soon as she saw Forsky and the prostitute, who was handcuffed to the pipe fence rail. The officers identified themselves, and Thompson put a cuff on the woman's left hand.

Forsky had hold of her right hand. "Wade, there's no way to handcuff her. She's too wide, and her arms are too short."

Fat Woman replied, "You don't need to handcuff me. I don't ever cause you all any problems."

The detectives were relieved to know they would not have to ride around on the woman before arresting her. Neither cared to transport an uncuffed prisoner, but sometimes it could not be avoided. As Forsky and his prisoner were getting situated in the back seat, Thompson glanced at his prostitute. She was actually wedged into the front seat. There was no real danger of her escaping; just getting out of the car would take some planning on her part. The worst she could do was to shift the loaded weight of the car as Thompson rounded a corner.

As they drove toward the office, Forsky, seated directly behind Thompson, leaned forward and said in a low voice, "You know you just put everyone else out of the running for the April Steamer award?"

Grinning, Thompson replied, "Yeah, I know. I won."

CHAPTER 9

When Thompson arrived at work Monday evening, he found three messages from Jan Doxee. He studied them briefly. The times of the messages were only about an hour apart beginning at 2:00 P.M.

Forsky walked in, found he had four messages from her and said to his partner, "What's the deal with all the messages from Jan?"

"I don't know. I've got some too," Thompson said, waving the slips of paper for Forsky to see. "It's either something very important or she's real drunk."

Forsky added, "Or both. Why don't you call her?"

"You call her! You have more messages!" Thompson said.

Forsky threw the slips in the trash and said, "Not anymore. You call her, you deal with her better than I do."

"Alright," Thompson said with great reluctance.

He was not looking forward to speaking with the woman if she was drunk, but he was curious to know if she had developed additional information on the escort service she had told them about. In addition, with what Jan's mother had told them, Thompson's estimation of her cunning mystique was elevated to a higher level.

Jan Doxee answered on the fourth ring.

"Hello!" she said, her voice having the gruffness reserved for a telephone company solicitor trying to sell the purported best in long distance service.

"Wade Thompson, Jan," he said, frightened by her pseudo-greeting.

"It's about time, Wade. I left a bunch of messages for you and John this afternoon and you wait until 6:30 to call me. You think I'm not very important, is that it, Wade?" she said, trying to pick a fight.

Thompson explained, "Jan, we're working evenings now. I thought you knew that. We just got to the office a little while ago."

"Well, it doesn't matter anyway. Why don't you come over and see me?" When she was drunk, Jan became very lonesome.

"Jan, we're busy. You said you were going to find out about the escort service. Have you done that?" Thompson asked, in no mood to deal with the woman in her state.

"Yeah, I got it. I told you I would, didn't I? I have the usual notes and everything else," she said, hurt that Thompson would even imply that she had failed on a mission.

Despite her being in a drunken, obnoxious condition, Jan Doxee was still capable of making sense. He and Forsky would chance a visit. A refusal to meet with her because she was not sober would be a terrible insult. She would discard the information and refuse to speak with the detectives for a few days. Then she would call and apologize and all would be fine. However, it would cost Thompson and Forsky a week. They had been down this road before, and there was no point in traveling it again.

"Jan, we'll be there in thirty minutes, okay?" Thompson told her, hoping she would become more pleasant.

"I'm waiting," she said before slamming the receiver in its cradle.

Forsky asked, "How drunk is she?"

"She's in the obnoxious and lonesome stage. We've seen her worse," Thompson replied.

With reluctance befitting for a prostate exam, Forsky

remarked, "Let's get it over with, then."

It seemed to Thompson that Jan opened her door too soon after the knock. It was as if she had been standing there in anticipation, one hand on the doorknob, the other holding a glass of vodka. The vodka had a spoonful of Coke in it, just enough to make it look like weak iced tea.

"Hi, Wade, hi, John…I am so glad to see you both," she said in a meek and elegant tone quite different from her earlier telephone voice. The 5 foot 6, 120 pound woman stood before the detectives wearing a pale gold silk blouse, and tailored black pants. She wore no jewelry, but her makeup was perfectly applied to accent her turquoise blue eyes. Using the tapered and professionally lacquered nail of her left forefinger, she brushed her shoulder length black hair behind her ear, displaying the plane of her high cheek bone. With a nod, she welcomed the detectives to her apartment.

"Good to see you, Jan," Thompson said. He never failed to notice her good looks, but he felt secure in his ability to hide his appreciation of her charms.

Forsky stared at the halfway point of a huge old pecan tree towering just outside her third floor balcony as he said, "Hello, Jan." She was glad to have the company and never caught the slight.

Being the ever-gracious hostess, Jan Doxce offered the detectives a drink and some cheesecake. She was an excellent cook, and always had something prepared for guests.

Thompson declined, but Forsky settled for a slice of the cheesecake. He would have preferred a salami sandwich with mayonnaise on white bread and some potato chips, but Jan did not keep such food in her kitchen. Forsky had inquired before.

Thompson and Forsky sat on the couch. On the coffee table before them was a manila folder. Many times in the past when Jan had assisted the officers, she had handwritten a summary of her work and placed it in such a folder. This was a strange degree of orderliness for an informant. The facts were there, but she always interjected personal comments, opinions, and suggestions as well. The woman was proud of her efforts, and like to be praised for them. Thompson and Forsky played that game well.

Jan sat in a recliner across from the detectives. She pointed at the folder and said with a slightly detectable vodka-induced slur, "There's everything on Luscious Lovelies, the dirty bastards."

Thompson picked up the folder, opened it and began reading. He recognized the names of the two owners. Both were broken-down bookies who had made other unsuccessful ventures into the escort service business. As he handed the folder to Forsky, Thompson told Jan, "As always, Jan, a good job."

She said nothing, but the edges of her lips curved upward. It was apparent the woman welcomed the words of praise. Thompson saw that her ego had been bolstered just enough to make her pleasant to deal with for the remainder of their stay.

Forsky noticed the same names Thompson had recognized. He knew Oscar Mortimer and Cecil "Dildo" Delaney all too well. He grinned and said to Thompson, "I see we've got a couple of old friends here."

Jan interrupted and directed her question at neither officer in particular, "You know these people?"

"Yeah...in fact, I'm surprised you don't know Mortimer and Delaney," Thompson said.

"Why's that?" Jan asked, very much on the defensive. "Do you think I know every criminal and whoremonger in town?"

Forsky explained, "It's just that these guys are both bookies, or at least they were last time we heard anything about them. As many bookies as you know, we just figured you might be familiar with them."

Feeling compelled to guard her reputation, Jan replied, "I know a few bookies, but have only one who is a very good friend. Period."

Thompson said, "Oscar Mortimer and Dildo Delaney are in their late sixties. I wasn't sure either one of them was still alive. Oscar's been a bad alcoholic for years and I think Dildo sucks on an oxygen tube all the time. These guys are first-rate losers. Every time they get involved in something besides the bookie business, all kinds of bad things happen to them. They get robbed, an employee snitches on them, somebody shoots at them…Oscar's car was torched in his driveway one time. Dildo got caught tryin' to cross back into Texas at Del Rio once with two-thousand Mexican rubber peckers in his trunk. He was going make a fortune wholesaling to the bookstores. Instead, he lost his inventory and his Cadillac. That's the kind of swine we're talking about here."

"Well, pardon me for providing information on criminals of such lowly stature!" Jan said.

Thompson realized he had overstepped his bounds. He looked to Forsky for help, but Forsky had returned his attention to the pecan tree.

Thompson placated, "Jan, I was trying to give you a little background on these people. I wasn't being critical of your information."

"That's not an apology, but I'll accept your explanation as you say it was intended," Jan said, appeased for the time being. It was time to leave.

Thompson said, "Jan, we do appreciate your help."

"I'm just glad to be of assistance, you know that," she said with a grin. "But, I do hate to see you go so soon. I'll prepare an excellent meal, if you'll both stay. I know neither of you have eaten this early in your shift."

"Jan, we can't. Thank you, though," Thompson said, wanting to get away from the woman as soon as possible.

With a dejected look, she replied, "I don't understand, but I'll try. Until next time, goodbye."

As she closed the door, Thompson knew that four or five more drinks would offset her loneliness, and then she would pass out for the evening.

As they approached the car, Forsky asked Thompson, "Wade, you don't really want to work on Oscar Mortimer and Dildo Delaney, do you?"

"Not in a million years! I have no interest in working on a couple of broken-down bookies like those two characters," Thompson replied, "and I know you share my sentiments."

Forsky said, "They'll go under quicker if we leave them alone. Besides, they would both require medical care. Can you see standing in front of the jail sergeant with a couple of desperadoes like them, Oscar with the DT's and Dildo with his oxygen tank? We'd probably have to incarcerate them in a rest home somewhere."

"They would both probably die before we could complete the prosecution reports," Thompson added.

Forsky thought of a solution. "Let's give it two weeks... if they're still in business, we'll make cases on a couple of girls, get affidavits, maybe run a search warrant. We might be able to get them released on their own recognizance, if they'll agree to stay out of the whore business for the remainder of their natural lives, which shouldn't be too long."

"Good idea. I'm in total agreement. I have no desire to put those almost dead guys in jail," Thompson said.

"To change the subject," Forsky said, "when are we gonna talk to Raeburn Compton?"

Thompson suggested, "If we can find him on Long Boulevard, let's do it tomorrow night."

"Okay, let's make a few copies of the tape, one for each of us, one for Sanderson, and another for Raeburn," Forsky suggested.

For the next hour, they remained sitting in the old Pontiac, discussing the Raeburn Compton project. They ironed out the details of the proposed confrontation. Then the topic turned to the Jan Doxee investigation.

Thompson asked Forsky, "You given any more thought as to how we're gonna work on Jan?"

"Actually, I've tried to avoid giving it any thought. I hate to work on someone that's as smart as I am," Forsky said, grinning.

"I hate working on someone that's smarter than I am," Thompson replied, without the grin. "I've given this a good deal of thought and agonizing reappraisal. I've come up with nothing satisfactory so far."

Forsky said, "You know, Jan is probably the only crook in town who doesn't have a cell phone. Anyone involved in the operation of an escort business has to be using the phone quite a bit. What about doing a trap n' trace on her home number again?"

"Guess it wouldn't hurt. It's been a year. We never come up with anything, though. This will be the fourth one, maybe we'll get lucky," Thompson said, trying hard to convince himself the undertaking would be worthwhile.

Forsky suggested, "Let's go to office and do the paperwork now. We can come in a little early tomorrow, walk everything through the DA's office, and get the subpoena to the phone company before they close."

"To the office, then," Thompson replied, admiring Forsky's readiness to make decisions.

CHAPTER 10

Bullethead Bentley and his partner J.C. Cook came to the office with four Jackson Street hustlers chained on a stringer, the fruits of a successful hustler tournament. Two patrol officers followed the group. A tournament often involved the entire squad of four detectives. On an occasion when Jackson was swarming with hustlers, like a sweltering night in August, the officers would set up a temporary command post and makeshift holding facility.

A stringer was a ten-foot-long chain with a single handcuff attached every foot or so along the chain's length. The chain would be cuffed to a solid object such as a parking meter, decorative wrought iron fence, or fire hydrant. Prisoners could be safely held in this manner without tying up a lot of manpower. Patrol officers transported the hustlers. If they were not busy, these officers would often hang around during the event and keep an eye on the stringer's catch.

From the looks of Bullethead and J.C., they had to ride one of their prisoners before taking him into custody. Bullet had a knot on his shiny noggin. A pocket on J.C.'s Hawaiian shirt had been ripped downward, but was still attached by threads. His white Panama hat had been trampled and the grease marks on it matched those of his knee-length yellow socks and white shorts.

Most people give no thought as to how nasty downtown streets are. So much vehicular traffic passes over them on a daily basis that the surface becomes highly polished, slick, and non-porous from the grease, oil, and gasoline residues. An inexperienced observer could easily determine which hustler had been less-than-cooperative. J.C. had ridden the big twenty-one-year-old into the ground in a literal sense as evidenced by the grease stain that covered the left side of the kid's face.

Lieutenant Pricklee came out of his office and walked into the squad room where all four detectives were busy. Also in the room were the four prisoners and two patrol officers. Before he could say anything, Pricklee caught the aroma of unwashed hustler and made a hasty retreat. J.C. and Bullethead both noticed this, looked up from their typing, and gave one another the appropriate irreverent, pleased smile.

The next afternoon, Thompson and Forsky took care of the trap n' trace subpoena for Jan Doxee's phone records. The request was for a thirty-day period. Perhaps there would be something useable this time.

As the detectives each devoured a hot link basket on a park bench in the heart of Raeburn Compton's northwest Dallas stomping grounds, they ironed out their strategy for a second time regarding their meeting with the sleazy activist.

In his practical-minded way, Forsky said, "Let's let him view it on the monitor and emphasize that we'll do what we can to protect his good name."

"Okay...I know we were going to give him a copy, but do we really need to? He's not going to show it to anyone, that's for sure. Let's treat him as if he's a decent person and recommend he stay away from bookstores, bars, shady folks and whores or whoever produced the video might try to undermine his paltry political career...something along those lines," Thompson suggested.

Forsky replied, "I guess a copy for Raeburn really wouldn't serve a purpose. In fact, not giving him one might heighten his fear that he could be exposed for being the swine he is...yeah, let's do it that way."

That evening, the detectives found Raeburn Compton's car

parked in front of Breezy's, another Long Boulevard beer joint. Thompson and Forsky were unaware that Compton ever went to Breezy's. It catered to an over-fifty ex-con alcoholic crowd. This was a sad lot of folks. Old career criminals develop health problems and find it difficult to ply their trade anymore. Most never worked legitimate jobs long enough to amass much in the way of Social Security benefits, profit sharing, or retirement. They could still peddle a few pills, do an occasional check or credit card scam, fence stolen goods, or maybe pull a swindle. While not steady work, such opportunistic ventures did not require much effort.

Over the years, more shootings and murders had occurred at Breezy's than all other Long Boulevard bars combined. A witness was never to be found after one of these incidents. Invariably, all twenty or thirty bar patrons had been in the bathroom at the crucial moment when the shot was fired. Raeburn Compton may well have been the reason Breezy's was still open and had all the required permits to serve beer and wine.

"It's almost nine. Let's wait him out. He won't stay past ten on a week night," Thompson said with the assurance of one that knew Raeburn Compton was more a creature of habit than most creatures.

In anticipation of a potential kink in the plans, Forsky stated, "Hope he doesn't come out with some filthy whore."

"I'm not sure whores even work Breezy's...too rough. Besides, that group in there isn't going to pay for sex when they have one another and one another's wives and girlfriends. I think Raeburn'll leave by himself," Thompson replied.

"Wade, your insight into the behavioral pattern of the human animal is nothing short of astonishing-distorted and debased, but astonishing," Forsky said.

At nine-thirty, Compton walked out of the bar and staggered to his car. Before opening the door, he paused, appearing to be confused for a moment. Then he turned to the car parked next to his, unzipped his pants, and urinated on the front tire. The detectives watched Raeburn Compton through binoculars.

Forsky remarked, "Just like a foul dog, pissing on somebody's tire!"

"Let's go, John. We need to catch him before he gets in his car," Thompson said, ignoring Forsky's remark.

The Pontiac roared to a halt behind Compton's Lincoln, startling the inebriated man and causing him to pee on himself. The old crook was frightened. The detectives held their badges and ID's up, plainly visible, so that Compton would know they did not intend to rob or harm him in some way.

Thompson said, "Mr. Compton, we're police officers and we need to speak with you."

Raeburn Compton regained as much composure as possible under the circumstances and replied, "Sure officers. You had me worried there for a minute. Thought I was fixing to get clubbed in the head and hijacked. I done pissed all over myself."

Forsky told Compton, "We can't talk here, Raeburn. Hop in our car, we'll pull across the street."

Compton was caught off guard. He had no idea what was going on and followed instructions without question. In the detectives' favor, Compton's slight stupor added to his cooperative attitude. Still, Raeburn did not want any of his cronies to see him talking to cops. Pants unzipped and with six inches of starched shirttail protruding through his fly, Compton got in the backseat of the Pontiac. The trio parked behind a vacant building. Forsky turned on the dome light for a few seconds to ready the camera's monitor for the viewing of the tape. Compton paid no attention to Forsky's actions. Instead, his gaze fixed on the car's fallen headliner. Forsky turned the light off.

Posing as the concerned advocate of the common man, Compton asked Thompson, "Is this the best vehicle the police department can provide you officers with? This thing looks like it needs a little work."

"It needs more than a little work, Raeburn," Thompson said, "and, yes, this is the best the department can provide."

For some reason, Thompson was glad to have been given the opportunity to voice his opinion, despite his knowledge that Raeburn Compton had no benevolent feelings for the police department or the condition of its equipment.

Beginning to get nervous, Compton asked, "Okay, boys, now what can I do for you?"

Thompson said, "Raeburn, we are aware of a homosexual encounter that you were recently involved in with a known prostitute. Your sexual preference is, of course, none of our business and we're not here to criticize. Other people, however, those more narrow-minded, might not be as tolerant and understanding as we are."

Compton interrupted, "What is this, this homosexual thing you talk about? I ain't standing still for some kind of shakedown!"

Thompson took charge and said, "We assure you this is no shakedown, Raeburn. No one wants a dime from your greasy pocket. It would be to your advantage to listen and speak when spoken to. Are you able to understand that?"

"I understand, sorry," Compton said, again lapsing into a confused state, not knowing where the conversation was headed.

Forsky had the video camera ready, and said, "Raeburn, watch the monitor here for a few seconds."

The man could not believe what he was seeing, his zenith of nightmares captured on film. Forsky turned the camera off. Compton was speechless. For effect, neither officer said anything, as they waited for Compton's eventual verbal comeback, if there was to be one.

Raeburn Compton said, "I know what you saw, but it's not what you think. I didn't know he was a man."

In his most professional manner, Thompson replied, "Raeburn, you owe us no explanation. We just thought you should be aware of the existence of this video. Other copies may exist. It's hoped that no one will use it against you. Now if you think you could explain the content to the satisfaction of others, then there's no cause for concern and we apologize for wasting your time."

"You know I can't explain getting punked by a he-she whore…nobody could," Compton said in frustration, "What do you all want out of this, anyway?"

"May we make a suggestion, Raeburn?" Forsky asked.

His tone angry, Raeburn said, "Make your suggestion."

"It would be to your advantage to clean up your part of town, and distance yourself from the criminals. You might refrain from the shakedowns and stop pounding the whores, in particular the underage ones," Forsky said.

Compton's anger and the alcohol in his system had instilled confidence as he asked," If you know about those things and think I did them, why not prosecute me?"

"Raeburn, that can be done if you want it that way. You know you're a sack a' shit and we do, too. Proving up a case on you wouldn't be difficult. A lot of good people have had their eye on your shady dealings for a long time," Forsky answered, hoping the amateur politician would buy into the bluff part about the ease of prosecution.

Raeburn was quiet for a minute. He was giving it all some thought.

Thompson said, "Raeburn, you've got a lot of decent people in your district and you don't treat them well at all. Yet you encourage the criminal activity. Many good people live in your part of town, others own businesses here and many of them are old folks, but most of them are smarter than you and your swine cohorts. If they get together, you and your criminal buddies have had it, believe me."

Compton would not admit defeat as he said, "There are constituents, 'swine' as you call them, that I may owe favors to. What do I do about them?"

Thompson replied, "That's your problem, Raeburn, but I think you have a lot less to lose from a strained relationship with your constituent thugs than you do with the good folks. The righteous ones will hang you, Raeburn. They've had it. Just wait and see, if you want to take the chance."

Thompson was completely out of practical reasons for Raeburn Compton's planned conversion to virtuosity.

"If I choose to do what you suggest, what's my first step?" Raeburn asked, nervous again.

Forsky answered, "We're not telling you what to do, Raeburn. You need to understand that. It would be wise to start doing things the right way. Maybe you need to get together with the decent citizens in your district. The ones you've ignored since you became an activist and sold out to the hoodlums. I think they can steer you in the right direction."

"Wait a minute!" Compton said. "I haven't ignored anyone. Those old folks don't like me. That's been the problem all along. They don't want to work with me!"

"Raeburn, grow up. They don't like you because you're a crook!" Thompson said.

Following a speechless moment, Compton told the detectives, "If I do things 'right', as you say, I'm finished as far as politics. I'll do good to serve out my term on the boards I'm on, and I sure hope I could do it without getting whacked. There's some rough folks in my neighborhood, you know."

Forsky looked at Compton and said, "It's up to you, Raeburn."

Thompson and Forsky both felt ahead of the game, and were ready to call it quits for the night. Thompson said, "Raeburn, you've had to much to drink to drive home. Leave your car where it is and walk over to your playroom at the Uptown Downtown to spend the night. You don't want to risk a DWI."

"No, no, I don't need no DWI. All this has pretty well

exhausted me anyway. Guess I'll be hearing from you fellows again?" Compton asked.

Thompson said, "I don't think so, Raeburn. Just get busy making things right."

In a series of unsteady movements, Compton stood up. Holding the door open, he bent down and said to the detectives, "Yeah, I know what to do. It's easy to say. But none of us knows how difficult doing it is going to be."

He was so right and Thompson and Forsky knew it at least as well as Compton did. Compton slowly closed the door and walked in the direction of room #8.

The detectives felt good about what had transpired. The project had turned out better than anticipated. They drove toward the office in silence for several minutes. Both were in a state of semi-shock. After a while, Thompson could not resist any longer, but he knew he would have to downplay the episode to discuss it with Forsky.

"Well, what do you think, John?" Thompson asked.

Forsky replied, "You know what I think, Wade. We beat the old swine! You know as well as I do that this is not an everyday occurrence. And, we did it without endangering good folks like Robert and Dorothy Johnson or their kid, Tonya. I feel good about it, and you should too."

"Yeah, I do, but it's a shame we can't tell anyone except Tal Sanderson how things went," Thompson said, no longer trying to hide his true feelings on the matter.

Forsky smiled and replied, "I'm glad we don't have to tell anyone but Tal."

Sergeant Sanderson was in his office when the detectives arrived downtown. The supervisor looked up from his desk when they walked in. Forsky said in a mischievous way, "Talbert, we need to talk to you for a minute."

"Boys, my time is yours," Sanderson said, confident the

news was good.

Thompson shut the door to Sanderson's office. He and Forsky were too wound up to sit. Forsky said, "Raeburn Compton's guilty conscience got the better of him tonight, and he's chosen to mend his ways."

"We need to get the people in his district, at least the ones who aren't criminals, to put some pressure on him right now," Thompson said.

Sanderson said, "Let me take care of that. I'll get in touch with Abraham Fishbein tomorrow. Believe me, one phone call will be all that's necessary. Abe and his citizens' group will be a thorn in Raeburn Compton's side, like they've never been before."

Eighty-year old Abraham Fishbein was a retired attorney and had been president of a neighborhood property owners group in Compton's stronghold for years. He had tried everything short of assassination to get something done about the corrupt activist. Fishbein had, at various times, confronted city council members about Compton. All had ignored the old lawyer. They were afraid of Compton. While Fishbein's fervor on the issue had never diminished, support by group members had. Many had just given up.

For some time, Raeburn Compton had refused Abe Fishbein admittance to his office. Compton had instructed his staff to give Fishbein any of a myriad of excuses as to why the politician was unable to meet with him. If Sanderson even hinted that now was an opportune time to confront Compton, Fishbein would be camped on the activist's doorstep in short order.

Like most cops who have been at it for a while, Talbert Sanderson did not care to do police work during off-duty hours. This would be a rare exception, however. Even though he did not get home until 2:30 A.M, he set the alarm for 7:30 A.M., so he could contact Abe Fishbein. The lawyer still maintained a one-man office located in downtown Dallas. He arrived around 7:00 A.M, five days a week. Fishbein did a limited amount of pro bono legal work, and was involved with a number of local civic and charitable organizations. He had more money than ten people could spend in their lifetimes and he was generous with it, but few knew of his philanthropic efforts.

One time, Fishbein needed two witnesses and a notary late at night. He called the only late-night notary he knew who could keep his mouth shut, Tal Sanderson. It seemed Fishbein was giving some money to an organization that at the last minute required the kindly donor to sign paperwork attesting to the fact that he was sane, and would not demand the money be returned. Sanderson arrived at the attorney's home with Thompson and Forsky in tow as witnesses. It was obvious that the tactic employed by whatever organization it was had embarrassed Abe Fishbein and hurt the man's feelings in a needless way. Sanderson and the detectives knew what kind of man "Mr. Fish" was.

"Hello, hello. Abe Fishbein speaking," an impatient voice said when the sergeant rang his number.

"Mr. Fishbein, this is Tal Sanderson. Are you busy, sir?" the sergeant asked, knowing what the answer would be.

"Sergeant Sanderson, it is always good to hear from you, and yes, I'm very busy, I'm always very busy. Don't bother to contact me when I'm not very busy because I'll be dead," Abe Fishbein said in his strong New York accent, diminished minimally during the fifty years he had lived in Dallas.

Before Sanderson could speak, the old man continued, "What would prompt your call so early in the morning, sergeant? I believe you are working nights this month, correct?" Few people outside of his unit, other police officers included, would be aware of Sanderson's work schedule.

"Mr. Fishbein, I won't go into detail, but Raeburn Compton might be in a very civic-minded mood at present. He would be most accommodating to the needs of your neighborhood organization," Sanderson said.

Abe Fishbein respected Sanderson and there was no need

for questions as he said, "I'm sorry...I thought this call was from someone I knew, but I am mistaken. Some anonymous callers are very credible persons, however. Thank you very much."

"You're welcome, Mr. Fish...good luck," Sanderson replied, quite pleased with the old man's response.

Neither said goodbye. Fishbein hung up first, anxious to clear the line so he could make an appointment with Raeburn Compton.

CHAPTER 11

Jan Doxee sat in the lounge area of the elegant mountain estate outside of Lake Placid, New York. She enjoyed her first imbibement of the day, vodka and water mixed with care so that the volume of water did not dilute the full-strength taste and accompanying kick of the vodka. In a pinch, the water portion was unnecessary.

Her couch companion was known to everyone as Mr. Western. His first name was Charles, but few people called him Charles. Western may have been his true last name. Mr. Western was a CPA in Houston, Texas. In his fifties, Western no longer did much work with numbers and taxes. He had plenty of smart, eager, and well-educated youngsters that did that sort of thing for him. When Western made the infrequent visit to his office, it was only to measure his current level of wealth. He had built a tremendous practice in the Houston area over thirty years; his firm did work for a large number of oil and gas businesses.

Never in danger of being referred to as a handsome man, Western needed a good dose of sunlight; his complexion had the pasty pallor of a corpse. His skinny frame could have belonged to a third-world, worm-infested victim. He manipulated his ill fitting false teeth, rattling them inside his mouth, with irritating frequency. His clothes were cheap, and his Hush Puppy loafers rang of John Forsky-the ultimate in practicality, if not fashion. He reinforced his overall image with an off-brand can of domestic beer, smuggled into Lake Placid in his luggage.

It was almost 10:00 P.M. when Thompson and Forsky arrived at the vice office with two Long Boulevard prostitutes. Identical twins, twenty-two years old and dressed in matching street whore outfits testified to the fact that vice work was never dull, let alone routine.

As the young ladies stood on the shoulder of the road, eight cars were in line, their drivers waiting for a turn to talk to the new girls on the block. Forsky called a nearby patrol squad to disperse the prospective tricks, so that he and Thompson would be the only customers. Making the cases involved no sporting opportunities whatsoever; they were too easy.

When the detectives got to the office with the twin tarts, they heard the loud voice of Herbert Greenlee. Greenlee was the chief over the vice, narcotics, and intelligence divisions. Seated at a desk in the squad room, he was on the phone providing a big chief, or even the number one chief, with information. If a chief was in the vice office at night, it was in response to a most serious situation.

Nevertheless, in his harried state, Greenlee waved and grinned at Thompson and Forsky. He stood and they shook hands. Lieutenant Pricklee came in the room and gave the chief a handwritten note. From the way he took hold of the paper, it was of extreme importance. He relayed the information to his boss.

Bullethead Bentley and J.C. Cook had been working hustlers again. Cook was driving an old British convertible that actually belonged to John Forsky. Everyone used it as an undercover car from time to time. Forsky did not drive the car on a regular basis and left it parked with the other undercover vehicles. Cook picked up a huge hustler who tried to rob the officer. The hustler pulled a knife and poked Cook's belly with it a couple of times as Cook was driving. He demanded that Cook pull over and hand him his billfold. Instead, Cook pulled over to the curb and with his left hand picked up the revolver he kept under his left leg. With the knife blade still touching Cook's abdomen, the detective shot the nasty male whore twice from a distance of two feet, killing the miscreant instantaneously with two rounds to the sternum.

Greenlee and Pricklee had already been to the scene. Tal Sanderson was at the location with representatives from the other police department divisions that respond to such incidents. The volume of paperwork generated by an officer-involved shooting was tremendous. Sanderson and Cook would spend considerable time for several days on direct and peripheral matters related to the shooting. As it turned out, the hustler had been handled for murder twice and served one pen term for the charge. His second trip to the joint was for armed robbery. He had just received his final conviction and sentence from which there was no appeal or parole, all at minimal taxpayer expense.

Greenlee hung up the phone. Instant relief was apparent from the look on his face. Trying to avoid a smile, he stared at Forsky and said, "John, your little convertible's a mess. It's not only bloody, but one of J.C.'s bullets exited the hustler's back and penetrated that flimsy British door, breaking the rolled down window glass in the process. We'll see if..."Greenlee broke out in great unrestrained laughter, knowing how frugal Forsky was.

Forsky said, "I really don't see what's so funny here, Herbert. After all, it's not your car."

Greenlee regained his composure and said, "What I was going to say before I rudely broke into laughter was that we'll see if we can come up with the funds to fix it."

"It would be most appreciated," Forksy said, his reply laced with sarcasm.

Two patrol officers came in with a handcuffed transvestite. He was six-foot and weighed two hundred pounds. From all appearances, he had required a bit of riding. The uniformed officers had transported "Claudia" for two vice detectives on the other squad.

They found Claudia performing favors in the arcade

section of a bookstore. After Barney Fawcett made a prostitution case on the beast, he was unable to lure the whore outside to make the arrest. Fawcett's partner, Niles Goldman was waiting near the door. Both detectives went into the arcade again. Behind a partially open booth door, they found Claudia "glory-holing" a customer through a hole cut through the common wall of two adjacent booths. An old guy was in the next booth, pants around his ankles. He had backed up to the hole as the he-she performed an anal operation with his unclean instrument.

Claudia went berserk at the interruption. He grabbed a pencil from his purse and stabbed Barney Fawcett in the left temple. Fawcett was dazed as blood flowed in profusion. He and Goldman were able to get Claudia on the floor and handcuffed him. The detectives made a stop at the Dallas County Hospital emergency room where Fawcett's injury was tended. While it looked like a bullet wound, no stitches were required.

Fawcett and Goldman arrived at the vice office. It was evident Barney was experiencing considerable discomfort despite the pain-killing injection he received at the hospital. He was in no shape to type an arrest report.

Captain Holland approached the injured officer and said, "Barney, I'm going to get someone to take you home…you don't look so good."

"I am feeling rather poorly, Captain. I'd like to lay down… it feels like that pencil is stickin' out the other side of my head right now," Fawcett said.

Barney Fawcett was a good vice cop and a hard worker. Anyone could work with Barney. While he did not preach to others in the office, he was quite religious. However, Barney was the biggest gossip and nosiest person Thompson had ever known. Barney would stand over someone doing paperwork and attempt to read even dull, insignificant material. To make matters worse, he would try to give the appearance that he wasn't reading over someone's shoulder. If Barney heard an office rumor, most notably about someone's personal affairs, he made an effort to discreetly interrogate everyone in the office. Different people, including Thompson and Forsky, had intentionally fed Barney bizarre, erroneous information on occasion. The tactic had served to embarrass Barney Fawcett more than once, but he never seemed to get the message.

Niles Goldman, Barney's partner, could best be described as an almost non-speaking person. He gave the impression that everytime he actually said something, it had been very well thought out. Like Fawcett, Goldman enjoyed working. The two got along in a splendid manner.

Chief Herbert Greenlee and Captain Arlie Holland concluded the preliminary cursory look into the shooting episode. There was no question it was a self-defense issue, but over the next few days Greenlee and Holland would justify the case to the news media and Monday-morning quarterback groups within the department and the community. In addition, there were various fleeting libertarians, closet politicians looking for a cause to exploit, no matter how feeble the issue.

Herbert Greenlee had served in vice as a lieutenant many years earlier. He was Thompson's boss when the young detective transferred to vice. Like Arlie Holland, Greenlee was well liked by the detectives and supervisors. He treated cops, citizens, and criminals fairly and went by the book only when pragmatic methods failed. Greenlee was disliked by several other chiefs and supervisors of various ranks. It was no coincidence that these same people feared Greenlee. He made public ridicule of others of equal or higher rank when it came to their petty jealousies, extra-marital affairs, poor decision making, mistreatment of subordinates, or any other issue that was good for both a laugh and / or much-needed exposure. Chief Greenlee had embarrassed many persons that deserved embarrassment with his witty, watchdog ways.

When Thompson got to the office the next evening, he

found a large manila envelope in his in-tray. The address label had been typed and there was no return address. The contents were an inch thick and the weight of the package accounted for its six-dollar postage fee.

John Forsky was busy filing a case and did not bother to look up when Thompson walked in. Forsky preferred not to be disturbed if the only reason was to say hello. Thompson opened the package and his usual serious look turned to a smile.

He said to Forsky, "John, Virginia Baccus came through for us!"

"Jan's records?" Forsky asked.

Thompson was anxious to let his partner know what sort of treasures the envelope contained. He could already see financial transactions, customer information, credit card statements and more.

Thompson said, "I'm gonna find a vacant office where we can spread this out … finish your case…we'll get started when you're through."

"Give me ten minutes," Forsky replied, glad to wind up the wearisome paperwork.

Arlie Holland had a small conference table in his office that was seldom used and he would not be around this night anyway. Thompson attempted to lay out everything in some semblance of order. It appeared that Virginia Baccus had copied the material randomly, not necessarily in the order she found it. Lack of organization was out of character for Jan Doxee.

Forsky entered Holland' office and paused to look at the mess on the table. Thompson had noticed stick-on yellow notes affixed to many of the copies. Forsky saw them as well.

"Virginia do her own critique on all this stuff?" Forsky asked.

Thompson replied, "Looks that way."

Forsky picked up a page with an attached note on it and said, "Listen to this, Wade. She says 'Pay close attention to this credit card statement. Jan charged over $400.00 at one liquor store in one month'...I must say that's really useful information."

Thompson was preoccupied and made no response.

Forsky said, "I suppose I shouldn't be critical. We're fortunate we got this stuff."

After a couple of minutes and with a hint of discouragement in his voice, Thompson said, "I don't really know what's here, John, but we ought to be able to make an evaluation in an hour or so."

"Let's start by having a square meal. We've got until 2:00 A.M. to go through all this," Forsky suggested.

"Thompson replied, "Fine, let's eat."

To Forsky, "square meal" meant cafeteria food, something balanced as opposed to their normal unhealthy trash diet of Mexican food, hot links, barbecue, or fried chicken. Thompson also welcomed a cafeteria meal.

As they drove through the downtown streets, Thompson gave thought to the paperwork spread on the captain's conference table. He was disappointed in what he had seen so far, but did not know why. It just seemed something was missing, but how could he reach such a conclusion so soon? He had a strong feeling that the copies of Jan's records were of questionable worth.

Upon their return to the office, they noticed Lt. Pricklee seated at the conference table reading a newspaper. The detectives did not have a key to the captain's office, so they could not lock the door when they left. As far as they knew, there was nothing in the pile of paperwork that the lieutenant should not see. However, they did not like the idea of him snooping.

"Hi, guys. How's everything this evening?" Pricklee asked.

"Fine, lieutenant, just fine," Thompson said.

In an insincere monotone, Forsky chimed in, "Great, lieutenant."

"I don't know what you all have going here, but somebody

buys a lot of booze according to those credit card statements," Pricklee said.

He had been snooping. Neither detective responded to Pricklee's remark. Instead, they immersed themselves in the records. Now feeling unwelcome, the lieutenant made no further comment and left the captain's office.

Forsky said, "Well, he's almost as good a detective as Virginia Baccus, and I say that as a true compliment to Pricklee. I wasn't aware he had that much insight into police work."

"Yeah...so far we've got two expert opinions that we're dealing with a problem drinker," Thompson remarked.

"I think I have all the wire transfer copy receipts. Looks like seven back to the first of the year," Forsky said.

Thompson replied, "Those things never have much information, on purpose. We won't know much without a subpoena on each one."

After two hours non-stop, Thompson and Forsky both became weary of looking at the paperwork. They had combed through ninety-percent of it, and Thompson's initial assessment of its worth was unchanged. Forsky's estimation was one of indifference.

"I'm going to draw up the subpoenas now. I'm tired of looking at all this for the time being," Forsky said.

As usual, John Forsky was planning. He had court the next morning. While he was at the courthouse, he would get the required judicial signature on each subpoena and fax a copy to the various banks for compliance. Banks and other financial institutions were, as a rule, very cooperative with law enforcement agencies regarding such research despite the fact that they received no payment for their work. For anyone else, a flat hourly research fee was charged. Most detectives tried to limit requests for records to the bare minimum, so as not to take advantage of the hard working clerks who provided this much-needed gratis service.

There were numerous deposit slips and bank statements

for two local checking accounts, as well as a savings account at each bank. Neither checking account ever had more than a fifteen hundred-dollar balance since the first of the year. Only a few checks were written monthly on either account, and they were all to area businesses or to pay rent or utilities. The credit card companies were also paid from these accounts. Credit card billings always averaged under a thousand dollars monthly, well under. In addition, almost all of that was for vodka or other liquor. The rest was for clothing. Thompson knew that Jan flew on occasion, but there were no airline tickets charged on either credit card for the entire year so far. Neither were there rental car charges, meals, or anything else from out of town. In fact, based on the paperwork scattered on the conference table, there was nothing to indicate she ever left Dallas. All businesses she dealt with where a credit card was used for payment were almost within walking distance of the woman's apartment.

    The two savings accounts provided little or nothing in the way of clues, either. There was nothing questionable. One account had just fewer than four thousand dollars; the other, a twelve-hundred-dollar balance. Activity in the form of deposits and withdrawals for each was infrequent.

    Just as Virginia Baccus had said, there was handwritten information regarding escort service business and a list of suspected vice cops. Most of this was several years old. Thompson and Forsky had seen very similar notes or possibly even the same material when they ran a search warrant at the apartment some years before.

    Thompson still wanted to believe he had been incorrect in his earlier assessment of the information Virginia Baccus had 'skulked' from her daughter's apartment. His only hope now was that the wire transfer records would provide something useful. Also, the trap n' trace on her telephone might prove worthwhile.

    As Forsky finished the fill-in-the-blank subpoena forms for the wire transfers, Thompson sat on the edge of his partner's desk.

Forsky paused, looked up at Thompson, and said defeatedly, "Jan's records are worthless, right?"

"Right… at least so far, but maybe the subpoenas will do some good," Thompson replied.

CHAPTER 12

It was 5:00 P.M., Wednesday. Tal Sanderson came in at four to attend a brief, but regular, weekly vice supervisors' meeting. As Arlie Holland was on his way home for the day, he stopped by Sanderson's office, giving him a handwritten note regarding a vice-related complaint.

"Tal, would you have a couple of your guys look into this?" Holland asked. "May be nothing to it; an anonymous source called the chief's office."

Sanderson glanced at the note and replied, "We'll take care of it, Arlie."

"Thanks, Tal. See you tomorrow," Holland said, and walked out the door.

It was "changeover" time when Forsky got to the office. The cramped squad room became particularly tight as the 10-6 detectives came to the office toward the end of their day and 6-2 people arrived to begin their night shift. Two of the day detectives were typing up a couple of prisoners arrested in a downtown adult theater. In irony, the only four such theaters in downtown Dallas were all within close proximity of the police building. In fact, during daytime hours it was more convenient for detectives to walk to these establishments than to drive and have to hunt for a parking place.

Conventioneers often filled hotels in Dallas' central business district. Some of these people provided a questionable boost to the local economy by patronizing the various adult establishments. One of the prisoners, in town for a seminar, had sought companionship at the El Rauncho Theater. The El Rauncho was, without a doubt, the seediest of Dallas' adult locations. The man found a willing partner in the form of a sunlighting hustler supplementing his nighttime earnings. As this butt pirate was playing hide-the-sausage with the out-of-towner in the romantic setting afforded by an arcade booth, he was also lifting the man's wallet and money clip.

The two vice cops had been lurking in the aisleway when they heard a commotion coming from a booth. Next came one horrendous crash as the flimsy paneling forming one wall of the booth flew off. The two men were exposed (?) and the hustler was still engaged in a mobile anal aggression on his victim. Both men's pants were around their ankles. Suddenly losing balance, they fell to the floor. Paper money was scattered about. Despite all the adversities, interruptions, and an audience, it appeared the hustler never missed a stroke. After handcuffing the two lust birds, the detectives corralled ten patrons who had witnessed the event and got their names and other vital information for inclusion in the arrest reports. The term 'unwilling witnesses that don't care to get involved' takes on new meaning in such a setting.

When Thompson got to the squad room and glanced around, he gave up all hope of finding a chair to sit in. About that time, Sanderson approached with the note from the captain in his hand.

"Wade, you and John come in my office for a minute. I've got an assignment from the boss."

The noise level in the squad room increased. Thompson stood in the doorway and motioned Forsky to come to Sanderson's office. As the detectives seated themselves, Sanderson handed Forsky the note. He read it and handed it to Thompson. As Thompson was reading, Sanderson began explaining the gist of the message, as he understood it.

"This came from an anonymous source through the chief's office to the captain. Apparently, there's some sort of wife-swapping activity in the theater at the Carnal Club on Friday and Saturday nights. I know it goes on in most of the stores and you all have better things to do, but it has to be checked out. It sounds like this one is an organized affair. It starts at 1:00 A.M., they don't allow single males in, couples only, supposed to be running a bar, and so forth. See if you can find a couple of female officers to go with you on Friday night," Sanderson said.

"We really do have better things to do, Tal," Thompson said, half-joking.

Forsky said nothing, already looking forward to the assignment. Sanderson said, "I know, but it's been a while since I gave you guys one of these. Work it however you see fit."

Sanderson was right. He was fair to a fault in handing out assignments. It had been some time since Thompson and Forsky had received such a complaint to work. One like this usually came from a jealous competitor, rather than a concerned citizen. In this way a sleazy, greasy bookstore owner could get vice to work for him instead of against him.

"Well, Tal, much as we've enjoyed visiting with you, we have to get busy and find dates for the movie," Thompson said.

By this time, the crowd had cleared from the squad room, and the detectives could sit at their desks. "Who are we going call, John, particularly with such short notice? Whoever we get, they need to be a little rough, don't you think? We've got to do this tomorrow night," Thompson said, fearful there was insufficient time to prepare for the assignment.

Forsky replied, "Let me take care of everything. I've got some ideas."

"It's all yours," Thompson remarked, somewhat relieved.

Forsky asked, "Wade, you remember Wanda Winchester?"

"Is that a whore, a stripper, or both?" Thompson answered

with a question.

"She's a patrol officer. We used her last summer for a decoy prostitution detail on Long Boulevard. She really raked in the customers. Tall girl...you remember her... she's actually Dr. Winchester, a former English professor who got bored with Shakespeare and sentence diagramming," Forsky remarked.

Forsky's hints aided Thompson in remembering Wanda Winchester.

"Okay, I know who you're talking about. Real attractive girl, but she could probably pass for whore or stripper with the right clothes and makeup," Thompson said.

"You did say rough, remember?" Forsky reminded his partner.

"Yeah, she'd be just fine," Thompson replied.

"I'm sure you don't know Lottie Symington, but she works the same patrol detail with Wanda. I met Lottie at a party, but she's worked decoys a time or two with the B-team. She would be perfect, believe me," Forsky said. He was becoming very enthused about the Friday night adventure.

Thompson and Forsky referred to the other vice detail as the B-team, and it was not meant in an entirely joking manner. Productivity was lower and personnel problems had been a chronic plague for the group for a long time, despite numerous changes in detectives and supervisors. Even some members of the group referred to themselves as the B-team.

"When I hear the name 'Lottie Symington', I picture a woman five feet tall, weighing about one-eighty and wearing a sack dress. She needs to shave her underarms; she has most, but not all, of her front teeth," Thompson said.

As he dialed the number for the patrol station, Forsky told Thompson, "That's not an accurate description. They should be working tonight, unless their days off have changed."

Even if the women agreed to work the assignment, Forsky would have to get formal approval from their supervisors. This was always done as a courtesy gesture. On a very few occasions, supervisors had refused to allow subordinates to work temporary vice assignments. No reasons were required, but Thompson suspected religious or moral convictions might have influenced such decisions. He respected those choices. However, he did not understand the misconception that some persons, police officers and civilians alike, had about vice work and the people that did it. Some of these persons preferred to remain ignorant of what they believed were trashy people doing trashy work. Vice personnel were likely more streetwise than citizens and many other police officers. There was nothing wrong with that. In fact, it was an obvious asset for vice work and one developed over time. Good vice cops are actors and actors are creative. Creativity is a prerequisite for success in vice work. Some persons lack creativity and imagination and would perform poorly in an undercover setting. Then, these same people possess talents that better qualify them for other types of police work, areas where good vice cops might perform poorly.

Vice is the best available training ground for narcotics or intelligence work. Those officers going into these fields without a solid vice background suffer. It can be likened to a college student taking an advance course without the basic prerequisite course. The course can be passed, but it will often be needlessly difficult.

Some would-be undercover officers, including ones that might be assigned to vice, think that all one needs to do the work are starched jeans, a huge Buick hubcap-style belt buckle, cowboy boots made from a reptile carcass, an enormous white cowboy hat, and a beard. Outfitted accordingly, criminals fall at the officers' feet and give compelling confessions as to their errant ways, demanding incarceration. As a rule, such officers are harmless and quite ineffective. However, they give the true undercover detective an undeserved bad name. They are too busy being self-possessed to do much in the way of real police work. From a general standpoint, their undercover careers are short-lived and uneventful.

Within an hour, Forsky had spoken with both female officers. Each was excited about the assignment. Since it was only for one night, he had no problem getting the approval of their supervisors. It was decided that everyone would meet at the office at 11:00 P.M. Friday night.

Thompson thought about the Carnal Club assignment on his way home. He was not looking forward to it, but was not sure why. When he had similar thoughts about other assignments he always reasoned that he had worked vice for too many years. However, each time he became involved in the actual assignment, it turned out better, often much better, than anticipated. Thompson tried to convince himself it would be no different this time.

Barney Fawcett got to work Friday evening and immediately looked at the detail board. This showed who was working that day, and who was on a day off. It also indicated a temporary change in hours to accommodate a particular assignment. Fawcett noticed that Thompson, Forsky, Sanderson, and two patrol officers on temporary duty were working 11:00 P.M. to 7:00 A.M., very odd hours indeed. Fawcett wasted no time to begin his investigation into the matter. He questioned everyone in the office, and no one could provide an answer.

At 10:00 P.M., Barney and his partner came in the office with a prisoner. Tal Sanderson got to work early, in fact he followed Barney to the vice office. When Fawcett saw Sanderson go into his office, the detective made a bee line to the door.
"Evening, Talbert," Barney said.
Sanderson grinned and said, "Hi, Barn."
Barney Fawcett began his line of questioning and said, "I see where you, Thompson and Forsky are working some strange hours tonight. What are you all doing?"

Sanderson had survived many such Barney Fawcett interrogations.

"It's pretty big. I'm not sure I should discuss it, Barn," Sanderson said. "Tell you what, though, if we need some help, I'll call you."

The assignment was no secret, but this is how people dealt with Barney during one of his nosy routines. Fawcett never gave up when something was none of his business. However, Barney had struck out so far.

At 10:30 P.M., Forsky and Thompson came into the vice office together. Thompson was pre-occupied with the Jan Doxee investigation and could not muster the enthusiasm he needed for the movie date. Forsky was excited and eager for the girls to arrive.

"Wade, I know you can hardly wait to get to the theater, but you'll just have to relax for now," Forsky said, hoping his partner would cheer up a bit.

Thompson's voice lacked any hint of eagerness as he replied, "Yeah, John…I'll try to settle down."

A dark-haired woman in her mid-forties walked into the vice office and stopped at the reception area. She saw no one in the main office and took a seat next to the receptionist's desk. Five-feet-seven and conservatively dressed in khaki slacks, green knit cotton shirt, and walking shoes, she was quite attractive and shapely at perhaps one-hundred -twenty pounds.

Thompson came from the squad room and noticed the displaced female. There was no receptionist or other civilian clerical personnel on duty after 6:00 P.M. It seemed odd for someone to be seated there at night. He introduced himself, "I'm Wade Thompson and you're Lottie, right?"

"I'm Lottie Symington and I'm very pleased to meet you," she said with a big smile displaying perfect teeth as she stood and shook Thompson's hand.

Lottie was about ten years older, much taller, much lighter, and far better looking than what Thompson had imagined. She had well-manicured long fingernails-real ones, not the fake kind. For as long as he could remember, he had noticed the hands and nails of other persons, particularly women, as if such features gave him insights into their personalities and characters.

Thompson would not characterize Lottie as 'rough' by any means. However, she did give the impression that she had enough worldly experience to handle any vice assignment. She smelled good, too, not a perfumy fragrance, but a pleasant one from fine soap or body lotion.

Thompson said, "Make yourself at home, Lottie. As soon as Wanda Winchester gets here, we'll all sit down and talk about what we're going to do tonight. I understand you've done some temporary work in vice before."

"I've done decoy work on the other detail, but I hope there's more to vice than that," she said, expressing obvious disgust with being propositioned by a bunch of old, creepy, foul-smelling fat guys.

Thompson replied in affirmation, "There's a lot more to it than that. A lot of the work is quite interesting." But, he realized he was being less than truthful as he thought about the old, creepy, foul-smelling fat guys who had accosted him in adult bookstores.

In walked Wanda Winchester as Forsky came out of the squad room. When she saw John Forsky, she smiled. He said, "Dr. Winchester!"

"John, it's been a long time. How are you?" Wanda Winchester said with spirit as she hugged Forsky.

Wanda was younger than Lottie, but had to have been forty. Unnaturally blond, she was five-feet-eight, one-forty, and looked like she ran and lifted weights. No doubt the woman was attractive, although her teeth, chest, and fingernails were not factory originals. A short skirt and sleeveless blouse revealed tanned and muscular arms and legs.

"Wanda, this is Wade Thompson," Forsky said. She and

Thompson shook hands.

"Good to meet you, Wanda. Hope you enjoy working here, temporary as it may be," Thompson said.

In her outgoing manner, she replied, "Wade, I met you when I worked the decoy prostitution."

"That's right," Thompson said, almost with enthusiasm, "I remember."

The foursome adjourned to the break room where Thompson and Forsky went over the basics of the assignment. Thompson was quite impressed with Forsky's selection of officers. In his opinion, these women appeared to be streetwise and would be easy to work with. However, they were both lookers and that might present a problem once inside an adult theater. Some greasy swapper would want to trade his beast of a wife or girlfriend for Wanda or Lottie, at least for a few minutes.

They left the office at 12:30 A.M. and drove to the Carnal Club. Tal Sanderson followed in his car. The Carnal Club theater was located inside Bookstore Impure. Although both businesses were under the same roof on Long Boulevard, they had two different owners. This was indeed an odd setup in comparison to the other adult locations.

Organized crime factions allegedly controlled the adult entertainment business in the United States. "Influenced" may be a more appropriate word than "controlled". It is unlikely a direct descendant of Lucky Luciano operates the local adult bookstore. Just because the owner of an adult business may be an ill-educated shady character in no way means he is a bona-fide gangster or has ties to such criminals. Many persons, including quite a few in law enforcement, stereotype these persons. By doing so, they assume a good deal of inaccuracies. These assumptions tend to become 'factual' over a time. Like real gangsters, however, bookstore owners use altered paperwork, fictitious names, and dummy ownerships to hide the true particulars about their sleazy business. That is all simply good business acumen for one running an operation that the IRS or state comptrollers' office might have a keen interest in.

The production and distribution of adult movies and magazines, the manufacture of novelties and sexual devices sold in the stores, arcade booths, and video equipment are different matters entirely, from the standpoint of traditional organized crime. This may be where they have a foot in the door. That foot might wear a size fourteen.

Forsky and Thompson had prepared to arrest a large number of theater patrons, perhaps twenty or more. Two two-man patrol units would wait in a nearby parking lot. In addition, a paddy wagon had been borrowed for the evening. It could accommodate dozen or more prisoners. Sergeant Sanderson would remain at this staging area.

John Forsky and Wanda Winchester went in first. It was 12:50 A.M. Thompson and Lottie Symington waited five minutes and entered. The management did not allow theater entrance to anyone before 1:00 A.M. Most adult theaters did not have regular hours and showed films on a twenty-four hour basis if one customer was present. Fifteen, maybe twenty, anxious couples were either waiting at the theater entrance or milling about the bookstore. Wanda Winchester became engaged in conversation with a store clerk who showed her a sampling of adult toys. He demonstrated a $65.00 deluxe crank-operated dildo. While casting no dispersions on the woman's character, Thompson could see that Wanda was more comfortable working vice than most male vice detectives.

While Lottie Symington was a bit more reserved, the bookstore atmosphere did not appear to bother her. The theater door opened at exactly 1:00 A.M. Admission was fifty dollars per couple. According to an official-looking sign from the local fire marshal that was posted at the entrance, maximum capacity of the theater was eighty persons. When Thompson and Lottie Symington entered, there were at least thirty people seated and the line outside the door was getting longer. Forsky and Thompson had no idea the place did this much business. Most of the theaters did swap/exhibition business on weekends, but not on this scale. The Carnal Club had become the Dallas mecca for weekend swap meets. The word was out, and if a couple did not get there early enough, they would have to settle for group grope activity at one of the lesser establishments.

Many patrons were crowded around the portable bar. Dare say this place had no liquor license, mixed drink permit, or anything else that would make the serving of alcoholic beverages legal. This violation would hurt the ownership far more than a few lewdhead cases. Forsky and Wanda had already purchased mixed drinks. Lottie found a couple of back row seats next to an aisle as Thompson bought drinks. Forsky and Wanda were seated on the same back row, but adjacent the opposite aisle.

Thompson had intended to purchase mixed drinks but after he got a good look at the bartender, he bought two canned beers instead. The guy was about thirty-five, five-feet three, and over two hundred pounds. His once-white shirt had great yellow perspiration stains under each arm. His slicked-back greasy hair had not been washed in recent times. His long fingernails trapped masses of filthy tallow.

Thompson handed Lottie a beer as she said, "I'm glad you got something that creature couldn't drip sweat into."

"Oh, so you got a look at Mr. Foul the bartender?" Thompson asked.

"All I wanted and then some," she remarked as she took tissue from her purse and wiped the top and sides of both cans.

"Sad to say, but a lot of people in here don't look much better than the bartender," Thompson said. Lottie was silent.

Across the aisle, Wanda told Forsky, "I've always been intrigued by swapping activities. I've never done anything like that, just curious, you know."

Forsky laughed and said, "Remember, you're here to observe what goes on. Please let me know if you get a strong urge to be an active participant."

Wanda realized too late that she should not be thinking aloud and was embarrassed by her own remark.

The theater was large as bookstore theaters go, perhaps fifty feet on a side. Thompson counted the seat rows. There were an even hundred seats, even if the fire marshal said twenty of them could not be used. The front row was fifteen feet from the screen. In an open area on either side of the screen sat very large beanbag chairs. Audience amateurs would give impromptu performances on the bean bags whenever the urge struck. The chairs were covered with a thick vinyl. One could only imagine the horrible residues and organisms present on this material.

Just like a regular theater, overhead lights were dimmed as the movie began. Unlike a regular theater, they were not dimmed nearly as much, so that patrons could get a good look at everything that happened around them. The movie was some untitled bookstore trash that starred the infamous Jerome Renauld, an AIDS-infected actor who had died from the disease a year ago.

Speaking of AIDS and other social diseases that were difficult to shake, some of the crowd appeared to be in poor health. More than a few of the men and women were alcoholics. At least three couples were in their sixties, about that many in their twenties, with the majority in between. With the exception of a few couples, the crowd appeared to be very blue collar in makeup, just the opposite of arcade clientele. Thompson found it intriguing to size up a crowd like this. The results of his informal surveys meant nothing to anyone but him. Even most vice cops cared little about such matters.

The theater was packed. One hundred had been admitted and the door was closed. A store employee, who was also a Liberace impersonator, had been posted at the door. Liberace checked ticket stubs of patrons who used the lobby restrooms and returned to the theater. No one in the theater was naked yet, but there was subtle action in several rows, and oral sex with your own partner was rather subtle for these people.

Wanda asked Forsky, "Is it safe to go to the bathroom here?"

He replied, "Probably not, but if you gotta go, you gotta go. I go out on the parking lot."

"Well, I can't do that," Wanda said with impatience, "I'll be back in a minute."

In a low voice, Thompson told Lottie, "See these folks going at it? We know what they're doing, but unless you witness skin-on-skin contact, you don't have a case. When you have a good case, just remember who's doing what to whom and the time it happened. I know that's a lot to keep up with. If you forget a few or get confused, don't worry about it, we'll let them slide. You'll remember the most bizarre ones for sure."

Thompson hoped she understood. He was not a teacher and did not give instructions well. It was difficult for him to describe a process in a way that most persons could easily grasp. He knew this all too well; it was a shortcoming he had never been able to improve upon.

Fresh from the ladies' room, Wanda attempted to seat herself next to Forsky. As she did so, she felt, and heard, a mild slap on her bottom. Forsky heard it, too. He and Wanda both stared at the middle-aged man seated directly behind her. He wore a dirty tank top and his head was shaved. He grinned at Wanda, revealing his need for some heavy-duty dental work.

As he extended his hand toward the policewoman, he said, "Hi, mah name's Orville and this here's Flo," as he put his arm around the little lovely sitting next to him.

Flo smiled with big brown teeth. She wore a tank top that matched the one Orville had on, except Orville's was cleaner. Orville and Flo had both eaten garlic sandwiches or something similar for supper that evening.

Orville cowered as he noticed the fire in Wanda's brown eyes. Her once surprised expression had turned to one of rage. She got in Orville's face and said in a low voice, "Touch me again and you'll have some serious regrets!"

Orville seemed relieved that Wanda did not hit him and said, "Hey, I'm sorry. I thought that's what we all came here for. I didn't mean to upset nobody."

After Wanda turned around, Forsky whispered to her, "That's really not good enough for a lewdhead case, but I have a feeling Orville and Flo will be leaving with us anyway."

"I certainly hope so!" replied a vengeful Wanda.

The officers had been in the theater an hour. Between the two couples, they had cases on fourteen patrons. Mr. Foul, the bartender, was selling a tremendous number of mixed drinks. Perhaps some of the people needed a few drinks to loosen up enough to give a public performance. At eight dollars for a drink with sweat in it and five dollars for a can of beer, Mr. Foul would be a prime target for a hijacker as long as the hijacker did not have to touch him.

Lottie asked Thompson, "Have you noticed that this crowd is one hundred percent white? Not one Hispanic, black, or other minority in the whole group. How come?"

"That says a lot for white folks' morals, doesn't it? I've seen some Hispanics and blacks at swap meets, but very few. I can't tell you why it's like that. Maybe the few that do go are there out of curiosity. I don't recall ever arresting a minority at one of these events. I know that didn't answer your question, though."

"No, but I guess your thoughts on the subject are worth something," Lottie replied.

A drunk man in his forties was seated two rows in front of Forsky and Wanda. He stood and, for a moment, appeared to be disoriented. After he gained some composure, he walked up and down the aisles handing out business cards for his insulation business! The guy was an ultra-skinny version of Orville. He was wearing a hospital scrub bottom that had been cut off above the knees. He wore no underwear and had taken off his shirt and shoes once inside the theater. He looked malnourished, but his wife who was still seated, had never missed a meal. She was also drunk. Following the advertising session, Mr. Insulation went back to get his wife. She was dressed in a worn see-through lacy remnant that came from a garage sale. It was made for a much smaller woman; she had on no underclothing.

It did not take the couple long to disrobe as they stood over a beanbag chair. The woman ripped her outfit trying to get out of it. She would never get it back on. What was left of the worn lace would not stand the strain of another stretching over her massive carcass. The couple attempted to engage in all sorts of sexual activity for about five minutes, but was unsuccessful. Mr. Insulation became exhausted. He lay on his back and was asleep within seconds. No volunteers from the audience offered the pitiful woman assistance. Because of her level of intoxication, she was in no way embarrassed. She left her passed out husband and returned to the seat, throwing around her the robe she had worn into the theater.

Thompson had seen all this many times before. He wondered what they were doing in this place. He had that familiar thought again about having worked vice too long.

Just then, Lottie bumped Thompson's arm and said, "Hey, we're fixing to see some real action here, Wade. These people are actually sober!"

Two couples in their thirties approached the unoccupied bean bag and undressed. They did not give the appearance of being blue collar like everyone else. Nor were they grotesque specimens of humanity. The women were rather nice looking and the men had a clean-cut appearance. For a short time, each couple engaged in various sexual activities. Both couples seemed to be known by other theater patrons. Three more couples approached them. Within minutes, ten people were going at it, on top of and around the beanbag. At random, they would change partners every ten minutes or so.

With all their years in vice, Thompson and Forsky thought they had seen just about everything perverted, bizarre, disgusting, and offensive that man was capable of doing. An occasion like this provided the realization that they had not seen it all and never would. Neither would anyone else.

Lottie was awestruck. Even Wanda was speechless. For that matter, Forsky and Thompson had had enough. Thompson got Forsky's attention. Pre-arranged, they knew to meet one another in the men's room.

Before Thompson stood up, he told Lottie, "We're fixing to call in the cavalry. Just sit tight."

Lottie responded, "Not too soon for me."

Forsky told Wanda, "It won't be long, now. We'll be back in a minute."

Wanda Winchester was ready and said, "Fine. I was afraid you wanted to watch more of the show."

Before speaking to one another in the men's room, Forsky flung open the three stall doors to make sure no one else was around.

Thompson said, "John, I've had all of this I can stand. Are you ready?"

"Ready," Forsky replied.

"We need more patrol officers. This crowd is too big and we're gonna have a bunch of prisoners. I'll put two on the door and have the rest come inside with me and Tal," Thompson told Forsky.

"Sounds good. I'm going back in," Forsky said.

Thompson walked across the street and behind a building where the officers waited. A very young and hyperactive policeman, freshly off training, got out of his car as Wade Thompson approached.

"Sir, are we ready to hit the place?" he asked.

Thompson answered, "Please don't call me 'sir'. 'Wade' will be fine. We've got a hundred people in the theater. Maybe thirty or more prisoners and some of them are drunk. We need at least six more officers, as soon as you can get them."

"I'll take care of it, sir," the youngster responded.

Within minutes, three more two-man squads arrived. This was surprising on a Friday night when patrol squads were busiest. In addition, the call load in this part of town was, by comparison, very heavy.

Thompson explained his plan to the officers. They parked around the bookstore and ten officers and Sgt. Sanderson accompanied Thompson into the place.

As the contingency of cops walked past the counter, the clerk said to Thompson, "Hey, I tell those people not to do that shit in there, but they just don't listen."

Bookstore employees deny knowledge of illegal activity that occurs in the stores. They believe it is a good ploy for court, but it does not work. The officers had no prosecutable violation on the clerk anyway, but he was unaware of that.

At Thompson's request, the clerk turned off the movie and turned on all the theater lights. Two officers blocked the theater entrance after everyone else went in. When theater patrons saw all the cops, they scurried about like a bunch of surprised rats, except these rats were attempting to put clothes on. Mr. Insulation remained passed out on the beanbag, oblivious to all the activity. Mrs. Insulation was on all fours behind the portable bar, getting hit from behind by none other than Mr. Foul, the bartender.

The four undercover officers were busy separating those they had cases on from the rest of the clientele that would soon be allowed to leave. Lining them against the walls, there were forty-one to be transported. For the first time that night, Thompson noticed the offensive smell created by the mixture of the various aromas of stale beer, body odor, sex, cigarettes, and cheap perfume. The air had become stifling and the theater's malfunctioning air conditioning system was unable to handle the volume of grossness.

All the officers began searching the arrestees. Obviously, rubber gloves were a necessity when searching people that had had sex with multiple partners. It was hoped that no one would have drugs or weapons on them. This would require additional charges and paperwork. With this many prisoners, however, paperwork would be monumental anyway.

Most of those arrested acted in a decent manner and caused no problems. Several had been arrested for public lewdness before. As one woman, a college instructor in her fifties explained, "After you've been married for a long time, you look for a little extra in the way of excitement. That doesn't mean you're bored with your spouse, in fact, it may mean just the opposite. It's an enhancement for both of you. The chance of getting caught provides a certain thrill in itself, but I can assure you there is no thrill in being arrested."

As Thompson and Forsky had suspected, the clientele knew the two couples that had initiated the beanbag orgy. These four made the rounds of all such theaters on the weekends. One of the men operated a large medical supply company that was owned by his family. The other man was president of the company and the most obnoxious of all those arrested. He lectured the detectives, uniformed officers, and other prisoners in an incessant way whether anyone listened or not. He made everyone aware of his level of arrogance. It was an unconscionable act to arrest a person for having sex in a public place, according to this man. Forsky had observed Mr. Obnoxious get punked by a beefy butt pirate, but could not identify the pirate. The prisoner's degree of despicability was further heightened, in Thompson's opinion, because he used such hackneyed terms as "on the same page", "I'll be honest with you", "role model", and "survivor".

Among trades and professions represented by this group of folks were the following: teaching, sales, mechanics, plumbing, carpentry, clerical, and computer science. Not nearly as blue collar as Thompson had originally thought. Mr. Foul, the bartender was a waiter at a very exclusive Dallas restaurant and had been so employed for a number of years.

As Thompson and the female officers handled the arrest reports, Forsky briefly interviewed every arrestee. He gave a spiel to each regarding "working their case off". The you-scratch-my-back appeal was very important with this group of people. Some swappers will do just about anything, in a very literal sense, when it comes to sexual activity. Some in the group might engage in bizarre practices such as bondage or fetishism. While they may not be involved in child molestation or child pornography, they often have access to a very resourceful perverted subculture with deviates that do participate in unspeakable offenses where children are victims. Granted, these ties may be distant, but swappers have a distinct edge over law enforcement when it comes to avenues of approach for extreme clandestine activities. It was unlikely the detectives would ever hear from any of the Carnal Club theater crowd. Nevertheless, it was not a waste of time to interview these persons.

The paperwork and booking process was completed at 10:00 A.M. Saturday. Even Forsky was tired. The female officers had willingly pitched in and done as much work as anyone, and neither complained about the long hours.

CHAPTER 13

Thompson, Forsky, and most other detectives and supervisors preferred not to have women working in vice on a full-time basis. From a physical standpoint, they did not "ride" an unruly prisoner as well as a man. A woman was far more limited in the work she could do in vice. This was not an issue created through male prejudice, it was based on fact. Nevertheless, the general attitude of vice personnel had a distinct telling influence on the number of women who would want to work in a vice environment on a regular basis.

When Thompson arrived at work Monday evening, he had a message to call Lottie Symington at home. He was curious and called right away.

"Wade, there may be nothing to this," she began. "Let me tell you the story and you decide. I was much too exhausted Saturday morning to mention anything and I figured it would keep for a day or two anyway..." she paused.

"I'm listening," Thompson said. He wondered if Lottie had paused midstream because she thought he was uninterested.

She continued, "Apparently, the other night, you or John talked to the nasty bartender. I did his paperwork, and I don't know whether or not you are aware, but in addition to the public lewdness and the alcohol violations, he had ten grams of cocaine on him. I guess he was selling in the theater. Anyhow, he has all these charges, but he's real worried about the dope case. Just as

I was leaving the jail, he said he'd be willing to work a trade if we can keep him out of the pen. He's on probation for dope now. He claims to know lots of whores and said he can help you guys out."

Thompson did not want to appear disinterested since Lottie was thoughtful enough to call him. He asked, "Anything else that you can remember...any details?" He knew there were none.

"Not really. That's about it," Lottie replied.

Thompson said, "It's okay, Lottie. We were all tired. I wouldn't have interviewed the guy right then anyway. I'll call him this evening and let you know what happens."

"Thanks, Wade. By the way, you know what he does for a living?"

"Yeah, he's a waiter at the Bull Baron Steakhouse. Don't ever eat there!"

"I won't ever again, believe me. Bye."

Forsky walked into the office, and said, "I don't know about you, Wade, but I'm still tired. I doubt the fact that I fished for fourteen hours on Sunday has anything to do with my present state of exhaustion."

"We'll take it easy tonight so we can regain our former strength," Thompson said with a smile. "By the way, I just talked to Lottie Symington. Mr. Foul, the bartender, wants to work. He had a bunch of dope on him the other night and he's on probation now."

Forsky replied, "If he's on probation, we'll have to get permission from the judge before we can use him."

"I know. I thought I'd call him tonight and see what he's got. It may not even be worth working."

Forsky added, "With everything that guy is charged with, he's gonna have to do something like the French Connection to take care of his cases."

"Yeah... He's not in exactly the ideal situation," Thompson said, a tiny spark of optimism in his voice.

Thompson rummaged through the stack of arrest report copies from the big adventure at the Carnal Club theater. He did not know Mr. Foul's real name, but he was the only one with a serious dope charge. He found the report and called the home number listed on it.

"Hello, Herschel speaking," a male voice said.

Thompson replied, "Herschel Fowler, this is Wade Thompson with the police department. I understand you wanted to speak with someone from vice."

With no hesitation, Herschel asked in a desperate tone, "Can you help me with my cases?"

"I don't know Herschel. If you're on probation, we've got to get permission from the judge who put you on probation. Can you come to our office right now? Give us a brief rundown on what you can do. If it's worthwhile, we'll talk to the judge tomorrow. Fair enough?"

Herschel was eager. "I'll be there in twenty minutes. I hate to say, but I know where your office is."

"John, Mr. Foul's real name is Herschel Fowler. He'll be here in a little while," Thompson said, knowing Forsky would comment on the name.

Forsky replied as predicted, "If that was my name, I'd go by Mr. Foul."

Thompson was staring idly at the doorway when Herschel Fowler arrived. The man was sweating, as if he had run the distance from his home to the vice office. He was just as nasty as he had been several nights before. Thompson grimaced as he shook hands with Herschel. Forsky went through the usual ritual he employed when he wanted to avoid shaking hands with someone like Mr. Foul. He kept a bottle of cheap hand lotion in a desk drawer. Making sure the offensive person noticed, Forsky squirted a copious amount of lotion in one palm then rubbed his hands together.

"Sorry, Herschel, I just put some lotion on my hands, can't

shake right now. I have very dry skin. Glad to meet you, though," Forsky said.

"Likewise," Herschel replied. His hands were greasier than Forsky's, and he had not used any lotion.

The three sat at the conference table in the captain's office. Thompson had made a few notes. He was always concerned he would forget an important point.

"Okay, Herschel, as I mentioned on the phone, we have to get the judge's permission for you to work. If he gives us the okay, you're looking at having to do a considerable amount to take care of all your cases. The dope case alone will require a couple of high-powered felonies. You understand?" Thompson asked.

"Yes, and I'm capable. I know people you're interested in, and I don't want to go to the pen," Herschel replied.

Forsky said, "Herschel, we're not gonna spend much time on this before we talk to the judge, but, from a general perspective, what sort of information do you have?"

Herschel began, "Let me tell you a little about myself. I'm somewhat of an anomaly as far as criminals go. I'm fairly well educated. I've had a steady job as a waiter at a very fine restaurant for a long time and I make a decent legitimate living. I use drugs on occasion and I sell them on occasion. I've been dating whores, street whores, escort whores, bar whores, you name it since I was seventeen. I've never had a date with a regular woman. I mean, look at me, I'm not very appealing to women."

Neither detective would argue the veracity of that last statement.

Thompson interrupted, "Herschel, keep in mind we're not really interested in making a bunch of individual, unrelated whore cases. Our interests lie with management, so to speak."

"I follow you one hundred percent. I know pimps, too. I've even done a little amateur pimping on my own... out-of-town rich guys, customers from the restaurant... even couples I've run across at theater swap meets that need to rent a whore for the night," Herschel replied.

Without getting into specifics, Thompson could see that the three of them had carried the discussion as far it could go for the first meeting. He said, "We've discussed about all we can for now. We'll call you as soon as we've talked to the judge."

Thompson handed the would-be informant a business card as they walked out of Arlie Holland's office. Herschel studied the card, holding it in both hands. He continued to stare at it as he walked toward the hallway. Without looking at either detective, Herschel said, almost inaudibly, "Thank you very much for your time."

"Thank you for coming in, Herschel," Thompson replied as Herschel disappeared into the hallway.

"Wade, I think the guy can do us some good if we steer him in the right direction," Forsky said.

Thompson replied, "Based on what he said tonight, it's hard to tell, but I hope you're right. I'm about ready to drop this thing with Jan and do something productive."

"Speaking of Jan…the wire transfer info should be here any day. I asked the banks to mail it to the office," Forsky said.

Thompson replied, "If that leads us nowhere, then that's it. The more I think about it, the more I think we've done nothing but waste time."

"It makes no sense for her to be involved in this alleged big escort operation when she's already doing so well, money-wise," Forsky said, also eager to drop the investigation.

Thompson said, "We still have to make some sort of disposition on this Luscious Lovelies investigation. It's been almost two weeks and it hasn't self-destructed yet, far as I know… and I haven't seen Oscar's or Dildo's name in the obituaries, either."

"Let's get it over with. Why don't we get a room tomorrow night, make a couple of cases, and see if we can get affidavits on Oscar and Dildo?" Forsky suggested.

"Well, May first is Thursday, so we've only got two more nights of evenings. Okay, tomorrow night it is," Thompson said in agreement.

CHAPTER 14

Jan Doxee had breakfast in the historic Grand Eastern Hotel restaurant in downtown New Orleans. Six spoonfuls of vodka from a half-pint flask made the bitter chicory coffee far more palatable. In fact, the flavor was improved to the point where she would have two more cups of the concoction. Joining her was Lenora Ludlow, a former Dallas dominatrix.

Lenora was well known among a profoundly discreet group of men, and to a far lesser extent, women, who paid her to brutalize them and perform a variety of other malevolent and repulsive acts. Lenora was forty-five, and almost six feet tall with a very muscular build. Her long blond hair was always pulled back in a very tight and neat bun. If Lenora was in a crowd of a thousand men and women, and someone was asked to select the one person from the group, male or female, that would look best as a uniformed Nazi interrogator with a riding crop in one hand, Lenora would always be the first pick. Lenora Ludlow could be frightening. While she did accept conventional prostitution dates on occasion, her specialty practice kept her adequately busy.

Lenora did not discuss work with Jan or anyone else. The two had been friends in Dallas when Lenora lived there in the 'eighties. They visited with one another a couple of times each year, whenever Jan traveled to New Orleans.

Wade Thompson and John Forsky had arranged for adjoining rooms at the Hotel Greater Dallas Tuesday evening. The Greater Dallas was downtown within walking distance of the vice office. It was a very old hotel but well kept as witnessed by the different areas in the building that were rotationally in various stages of remodeling.

The detectives each kept a packed suitcase in the office for such an occasion. Along with the suitcase prop, each officer had adequate fictitious identification, business cards, etc. that could withstand scrutiny and verification with one hundred percent reliability. Most escort services that planned on being in business for any length of time verified as much information as possible on any potential client before sending a girl to a location. The services did their utmost to make certain they never dispatched a prostitute to a vice cop's room.

Forsky called Luscious Lovelies. The voice answering the phone belonged to a goofy eighteen-year-old female. "Luscious Lovelies. How may I assist you this evening?"

Acting shy, Forsky replied, "I desire companionship for an hour or so tonight. Could you possibly accommodate my need with two girls?"

"We'd be happy to, sir. Our rates are $150.00 per hour per girl, tips are extra. What sort of girls did you have in mind for tonight?" Miss Goofus inquired.

"First, I must confess I have never called one of these services before, so I am quite unfamiliar with the procedure. I did not realize I had a choice in the women, however, I am not particular as long as they are young, not over twenty-five. Can you furnish ladies like that?"

"We certainly can, sir. In fact, I have two lined up for you right now that you'll be very pleased with. Their names are Brook and Brandy. They are both twenty-five and gorgeous. They can be at your room in an hour. How do you wish to pay, cash or credit card?" the youngster asked.

Forsky replied using almost a whisper, "Cash… definitely cash."

"Well that's just fine, sir. Now I need to get your name

and some other information and where you would like the girls to meet you tonight. By the way, this is all very confidential," she said, lowering her voice almost to a whisper.

Forsky furnished the girl with all the usual bogus information. Forsky knew that Brook and Brandy had real names, were over twenty-five, and were not gorgeous. As far as making a whore case went, none of that mattered anyway. He told Thompson, "Two luscious lovelies en route; estimated arrival time about an hour."

Both detectives knew that 'an hour' almost always meant at least two hours when dealing with an escort service. Of the hundreds of escort cases they had made during their careers, neither could recall girls who had shown on time.

Thompson was watching TV and made no comment. He still did not want to file pimp cases on a couple of barely alive old men.

There was a knock on the door after a two-and-one-half-hour wait. Thompson went to the adjoining room and locked the door. He kept his ear to the door so he could hear all that happened in Forsky's room. Thompson's revolver, ID, and handcuffs were at the ready and he could quickly re-enter if necessary. Otherwise, Forsky would knock on the door or call Thompson's name when he was ready to make the arrest. While neither detective ever had a prostitute or pimp attempt to rob or harm them in any way in a hotel room, the potential was always there.

Forsky opened the door. For effect, he wore an outlandish red and blue satin smoking jacket. It looked like something from a 1940's movie and was extremely worn when he bought it ten years ago at a second-hand store. Prostitutes were always taken aback when they caught the first glance of Forsky in his outfit. To his advantage, they were thrown off-guard and some women even forgot to ask if he was a cop. He could not wear the jacket frequently, however, as the word would get around.

"Good evening, ladies," Forsky said as he opened the

door, a mischievous smile on his face.

The women were in their late twenties, both about five-foot-five. One had long, straight blond hair and was thirty pounds overweight. The other, a brunette, was more slender, but not thin by any means. She was smoking a cigarette, had rings on every finger, and was a nail-biter. Both were dressed appropriately for a wrestling match or moto-cross tournament.

The nail-biter appeared to be the more experienced of the two. She said, "Hi, are you Mister Topper? I'm Brandy and this here's Brook."

Brook had yet to speak.

"Please call me Cosmo," Forsky told the girls.

Forsky had never encountered a prostitute under the age of forty-five who had ever heard of Cosmo Topper, the main character in the 1950's TV comedy series, "Topper".

In her most intelligent manner, Brandy asked, "What kind of name is Cosmo? Is that Eyetalian? Don't get me wrong, now. I like your name, Cosmo."

"Young lady, you have a most discerning ear. Yes, it's Eyetalian," Forsky said in an attempt to see how far he could carry the ridicule.

"Okay, Cosmo, we need to get business out of the way before we do the fun part. You got a driver's license, business cards, stuff like that to prove who you are?" Brandy asked in the most businesslike tone she could manage.

As he retrieved his billfold from the dresser, Forsky asked, "My heavens, of course I do. Why do I need my identification?"

"We got to be careful, you know, weirdoes and all," Brandy said.

Forsky handed the girl an Alaska driver's license with an Anchorage address on it. He also handed her a 'Topper Marble Company' business card.

"Now, will that suffice, or do you require more?" Forsky asked.

"No, this'll be fine. What do you do Cosmo? Sell marble statues and bathtubs and things?" Brandy inquired as she made her best attempt at intelligent conversation.

Forsky answered, "No, actually, I sell tombstones. In fact, I'm attending a seminar being held in this very hotel."

"Oh, okay. You got three hundred cash, Cosmo? That's for both of us for an hour. That all goes to the agency. We work off tips. We model nude, but there ain't no touching for the three hundred. Now, if you want a straight lay or half-and-half, that's a hundred for the former and a hundred-and-fifty for the latter. That's for each girl… you understand, Cosmo?" Brandy recited, smiling because she was proud of using words like 'former' and 'latter' in her sales pitch.

Forsky was mentally preparing his arrest report.

"I want a straight lay, so I will owe you $100.00 for that service in addition to the agency fee, is that correct?" Forsky asked Brandy.

"You're a sharp guy, Cosmo. That's it," she said in confirmation.

Forsky, directing his attention to Brook, asked, "Brook, I would also like a straight lay from you, okay?"

"Okay, but it's still a hundred," she said.

The girls were so easy, Forsky decided to forego his usual haggling for lack of sport. Each would cut their price by at least fifty percent with little effort. He knocked once on Thompson's door, but gave the girls the appearance that he had bumped his elbow.

Thompson entered the room with his ID and badge displayed and announced, "Ladies, we're police officers and you're both under arrest for prostitution."

In a simultaneous move, Forsky snatched both purses from the bed.

Brook sat on the bed and cried.

Brandy gave Forsky a mean stare and said, "Cosmo, I

knew you was a 'vice'. I thought about leaving the minute you opened the door." She had had no such suspicion, but saying so made her feel better about being duped.

Forsky read both girls their rights. Brook regained her composure. To Forsky's surprise, she admitted to being arrested for prostitution once before. Brandy had not. Thompson went through the standard line about working off the cases as the officers handcuffed the women. Thompson and Forsky gathered their belongings and everyone went to the vice office.

In the vice office, Forsky typed the arrest reports with both prostitutes seated across from his desk.

Thompson asked them, "You girls give any thought to what we talked about before we left the room?"

Brook answered first, "Yeah, I don't need another whore case, but I'm not sure I can help you."

"Who hired you? How long have you worked for the agency?" Thompson asked.

Brook responded, "I went to work last month. Two old men hired me."

Brandy said, "I been there four or five months, but I known Oscar and Dildo since I was little. They're bookies. They used my dad to collect from deadbeat gamblers."

Thompson took Brook aside and asked, "What did these guys tell you about the prostitution part of the business?"

"They told me they got all the agency fee, and ten percent of what I made for tricks. They told me to watch out for cops," Brook recited.

"Which one of them told you this?" Thompson asked.

She replied, "It was Dildo, but Oscar was sitting right there next to him."

Thompson said, "Okay, you want to write an affidavit to that effect? In other words put on paper what you just told me?"

"Yeah, I can do that. I might need some help. Will it help

me?" Brook asked.

Thompson replied, "Yeah, just be truthful. Use dates and times if you remember, if not, approximate them as best you can."

Thompson seated her at a small table in a tiny interrogation room. She was given pen and blank affidavit forms.

Forsky had done the same with Brandy in the other interrogation room.

The girls had been writing for the better part of an hour when a cocky, well-dressed man in his late fifties strolled through the door of the vice office. He clutched an expensive monogrammed leather portfolio. The heavy payload of hairspray on his silver mane reminded Thompson of a shady TV evangelist in search of an open billfold. Forsky glanced at the stranger. No doubt he was an attorney representing 'Luscious Lovelies'. The detectives did not want this character to speak with either Brook or Brandy until the girls had completed the affidavits.

Thompson approached the attorney. They shook hands.

Thompson introduced himself, "I'm Wade Thompson. Can I help you?"

"Yes, I believe you can. I'm Rex Swearingen. I represent Mr. Mortimer and Mr. Delaney."

Before Swearingen could continue, Forsky interrupted with his usual line, "We need to see your bar card."

Forsky refused to talk to any defense attorney in an official capacity without seeing his bar card first. Some attorneys balked at the initial request, but they always presented the card to the detective.

Exuding arrogance, Swearingen retorted, "Why? I've never shown my bar card to a cop before."

"We need verification you're an attorney licensed to practice law in the State of Texas. If you're unwilling to cooperate, then please leave. We're very busy," Forsky said.

Swearingen's faced turned red as he dug through the

contents of his wallet, found the bar card, and dropped it on Forsky's desk. The attorney said nothing, but it was no secret the humbling experience irritated him considerably. Forsky looked at the card, but never touched it.

Thompson rushed Swearingen into the captain's office and closed the door. Forsky had to hurry the prostitutes into completing their affidavits. He would have to review them, then take the women upstairs to the jail office. The affidavits would be signed and notarized and Brook and Brandy would be booked into jail.

Neither young lady had requested the services of an attorney and Thompson and Forsky had not anticipated one showing up at the office. Someone at the escort service assumed Brandy and Brook had been arrested due to the length of time that that had elapsed since they were last heard from.

Had Rex Swearingen observed either girl writing an affidavit, he would have advised them against doing so. The attorney had no real concern for Brook and Brandy, despite the fact that from a technical standpoint, he represented them. Oscar and Dildo paid the man's fee, however. Swearingen was at the vice office to make sure the girls said nothing about his real clients' whore business. Alas, he was too late, even if he did not know it yet.

Swearingen sat at the conference table, drumming his fingers against his briefcase. He said, "I'm not here for small talk, officer. I want to get those girls released as soon as possible."

Thompson replied, "I know. They're probably upstairs in the jail at this very moment and they'll be booked soon. I'd give them at least another fifteen minutes. You can go up there now if you want, but you'll have to wait."

As he stood, Swearingen said, "Well, if it's all the same to you, I'll wait up there."

"Makes me no difference, Rex," Thompson said.

As Thompson got up from the captain's chair, Swearingen

asked, "Before I leave, can you give me a brief rundown of why you arrested these girls?"

"We made whore cases on two girls who work for Oscar Mortimer and Dildo Delaney," Thompson said, careful to give the lawyer no information he did not already have.

Swearingen said, "Oscar Mortimer and Cecil Delaney, or 'Dildo' as you call him, are trying to run a legitimate business. These men are elderly and not in the best of health. Granted, they have been in trouble before, but they're long past being criminals now."

"You can defend them in court. No need to do it here," Thompson replied.

"You know as well as I do this won't go to court. Are you going to file cases on my clients?" Swearingen asked.

Thompson said, "Tell you what, Rex, if we file cases, I'll call you and you can turn them in yourself. We won't come out and get them." Thompson knew Swearingen would see such a gesture as a favor to his clients. Better yet, Thompson and Forsky would not have to put the two old sickly guys in jail. Swearingen smiled for the first time since he had walked into the vice office.

"That would be most benevolent of you, officer. Please do call me if you file cases. I'll surrender my clients right away. Thank you. I'll go upstairs now."

"Glad we could do business, Rex," Thompson replied.

Forksy and Swearingen passed and ignored one another in the hallway. Forsky was out of breath when he got to the office.

Thompson said, "Our timing was pretty good, John. Are the affidavits okay?"

"Brook and Brandy ain't exactly journalistic scholars, but yeah, the affidavits are fine."

Thompson replied, "Good. Swearingen's fixing to find out they wrote them. He never asked me a thing about it while he was here. He did say he would turn in Oscar and Dildo, if we file cases. We won't have to stand in front of a jail sergeant with them after all."

Forsky said, "Let's file the cases tomorrow night, then, while they're still breathing."

CHAPTER 15

In a luxurious suite at the Denver New Victorian, Jan Doxee had just finished lunch with an elderly investor. The horrendous headache precluded her enjoyment of the lobster. She had not had a drink in several hours, but that problem would be remedied in minutes, even if it worsened the headache.

Forsky's mail tray in the vice office was stuffed. It did not hold much to begin with. One of the day clerks took everything out and placed it all in a large manila envelope. She left the package on the desk Forsky shared. When he got to work the next evening, he began sorting through the envelope's contents. This was a task Forsky did no more than once a week, despite Thompson's and Sanderson's best efforts to reform the detective.

Forsky suddenly exclaimed, "Wade, we've got the wire transfer information, and we also have the trap n' trace records from the phone company! It probably all came in today."

"It's probably been there a week, John. I wish you'd just check your mail once in a while," Thompson replied.

Forsky ignored his partner's last comment and said, "Come on over here, Wade. Let's see what we've got."

Thompson sifted through the phone company information as Forsky looked over the wire transfer material. It took Thompson all of thirty seconds to determine they had struck out again. There were mostly local calls, numbers he recognized right away, the same numbers that were on previous trap n' trace requests. It was the same for long distance calls. Thompson said, disappointed, "No luck on the telephone company stuff, John. Same numbers we've seen before, almost all local."

"I was afraid of that," Forsky said, preoccupied. "Let's see what we have here."

Thompson picked up some of the bank paperwork and examined it. They had not discussed it, but both detectives believed that if a clue existed regarding Jan Doxee's alleged escort service operation, it would be found amid this paperwork. They traded forms. Thompson quickly saw the scheme. Forsky did, too. They stared at each other for a moment. Neither wanted to speak first for fear one might have overlooked something. Both realized there was nothing to overlook; a sixth-grader with a basic knowledge of math could see through the ruse. In fact, there was no ruse, con, or scheme, at least not like anything the detectives had encountered before.

Forsky said with disgust, "This is crazy, or I've missed something very obvious."

"No, you haven't missed a thing. I see it exactly as you do and it makes no sense to me, either," Thompson replied in frustration.

A little more than $72,000 had been shuffled from one bank account to another via the wire transfer process. All five banks were in Dallas or the Dallas vicinity. No pattern existed as to time, date, or amount. Each account was a regular personal savings account. While not illegal, it seemed to Thompson that someone in the banking system might have been aware of the strange repeated transactions. Of course, with the volume of business that Metroplex banks handled, maybe such money transfers would never merit a second glance. Neither detective had a formal banking or financial background, but both knew that the IRS was notified of cash transfers of $10,000 or more.

Forsky offered his immediate appraisal of the situation, "I think Jan's alcohol-influenced reasoning ability and her paranoia may explain what we can't."

Thompson replied, "I doubt Jan could interpret this even if we confronted her with it. It makes no sense and leads us nowhere again. She makes a living as a whore and we've known that all along. We don't need to waste any more time on this," Thompson said.

Forsky agreed and said, "Okay, let's do some real vice work."

Thompson knew what that meant. Last night on evenings, tomorrow is the first of the day shift month; 10:00 A.M. to 6:00 P.M. The pair would take off early tonight, no later than midnight. A downtown hustler or two would take up the rest of the evening quite well. But first, he had a call to make.

Thompson felt obliged to contact Virginia Baccus and let her know they would be closing the investigation on her daughter. "There's just nothing there," Thompson told the woman.

"I think, I think, I think...you're mistaken, Mr. Thompson, but it's your decision," Virginia Baccus said. She was in a moderate state of inebriation. Thompson should have called earlier.

"We appreciate you providing the information," Thompson concluded.

"Very well, very well," Baccus said as she abruptly hung up the phone.

As Thompson replaced the telephone receiver, Forsky said, "Let's see if we can snag a rump ranger, want to?"

"Not really, but I know your heart's set on it. Let's go," Thompson said with a smile.

Thompson ducked down in the seat as Forsky drove down Jackson Street. There were ten hustlers in four blocks. In vice lingo, it was "swarming". Forsky blew kisses or yelled "Hi, sweetie" to the street punks.

"Got some hungry ones out here tonight, Wade," Forsky said.

Thompson replied, "Find a good corner and let me out."

At least one male whore was staked out at or near every intersection along the most desirable six-block stretch of Jackson. Others were on side streets. Forsky found an unoccupied corner several blocks from the prime area, and let Thompson out of the car. Both detectives knew it would be well under five minutes before Forsky bagged one. In about half that time, Forsky pulled alongside Thompson with a tall, scraggly-looking, thirty-year-old gutter urchin.

The male whore asked Thompson for directions. Thompson bent over and rested his arms on the door, face-to-face with a man wearing glasses that had the thickest Coke-bottle lenses the detective had ever seen.

Something spooked the hustler before Thompson or Forsky could initiate the arrest. Mr. Hustler shoved the door open in a violent gesture, knocking Thompson to the sidewalk.

As Thompson was down, he kicked the door, blocking the whore's exit. As Thompson regained his footing, Forsky reached his arm around the skinny neck of the wild man. Thompson managed to divest the man of his glasses as the hustler kicked the door trying to gain his freedom, which he did. He knocked Thompson down a second time with the car door while breaking Forsky's grasp around his neck. Forsky never had a secure hold, anyway, because the hustler had weeks of built-up grease and slime on his neck.

He hotfooted down the sidewalk like a hound after a deer. Thompson and Forsky were behind him, but moving with the speed of cattle after a hay bale. The swine ran head-on into the side of a slow-moving city street sweeper. The detectives were relieved to see the pavement punk on the sidewalk. The truck never stopped, the driver oblivious to the collision.

Slowing as they approached the accident scene, Thompson, out of breath, said to Forsky, "The guy's blind without his glasses. He never saw the truck."

"What happened back there? What spooked him?" Forsky asked with heavy breath.

Thompson replied, "I don't know. Hey, he's getting up! Let's not lose him again!"

The hustler regained strength even if he could not see. As he attempted to stand, the detectives could see his face was a bloody mess. Thompson identified himself, but dropped his credentials as the man swung at him with a closed fist. Forsky managed to get a more secure hold of the grimy neck. The hustler hit Thompson in the stomach, causing the detective's snubbed-nose .38 revolver to fall from his waistband and land on the sidewalk. Not one of the three missed the moment. Before Thompson could retrieve the gun, Forsky and the prisoner fell to the sidewalk. The hustler was face down with Forsky on his back. The gun was under the man's stomach, and he grabbled for a hold on it. Forsky's weight on his back was the only hindrance, as Thompson tried to retrieve the handgun. The suspect had a firm grip around the entire frame. He only needed to reposition his fingers slightly to fire the weapon. While not an occasion for profound meditative deliberations, Thompson likened the situation to holding an armed hand grenade. The device was safe as long as a firm grip on the plunger was maintained.

Forsky choked on the hustler's neck to no avail.

"Keep choking him, John. I'll have it here in a second!" Thompson yelled.

His jaws clenched, an exhausted Forsky exclaimed, "May have to call a time out if you don't get that gun pretty soon!"

Suddenly, the hustler emitted a blood-curdling scream. Thompson had bent the man's index finger in a desperate attempt to force him to relinquish the gun, snapping bone in the process. His whole body went limp from the pain for just a moment. Little effort was required in handcuffing the errant heathen.

A patrol officer arrived on the scene. He had been dispatched on a call regarding two old guys attempting to rob a young man. The hustler had a cut on his cheek that would need stitches in addition to the broken finger. Forsky and Thompson were uninjured, but they smelled as bad as their filthy prisoner. They would spend two or three hours at the county hospital with their vagabond before they could do the paperwork and place him in jail. So much for taking off early. Perhaps they could rush home and get a shower and a couple of hours sleep before returning to work at ten the next morning.

CHAPTER 16

Thompson overslept the next morning, but managed to show up at work by 10:15. His bloodshot eyes were sensitive to the office's bright fluorescent lighting. Forsky was preparing his vice activity summarization for the previous month. Tal Sanderson sat in the squad room reading a newspaper.

Sanderson sneered at Thompson and said, "Stay up late last night, Wade?"

"I had this horrible nightmare where I had to fight a filthy hustler for my gun. Forsky was in the dream, too, but he wasn't much help," Thompson replied.

Forsky only grinned. He showed no sign of fatigue.

"Tal, if it's okay with you, I'm gonna do a little paperwork and a couple of other things, but when I feel nap time approaching, I'm gone for the day," Thompson said.

Sanderson understood and replied, "Leave whenever you're ready."

As Thompson sat behind a desk, Barney Fawcett came in and said, "Wade, a woman named Jan called a while ago. She wants you to call her when you can. What have you got working with her, anyway? Is that the escort service girl?"

"Yeah, that's her. Thanks, Barney," Thompson replied.

Fawcett would not give up and asked, "She the one that drinks quite a bit?"

"You're right again, Barney," Thompson said, a slight irritation in his response. Barney Fawcett sensed he might have overstepped his bounds with the last remark and walked away.

Thompson called Jan. She was sober and in an apparent good mood.

"Stay out late last night?" she asked.

"Very late," Thompson replied, not wanting to get into the hustler story.

She laughed and said, "Maybe you'll keep me out late some night."

"Don't count on it, Jan. It's an idea my wife doesn't care for," Thompson told her for the millionth time.

"Wade, don't you think I know Rose has left you?"

"What? How'd you know that? Nobody knows about that."

"And, neither did I for sure, until just now," Jan cooed. "But, that's not what I want to talk about right now. First, thank you for returning my call, and secondly, thank you for working on that wretched escort service. I hope you send those owners to the pen."

Thompson's head reeled from Jan's statement about Rose, but he was grateful she had dropped the subject. He also had no idea she knew anything about the escort service arrests. He asked her, "How did you find out about that?"

"Wade, my dear, the community of escort service people is very small and word travels in a hasty manner. I have many excellent sources for all kinds of information."

Thompson knew that, and wondered why he had asked such a question, particularly of this woman. It was too late to save face.

"Their phone lines have been disconnected and it looks as if they moved out of the office in a hurry. There's junk and trash everywhere. I just wanted to let you know," Jan reported.

"Maybe Oscar and Dildo are going back into the bookmaking business," Thompson replied.

The 'call waiting' feature on Jan Doxee's phone indicated she had a call from Charles Western. She would not interrupt her conversation with Thompson, however, as she knew how rude he believed such interruptions were. His telephone etiquette precluded him treating anyone with pomposity, and he hung up on those who dared to deal with him in such a manner. Mr. Western would just have to wait. He was calling from a pay phone that he often used. He seldom called Jan, but when he did, he always gave her fifteen or twenty minutes to return the call. Both preferred to meet face-to-face at pre-determined locations.

Thompson said, "Got to go now, Jan. I have a lot to do."

"Okay, thanks again, and please stop by soon so we can visit," Jan concluded.

Captain Holland was in the corner of the squad room talking with a couple of the detectives when Lieutenant Pricklee approached him. The detectives moved. Holland sensed that Pricklee wanted to speak to him in private, but the squad room would have to suffice. It was too early in the day for the captain to have to deal with Pricklee. Thompson was unable to hear the entire conversation, mainly because he did not hear well anyway, but he did make out words and terms such as 'closure', 'zero tolerance', 'politically correct', and 'ducks in a row'. Anyone using that many relevant terms in a two-minute conversation could not have much to say that was of any importance.

Pricklee left the room. Thompson, Forsky, and Holland were the only ones left. Directing his attention to both detectives, Holland said, "This hustler last night…he's got some attorney who called the chief's office, ranting about how you guys brutalized his client. Anything to that?"

"Not in the least. You know that, Arlie," Thompson said with a solemn expression on his face.

"That human filth is very fortunate that he's alive to complain. Does his attorney even know what happened?" Forsky asked.

"Of course not. He only knows what your boy whore told

him," Holland said.

As Holland got up to leave, he told Thompson and Forsky, "I know what happened. We all know each other well enough that it makes this whole conversation rather senseless. I'll take care of it."

Thompson and Forsky knew that would be the end of the frivolous complaint, even if Pricklee thought he had a couple of sadists working on one of his 'teams' as the bonehead preferred to call the squads.

CHAPTER 17

Jan Doxee drove to the liquor store just down the street from her apartment. Before she purchased some necessities, however, she called Charles Western from the pay phone in front of the store.

Tal Sanderson walked around the office and squad room distributing a training brochure developed for the upcoming Republican National Convention. Everyone was given two weeks to read and review the material. This would be followed by a mandatory eight-hour class and training exercise conducted at the police academy. Since January, every officer in the police department had received periodic briefings and training regarding the big event to be held in Dallas in August, still three months distant.

While everyone had a part to play, the role of vice personnel was markedly different. From official and political perspectives, and from the standpoint of police administrators, vice would also function in a security capacity. Then there was the real world, a world of human weaknesses and shortcomings. The sole function of vice detectives was to prevent the city's embarrassment not only by the local whore population, but from the many visiting mercenary prostitutes, and perhaps some pimps who would be in Dallas to exploit the occasion. The whole point was moot at best and the vice detectives did not mind being relegated to second-class duty. On the contrary, they would have a far better job than most, and with plenty of overtime.

All hotels and motels within fifty miles of Dallas would be booked to capacity for more than a week. Upscale bars and restaurants in the Metroplex would do phenomenal business. Such places nearest the downtown convention facilities would be the busiest. Opportunistic convention prostitutes have a tendency to rob or steal from clients on a more frequent basis than everyday working whores do. City administrators and police officials preferred visitors to leave Dallas with pleasant thoughts of a great city, one they would visit again. What public leaders did not want was a U.S. Senator or editor of a conservative political publication to be shaken down for his Rolex and a wad of cash while such person was in a horny, drunken stupor. Such an unfortunate situation would certainly skew the victim's image of Dallas.

Thompson, Forsky, and the other detectives looked over the material.

Forsky remarked, "You know, Wade, I'm not so sure I'm looking forward to this convention."

"Hate to hear that, John. I'll do my best to provide the enthusiasm we'll need," Thompson replied with a grin.

Forsky said, "Do you realize this will be the largest gathering of big-headed pomposity in the world? And we always vote Republican and probably always will. It saddens me to no end."

"You think it would be any different if it was the Democratic Convention?" Thompson asked.

"Not really. Arrogance is probably infectious with those people, too. To my way of thinking, a way unaffected by prejudice, bias, or narrow-mindedness, there is only one basic difference between swines of the Republican Party and swines of the Democratic Party. It's more difficult to catch a Republican with his pants down, from both figurative and literal perspectives. I must admit I don't know why that is. From a pure conjectural standpoint, one that could be affected by prejudice, bias, or narrow-mindedness, it might be because they're shrewd, smarter, and more discreet," Forsky said in conclusion of his political diatribe.

"Whew!" Thompson sighed, "I won't bring that up again!"

"May I remind that you are the one who asked the question with the many veiled politically philosophical undertones," Forsky replied.

"I guess I asked for it then. That's good incentive for me to go home and take a nap," Thompson said.

Forsky immersed himself in the training literature, more as a matter of curiosity rather than a fervent quest for knowledge.

As Thompson drove home he thought about Rose. She had left him three weeks earlier. Such a thing would never happen, he thought, because of the stability in their relationship. Stability was the only common thread they shared. Maybe stability had nothing to do with love, happiness, or anything else that mattered in a relationship. Thompson had placed undue importance on a trait that was not worth much in the eyes of many, including Rose. It would be easy to say the couple 'drifted apart' using a really haggard expression, but for such a thing to happen there had to be a central point to drift from. Thompson was not sure a central point ever existed.

Rose was a scholar, a real scholar. She had been a professor of English at a prestigious sectarian Dallas university. She was offered a department head position at an even more prestigious school in the Northeast. A good deal of extra money that went along with the job would provide incentive for most people, but money was always secondary to Rose. The overall environment of top-level academia meant far more to this woman. That alone was a type of high pay, something few persons, Thompson included, would understand.

Rose took very little when she left. The house, bank accounts, and everything else was pretty much intact. To say

Thompson was hurt by the ordeal would have been grossly understating the fact. He knew he would not find anyone else as close to his definition of "practical perfection" as Rose had been. He also knew he would not try. While work was not as enjoyable as it had once been, Thompson still liked his job. He could not imagine doing anything else and he knew anything else would be boring, very boring, after more than twenty years of vice work. His general outlook on life saved him from the depressive state that many would be relegated to, given his situation. Thompson had not discussed Rose with Forsky or anyone else. It was no one else's business, and he wondered again just how Jan Doxee knew about the separation.

Fault or virtue, Wade Thompson spent too much time remembering the past. His memories were usually quite favorable ones and there was a good chance many of these were inaccurate. Life could not have been as pleasant as he remembered it. Childhood, school, early years in police work, it made no difference. He enjoyed reading and he preferred reading about the past.

Thompson liked a variety of music, but to him, music produced from the late-1940's to the late-1960's was the very best. Pre-television childhood memories included listening to music by Frank Sinatra, Patti Page, Rosemary Clooney, The Mills Brothers, Mel Torme and many other popular singers of the day. The family had a large wooden-cased radio in the living room of a tiny home in northeast Dallas, the first home Thompson remembered. The radio was playing on a Sunday afternoon in the spring. The day was calm and sunny. Doors and windows were open; the temperature outside was almost eighty degrees. Everything was perfect. Thompson's family and his whole world were at peace. Life could not have been improved in any way.

Thompson thought about this non-existent perfect world to an unhealthy extent. In the reality that his memory may have avoided, the setting might have depicted a radio with static in the background. The windows and doors were open, but it was not springtime. The month was August and it was 105 degrees, muggy and miserable. Thompson preferred his flawed memory.

One memory that remained was painfully accurate. It had been relived countless times in the more than two decades since it had occurred. This reliving had become much less frequent in recent years, however. It was no longer obsessed about several times daily as it had been at one time. This must have provided a measurable degree of solace, Thompson thought, but its evolvement had been so gradual as to go unnoticed, and perhaps, unappreciated. He had discussed the matter with no one but Rose. Even with her, he had been careful and somehow internally compelled to expose his feelings only a minimal amount. He would not bring every aspect into the light and never would. Rose understood all this, as well as anyone could who had been provided with only a limited amount of information.

A fellow officer Thompson not only worked with in patrol, but had gone through the academy with, had been killed in a violent confrontation with an ex-con kidnapping suspect. Late one night, Thompson observed a car with fresh body damage and a piece of mangled chrome trim dangling from a wheel well. Assuming the driver was a DWI suspect that had just been involved in a hit-and-run accident, he stopped the car. As he approached the stopped vehicle, Thompson noticed the driver engaged in a mild struggle with a passenger who was in the floorboard and had apparently been there since Thompson first saw the car. At the moment he observed this, the driver sped off, turning onto a major east Dallas thoroughfare. As the criminal's car approached 110 miles per hour with Thompson in pursuit, the distance between the cars lengthened. It was clear to Thompson he wasn't going to overtake the vehicle.

The other officer did. The suspect lost control of his car, which landed against a hedge in a front yard. The driver ran from the car with the other officer chasing him on foot. As Thompson approached the scene, he was distracted by the kidnap victim who stood in the street and screamed in hysterics at him. Thompson heard two gunshots from very close by, but saw nothing. Running in the general direction of the reports, he found the officer, mortally wounded from two bullets fired at point-blank range into his back. The suspect was gone. The officer was alive, but barely, and that condition did not last long. The killer was arrested at his home within hours. As it turned out, the suspect was the first person tried under the new Texas law making it a capital murder offense to kill a police officer in the performance of his official duties. He received a death penalty which was prematurely carried out when a fellow inmate stabbed the man in the penitentiary.

According to the kidnap victim, the suspect had a cheap automatic pistol hidden in his hand when Thompson had first approached the vehicle on that unseasonably warm winter night in 1974. The man told the victim to keep quiet because he was going to shoot the officer. Thompson focused on the front-seat struggle as the suspect pulled the trigger, the pistol pointed at Thompson's chest. The gun misfired, and that was when the suspect sped off. Another handgun in the suspect's possession had just been stolen from an off-duty officer along with the vehicle the suspect was driving. The revolver worked properly, and it was with that gun that Thompson's friend and fellow officer was killed.

Thompson often pondered "what if" regarding the ex-con's choice of weapons. Why did events unfold the way they did? The deceased officer left a wife and young child. Their lives were forever altered by the horrid events of that night. Thompson's life was also altered, but he did not think about that. Was the occurrence his fault? Fault and blame…the big and important issues…In retrospect, Thompson was sure he could have handled things better than he did. At least, in his mind, that was the way things were and no one could convince him otherwise, despite the years. The guilt feelings diminished with time, but they never went away. His overactive memory and conscience made certain of that. He wondered if the crack in his relationship with Rose had begun on that night, so long ago.

CHAPTER 18

Jan Doxee met Lilly LaMarque in the lobby of the Ranch House Bed and Breakfast. Located near a large ski resort, the Ranch House was not a typical bed and breakfast. Once an exclusive hunting retreat for wealthy clients, mismanagement and hard financial times had forced its closing in the late 1960's.

The main lodge and the half-dozen cabins fell into a state of disrepair and abandonment for almost twenty years. The new owner had pumped several hundred thousand dollars into the restoration, making it far more luxurious than it had ever been. The main lodge housed a conference room with seating for fifty; the dining room could accommodate one hundred. The restaurant had become popular with the ski crowd and tourists. With the guests staying at the ranch house and the public who dined there, the eatery was packed nightly. It was open to the public during the evening hours only and reservations were required. A small but elegant bar was on the backside of the dining room. Food and drinks were excellent, but prices indicated everyone was being gouged to the extreme. A common practice in resort areas, but no one complained.

Each cabin was set up as a small home, complete with two bedrooms, two baths, a living room, and kitchen. One cabin was never rented to the public. It was used strictly for illicit purposes.

No one named a newborn Lilly LaMarque. Even if that was not her real name, no one cared. Lilly and a couple of cohorts took care of the planned activities that occurred in the special cabin. While it became apparent after a time that something about *this bungalow was not quite right, no one said anything. Many people in lavish resort areas have a knack for keeping silent about the affairs of others. They often have skeletons in their own closets that reek of decadent lifestyles, including drug use, infidelity, and white collar crime.*

Lilly, the whore, was quite a good-looking forty-year old single woman. She was an expert skier and would never leave the area even if she became too old to work. Besides, there were plenty of men that would be all too eager to take care of Lilly forever. Dark in hair and complexion, Lilly was a small, slender woman with no artificial attributes. Man could not enhance upon her natural features.

Thompson looked through several telephones messages at work the next morning. All had come in late the day before after he had taken off early. He was interested in each. One was from Raeburn Compton, another from "Mr. Foul", the bartender, also known as Herschel Fowler, and the third was from Jan Doxee.

He called Raeburn Compton first.

"Raeburn Compton speaking."

"Raeburn, this is Wade Thompson."

Compton responded in a humorous tone, anxious to toot his own horn, "Detective, I just wanted to give you a report on all the good deeds I've done in my district lately. Of course, Abe Fishbein has provided me with some assistance."

"Well, Raeburn, I'm glad to hear you're doing good things, but don't feel like you need to give me a report. Just work with the decent people and piss on the crooks," Thompson said.

Compton said, "That's what I've been doing. I can't even get a free drink anymore. Well, you must excuse me, I've got a meeting."

"Thanks, Raeburn," Thompson said.

Thompson called Herschel Fowler next.

"Hello," Herschel answered, obvious irritation and

impatience in his voice.

"Wade Thompson, Herschel, returning your call."

The waiter replied, "Sorry, Detective Thompson, I didn't mean to sound gruff. I was just on my way out the door. I'm going to work."

"Why not just call me when it's convenient?" Thompson suggested.

Herschel replied in desperation, "I don't want to be a pain in the neck, but I'm worried to death about going to jail. I'd like to get my cases taken care of as soon as possible, particularly the drug case. Can I come in tomorrow or the next day and talk to you guys?"

"How about in the morning? I think Forsky talked to the judge yesterday afternoon. If for some reason we don't have permission yet, I'll call you. Otherwise, be here at ten," Thompson said.

"I'll be there. Thank you," Herschel replied.

Forsky walked in just as Thompson hung up the phone.

"John, did you talk to the judge about Mr. Foul?" Thompson asked.

Forsky answered, "Yeah, we can use him as long as we don't have him making drug cases. If we use him successfully, the judge wants to know what he did. You know, something official in writing, I suppose."

"Good. He'll be here in the morning at ten," Thompson said. "He's real eager to work. The guy's terrified of going to the pen."

Forsky responded with a laugh, "Mr. Foul's got nothing to worry about in the joint. No one there is that hard up for a boyfriend."

Thompson was reluctant to call Jan Doxee, but he wanted to get it over with. He hoped she was sober. The later he waited to call, the greater the chance would be that she was not.

"Hello," she said. She was sober.

Thompson said, "Jan, how are you? Did you call last night?"

"Yeah, I did, Wade. I'd like to explain this in person, but I know you won't make a social call, so I'll mention it on the phone." she said.

Thompson tried to prepare himself as he said, "Okay, what would you like to mention?"

"Wade, I've been having this pain in my chest, and I went to see my doctor. I thought I was having a heart attack, but he says I have a duodenal ulcer. He told me if I don't stop my drinking, I will soon be dead. I could just bleed to death internally. Wade, I'm really scared. I don't want to die. He's recommended a treatment facility here in Dallas. I'm scared to death to do it. What do you think?" Jan asked, expressing a need for help and comfort for the first time.

"Do it!" Thompson exclaimed, so surprised he could think of nothing else to say.

Jan said, "I'm ashamed to discuss this with my family and I have no real friends. I'll bare my soul and say you and John are as close to being true friends as I've ever known. I can't do this alone. A staff psychiatrist at the institution has interviewed me. They want me to stay for thirty days. I'm going to put you on the spot, here, Wade. I'll do this if you will accompany me on the day I'm admitted and visit me once in a while. I must have your support or I can't do it...I won't do it. I guess I'm a coward."

Thompson said, "I'll go with you, just don't ask me to handle your business affairs during your absence."

Jan replied, "Thank you, Wade. It means a lot to me. I anticipated that you would say yes. Pick me up tomorrow at 1:00 P.M. I've told everyone I'm going on a month-long vacation and they will be unable to contact me. No one but you will know where I am."

"I guess I'll see you tomorrow afternoon, then," Thompson said.

"Thanks again, Wade. I've got to run to the liquor store and pick up a few things," Jan said. "I'm just kidding… I haven't had a drink since dinner last night. I'm shaking so bad I can hardly hold the receiver. I may have the DT's when you get here, but I'll be sober."

"I hope so, Jan."

She replied with commitment, "I'll be okay."

Thompson told her goodbye. He doubted that she had the strength to ward off the demons. His doubts were strong and justified.

Thompson told Forsky, "Let's eat lunch, John. I have some interesting news."

"Square meal?" Forsky asked.

"Square meal it is," Thompson conceded.

As they ate, Forsky asked, "So you think the cure will take?"

"I sure hope it does, but I don't know," Thompson said.

Forsky remarked, "I hate to be negative about something like this, but the only 'treatment' I can visualize is when she 'treats' herself to a vodka collins at the nearest bar on her way home to the hospital."

"We're not stopping at a bar," Thompson said with slight irritation.

Herschel Fowler arrived at ten A.M. The detectives talked Tal Sanderson out of his office so that they would have a suitable place for an interview. Before everyone was seated, Herschel said, "In the interest of efficiency, I've made some notes for your use. I've dealt with perhaps twenty escort services in the Dallas area and elsewhere. I average calling them about twice a month. Almost everyone in the business knows Herschel. You can use me as a reference if you wish."

Thompson and Forsky examined Herschel's notes. The detectives were familiar with several of the agencies.

Forsky asked Herschel, "What's the story on these services with toll-free numbers?"

"That's really nothing new... they've been around for a while. You call the number and tell them what city you're in. They contact a local hooker and have her come to your location, or you can meet her someplace. They're very accommodating, but are higher priced than the ones advertising in the yellow pages," Herschel volunteered.

Thompson found Herschel to be somewhat of a bewilderment in comparison to other informants he had dealt with. Despite his physical appearance and his unquenchable thirst for whores, Mr. Foul seemed to be intelligent and was very forthright with the information he provided.

Forsky asked, "Where did you get these 800 numbers? I know they're not in the yellow pages or the Dallas Back Door."

The Dallas Back Door was a local 'underground' newspaper. It served as a popular advertising medium for escort services, male and female freelance whores, weirdoes, con games, and shady businesses. There was always a current edition in the vice office.

"Oh, they advertise in places where you guys probably wouldn't look...magazines like "Modern South Lifestyle", "Contempo Texas", legitimate stuff...and that's just in this part of the country. There are lots of other publications all over the nation. Look in the classifieds of one of the magazines. It'll be a simple ad, something like, 'Girls!' followed by an 800 number," Herschel explained.

Thompson replied, "Herschel, you have considerable knowledge of the organized whore business."

"I'll take that as a compliment, but it's not something I'm real proud of. Hey, it's after eleven, I need to get to work if it's okay with you all," Herschel said.

As they all stood, Forsky told Herschel, "Sure, go to work. We'll look over your notes and give you a call."

Herschel said, "Just help me out of this mess."

"I think we can do that," Thompson replied, as Mr. Foul hurried toward the hallway.

CHAPTER 19

Thompson arrived at Jan Doxee's apartment shortly after 1:00 P.M. She opened the door and at her feet were a small overnight bag, briefcase, and her purse. Jan had on little or no makeup. The very noticeable dark circles under her eyes had never been there before, or perhaps they had been hidden. The woman had cut off her long nails. She wore a plain, loose dress that fit like a bag. Jan looked as if she were going to her own execution. Both hands quivered. She had not been drinking, and appeared sick.

As they drove away from the apartment, Jan said, "Wade, I'd like another favor."

"What is it?"

"I can't bring any money into the hospital. I have some cash in an envelope in my purse. Keep it for me until I get out. You could just put in your car trunk if you'd like," she said.

Thompson replied, "Jan, I've got to draw the line somewhere. I won't hold your money. I can't and you should know that. Let's go by your bank now, and you can deposit it."

"Okay, I know. I thought I would ask anyway. Go by the Overland Trail branch. It's right before you get to the hospital," she said.

As he entered the parking lot, Thompson drove toward a drive-in teller.

Jan said, "No, no, I don't use those drive throughs. Pull up in front. When I go to a bank, I do business inside."

Thompson was silent as she got out of the car.

She returned in a few minutes and remarked, "Thank

you very much. I shouldn't have been carrying cash around, anyway."

Thompson was curious and asked as he drove, "It's not my business, but how much cash did you have?"

"You're so right, it's not your business, but I had about twenty-thousand dollars, all large bills, of course," she said matter-of-factly.

Thompson asked in amazement, "You were going to leave twenty-thousand dollars in my car trunk for a month?"

She smiled for the first time since Thompson picked her up and said, "I trust you, sweetie, but when all the alcohol is out of my system, I may not."

With a slight grin, Thompson replied, "When all the alcohol is out of your system, I hope the good sense I assume you once had returns."

As they pulled into the hospital parking lot, a still smiling Jan said, "That's a very hurtful remark, Wade."

Thompson parked. When Jan realized where they were, the smile vanished.

"Wade, I have never been so terrified in all my life," she said as she firmly squeezed his right hand with her sweaty and shaky left hand.

"Everything will be fine," Thompson replied, knowing full well that was far from the truth.

Jan released her grip and said, "Can we sit here for a while? I could really use a double vodka right now, and I'm not kidding."

"I know you're not kidding. No, we won't sit here. Let's go," Thompson said with all the firmness he could muster in the sad situation.

They were almost at the front door, when Jan said, "Wade, don't get upset, but I listed you on the admitting paperwork as my brother. I had to have an emergency contact, and you're it."

Thompson did not like surprises. He was becoming

irritated and regretting his involvement. "What name did you use for your brother on the paperwork? And what else haven't you told me that I need to know?"

"I used your name and gave them your work number and pager number. Don't worry, they won't call unless I hang myself or run away or do something else foolish. Relax... there are no more surprises," Jan said, appearing to be more at ease as a result of the mild confrontation.

As they entered the spacious lobby area, a well-dressed woman in her late-fifties approached. Her hand was extended first to Jan, and then to Thompson. She had a huge, warm smile on her face. Thompson instantly liked the woman, even before she spoke.

"Jan, you may not remember me, but I'm Doctor Virginia Edmonds. I sat in briefly on your initial evaluation last week. I'm quite pleased to see you here," the woman said.

Jan managed a weak smile and replied, "I wish I could say I'm glad to see you and tickled to be here again, but I won't."

Jan introduced Thompson to Doctor Holland, but she did not say he was her brother. The doctor appeared eager to assist Jan with her admittance.

Jan shook Wade Thompson's hand and said, "I can't use the phone during the first two weeks, but I'll call you after that. Thanks for the help and support. Please leave now. This is becoming very difficult."

The doctor stood in silence. Wade Thompson felt awkward and uncomfortable, and sad for Jan. Tears were forming in her eyes. He said, "Goodbye, Jan. Good luck to you."

Neither Jan nor Doctor Edmonds said a word as Thompson turned and left the building. All he could think about as he drove to the office was how difficult and humiliating it would be to experience what awaited Jan Doxee.

Forsky and Thompson met in the hallway just outside the vice office.

Forsky asked, "Did you all stop off for a cold beer on the way to the cure?"

"No, John, we didn't stop for a beer," Thompson replied, a bit upset at Forsky's cop humor. He knew, however, that Forsky also wanted Jan to get well. He changed the subject and told his partner about the cash Jan Doxee had in her purse.

"Twenty-thousand dollars? And she wanted to leave it in the trunk of a five hundred-dollar car? I'd say she's got more problems than being a drunk," Forsky said.

Thompson continued, "We went to the Overland Trail branch by the hospital. That's one of the banks where she was wire transferring funds back and forth."

"If anybody makes a case on her, it's gonna be the IRS," Forsky said.

CHAPTER 20

When everyone had shown up for work, Tal Sanderson entered the squad room and announced a meeting that would take place in the next half-hour. The captain was in a staff briefing with the big guys and would be in the office shortly to inform all supervisors and detectives about some matter of importance. Most assumed the meeting was in some way related to the political convention.

Forsky asked Thompson, "You want to start on that Herschel Fowler stuff today?"

"Yeah. We need to check out some of the people and agencies we're unfamiliar with, and maybe get subpoenas ready on those phone numbers," Thompson said.

Escort services often advertised a fictitious address in conjunction with their real telephone number. Whether they did this to avoid detection by law enforcement or as a way to appear legitimate to prospective customers was unclear. Perhaps the ploy was designed to serve both purposes, but it was ineffective.

Captain Arlie Holland came into the squad room, a look of concern on his face. The room was packed; all eight detectives, two sergeants, the lieutenant, and captain crowded in. Lieutenant Pricklee shut the door.

The captain said, "I'll make everyone aware of the information I have at this point. The chief is retiring. He has had his fill of planning this convention. Outside agencies have been trying to assume the role of the police department instead of cooperating with it. City management has been doing the same thing. Within the department itself, some petty jealousies and in-house bickering have kept some things from being done as scheduled. I've been involved in a good deal of the planning, and can testify that the chief has had a lot of people working against him. Now he's given the arrogant jerks and incompetents the opportunity to run the whole show themselves. The new chief will likely be Theron Thomas. He may be the finest chief we've ever had and we need to be supportive of the man. He's coming in at a difficult time. He lacks experience, and he's the first to admit it, but that may not necessarily be detrimental. That's what I know at the present. Anything new happens, I'll make you aware."

Everyone vacated the stuffy squad room for the breathing air available in the main part of the vice office.

Thompson asked Forsky, "You know Theron Thomas?"

"I know he's an affirmative action sergeant that made deputy chief. That's certainly nothing in his favor, but some of those guys have turned out okay. I've never heard an adverse comment about the man," Forsky said.

"Well, John, if you can't say anything bad about someone, they must be alright," Thompson replied.

The basic affirmative action concept had received a liberal interpretation and a generous implementation within the police department. To use ethnicity or gender as a basis for promotion was wrong and there could be no logical argument there, but Thompson's outlook on the matter was very positive. He felt certain that in time the right people would see the shortcomings of the system and would work to turn things around. These "right" people might be male, female, black, white, green, or chartreuse. It made no difference. Additionally, there were some officers who had been promoted without the benefit of affirmative action who were horrible supervisors. Lt. Pricklee was a perfect example.

"Let's do some work," Thompson suggested to Forsky. "I'll get started on the phone numbers if you want to check on the agencies and names we're not familiar with."

Forsky replied, "About time you did some phone subpoenas."

Both detectives were somewhat embarrassed about being unaware of the toll-free whore services Herschel mentioned. They did not discuss it. It's doubtful anyone else in vice knew of their existence, either, but Thompson and Forsky worked the services more than all the other detectives combined. They should have known.

The many thousands of jurisdictions around the country were usually under no obligation to honor out-of-state subpoenas. On occasion, one would be recognized and acted upon by a jurisdiction in another state. This was done as a courtesy measure and for information not deemed critical or highly sensitive. Sometimes, a helpful district attorney's office located in the appropriate state would be willing to do some of the legwork, obtain the subpoena, and serve it.

Through regular sources, Thompson found that all four toll-free numbers were located in the San Antonio, Texas area. That would save out-of-state red tape, but subpoenas still had to be prepared to get the particulars. Thompson would prepare them, have them signed at the courthouse, and deliver them to telephone company security that day.

Forsky was busy on the computer, doing criminal backgrounds on the names provided by Herschel Fowler. It dawned on Thompson that neither he nor Forsky had mentioned anything to Sgt. Sanderson about what they were working on. He walked to the doorway of Sanderson's office, and asked, "Got a minute, Tal?"

"Come on in, Wade," Sanderson said in a manner that indicated he wanted to talk to Thompson anyway.

Thompson sat down and hit the high points of the toll-free whore service investigation. He concluded with, "As soon as we get the information on the phone numbers, we'll probably need to make a trip to San Antonio...maybe get their vice guys involved in this, too."

Sanderson's reply indicated he was preoccupied, "Whatever you need to do…Wade shut the door."

Thompson closed the door and reclaimed his chair.

Sanderson said, "I'm going to discuss this with everyone, but since you're the first one in my office after that meeting with the captain, I'll take advantage of the opportunity."

Thompson was baffled and hoped his boss would get to the point.

Sanderson said, "I don't know whether or not you know Theron Thomas. He will be the new chief, that's for sure. The city manager will make an official announcement tomorrow or the next day. When that happens, there will be a very divisive atmosphere within the department. A 'let's get even' attitude will prevail. The important people on the command staff will be minorities. A few others will be carefully chosen 'yes' men who will be harmless to the new regime. The department will undergo significant changes, and won't be the same as we've known it. Our captain will likely be replaced. So will our deputy chief, Herbert Greenlee. You know as well as I do that you won't find more competent characters than those two."

Thompson interrupted, "Tal, you're preaching doomsday stuff. How could you possibly know all this?"

Sanderson was evasive as he replied, "It will happen and I want everyone to be prepared. I'm not really sure what good the knowledge will do any of us, since there is nothing that can be done about it."

Thompson knew better than to question Sanderson on something like this. Sanderson was known, respected, and trusted by many of the higher-ups and their assistants. Over the years the sergeant had mentioned other things that Thompson had thought were nothing but wildly exaggerated rumors. Not only did these things occur, but even minor details were accurate to a reasonable degree.

Thompson and Sanderson gave one another a momentary pensive stare.

Sanderson said, "Wade, you and me and a lot of others in this office are in a position to retire or will be soon. If you have any plans along those lines, now might be a good time to give them due thought...but for now, go to work, I'm through brightening your day."

Thompson grinned and said, "You've done that alright, Tal."

With a cup of coffee, Thompson sat at his shared desk and began to work on the phone subpoenas. After only a few seconds, he started daydreaming about retirement, something he had not given much thought to before.

Thompson hunted elk in Western Colorado every fall. He enjoyed it immensely, and had fantasized about being an elk guide for wealthy clients. However, he had never given the idea serious consideration once he returned home from a hunt. Now he looked at the possibility in a different light, and with far more interest than ever before.

The detective caught himself in the midst of his daydream. He remembered a phrase Forsky had coined years before that described his partner's yen for vice work. Forsky had said: 'there's no life after vice'. He meant that any other job in police work or elsewhere would be dull, very dull, and very lacking after working vice. Thompson had been in agreement with Forsky on the subject. Now, for the first time, he had doubts. He wondered if maybe there was something else out there he might enjoy doing. He had done nothing but police work for almost thirty years and had enjoyed most of his career to an immense degree. It was almost as if he had not worked for a living. Few people experience such luxury in a profession. If he ever did switch careers, it could only be for something that offered equal enjoyment. Anything less would be a "job" and no amount of money could make a "job" pleasurable, exciting, and interesting.

Thompson realized his idle thoughts were of little help in getting the paperwork completed. He tackled what was left and finished the subpoena forms in less than an hour.

During lunch, Thompson gave Forsky a summary of Tal Sanderson's dismal forecast for the department's future.

"If it happens, it happens," Forsky said, not at all unsettled by the news.

"Your attitude surprises me," said Thompson.

Forsky continued, "Look at it this way, we've had a pretty decent job for a long time. For reasons unknown to us, things change and oftentimes it's not for the better. There may be no life after vice, but I can fish and I'm not talking about sitting under a willow with a cane pole and drinking cheap beer. I've given it serious thought for the last year. I'd like to run a guide service year 'round, and fish in tournaments. That would be a very close second to vice, at least for me."

Thompson was taken aback by his partner's remark. Forsky had it all planned, and it was a comfortable plan. If changes made the vice job unpleasant, he had an almost perfect alternative, ready to set into motion.

Thompson said, "Looking at it that way, John, you can't lose."

"That's exactly right. Now don't worry about any of this until it happens. It may not happen at all. If it does, be prepared. You can go to the mountains, and let rich guys pay you to gut dead elk just as easy as I can catch fish."

Jealous of his partner's contingency plan, Thompson no longer wanted to discuss the issue. The whole idea was discomforting to him.

CHAPTER 21

"Find anything of interest in those names Mr. Foul gave us?" Thompson asked Forsky.

"Not yet. I've run all the criminal backgrounds, but I haven't looked at them."

Thompson remarked, "We've got that to do, and we'll have to wait a few days for the information from the phone company. We've got to check out this San Antonio angle, but we don't need any of that to make a whore case or two right now."

"Okay," Forsky said, "let's set up at a hotel tomorrow. I'll bet this service has daytime whores."

About eighty percent of escort services did not take calls until late afternoon or early evening. Vice detectives seldom worked the services during the daytime for no particular reasons. Agency operators were well aware of this, but apparently, there were not enough daytime clients to make the practice worthwhile for the escort businesses.

Thompson went through his regular contact to get a couple of complimentary rooms at the Hotel Greater Dallas. The day security man was a retired traffic cop in his sixties. He never asked questions, and told no one except the manager that vice was working in the hotel.

During the early afternoon the next day, Thompson and Forsky lugged their prop luggage down the street and checked in. Thompson called one of the 800 numbers provided by Herschel Fowler. Harried and impatient, a young woman's voice with a distinct Texas accent answered, "What city, please?"

Thompson was startled for a second; at first he thought he had a phone company operator. He responded, "City? uh...I'm in Dallas."

"Very well... give me your name, credit card number, expiration date, and a phone number. The initial fee is one-hundred-fifty dollars. I'll have a young lady call you soon. She will explain the details to you and answer any questions you might have. I'm ready to take your information now," the fast-talking girl said.

"I'm Franklin Wood," Thompson said, and proceeded to provide everything requested, including driver's license information and questions about his work. The entire call could not have lasted two minutes. An efficient production line operation, the detective thought, unlike any whore service he had dealt with before. "A whore will call shortly, or so the girl implied," he told Forsky.

With less optimism in his reply, Forsky said, "Yeah... probably within an hour."

Five minutes later the telephone rang and Thompson answered. A female caller said, "Franklin Wood, please."

"This is Franklin."

"Franklin, my name is Jackie, and I'll be at your room in the next half-hour if that's convenient."

"That's fine," Thompson replied. "I look forward to meeting you."

Forsky had a surprised look on his face as Thompson said, "She'll be here in thirty minutes."

"You know, I think she really will be here soon. Forgive me for stereotyping all escort services as being less than punctual. A breach of professionalism on my part, I suppose," Forsky responded in his unrepentant apologetic manner.

After twenty minutes, Forsky went into the adjoining room. Thompson sat on the bed, flipping TV channels in his nervous state. The nervousness was a response to a perceived fear of the unknown. While it never subsided to a noticeable degree, it had become easier to accept and deal with over the years.

There were three faint knocks on the door. Thirty-five minutes had elapsed since Thompson had spoken with "Jackie". Record time for an escort service whore, truly record time, Thompson thought. He opened the door.

"Hi, Franklin, I'm Jackie," said the comely early-thirties woman, a sincere-looking smile adorning her face.

"I'm very pleased to meet you, Jackie, and I'm impressed with your promptness," Thompson said. He stepped aside, and Jackie walked into the room. He closed the door.

She stood next to the bed, and asked, "May I sit here?"

"By all means, make yourself comfortable," Thompson replied.

He was not accustomed to escort service whores who were punctual and well mannered. Jackie did not wear cheap clothes and reek of cigarettes and nauseating perfume. She wore only one ring, and her nails were real and manicured. The woman was very unhooker-like.

In a businesslike and authoritative way, the young woman said, "Franklin, I must explain a few things of a financial nature before we proceed. I receive none of the money from the agency fee you have already paid by credit card. My earnings come solely from tips. I will accept a credit card or cash for my services. How do you wish to pay, and what exactly did you have in mind?"

"I'll pay cash. I wanted a straight date, if you know what I mean," Thompson said with confidence. No challenge would be presented in making a prostitution case, unlike he had anticipated.

Jackie replied without hesitation, "Yes, I'm well aware of what a straight date is, and my fee is based on the act; it's not an hourly rate. A straight will cost you $250.00."

"A little high-priced aren't you? I'm sure you're worth it

though," Thompson said as he bumped the door to Forsky's room with his elbow.

Forsky burst into the room with badge and ID in hand. The woman shrieked, but soon realized what was happening. Thompson presented his credentials, and arrested the woman. Indignant, she remarked, "I've done nothing, you can't charge me with prostitution."

Forsky retorted, "If you believe that, you've been coached by an idiot or a shyster, maybe one in the same."

Jackie crumbled onto the bed, and cried. "I didn't check you out. I let my guard down. I felt comfortable, and knew you just couldn't be a cop."

"Most women think I do look like a cop, whatever look that is," Thompson replied.

As Thompson gathered up props, Forsky read the girl her rights. He also went into the procedure for working off a case. "Are you interested?" he asked.

She replied, "I'm very interested…I have two prostitution convictions."

Thompson listened with amazement when she mentioned convictions, but the woman was not very streetwise. Jackie had allowed green dollars to numb what should have been a far more cautious nature.

As the trio made the short trip to the vice office, Forsky inquired about the woman's background. Both detectives were curious, since Jackie was unlikely material for career whore work.

"I teach political science in the Dallas County College District," she said, "I make a good salary, but this also pays well. I only do a couple of dates a week."

The detectives stared at each other. "How long have you worked for this agency?" Thompson asked.

The woman answered, "I've been with them over a year. In fact, this is the only agency I've ever worked for."

Forsky inquired, "Were your previous arrests in Dallas?"

"Neither of them were here. One was in Oklahoma City, and the other was in Shreveport," she replied.

Both officers were puzzled and the woman saw it on their faces.

"Please continue," Thompson said. "Why were you working in those cities?"

"I'm getting to that," she said, as they got off the elevator on the vice office floor.

Jackie explained, "The agency sometimes comes up short in other cities if there's a heavy demand for services... conventions, things like that. They'll fly you or pay you mileage if you drive and they pay all other expenses, too. You will normally stay over a weekend. After I get through with agency business, I might do a little freelancing. That's what happened both times when I was arrested. In Shreveport, I tried to work a casino and picked up an undercover cop. In Oklahoma City, I was in a hotel bar. I'm about ready to give up this work. I'm a far better teacher than prostitute."

Thompson had to agree with the woman but kept the thought to himself.

"What's the name of this agency you work for?" Thompson asked.

"Silly as it may sound, I have no idea," she answered, you won't find a name in any of the ads, only an 800 number."

She spoke so freely, Thompson and Forsky decided to keep her talking and worry about the arrest paperwork later. They all got comfortable in Sgt. Sanderson's office.

Forsky asked, "How were you hired?"

"I saw an ad and called. In fact, I was in my office reading a journal and noticed a tiny advertisement in the classifieds. It said something like 'escorts / companions anywhere in the USA' followed by a phone number. I called and they took my name and number. A few days later, someone from the agency called and told me to meet a man at a coffee shop. I did, he interviewed me, and I was hired," Jackie told the detectives.

Thompson asked, "Do you know who this man was? Did he give you a name? What did he look like?"

"He told me his name was not important. If I ever needed to speak with him again, call the agency. They would contact him. He was in his fifties, tall and thin. He was dark and his skin was very wrinkled, like he'd spent his life on a beach. He was well dressed but not well educated...something about the way he conversed. I had to show him my driver's license, voter registration, credit cards, checkbook, just about everything in my purse," Jackie said.

Amazed at her naiveté, Forsky remarked, "You let a strange man go through your stuff like that?"

"Well, yes, I did," she replied, "how else was I going to get hired?"

Thompson asked, "What did you and he talk about?"

"Well, he explained about the money, how the service received the agency fee and I worked for tips. He told me never to charge a low fee for any reason. If I did and word got back to the agency, I would be fired. He said the agency did not want its image among customers to be cheapened by hundred dollar hookers. I was told never to charge less than $200 for a straight date, $200 for oral sex, or $350 for a half-and-half. He mentioned checking out clients to make sure they weren't cops and if I got arrested I was on my own. If I wasn't punctual for a date, I'd get fired. Oh, yeah, if I took a credit card for payment for sex, I should fill out the credit card slip in the hotel room. He gave me a whole stack of the slips. To be paid, I'd call the agency. They would send this same man to meet me. I would give him the slip and he'd give me cash, less fifteen percent for his trouble, " Jackie said.

'Factoring' is a common practice among escort services. Credit card companies prefer not to provide accounts for shady businesses, particularly those that are involved in prostitution.

Nevertheless, disreputable characters do have accounts. They charge other slime a percentage to cash credit card slips. Often, when a customer receives a monthly statement, a particular charge may show to be from a florist or catering service. The credit card company, unfortunately, gets wise to the scheme after several customers balk at paying $300 dollar charges for flowers. A customer may claim a blatant error in billing and refuse payment.

"Have you ever met anyone else connected with the service?" Forsky asked, confident he already knew the answer.

She replied without hesitation, "That's it. There's no one else."

"Would you be willing to call the agency and tell them you've done a credit card transaction so they'll send out the man you met?" Thompson inquired.

Jackie replied, "Sure, if it'll help me."

"Okay," Thompson said, "first, we'll do your paperwork and you'll be placed in jail. The bond will be low. You can make it yourself. An attorney won't be necessary unless you just want one. When you get home, call the agency. Don't mention the arrest to them or anyone else. Just tell them you need to cash a credit card slip. The man should call to arrange a meeting. Do it in the daytime so we can get a look at him, his car, license plate and so forth. I'll give you a name and credit card number to put on the slip. Alright?"

Jackie replied, "Yeah, but I have classes until noon tomorrow. Maybe he can call my office after that."

"That's fine, but you call us right away and let us know. For our surveillance and your safety, meet him someplace very public like a coffee shop, restaurant, or shopping center parking lot. And give us an hour's notice," Forsky said.

"Got it," the woman said.

The detectives hurriedly completed their paperwork.

The next day, Jackie Spencer paged Forsky at 1:30 P.M.

He called her office number.

"Jackie, John Forsky. Did you hear from him?" Forsky asked.

"Did I...the guy's got a regular route. He said he would be in my part of town in the late afternoon. I'm to meet him in the parking lot of the restaurant where I met him the first time. He said to be on time because he has to meet other people, too. The man was just short of being rude," she remarked.

Forsky said, "Go ahead then. Forget about us even being in the area. Get there early and park away from everyone else if the lot's not crowded. When you're through, go home or wherever you'd like. We want to make sure he doesn't follow you."

"I don't mind saying this makes me a bit nervous," the woman replied.

Forsky said with encouragement, "You'll do just fine, Jackie. Call us if anything comes up. Otherwise, we're in business."

Forsky briefed Thompson regarding the arrangements. They left the office at four. In the heavy afternoon traffic, it took forty minutes to get to the North Dallas location. Jackie Spencer was already parked when they arrived. The detectives positioned the old Pontiac among other cars in an adjacent grocery store lot.

At exactly 5:15, a silver Lexus drove alongside Jackie's Blazer. With binoculars, Forsky and Thompson got a good look at the driver of the Lexus. He was quite a bit older than the woman's estimate. Neither Jackie nor the man got out of their vehicles. Forsky wrote down the license number of the Lexus that pulled away after only six minutes.

Thompson and Forsky watched as the car quickly entered the northbound entrance ramp to the freeway. Jackie drove south. Keeping up with the Lexus in rush hour traffic was difficult and the detectives lost sight of it twice. After several miles, they took an exit with the silver car then watched as the driver entered the parking lot of a large insurance company high rise located next to the service road. The driver pulled next to a new Chevrolet pickup. Thompson could make out a female in her late twenties as the driver of the truck. Again, neither person got out of their vehicle. After a few minutes, both vehicles left in different directions.

Thompson and Forsky followed the Lexus toward the interior of the neighboring city of Richardson. At 6:20, the as-yet-unidentified male replayed the previous scenes as he stopped next to a twenty-year old, beat up blue Cadillac parked behind a fast food joint.

The driver of the junker appeared to be a woman in her mid-forties. In sharp contrast to her car, she was attractive, though old for a whore.

Forsky asked Thompson, "You want to follow this guy all night? I think we know what he's up to."

"No, we've done enough for this evening. I wonder how often he does this." Thompson remarked.

Forsky replied, "Who knows? For our purposes it really doesn't matter."

"Let's go home. We can run license tags in the morning," Thompson suggested.

The next day, Forsky was busy at the computer when Thompson arrived at work.

"Find anything yet, John?" Thompson asked.

He replied, "Our man is Rufus Mathison. I've heard of him. He's about as close to a real gangster as we've ever run across. He was a strong-arm for bookies and loan sharks. Intelligence had a file on him. I made a copy; it's on the desk."

Thompson got some coffee, grabbed the file, and sat beside Forsky. Thompson could spend hours reading extensive files on old criminals, particularly those with records dating to the 'fifties and 'sixties. The very different 'no-nonsense-to-the-point' paperwork forms the police department used then were interesting. Official memos that summarized investigations were typed on onionskin paper. Thompson was intrigued by the crude print so characteristic of a manual typewriter in the hands of the unskilled. The old black and white mugshots made everyone look far more sinister than they were. Adding to the effect, many males with hair of nominal length had it greased to the point where it looked as if it had not been washed in weeks. The old photos almost imparted the aromas of various popular men's hair creams and oils of the era.

Long before it became fashionable for people to be overly sensitive and to take full advantage of every opportunity to have their feelings hurt, the language of police narratives was markedly different. While not done with harmful intent, these narratives would be found by many persons, including police officers, to be offensive by today's standards.

The majority of cops several decades ago had far less in the way of formal education than those of today. However, Thompson could not help but think that the level of street wisdom of former generations of cops was keener than that possessed by contemporaries. The old timers also lacked the technology we have today, but made up for it by actual shrewd brainwork and cunning in order to be successful. Moreover, they were successful. Cop work may not be as advanced now as some would have us believe.

According to the file, Rufus Mathison was sixty-three years old. He had served three penitentiary terms, beginning in 1956 with a murder conviction in a hired-gun killing. His second pen trip in 1963 was for the sale of heroin. The last stay in 1969 was for armed robbery. Rufus had spent more than twenty years in jail. His lengthy record also included arrests for rape, counterfeiting, and safe burglary.

Forsky ordered a current driver's license photograph of Mathison. The two mugshots in his file were more than fifteen years old. Rufus had not been arrested in a long time. Factoring credit card charges was not as exciting as contract murder work but it was less stressful, the hours were better, and the chance of going to jail was slim indeed.

Thompson told Forsky, "Let's go by Rufus' place today and have a look...that is, if he lives at the address listed on his driver's license."

"You know where that is?" Forsky asked, with reluctance.

Thompson replied, "No, I was hoping you did."

"I know about where it is, practically in Frisco. Traffic's been a nightmare since half the world moved up there a few years ago. Roads are torn up and everything's under construction. Looks like Beirut, but whatever suits you just tickles me plumb to death," Forsky remarked as only Forsky could.

It took an hour to get to the address listed on Rufus Mathison's driver's license. The area was street after street of apartments and condominiums. There must have been fifty thousand people living on a hundred acres of real estate that was a cotton field four years ago. Rufus lived in a modest condo. The Lexus was in the driveway. Forsky's research indicated another ex-con and current bookie owned the place.

The detectives parked down the street. After a few minutes, Thompson said, "Let's get out of here. There's no good place to sit and watch that condo during the daytime. The neighbor's will be calling the cops pretty soon if we stay."

As Forsky pulled away from the curb, he said, "Yeah, and this car was probably built before most of the residents out here were born. We might stand out a bit."

CHAPTER 22

It was almost three before Thompson and Forsky returned to the office. They had more research to do on the national dial-a-whore case. Thompson was taking his turn on the computer when Jan Doxee called.

"Wade, how are you?" she asked, sounding very fatigued.

He answered, "I'm just fine, how are you...really?" That had not sounded as he intended it. Thompson feared it would put Jan on the defensive. It did.

"Sounds like you're anticipating a lie from me, but I'll ignore it because I feel good," she replied.

Thompson responded, "I didn't mean it that way. I'm glad you feel good. It's just that you sound very tired."

"They have me on some medicine that just wears me out. I could lie down and take a nap anywhere, anytime," Jan explained, "but I can stop taking it next week if I choose."

Thompson was curious about her treatment, but knew he had to be careful with the wording of his questions. "How has the program been so far? It's been two weeks."

"Wade, this may be difficult to understand. It is for many people, whether they are drunks or teetotalers. I'll be an alcoholic even if I don't drink for the next fifty years. I haven't tried to sneak out to a bar in the middle of the night, though I must admit the urge has been there, oh, thirty times or so. I don't shake any more. I haven't had a severe bout of depression. No more bad headaches. Overall, I can't remember feeling this good, physically or mentally. I know I sound drugged and I am at the moment, but I'm progressing. What's important is that the intensity of the cravings diminish daily."

"Jan, I'm relieved to hear all those things."

"Something else...I haven't smoked a cigarette in four days. They just stopped tasting good, and they definitely are not good for my ulcer. In fact, the smoke makes me a little nauseous. I get the urge for one now and then, but the urge is of short duration. I feel that if I am able to stop drinking, I can do anything."

Thompson said, "Your attitude is certainly more positive than it's been. Do you need anything?"

"Well, I'm lonesome, but I know you won't help me out there. I wanted you to visit but I have not put on makeup lately and I'd rather not be seen by someone who knows me. In answer to your question, then, I don't need anything. I'll call you every day or two if that's alright," she said.

"That's fine...I'm pleased to hear you're okay."

"I know you'll try and get rid of me if I talk too long, so I'll let you go. Thanks, Wade," she said. As Thompson had no use for lengthy phone conversations, she knew that he was anxious to conclude the call.

In his facetious way, Forsky asked Thompson, "Did she invite you out to happy hour at the asylum?"

"For your information, John, she's not only taken the cure but she's quit smoking, too."

"Jan Doxee quit smoking? I'd have to witness that to believe it. As much as she smoked, the stability of the tobacco market might be affected. That woman was doing her utmost to kill herself living like she lived...I'm glad she's doing well."

"John, did you ever come up with anything on those other two women that Rufus Mathison met with yesterday?" Thompson asked.

"Haven't had the chance, but since you're at the computer for a change, here's the license numbers," Forsky replied, as he handed his partner a piece of paper.

Thompson checked the license plate numbers for ownership and for any tickets issued to those tags. He checked the names for driver's license information and criminal backgrounds. It took an hour, but he was sure he had identified both women as known prostitutes. In fact, Forsky had arrested the older woman in the ragged Cadillac fifteen years ago. She had worked for an escort service then, too. Thompson remembered the distinctive name. The woman in the pickup also had a prostitution conviction.

Thompson smiled as he asked Forsky, "You remember Henrietta Skelton?"

"Do I remember Henrietta Skelton? Yes, I remember Henrietta Skelton. I remember her quite well. I wish I could forget Henrietta Skelton. That was her in the old Cadillac?" Forsky inquired.

"I'm sure it was her. The car's registered to Henrietta and she's had two tickets in that junkheap in the last year," Thompson replied.

Forsky remarked, "Henrietta must have been around thirty when we arrested her and that's been a long time ago. She ought to be retired from the whore business by now. I thought those cops at Northwest were gonna do a contract hit on me after we snagged that woman."

Henrietta Skelton used to hang out in some bars near one of the police substations. She did escort service work and had become "friendly" with several of the uniformed officers who worked the area. The cops were unaware the woman was a hooker. The day after the arrest, Forsky received a strange phone call from a patrolman he did not know regarding the case. The officer wanted the details because he "knew" the defendant. Figuring the officer had already read a copy of the arrest paperwork, Forsky mentioned nothing that was not in the report. A couple of days passed and another patrol officer made a similar inquiry. After the third such call, a close friend of Forsky's who worked at the substation came by the office. The officer said announcements were being made in all patrol details at the station to stay away from the tainted lady who was also a devoted lover of uniformed cops.

"John, what do you think about having Herschel Fowler arrange for a party and ask for maybe twenty girls? The people who answer the escort service phones are bound to know him well enough that they wouldn't suspect anything. The whores know him for sure, so they wouldn't be suspicious," Thompson said.

"It ought to work. We'd have to use new guys to make the cases, though. You get that many whores together, there's bound to be at least one who would recognize one of our regular guys. They'd scatter like quail. When the time's right, let's give it a try."

One of the clerks handed Thompson a large, thin manila envelope. Opening it, he found the subpoenaed information from the telephone company regarding the 800 numbers in San Antonio.

"John, come here and have a look at this," Thompson said. He gave Forsky four of the eight pages from the envelope. Both officers pored over the material in silence. After a couple of minutes, they traded pages.

Forsky remarked, "We've got four numbers coming back to the same location, each number with a different business name."

"Let's call the San Antonio vice people, give them a rundown on what we're doing, and drive down there in the morning," Thompson suggested.

"I guess we should, if we're going to do this right," Forsky said.

Thompson qualified his own suggestion, "Just for the day...we can be back by dark." Thompson had never liked overnight business trips for some reason. Forsky was well aware of his partner's quirk.

"Yeah, just for the day. We can leave around six and

be there by ten. We'll be on the way home by late afternoon. You won't have to sleep in a strange bed," Forsky responded, grinning.

"I'll run it by Tal," Thompson said.

Forsky said, "I'll call San Antonio Vice and see if we can get some help."

Thompson and Forsky took Tal Sanderson's car on the trip, since their old Pontiac had close to 200,000 miles on it. Thompson often told others in reference to the overall condition of the undercover fleet, "If these were airplanes, we'd all be dead by now."

Forsky wore a pair of beige shorts that were two sizes larger than his frame required. The blue and red striped shirt would have been a perfect fit if he were thirty pounds heavier. His tennis shoes and white socks with their monogrammed green bass above each ankle served to accent the ensemble.

Thompson commented when Forsky arrived at the garage, "You brought real clothes, too...right?"

"Hey, I like to be comfortable when I travel," Forsky replied in defense. "You should try it sometime."

Forsky drove. That way they would arrive an hour sooner than if Thompson had driven.

The day before, Forsky had a lengthy conversation with a new and very enthusiastic San Antonio vice detective. He also gave him several things to research. The officer was waiting for the Dallas detectives at a freeway exit on the north side of the city. Bert Perez was driving a late model Cadillac undercover car. Bert was all of twenty-seven and kept addressing Thompson and Forsky as 'sir' which they both detested. Bert could not seem to overcome using the proper and polite reference. He had been out of uniform such a short time that he still had all the cop mannerisms and looked like a cop. In fact, it was unlikely anyone would mistake him for anything other than a cop. In outline form,

Perez had typed the answers to Forsky's requests and included other information he thought would be helpful. He handed a copy to each detective.

While still on the side of the road, Bert Perez told Forsky, "Sir, you can follow me if you wish or I can take you around in my car."

Forsky did not have to give that one much thought as he asked, "Where can we park our car?"

Bert Perez suggested a nearby shopping center parking lot. The three went in search of the address where the four 800 numbers were located. Perez had already been there. It was a few miles from the freeway exit, still in the north part of town. The entire area showed the obvious signs of recent growth and commercial development. Strip shopping centers were everywhere. The address the officers were looking for turned out to be a single story structure next to a high rise office building.

Six offices were in the plain building. Thompson walked into one of them and made a phony request. He did the same in a chiropractic clinic. While he could only see the outer reception area of each business, it appeared the layout and square footage of all the offices was probably the same, perhaps twelve to fifteen hundred square feet. For an escort service phone center, this was huge. Thompson and Forsky had dealt with many such operations in commercial locations that occupied less than two hundred square feet.

Thompson recalled an office located in a derelict building across from the Dallas City Hall. He cracked open the unlocked door and found a small particleboard table with a telephone on it. A metal folding chair completed the room furnishings. A cotton rope had been stretched tightly across the middle of the room and a filthy bedspread had been draped over it to serve as a room divider.

Suite # 4 was the one Thompson was looking for. 'Mabry Consultants' was engraved on a gold nameplate that was affixed to the door at eye level. Thompson went outside to give a report of his findings to Forsky and Bert Perez.

When Thompson mentioned 'Mabry Consultants', Bert Perez interrupted, "Sir, I've already checked that out. I came out here yesterday afternoon to familiarize myself with the location. If you refer to my report, there is mention of the fact that no such business name is registered with the City of San Antonio or the State of Texas. The Better Business Bureau has no record of them either."

Thompson was embarrassed, as he deserved to be but had to admit to himself they could have done far worse than Bert Perez when they requested assistance. The guy was good, even if he lacked vice experience. He had saved Thompson and Forsky many hours of work even if they could not get used to being called 'sir'. Since Perez had both a computer and phone in his car, it was unlikely the group would have to venture downtown to the PD headquarters. They could better utilize their time right where they were.

Only about a dozen cars were parked in the area nearest the office building. Bert Perez was copying all the license plate numbers. After normal business hours, the only cars on the lot would likely belong to 'Mabry' employees. To be all inclusive, and since the detectives did not know how many people worked there or what their hours were, it would be necessary to check the lot several times a day for at least a week. Bert fed the list of license numbers into the computer. When he finished and was waiting for results, Thompson asked if he would be interested in making the random checks.

"I'd be happy to help out, but I'll need the approval of my supervisor. It will take several hours each day to do what you want," Perez said.

Thompson said, "If you can spare the time, we could use the help. After about a week, we shouldn't need much in the way of legwork, but we'll still need you as a contact should something come up."

"I understand and I really want to do this. I have nothing of any importance that I'm working on anyway. I'm the new guy…you know how that goes," Perez said.

Forsky attempted to provide a measure of reassurance as he told Perez, "Bert, this whole thing is kind of new to us; we've barely scratched the surface at this point, so you're more or less at the beginning of the investigation."

Forsky handed Bert Perez several pieces of paper that had been stapled together and continued, "This is a copy of our log and some notes. Read this and you'll be up to where we were yesterday afternoon when we made the last entry."

Thompson told the San Antonio officer, "Bert, since we're here, let's keep an eye on this lot for an hour or two and maybe get some more license numbers. There's no way we can wait in the lobby to see which people go into which office... not even a chair in the place."

"It's okay with me," the young detective answered. "It's only ten-thirty; I think we'll see more cars before long."

During the next two hours, they ate lunch, drove around the area and randomly checked license numbers of cars parked at the targeted location. There were not that many, but none of the businesses within the building were engaged in the sort of commercial activity that would generate heavy vehicular traffic.

At 1:00 P.M., Thompson turned to Forsky and asked, "You ready to head home, John?"

Forsky grinned and replied, "I expected that you'd ask that an hour ago. Yeah, I'm ready."

Bert Perez took them to their car. Thompson had the feeling it would have taken little coaxing to get Perez to stay in the parking lot until nightfall, recording license numbers.

Thompson and Forsky thanked the San Antonio officer and shook his hand again. He was eager to work.

As the Dallas detectives got out of Perez' car, he said

"Anything you need, anything at all, please call me. I'll fax the license numbers and any other pertinent information to you daily."

"Thanks again, Bert," Thompson said.

"You're welcome, sir."

As Forsky drove north on the freeway, he said, "Bert might be a little green, but damn, he's so enthusiastic. The guy makes me feel like a slug."

"I was afraid we'd get teamed up with some fat, lazy old-timer who hadn't allowed work to interfere with his career for the last twenty years. Yeah, we came out real well," Thompson replied "Tomorrow we can look over this stuff Bert put together for us. He's got tax roll information, utilities, all that."

"Go over it now, oh, I forgot, I guess you're gonna use that old carsickness ploy about how you can't read in a moving car," Forsky said as he started laughing.

Thompson rebutted, "It's no ploy, John. I get nauseous just thinking about reading in a moving vehicle."

"Then let's drop the subject. I don't want you throwing up near me," Forsky said.

When Thompson got to work the next morning, Forsky was reviewing the information Bert Perez had compiled. "Anything worthwhile, John?"

Forsky replied, "There may be, but none of the names or addresses mean anything to me, at least not right now."

"Why don't we get Bert and his people to make a couple of cases in San Antonio? I'm sure he'd jump at the chance. He may not be vicey enough yet, but some of the other detectives would be," Thompson said.

Forsky replied, "All they could do is turn him down. We've all had that happen."

"Okay then, but let's not bring it up until he's through with the parking lot surveillance. No sense in overloading him with any more of our work right now," Thompson remarked.

CHAPTER 23

It had been a full week since Thompson had spoken with Jan Doxee. He anticipated her calling daily since she was allowed use of the phone. While somewhat relieved that she had not called, he hoped that it was not influenced by a relapse or other lack of progression. Yet he was reluctant to call her, at least for now. Perhaps she would call soon and let him know everything was all right. He would wait a little longer. She would be released in another week. She would have to call then, so he could take her home.

Rufus Mathison finished his second gin and tonic as the brief commuter flight to Oklahoma City was three-fourths complete. During the forty-minute trip, there was only a fifteen-minute span where drinks were served. So was the domain of heavy-duty drinkers like Rufus.

The plane landed at 1:15 P.M. By 2:00, the factoring agent would have a car rented and be on his route. Rufus wasted no time and did not drink on the job. Neither did he eat. By 10:00 P.M., Rufus had handled almost sixty transactions for eighteen women. A good night's work, significantly better than this city's weekly average of forty-five. Even at that, the largest of Oklahoma's metropolitan areas always paled in comparison to other cities. A couple more drinks on the return flight were well deserved for the hard worker who arrived home just after midnight.

"This is Bert Perez, sir. I have some additional information for you that I did not include in today's fax."

"What have you got, Bert?" Thompson asked.

The San Antonio detective answered, "I don't know for certain, sir."

"I'm listening, Bert," Thompson replied.

"There's a car I've seen at the location twice in the past week. A white Oldsmobile registered to Mabry Consultants, but not at the San Antonio address. The registration address is in Houston. I've checked with the Houston PD, and there's no Mabry Consultants or anything even close to that in their city. I've just done preliminary work on it so far. The next step is to call Houston back and find out what is at the address where the car is registered," Bert Perez said.

Thompson replied, "Thanks, Bert, but don't worry about calling Houston. You already have enough of our work to do. I'll take care of it. We'll enter it in the log, and fax you a copy."

"Very well, sir. Now, let me give you the information on the car," Perez said, before ending the call.

It was very important to Thompson that Bert Perez feel as if he was a vital part of the investigation because he was. Thompson had seen numerous instances over the years where investigations had been stalled, unraveled, or suffered complete collapse because of inter-agency and intra-agency jealousies and bickering. Law enforcement agencies are notorious for refusing to share information with one another. Thompson never understood this immature concept nurtured by so many in his profession. Within his own department and even in the Vice Division, this blatant lack of cooperation happened far too often. Thompson attempted to undermine the practice at every opportunity. Certain investigations may be of a confidential or sensitive nature, but they are few. Thompson and Forsky both knew all too well to avoid dealing with any detective who was constantly secretive about self-perceived 'big deal' investigations. They withhold information vital to other detectives and their cases. Truly disgraceful individuals...

Thompson called Houston PD Vice. A vice supervisor sent a detective to the address where the car was registered. It was a business in a new, two-story structure, an office complex in a ritzy part of Houston. Eight businesses, mostly accounting firms, were housed there. The registration for the Oldsmobile in question had the address of the office complex plus a post office box number. It was registered to Mabry Consultants, suite #8.

"John, you want to drive to Houston in the morning?" Thompson asked.

"I suppose I'll be doing the driving again?"

"Only if you want to get there faster," Thompson replied.

"I do. Now why are we going to Houston?" Thompson explained the situation to Forsky.

As they were on the outskirts of the largest city in the state, Thompson called the Houston PD Vice contact he had spoken with the day before. The detective gave them directions to the intended location where they would meet. It was after 11:00 A.M. when Thompson and Forsky parked down the street from the building on Numeral Square Drive. It was in the heart of a giant business park that covered a couple of hundred acres. All the streets had names like Integer Boulevard and Digital Circle.

A blue Camaro parked behind the Dallas detectives. The driver got out and approached the passenger side where Thompson rolled the window down.

The man said, "Wade Thompson and John Forsky, I hope? I'm Ed Witkowski."

They all shook hands and Ed Witkowski sat in the back seat. Witkowski looked like a professional weightlifter. Six feet tall, two-hundred-sixty pounds, his blond hair in a freshly cut crew, the detective was around forty. He wore shorts, running shoes, and an extra large knit shirt that was a bit tight for his frame, particularly for his massive shoulders. His waist could not have been over thirty-four inches, if that.

"Okay guys, what's the story here?" Witkowski asked.

Thompson hit the high points of the investigation as Forsky went on a reconnaissance mission to the office building.

The lobby building directory had no listing for a Mabry Consultants or Mabry anything else. Suite #8 was CWA, Inc., whatever that was, and it was located nearest the building entrance. CWA, Inc. had twice the office space of any other tenant. It was really two large suites. Because of where they were situated, it seemed logical to Forsky that the two CWA, Inc. suites should have been #1 and #2 rather than both being #8. He needed to have at least a peek at the office arrangement, if he could manage to do so.

The detective walked into the spacious reception area. A well-dressed, middle-aged woman was sitting behind the desk, talking on the phone. Everything was lavishly decorated. The furniture was expensive, the carpet thick. This was no fly-by-night operation. The door behind the receptionist was ajar, but Forsky could not see enough to determine if it was an inner office, a large open area, or perhaps a hallway.

The woman concluded her phone conversation. As she made notes on a pad, she smiled at Forsky and said, "Good morning, sir, may I help you. Do you have an appointment?"

"No, but I do need some help. I'm looking for an investment firm, Wallace Dingel and Associates. I had this address and there is no such business in this building. May I trouble you for a phone book?" Forsky asked.

The woman seemed very willing to help as she handed Forsky two telephone books. As he thumbed through one of the books, the receptionist said, "There are no investment firms in this building. There are several accounting businesses and a couple of tax consultants. We own the building and all of our tenants have been here for a while."

Forsky retrieved a piece of paper from his shirt pocket and wrote on it as he alternately stared at a page in the phone book. He asked the receptionist, "Would you have a criss-cross city directory handy?" He hoped she would have to go to another room to get it.

"I believe we do. Give me a couple of minutes," she responded, in a tone that made Forsky feel as if he had just worn out his welcome and was fast becoming a pest.

As she disappeared behind the inner door, Forsky walked in the same direction. He gave the woman a few seconds lead before opening the door fully. There was a narrow hallway forty feet long with four doors on either side. At the end, the hallway continued to the right and left. Some of the office doors were open. He could hear a woman talking on the phone in the nearest office. Farther down the hall, two, perhaps three people were in another office, laughing. He had seen enough. This was no escort service. It was a legitimate business. Forsky sat on the couch in the reception room. The lady returned, carrying a criss-cross directory. From the look on her face and considering the length of time she was gone, the book had not been as easy to locate as she had anticipated. She handed it to Forsky, but had nothing to say to him.

"Thank you. I'm sorry to have been so much trouble," he said.

The woman faked a smile, hoping he would leave soon.

Forsky thanked the lady again and asked, "Is this strictly an accounting firm or do you also do tax work?"

"CWA does both...is there something in particular I can help you with?" the receptionist asked in a curt manner.

"Oh, no...just curious. I'll be leaving now, you were most helpful," Forsky said as he headed for the door. He had irritated the woman long enough.

When he got in the car, Forsky told Thompson and Ed Witkowski, "CWA, Inc. is a legitimate accounting and tax outfit. Nothing appears shady. The suite number is eight although they actually have two suites. There's no Mabry around here. Maybe we'll figure this out eventually."

"You think maybe some low-level employee at CWA might have involvement in the San Antonio thing?" Thompson asked Forsky.

"I don't know. I'm guessing CWA has thirty to forty employees counting CPA's, clerical help, and so forth. We can't do the old license number routine here unless we find the Oldsmobile, sit up on it, then get the driver ID'ed. See how small these parking lots are? They're probably for clients only. I'll bet employees park in the parking garage."

"Looks like there's one multi-story garage for every three or four of these office complexes and each garage will accommodate two- or three-hundred cars. We don't need to write down license numbers, but since we're here let's see if we can find the Olds in the nearest garage," Thompson said.

Thompson, Forsky, and Ed Witkowski drove through the six levels of the nearest garage. The car was not there, but it was lunchtime, and many office workers were leaving or had already left. The detectives decided to join the lunch crowd. They could check the garage again after 1:00 P.M.

When they were back in the vicinity of the parking garage, Witkowski asked, "So you guys think that whoever drives this Oldsmobile is involved in the operation of the San Antonio escort service?"

"It's just speculation now, but of all the registrations that have been checked in San Antonio, this is the only one that stands out for any reason," Thompson explained.

Witkowski replied, "Okay, if I understand this correctly, it stands out only because of the 'Mabry' connection between San Antonio and Houston. Is that right?"

"That's it," Thompson said.

Witkowski said, "Personally, I don't think that's a significant connection, especially in the escort service industry, but it's your case, not mine. What do you want me to do?"

Witkowski was a bit too frank for Thompson, but the Houston detective seemed willing to help.

"If you can spare the time, we'd like for you to do what we're doing now-look for the Oldsmobile. If you find it, stay with it, and get the driver identified. Could you do it for a week?" Thompson asked.

Witkowski replied, "I'll do it, but realize I have other investigations I'm working on. This one will take a backseat to my own stuff."

Thompson was relieved as he said, "Fair enough".

"It will mean coming out here mid-morning or mid-afternoon. A round trip from the office, plus the time I spend looking at all the cars in the garage will take two hours each day," Witkowski said.

At first, it was quite unclear to Thompson whether Witkowski wanted the Dallas officers to be aware of how much time their request would take or if the Houston detective wanted Thompson and Forsky to be beholden to him for his sacrifice. Thompson decided it did not matter. Witkowski was straightforward, and they were in this together. After all, we are dealing with people here and no one actually resided in Wade Thompson's perfect world, Thompson reasoned.

"We realize it will take a good bit of time. Here is a copy of our investigative log. It will bring you up to date," Thompson said as he handed Witkowski the paperwork.

Forsky exited the parking garage. The Olds was not there.

Ed Witkowski remarked, "I'll start coming out here tomorrow. If that's it for today, I need to get moving; I have a meeting in the office."

As the Houston officer was unlocking the door of the Camaro, he looked toward Thompson and said, "Call me if you come up with anything new down here. I'll try to check it out."

"Thanks, Ed," Thompson replied.

Forsky looked at Thompson as they started their two-hundred-fifty mile journey back to Dallas and said, "We've put more miles on Tal Sanderson's car in two weeks than he's driven in the last three months. Got any more trips planned?"

"I hope not," Thompson said.

Forsky stifled a laugh. Then he did it again.

Thompson asked, "Well, what's so funny?"

"Oh, nothing really. I was just thinking about how I would much rather have Ed Witkowski for a partner than you the next time a prisoner needs to be ridden or you have to fight a hustler for a pistol. I'll bet that guy can take care of himself and everyone else, too, any way he chooses."

"That really hurts, John, that you feel that way. But, yeah, Ed would be rather intimidating without ever saying a word. Most street swine would be terrified of him, or in love with him."

CHAPTER 24

Thompson and Forsky got to the office at seven P.M. Thompson had a message to call Jan Doxee. He had forgotten that she would be discharged the next day. He waved the note in the air, and told Forsky, "Jan gets discharged in the morning. I'll pick her up before I come to work. Would you tell the boss I'll be a little late?"

"Sure...hey, do you want me to go with you?"

"Would you?" Thompson asked.

"No, definitely no. Unless you demand I go, I want no part of it. A dried-out Jan may be worse than the pickled Jan," Forsky said.

Thompson smiled. "I hadn't thought about that, John." Forsky made no comment as he sat on a desktop staring at some papers he held.

The next morning, Thompson arrived at the psychiatric care facility at 9:30 A.M. He sat in the car for a few minutes in a futile attempt to relax. He did not understand the degree of nervousness and anxiety that he was enduring. Waiting only made it worse.

When Thompson entered the facility, he observed Jan Doxee seated on a couch in the waiting area. Her few personal belongings were neatly arranged on the floor next to her. Dr. Virginia Edmonds was in a chair directly across from Jan. Both were laughing. Neither had seen Thompson.

As the detective approached, Dr. Edmonds noticed him

first and stood. As he got closer, Jan remained seated, but smiled and extended her right hand. Thompson noticed that she again had the long, well manicured nails. The dark rings under her eyes were gone. She looked better than she ever had before. Jan squeezed Wade Thompson's hand tightly, and held on as tears formed in her eyes.

Dr. Edmonds said, "Mr. Thompson, we are delighted to see you. I know Jan is very anxious to go home, but I need to speak with you for just a couple of minutes. Please come this way."

Just as the doctor began to lead Thompson to her office, she turned to Jan and said, "We'll be back in just a minute, Jan," as if she were speaking to a small, frightened insecure child. Jan nodded in affirmation, but said nothing as she dabbed a tissue to her tears.

Once they were in her office, Dr. Edmonds said, "Jan is on no medication right now. That may change, depending on how well she does at home. She's enrolled with an AA group. And I suppose you know she quit smoking? That's a first in my experience with alcoholics who smoke, and almost all of them are smokers. Some quit after they've effectively dealt with the alcohol, but no one does both at the same time. I suppose that's an indication of a strong will. I don't need to tell you that she will have to be very careful about the company she keeps and the places she goes if she's to remain sober. She has had no appreciable problem with depression during her stay. Overall, her level of success has been far better than anticipated. From a professional perspective - I shouldn't say this but I will - her success has been just short of scary. If there are any problems whatsoever, call me right away. I really think Jan will call if anything comes up, but I wanted to let you know as well. I have developed a good relationship with Jan, and I believe she trusts me almost as much as she does you. Anything you want to ask?"

Thompson replied, "No, at least not right now. I do appreciate your concern. I think the best thing now is to get Jan home."

"Yes, she's ready and I won't keep you. By the way, I know who you are. Jan opened up to me in a way she thought she never could," Dr. Edmonds said with a smile.

Thompson was embarrassed. As he grasped for words that were not there, Dr. Edmonds shook Thompson's hand again and said, "It's okay…everything's confidential. I'm the only one who knows. Go now."

Thompson smiled at the doctor; still there was nothing he could say. She stayed in her office and did not accompany the detective to the waiting area. Thompson thought that strange for an instant, then realized the two had become far closer than either had ever imagined. The doctor knew that any further well wishing at this point might become an emotional matter that neither could deal with.

Jan Doxee was composed and there were no more tears when Thompson returned. She was standing with her belongings in hand. She forced a smile.

"Well, young lady, I suppose you're anxious to go home," Thompson said, trying hard to appear cheerful. The place had a distinct sadness about it, despite Jan's progress and the genuine goodness of Dr. Edmonds.

She replied without hesitation, but with a hint of impatience, "Yes please, let's go."

They walked to the car in silence. As Thompson drove from the parking lot onto the street, he asked, "Are you going to be alright, Jan?"

"Wade, once again, there's so much doubt in your question, but please understand, I'll not fail. I've been planning and I want to tell you about that. I'm retiring. Financially, I can get by okay. I want to get close to my family for the first time. I am going to travel some. I have become quite a reader again in the last month. I had all but forgotten what pleasure I get from reading. It's probably saved me. A good book helps immeasurably against the cravings for booze and cigarettes," Jan said.

Seeking confirmation, Thompson asked, "You're going to retire?"

"I must, I have no choice. My lifestyle has to change dramatically if I'm going to have a lifestyle at all. I'm too old to be a whore, everyone knows that including me. Until recently, though, I was too vain and greedy and drunk to admit it."

"Glad to hear it. I don't think you'll be bored in retirement," Thompson replied.

Jan smiled and said, "No chance of boredom. I'll have plenty to do. Wade, I'll not screw up this opportunity. My health is improving daily, and the future appears bright indeed."

Thompson made no response. Jan Doxee had never had a positive attitude about anything before. He thought a second time about how fine she looked as he helped her carry her things to the door of her apartment.

"You want to come in for a minute, Wade?" she asked, anticipating the normal refusal but knowing there was no harm in asking.

Thompson replied, "No, I have to get to work. You'll be okay."

"How did I know you would refuse my offer? Yes, I'll be okay. Now, go to work," she said, resigned to the fact that their relationship would never get past this point.

Forsky was doing computer work when Thompson got to the office. Forsky never looked up as he asked in his pre-occupied manner, "Well, how is she?"

"Doing very well," Thompson replied.

"That's good," Forsky said, typing away. They were both through talking about Jan Doxee.

After a few minutes, Forsky said, "Wade, you remember we talked about Herschel Fowler setting up a whore party? Why not go ahead and at least start planning for it right now?"

"Alright...this whole thing is moving slower than what we're used to."

"I'll call Herschel today," said Forsky, "but first, let's decide on a couple of things."

"What things?" Thompson asked.

Forsky replied, "Do we want Herschel at the party?"

"You concerned about his self-control, or lack thereof, around a bunch of whores?" Thompson asked.

Forsky answered, "Very much."

"We could probably do it without him, but I think his presence would make things go more smoothly...the girls would be more at ease. What if we assign someone to stay right with him the whole time?" Thompson suggested.

"That might be okay...and give him a good lecture beforehand, bring up the penitentiary and all that. You know how he's terrified of going to jail," Forsky said.

Thompson asked, "What else?"

"How many girls do we want? Manpower's going to be our biggest problem. If we have more than a few whores, we'll have to have fresh faces, not regular vice guys. We have sixteen people on both details; maybe three or four are new enough to work something like this," Forsky said.

Thompson responded, "Let's see what Herschel can do in the way of numbers and go from there. If we have to borrow six or eight temporary guys, that's going to take some time. Then we'll have to get approval and all that. We need to work something out with a hotel, too, and not one that we use on a regular basis."

"My guess is that it will take two weeks to set this up right," Forsky said, "and that's if we start on it today."

Thompson replied, "Call Herschel and see what he says... and what about the Houston and San Antonio vice people? Do we still want them to make some cases?"

"Why not? The only problem is that they can't do a party setup if we do it. Someone in the 800 outfit would smell a rat for sure," Forsky said.

Thompson had an idea. "We'll do the party here and get Houston and San Antonio to try for four or five individual cases each on the same night. If this whore operation is as big as it appears to be, a few extra customers in one night in two large cities shouldn't raise any eyebrows. Our party will be set up in advance, anyway. If nothing else, all three PD's should get some good intelligence from the exercise. Call Herschel."

"If you will recall, that's what I was attempting to do when you came up with all these additional thoughts," Forsky remarked. Thompson sat back, and smiled as he gave the whole thing some mental appraisal. Surely they had not covered it all in a few minutes.

Forsky left a message for Herschel at work. Within an hour, the waiter called the detective, eager to help himself by helping out.

"John Forsky, this is Herschel," he said.

Forsky asked the informant, "Herschel, how much trouble would it be to set up a party and invite a bunch of girls from this 800 number service?"

"It depends on who calls to set it up. If I do it, it'll work. They know me. If you call, you could probably get two girls, that's it," Herschel said, exuding confidence.

With slight irritation, Forsky responded, "I meant you, Herschel. I had a feeling your chances would be somewhat better than mine."

"How many ladies are you talking about…five or six?" Herschel asked.

Forsky dropped a bomb on the waiter when he said, "I was thinking about twenty."

"Twenty!…twenty! I don't know. I think they're capable of providing that many with ample notice, but I've never heard of them doing anything on that scale. I set up a party one time using six girls. Some rich guys I knew from the restaurant wanted me to arrange it. Actually, I made a few bucks on the deal, too. A little pimp work on my part, but that's in the past...okay, I'll try it, but let's give them a week's notice. Let me come up with a story," Herschel said.

All Forsky could think about was how sleazy Herschel was. If he was like most informants, he knew a good deal more than he was willing to cut the cops in on. Herschel had very good connections with the 800 service, but Forsky did not think it wise to push him at this point. Besides, Herschel might volunteer additional information on his own later if Thompson and Forsky did not figure out something. Herschel's type craved recognition. He would toot his own horn if not properly credited with what he believed was an outstanding achievement in his field of expertise.

With obvious trepidation, Forsky replied, "That's fine, Herschel, but we have to okay your story before you set anything up, understand?"

"Mr. Forsky, I understand precisely. I will not make a move without your approval. I'll give it some thought and call you in the morning with an idea," Herschel said.

The Eddie Haskell response served only to further irritate Forsky. He told the man, "Be sure you do, Herschel. We need to set this up soon."

"I'll call promptly at ten. Goodbye," Mr. Foul said.

"Yeah, bye Herschel," Forsky said as he hung up.

Forsky told Thompson, "Herschel's going to come up with a cover story and call us in the morning. He knows not to do anything on his own...we have to OK all of it."

"Did you mention trying to get twenty hookers?" Thompson asked.

Forsky replied, "Yeah, and it's workable. Reading between the lines, I think Herschel deals with someone other than the goofus who answers the phone in San Antonio. For the time being, though, Herschel owes allegiance to no one but us. However, I think he'd sell out his contact when the time's right. In short, I'm pretty sure Herschel can arrange for twenty girls or a hundred and twenty, if he wanted to."

"We'll see what he says in the morning," Thompson suggested.

Herschel did not call the next morning at ten A.M. Instead, he was in the hallway waiting area when Forsky arrived at 9:30. Forsky did not notice Herschel as he breezed through the main office door. The waiter got up at once and followed the detective.

As Forsky was getting coffee, he glanced toward the reception area, and saw Herschel waving. "Good morning, Mr. Forsky."

"Herschel, I didn't expect to see you; it wasn't necessary that you come to the office," Forsky said as he approached the man. Forsky preferred to deal with Mr. Foul over the phone, but it was obvious the informer was very excited about his role in preparing the hooker party.

As Forsky and Herschel went into Tal Sanderson's as-yet-empty office, Thompson arrived, just catching a glimpse of the informant. By the time Thompson walked in on them, the two were in deep discussion and neither acknowledged Thompson's presence. He was more tolerant of Herschel than his partner was, but not exactly to the point of best-friend status. Herschel used relevant irritating expressions such as 'world class' and 'on my watch'. With his perpetual greasy appearance, Thompson wondered how Herschel was able to hold a job at one of the finest restaurants in the city.

After a couple of minutes, Forsky told Thompson, "Herschel's associated with a group of folks that make business software. He's set up parties for them with the 800 service, but never asked for more than six girls. The service is familiar with the group, and it's not always the same individuals. That should work fine as a cover…"

Herschel interrupted, "Mr. Thompson, I'm almost certain they will be willing to provide twenty girls, but there's one thing I should mention. You know they normally charge an agency fee of one-fifty per girl, but for five or more women, they up that to two-fifty each. The agency fee for twenty would be five thousand dollars. They may require cash on something like this. If they do, they will send a runner out a day or two in advance to pick up the money."

"Five thousand cash?" Thompson said, astonished and wondering where they would come up with the money.

Herschel replied, "Now I'm not one hundred percent positive on this, but I'll know for sure after I call them."

Thompson said, "If it comes to that, we'll just have to see what we can do as far as scrounging the cash. Herschel...will it be necessary for you to be present at the party?"

"Oh, by all means. After all, many of the girls know me and I'll be in a position to vouch for any of your undercover officers. Of course, I'll never get a date with one of their whores again after the show's over," Herschel replied, a note of sadness in his voice.

Forsky said, "Herschel, that's fine and dandy that you'll be there to make sure everything flows smoothly. However, there is one very important aspect that you need to understand..."

Herschel interrupted again and said, "I think I know what it is...no sex, right?"

"You got it, Herschel. Frankly, we don't trust you. You will be under our watchful eyes at all times. There will be an officer assigned to you. Don't attempt to get out of his sight. If you screw this up, all deals are off as far getting your drug case dismissed. You'll be in the Texas pen system fast and your cellmate will be telling you what a fine wife you'll make," Forsky threatened.

Thompson could tell his partner's message had great effect on Herschel. Thompson knew he could not have said it nearly as well as Forsky did.

Herschel responded, "A simple warning would have been sufficient, Mr. Forsky… threats and intimidation are uncalled for." There was no doubt Herschel's feelings were hurt.

Forsky replied, "I wanted there to be no question as to where we stood on the matter."

"Believe me, there's no question," Herschel said.

Thompson told the informant, "We will give you a date, time, and location within the next few days. Right now, we're planning on doing this in the next two weeks."

"That should allow ample time for the service to make arrangements. I need to leave for work now," Herschel said, still hurt and uncomfortable after Forsky's penitentiary remark. He did not need to leave for work nearly so early. He just wanted to get away from Forsky.

Both detectives nodded in affirmation and Forsky said, "Sure, Herschel…go ahead. We'll call you with the details when we have them."

Herschel had nothing else to say as he stood. Thompson followed him to the hallway.

Forsky was still seated behind Sanderson's desk when Thompson went back to the office. Thompson smiled as he told his partner, "John, rest assured Herschel will be no problem at the party, thanks to your penitentiary spiel."

"That was my intent. I wasn't trying to hurt his feelings. Nobody in the joint would have his greasy fat ass anyway," Forsky replied.

Thompson pushed aside paperwork to expose Sanderson's deskpad calendar. He said, "What about the twenty-first? That's two weeks from today. I checked the convention log yesterday. There's nothing of any size in the entire Metroplex for that week, so we shouldn't have to compete for whores or rooms either one."

"If that's okay with Houston and San Antonio, it's fine with me," said Forsky.

Thompson replied, "I'll talk to the captain right now about the money. Why don't you call Houston and San Antonio?"

As Thompson stood in the open doorway, he saw Captain Holland seated behind his desk signing paperwork. The Captain looked up, and with a grin, said, "Can't you see I'm busy…what do you want?"

Thompson sat on the Captain's couch and replied, "Actually, I need some money, Arlie."

"Okay…this have anything to do with that escort service?" Captain Holland asked.

"Yeah. And we need five thousand cash to set up a party," Thompson said.

"Five thousand!… maybe you had better tell me a little more," the Captain replied.

"We have a spy working off a dope case. He's setting up a party with twenty girls. The spy says the escort service will require a two-fifty agency fee per girl. A runner collects the cash a day or two in advance of the party," Thompson explained.

Holland said, "Wade, I can tell you now that vice doesn't have the money. But the narcotics discretionary fund does, and we've used their money before. Our chief will have to approve it. Tell you what…write up a request in the form of a memo, something official looking I can present to Herbert Greenlee. No promises, but I think we can get approval and have the money within a couple of days."

"Okay, thank you, Arlie," Thompson said as he got up to leave.

The Captain said, "Wade, just a second. I wish you and John would tell Lt. Pricklee what's going on with your investigation. I know you don't care for the guy, but I have to keep peace and harmony in this office as long as he's here. Tal Sanderson drops him a bone now and then regarding what you're doing, but I don't think it's enough."

"Arlie, we haven't kept this a secret, but we'll talk to him,"

Thompson conceded.

The Captain responded, "Do this. I think it will help. Go through him with the memo, then he can present it to me. It's called chain-of-command. For your information, it's the way things are supposed to be done."

"I thought we only resorted to that method when we were unable to accomplish a goal in an efficient manner," Thompson said in semi-serious jest.

Restraining a laugh, the Captain said, "Consider this one of those times. Now get to work and stop irritating me."

As Thompson left the Captain's office, Forsky approached him. He said, "I talked with Houston and San Antonio. Probably yes for both of them, but they've got to get approval. Both will give us a definite word within a couple of days. Something else. We need to get busy on our recruiting effort for the temporary undercover people. You want to hit the point-control traffic detail tomorrow and ask for volunteers?"

"Yeah, but we'll need to get an okay from one of their lieutenants or a captain before we do that," Thompson said.

Forsky replied, "Already taken care of through the traffic captain."

"Okay, let's go over there in the morning and give them the sales pitch," Thompson said.

CHAPTER 25

Point-control traffic officers were assigned walking beats in the downtown central business district. They worked 10 A.M. to 6 P.M. and were off on weekends. Each man was responsible for a particular intersection where he directed traffic during the evening rush-hour period, 4:30 to 6:00 P.M. During the day, the officers had few responsibilities, other than to be seen by the public. They did almost no paperwork. If they made an arrest, they called a downtown squad to transport the prisoner and do the paperwork as well. Most of the point-control officers were past fifty-five years of age with several approaching sixty-five. Considered by many to be a desirable job, point control had never interested Thompson. He always wondered what the attraction was to that type of work. Of course, point control officers probably had the same thoughts about working vice.

Thompson and Forsky arrived early for the traffic detail. A few of the old guys were trickling into the detail room. It was a step back to another era for Thompson, an era he was too young to have known. Some of these men were ten or fifteen years older than he was. Their leather holsters and Sam Browne duty belts had been worn so long they appeared to be soft and comfortable. This detracted from pure functionality since police leather gear required at least some rigidity. Most of the badges had long since lost the original sheen and now had a dull, matte finish. Seniority, confirmed by the low badge numbers, was greater here as a group than anywhere else in the department. Some of the men had slight limps or grimaced a bit as they sat down or stood up, testifying to states of health that were no longer at their zeniths. While a few might discuss hemorrhoids or arthritis, the group was in decent shape overall, age considered. They got plenty of exercise walking and few were overweight.

Thompson, Forsky, and many others saw much credence in a widely held belief that as cops age, they begin to look less like cops. Perhaps the fact that many police officers age much quicker than the population in general has a great deal to do with it. The cumulative effects of poor diet, failed marriages, miserable working hours, financial difficulties, stress, and the occasional life-threatening situation contribute to the condition in no small way. Cops who do not look like cops can often open doors that would otherwise remain closed. A young undercover vice cop has to make up for the lack of years with imagination and creativity. He has to work harder to give the illusion he is not a police officer. The rub here is that the old guys care nothing about doing undercover work, at least on a regular basis, and the youngsters do not want to walk a beat downtown. Any prostitute with just a fair amount of street sense is suspicious of a man in his twenties or thirties who is willing to pay for sex. If a potential customer is fifty-five or sixty, the suspicions cease to exist in the mind of all but the wariest of hookers.

At about one minute of ten, the detail room filled with old cops. The roll call and various bureaucratic announcements lasted less than ten minutes. The detectives walked to the front of the room as the traffic captain introduced them. One of the officers seated on the front row asked, "Is that Forsky as in foreskin?"

There was laughter throughout the room. Accustomed to the un-original comment that he had heard since high school, Forsky remained unruffled. He responded with his standard comeback line, also from his high school days, "Yeah, that's right, but you're the dickhead!"

There was a second round of laughter. Forsky's comment had all but guaranteed his approval by the group.

"We're looking for volunteers to work a prostitution assignment from 6 P.M. to 2A.M. on the twenty-first of this month. We would like to get a minimum of six men from this detail, but we could use as many as twelve. Everyone will be required to wear a coat and tie. Detail will be held in the vice office. Any questions?" Forsky said.

Officer Dickhead raised his hand. Forsky knew what the question was. Someone in every group of prospective volunteers always asked it. Forsky beat the old cop to the punch when he said, "No, you cannot sample the wares. Did that answer your question?"

The officer was clearly amazed at Forsky's response. He admitted slight defeat as he turned around to the rest of the detail and remarked, "Hey, this guy's pretty good." Then he turned back to Forsky, and asked the time-honored beat cop question, "Will there be free food and drinks?"

"Food and drinks will be provided," Forsky improvised. He concluded, "Okay, if there are no more questions, that's all we've got. We'll be in the back of the room if any of you are interested."

The detectives watched the line form. They had ten volunteers! To Thompson's dismay, however, officer Dickhead was one of them, but he made no more comments. He was either out of smart remarks or felt he had met his match in Forsky.

As Thompson and Forsky walked toward the parking lot, Forsky said, "I'll bet some of those guys have leisure suit wardrobes that would put mine to shame!"

Thompson said, " You may be right. You did good in there, John, the way you handled that obnoxious traffic cop."

"Well, there was no harm done because you couldn't hurt that guy's feelings. I had to say something though, or he would have had total control of the room right in front of all his cronies. Nobody would have heard a thing I said," Forsky explained.

"By the way, what's the story on the free meal we're

providing? That was the first I'd heard of that."

"Uh, that was a-spur-of-the-moment thought, actually. I figured it would be added incentive to volunteer. Most cops are whores themselves when it comes to a free meal, you know that, Wade," Forsky replied.

Thompson said, "Can't argue with you there, we'll work out something later on the meal."

When they got to the office, Thompson had received a message to call Ed Witkowski in Houston immediately.

"John, Ed Witkowski called while we were gone. Says it's urgent," Thompson said as he dialed the number. Thompson's pager also beeped with the same message.

"Ed, this is Wade Thompson," he said into the phone, curious what had happened in Houston.

Witkowski replied, "Man, I'm glad you called. I got your mystery guy identified, the one driving the Oldsmobile. I had a dental appointment in that part of town at eight o'clock. On my way back to the office, I guess it was about nine-thirty, I decided to swing through the parking garage. I met the Olds coming down the ramp as I was going up. I was barely able to get on him in the traffic. I followed him seven or eight miles before I could get a marked squad to stop him on a traffic violation."

Witkowski was talking faster than a speedhead that just shot up.

Thompson interrupted the Houston vice cop and asked, "Just who was the guy, Ed?"

"Oh, I'm getting to that," Witkowski said. "He turned out to be a real jerk and the uniformed officer wrote him a speeding ticket, seventy-five in a fifty-five. While the cop was writing him, he noticed the inspection sticker on the Olds expired almost a year ago, so your man got another one for that. He was real upset. I gave the officer your fax number. He should be at his station soon if he's not already there. He'll copy the citations and fax them to you."

Witkowski's words had not slowed. Thompson asked "Ed, what was the driver's name?"

"Uh," said Witkowski, followed by a long pause. "Damn, I forgot to write it down, Wade. I'm sorry. I get a little charged up sometimes and forget things. Anyway, it'll be on the ticket. He said the car belongs to his company. He's the owner of CWA, at least that's what he said. You would think the owner of a business like that would be driving a much nicer car."

Thompson asked, "Anything else, Ed?"

"No, I think that about covers it. I'll get copies of the tickets, too, and run the fellow locally," Witkowski said, slowing a bit at last.

Thompson replied, "After you run him, you might have a look at his house, and maybe check on other vehicles he owns, the usual stuff. Ed you've been a big help, thanks."

Forsky had become quite bemused as he listened to Thompson's end of the conversation. He asked, "What was that all about?"

"Ed Witkowski spotted the Oldsmobile leaving the parking garage. He followed it and got a patrol officer to stop it. The officer wrote the driver a couple of tickets. They're faxing copies of the tickets us now. The driver not only owns the car, he owns CWA," Thompson related as the fax machine worked in the background.

Both detectives walked toward the apparatus as the single sheet minus a cover page slid into the receiving tray. Copies of both tickets covered almost the whole page. Without reading it, Forsky grasped the paper and made a copy which he began reading as he handed Thompson the fax.

The detectives studied the information with diligence as they sat behind the only vacant desk in the squad room. Nothing in the paperwork jumped out at either of them; the man was nothing more than another player in the game.

"So now we have a Charles Western who owns Charles Western Accounting, Inc., CWA. He's fifty-six years old and drives an Oldsmobile. Wonder what his connection is in the grand scheme of things?" Forsky asked, underwhelmed.

"I don't know, John. Maybe he does their taxes," Thompson said, bewildered himself. "That accounting business is legitimate, but why would he register his own car, company car, whatever it is, using a bogus company name? Mabry Consultants doesn't fit anywhere. But, it's still the only connection we have between the 800 number outfit in San Antonio, the Oldsmobile, and CWA in Houston where the car is registered. Charles Western may be the owner of CWA, but maybe someone else associated with the business registered the car and Western knows nothing about it. Other people may drive the car, too."

Forsky replied, "Maybe so. Today is the first time anyone connected with this investigation has seen the car occupied. We know it shows up in San Antonio on at least a sporadic basis. Perhaps Bert Perez will get lucky and find it occupied in San Antonio. We need to let him know about this."

"Okay, I'm going to see what I can find on Charles Western," Thompson said.

Thompson and Forsky still did not know what the man looked like. Thompson called the Texas Department of Public Safety in Austin and requested a copy of Western's driver's license photograph. It would take several days to receive it. Western had no criminal background whatsoever.

"John, Charlie the accountant is so clean I'm inclined to believe we should be looking at an employee of CWA rather than the owner," Thompson said.

Forsky replied, "Yeah, it just doesn't make sense."

Captain Holland came into the squad room. He stared at Thompson and Forsky for a moment, grinned, and said, "Alright. I just met with Herbert Greenlee and you've got the money. One thing, though, I didn't request five-thousand. I asked for fifty-five hundred instead, just in case there are some unforeseen expenses."

"There will be some unbudgeted expenses, like food and drinks," Thompson replied.

The Captain stood there for a moment without saying anything. It was apparent to the detectives that something was on Arlie Holland's mind that he was hesitant to mention. Finally, Forsky looked up from his paperwork and asked, "Arlie, you want to talk to us about something else?"

Arlie Holland was eager to respond, "If you need any more volunteers for your party, I'd be glad to personally help out."

Thompson almost laughed out loud. "You, Arlie? Sure, if you want to. We were going to give the traffic men a short course in making whore cases that evening before we go to the hotel. I guess there will be room in the class for one more student."

"Hey, I've made as many whore cases as anyone in this office. However, to your advantage, I haven't made any recently. There's no way any of the girls will know me," Holland said in a desperate attempt to sell himself. He was not quite sure if Thompson and Forsky wanted to use him.

Forsky looked at Thompson and said, "Wade, what do you say we give him a waiver on attending the class based on his life experiences? And he's old like the traffic guys. He might fit right in."

Thompson replied, "Alright, let's give him a chance."

Holland asked, "What about Tal Sanderson?"

"We turned him down for the same reason we're not going to be there. He's made a few escort service cases in the last couple of years. Too much chance someone will know him," Forsky said.

"Okay," Holland replied. "How many troops do you have at the moment?"

"Four from vice, ten from traffic, plus you, makes fifteen," Thompson said. That should be enough."

The Captain asked, "One more thing, do you have a hotel yet?"

"As a matter of fact, we don't," Thompson responded. "Got any suggestions?"

Arlie Holland said, "Yeah, I do. It might be worth a phone call. The Hotel of the Southwest on Stemmons opened a few months ago. They had a problem with some traveling hookers working the bar the first week it was in business. A couple of the guys on the other detail not only made cases on two whores, they recovered some jewelry one of the girls had lifted from a hotel guest. The manager couldn't thank us enough. I believe he would be accommodating to your needs for this party. His card's on my desk somewhere. The place is expensive, too. Rooms start at two-fifty a night."

"Thank you, Arlie. I'll give him a call," Thompson said.

Captain Holland left the squad room a happy man. He was going to get to do some undercover work one more time, even if it was only for two or three hours.

Thompson's phone rang as he again studied the traffic citation information on Charles Western. "Vice, Thompson," he said.

"Mr. Thompson, this is Herschel Fowler," the waiter said.

Thompson asked, "What can I do for you, Herschel?"

"I talked with the escort service. They will provide twenty girls as you requested on the twenty-first of the month. I told them I would give them the hotel location and room number at least two days before the party. I'm afraid the fee will be two-fifty per girl as I had speculated. I tried to get them to discount it since they know me and I'm a good customer, but they weren't agreeable to that. On the nineteenth or twentieth, a courier will call me and designate a location where I will meet him. He will pick up the five-thousand cash at that time," Herschel related.

Thompson replied, "Herschel, that's fine, but we're not giving you the cash. A vice detective will have the money and he will accompany you. He'll be the one to hand it over to the courier. That's the only way we can do it."

"Then that would be most acceptable. I just wanted to let you know, I have to get back to work now," Herschel said.

Forsky heard a portion of the call and asked, "Has Herschel got everything arranged?"

"So he says. He mentioned that he tried to get the service to give a better deal on the agency fee since we want twenty girls. According to Herschel, they wouldn't go for it. His sincerity reminds me of the car salesman who says he'll talk to the boss in hopes of getting a better deal for you. Herschel may be trying to shake us down, John," Thompson said.

Forsky replied, "That wouldn't surprise me at all. Let's not say anything to him until just before we're to deliver the cash. We'll do a shakedown on him before he has a chance to clip us."

"Okay," Thompson said. "I'm going to call the manager of the Hotel of the Southwest and see what he can do on some rooms for the twenty-first."

Forsky replied, "I forgot to mention, Bert Perez and Ed Witkowski both got approval to work the agency the same night we do the party. I know you see all sorts of problems with this investigation, Wade, but things are actually falling into place. Take my word for it."

"I will, John, I will."

CHAPTER 26

"I believe we can handle your needs, detective," Lyman Brotherton, the hotel manager said. "We have a large suite with a wet bar, hot tub, outer reception area, and an inner sitting room. It has three baths. It's like a luxury home within the hotel. It's never been rented. I'll comp it for the twenty-first if you want it. Now if you need room service, meals, drinks, snacks, what have you, I can't comp those items, but we'll let you have them at cost. That's an obscene savings."

"If we need room service at all, it'll be minimal. We do appreciate you providing the room, however. At the moment, I'm not even sure what name the room will be under. Will a two-day notice be sufficient for that?" Thompson asked, most happy with the ease of the arrangement.

"That'll be fine, just give me a call," the manager said. "You boys are welcome to work out of here anytime. Give my regards to Captain Holland."

"I'll do that and thank you very much for your assistance. Oh, by the way, Lyman, how much do you charge a paying customer to rent that room?" Thompson asked.

The manager replied, "I believe it's fifteen hundred per night, plus tax, of course."

"Of course, thanks, Lyman," Thompson said as he wondered who paid fifteen hundred a night for a hotel room.

He gave momentary thought to the good fortune of the Vice Division regarding their relationship with hotel management and security in Dallas. Most of them would do handstands for the vice detectives if the officers would occasionally work the bars and weed out prostitutes.

That thought triggered the memory of an over-accommodating security man that worked at one of the large downtown hotels years before. The hotel was very old, built around the turn of the century. Thompson and Forsky worked the place long after its prestigious era. While still a clean, decent hotel that did a good business, the interior was quite dated and in great need of remodeling. The security officer called Thompson and Forsky whenever a prostitute checked into the hotel. A hooker might work several downtown hotel bars for a few days or a week, but she would stay at the old hotel because the rooms were cheaper. The house detective would always know how many customers a girl took to her room, what they did, and how long they stayed. Thompson and Forsky figured the man could spot a prostitute, but thought he may have made up the other information that he provided, such as the sordid acts.

Despite this, the detectives made a number of prostitution cases over the years simply by knocking on a suspect's door and feigning the 'lonesome and need companionship' routine. Eventually, the security man felt comfortable enough with Thompson and Forsky to let them in on his "secret".

The room doors all had one-inch gaps between the bottom of the door and the floor. The hotel detective always carried a tiny mirror affixed to a six-inch thin metal shaft, the kind dentists' use to look in patients' mouths. The man used this homemade invasion-of-privacy device to spy on the prostitutes. His voyeuristic habits were likely not limited to the affairs of working women. Thompson and Forsky were spooked by the man's confession and stopped working the hotel. Based on an anonymous tip, hotel management caught the pervert a few weeks later as he "checked rooms" and fired him.

Thompson told Forsky, "We've got a room. Well, really,

that's an understatement. It's normally fifteen hundred a night. Should be big enough to accommodate our large crowd."

Thompson realized for the first time that things were working well and going smoothly, as they should. He and Forsky knew very well that the planning part of a project like this was of utmost importance. However, when the actual undercover operation took place, no amount of planning compensated for things that did not work out as intended. With almost forty people involved, it was a sure bet there would be some spur-of-the-moment ad-libs, last-minute changes, corrections, and cover-ups to assure a successful operation. Safety was always the primary concern, making good solid whore cases was next, and the avoidance of embarrassment to officers and the department was third. Number three would be number two in the eyes of administration. The transposed number two could really turn to number two, given the right circumstances. The potential for embarrassment was always great in a situation like the detectives were planning. A few drinks were fine, but no one could become intoxicated. That went for the whores as well. Most police supervisors, prosecutors, and judges looked with disfavor on cases made against a drunken harlot unless mitigating circumstances warranted a prostitution charge.

In the ideal setting, the entire act would be balanced so that no one, cops and whores alike, had more than two or three drinks, good cases were made, no one removed any articles of clothing, and arrests happened in a swift manner without incident. Thompson, and Forsky, to a lesser extent, preferred to be in total control of an operation like the one planned, but they would not even be in the room. This was unsettling to both of them. They could do nothing about it and they chose not to discuss it. The one comforting factor was that Arlie Holland would be there to oversee the whole show. They trusted that he could handle the affair.

The next morning, shortly after Forsky arrived at the vice

office, Ed Witkowski called. Forsky gave him a brief rundown on how they wanted the Houston vice detectives to work the 800 service on the twenty-first.

"Consider it done," Witkowski said. "My lieutenant wanted to do something like this ever since we first got involved in the investigation."

Forsky replied, "We'll get with you on the final details two days in advance, but I'd suggest you have your hotel rooms lined up by then."

"We'll do it. Hey, I did some research on Charles Western. Let me tell you about it," Witkowski said.

"Give it to me," Forsky said.

"He's been in business as CWA, Inc., for nearly thirty years. He owns the office building and it's appraised on the city tax rolls at $2.8 million. He's been divorced for a long time, no children, and lives in a condo pretty close to his office. I went by there. It's in a nice neighborhood, but nothing fancy. The tax roll appraisal on it is two hundred thousand. He lives frugally if you ask me. He has no vehicles registered in his name. The Oldsmobile registered to Mabry Consultants is the only one registered at the office address. No cars are registered to CWA, period, and no other vehicles are registered at the office address or the home address. It looks like Charles Western owns and drives the only company car."

"Strange," Forsky commented. "Fax me everything you have, Ed. Thanks for the help."

When the fax came through, Forsky looked at it then handed it to Thompson as he came into the squad room.

"This Charles Western is an odd fellow," Thompson said. "I'm still not convinced he's a suspect, but based on what we've all come up with, he's got 'bad guy' written all over him. Can you imagine what sort of legitimate income he must have from an accounting business like CWA?"

"I wouldn't venture a guess," Forsky replied. "I have no idea."

"I'll consider the man a serious suspect when someone sees him at the San Antonio office. Bert Perez is still checking that place, and it's been a while since he's even seen the Olds," Thompson said.

"If Western's our man, he'll show up in San Antonio again."

"What else do we need to do at the moment, John?" Thompson felt quite certain he had overlooked something.

"We're waiting on a few things, but that's about it for the immediate future. Why do you ask? Are you getting the urge to do some real vice work for a change?" Forsky asked.

"Well, we've spent an unhealthy amount of time in the office during the past two months. A little diversion from all this might be a welcome respite."

"Respite? Don't use words like that, Wade. 'Respite' sounds like something Herschel Fowler or Lt. Pricklee would say. Yeah, we've been in the office way too much lately. And we haven't had a steamer-of-the-month 'Wall of Shame' nominee since you made a case on that half-ton creature from Fort Worth Avenue."

"Okay, John, we'll look hard for a candidate this afternoon, but let's eat lunch first."

CHAPTER 27

Fort Worth Avenue was convenient. Thompson got out on a corner and stood at a bus stop as Forsky made the rounds in the Pontiac. He drove slowly through the parking lot of the Be Back Soon Inn, without a doubt the nastiest dump on the street. The afternoon was warm and many of the doors were open. This may have been the only motel in Dallas with no air conditioning, and its very reasonable room rates reflected the lack of summertime comfort.

As Forsky cruised through the lot, he heard a woman's voice, "Hey, come here."

He stopped and heard the same words a second time, but this time they came from farther away. Forsky had yet to see anyone, but knew the voice had come from the passenger side of the car. He leaned over, rolled down that window, and backed up several units.

Looking through the open front door, then directly through the open bathroom door, he saw a white female sitting on the pot with a newspaper in hand. She waved at Forsky with her free hand.

As the detective smiled and pondered the woman's unromantic pose, she said, "Hey, come on in, I'll be through in a minute. What are you looking for?"

"How about a half-and-half? Can you take care of that?" Forsky asked.

"Sure can, it'll be twenty-five," the prostitute replied.

Without spooking the girl, Forsky had to talk his way into

leaving so he could pick up Thompson. He asked her, "Got any rubbers?"

"Naw, don't use them. Nobody lives forever," she replied.

Forsky responded, "Well, I use them myself. Mind if I run down the street to buy some?"

"Suit yourself," she responded, her head buried in the newspaper.

When Forsky picked up Thompson, he related the story to him.

"She's on the pot? She's sitting on the pot?" Thompson asked, amazed.

Forsky answered with a measure of hopefulness in his reply. "Yeah, but she'll be through by the time we get back."

"The splendor of the setting overwhelms me, John. What if she's still on the pot when we get there?" Thompson said, laughing.

Forsky made no response. They parked several doors down from the room. The door was still open. As they approached, Thompson stayed back from the doorway as Forsky stood on the threshold and said, "Well, here I am."

To Forsky's dismay, the woman was just as he had left her a few minutes earlier. Her bowels might have moved, but she had not.

Again, never looking up from her paper, she replied with disinterest, "Yeah, here you are. I'll be through in a minute. I fried some onions and bell peppers for lunch. It tore my guts up something fierce, I'm telling you."

Thompson was able to hear the conversation he wished he had not heard. He longed to be spending 'unhealthy" time working in the office again. When it became apparent the woman did not intend to finish her business anytime soon, Forsky covertly motioned for Thompson to join him in making the arrest.

With reluctance, Thompson walked into the room with Forsky. The prostitute barely looked and said to Forsky, "You either brought your buddy with you or you guys are cops, which is it?"

Of all the prostitutes Thompson had arrested over the years, this was by far the calmest one. She was rattle-proof.

"We're cops," Forsky said as both detectives presented their badges and ID's to the hooker.

She replied, "Okay, I'm really through now." The woman unrolled five feet of toilet paper, finished up and flushed the commode.

As she stood and pulled her pants up, she told the officers, "I've got convictions, so this'll be an enhanced case, but I've served jail time before. You want to handcuff me?"

As they drove toward the office, Thompson remembered the frequent and humbling realization that no matter how long someone is involved in police work, every situation is a new one. It was difficult to understand a person having such total disregard for their very existence. Life itself had become so miserable in a routine and acceptable way that this woman saw jail as being on the same plane as everyday reality. No better, no worse.

When they arrived at the office with their prisoner, Forsky began the paperwork. The girl again triggered the recurring thought Thompson had about having worked vice too long. It seemed so pointless, so inconsequential. Did this woman deserve to be in jail? Is prostitution the only way she could make a living? Or was she just lazy and defiant? Did she harm others? In an age when perversely liberal politicians and psychoanalysts of aberration preach the non-acceptance of responsibility for one's actions, what can be expected? Deep, complex stuff, Thompson thought. No human being possessed the required insight to come up with the right answers. As usual, Thompson felt the immediate need to occupy his mind with far more simplistic thoughts.

CHAPTER 28

"Yes sir, that's correct. Everything has been approved for the twenty-first," Bert Perez told Thompson.

"Good. Houston Vice will be doing the same thing. There are still a few loose ends right now, but we'll give you plenty of notice," Thompson said.

"Okay, sir," Perez replied.

While he still had the San Antonio officer on the line, Thompson remembered, "Bert, I almost forgot this. I think John told you about Houston PD identifying the driver of the Oldsmobile. If you see that car parked at the agency phone center again, find out who's driving it. That's become very important."

"Yes, sir, I know. I'll do my best," Perez said.

Jan Doxee had not called in several days. Thompson did not care to have a phone conversation with her any more than he did with anyone else, but since he had not heard from her, he became concerned that she might be drinking again. He decided to call her, but told himself he would cut the conversation short if she was sober.

"Jan, how are you?"

"Wade, I'm so glad you called," she said. "I'm doing very well, thank you. I've refrained from calling you. I know you and John have been very busy, as always, and I didn't want to bother anyone."

Thompson was relieved. Her sobriety was unmistakable. She was cheerful and reasonable as well.

"I'm glad you're okay. I am busy, but I wanted to check

on you and make sure everything was fine. Have you been to your follow-up with Dr. Edmonds?"

"I have had my first follow-up interview and everything went well. I've declined medication and she doesn't think it would be of much benefit anyway, considering my progress," Jan said.

"Mighty fine," Thompson said. "Call if you need anything."

"Wade there is one thing, and I'm not bringing this up to upset you in any way. Don't be so distrusting. Maybe you've done cop work too long and expect the worst to come through in everyone. You're not as sly as you think. On the other hand, I know you have a genuine concern for my well-being, and I'm thankful for that," she said.

"I can't argue with anything you said. I'll do better," Thompson replied, knowing he would never overcome the ingrained attitude.

As Thompson drove to work on the morning of the nineteenth, he could think of nothing other than how busy the day would be. He and Forsky would begin the coordination of events that would lead to the much-anticipated success of the undercover operation. Thompson had not experienced that unique exhilaration in some time but he knew he would still enjoy it. The uniqueness was just that, one of a kind in the most pure literal sense imaginable. This was the part of police work that could never be duplicated in another job or avocation. It was simply a good feeling.

Forsky had been working for an hour when Thompson arrived thirty minutes early. Tal Sanderson was sitting on the desk half that Thompson claimed as his own, reading a newspaper.

"Good morning, Wade," Sanderson said.

"Hi, Talbert."

"Say, John was telling me about that slimy snitch you all are using. Is he trying to pull a fast one with our money?"

Sanderson asked.

"We don't know for sure, Tal, but I think we'll find out this afternoon. Mr. Foul and one of the undercover guys are supposed to meet a courier and give him the cash."

"Let me know what happens. By the way, the captain picked up your money this morning. It's in the safe," Sanderson said as he folded the newspaper and began to walk to his office.

"Okay, thanks, Tal."

Forsky said, "Wade, Herschel called. The courier wants to pick up the money behind that same coffee shop in North Dallas at 3:00 P.M. I told Herschel to be here no later than two."

"Let's hit him up about the money as soon as he shows up," Thompson said.

Forsky smiled that insidious Forsky smile and replied, "By all means."

Thompson called the hotel manager. The suite was put under the name of a fictitious business. However, should anyone attempt to check it out by phone, fax, or actually going to the business location, all would appear to be in order.

He also checked with the Houston and San Antonio PDs'. Everyone was ready. Hotel rooms were secured and preliminary briefings of undercover officers would take place today in both cities.

Forsky had enlisted the services of a former gambling informant who happened to own several Mexican restaurants in the Dallas area. Abel Goldstein was a bit of an oddity in comparison with other Mexican restaurant owners. He was Jewish, from New Jersey, and spoke Spanish with a strange accent. Twenty years ago, he opened his first restaurant down the street from the police building. Cops ate there all the time and it was during those early years when Forsky and Thompson got to know the man. Abel could be found in the kitchen at 6:00 A.M. making tamales and enchiladas. His business grew and Abel got rich. Abel had to be rich because he played poker with serious gamblers and lost most of the time. Abel's card-playing cohorts were bookies who played poker to feed their addictions, although they claimed it was a friendly game, a hobby, a diversion from work. Abel was cheated often. He, and the others, had been robbed at gunpoint during several card games. The little Jewish guy from Hackensack, however, never let obstacles and bad luck get in his way. He always jumped back in the game.

"Wade, come here a minute," Forsky said as he motioned to his partner.

Thompson approached Forsky's desk and said, "Yeah, John?"

"About the meal for the undercover people, I've taken care of it," Forsky said in a low voice that kept getting lower.

"Why are you almost whispering?" Thompson asked.

"The hotel management might not approve of the arrangements."

"What arrangements?" Thompson inquired.

Forsky replied, "I talked to Abel Goldstein. He'll cater a meal at no charge."

"What if the hotel catches Abel's people doing an unauthorized catering job?" Thompson asked, hoping this was a joke but knowing it was not.

"Don't worry, Wade, I've been through all that with Abel. They won't get caught. In fact, he said restaurants do it all the time. Now the hotel's going to get some business, too. I thought we'd get the hors d'oeuvre trays and drink set-ups from them. We'll buy the beer and liquor ourselves and take it over. We can save a little money there. It's all worked out."

"John, you're a true swine, and a cheap one at that," Thompson said, grinning.

Forsky replied, "Just trying to take care of the police department's budget like it was my own."

Herschel Fowler arrived at the vice office shortly before 2:00 P.M.

"John, Herschel's here. The captain's gone right now; let's use his office," Thompson told Forsky as he motioned for Herschel to follow.

Once in the office, Forsky closed the door. Herschel greeted the officers, "And how are you both today?"

Thompson replied, "We're fine Herschel. There's something we'd like to discuss with you before you and the undercover officer meet the courier."

"And what might that be?" Herschel asked nervously.

Thompson continued, "Understand, Herschel, we're making no accusations. This is regarding the agency fee of two-fifty per girl. If the agency's fee is really only one-fifty per girl and someone tacked on an additional 'service charge', then technically, we could file a felony prostitution promotion case on that person. You see, Herschel, that person would be reaping financial benefits from a prostitution enterprise. Sort of like indirect pimping. Do you follow me so far, Herschel?"

"Quite clear, quite clear, Mr. Thompson," Herschel said, hands shaking.

Forsky said, "Of course, if the person that did that dastardly double-cross was trying to work off a case and we found out about it, not only would the case not get dropped, we'd also file the one Wade mentioned. That person would be guaranteed a free bus ride to the pen where he could find a big, rough husband and live wretchedly for a long time."

Herschel was terrified.

Thompson asked the informant, "Now, Herschel, we may have misunderstood you previously, but exactly how much did you say the agency fee was? Think about it for a minute if you like."

"Okay, it's one-fifty per girl, three thousand total. But the extra hundred per girl wasn't going to be all mine. I had to split it with the courier, so we were going to make a thousand apiece. I know I shouldn't have tried it but I assumed your funds came from deep pockets. I figured we could make a few dollars and no one would be the wiser," Herschel confessed.

Herschel observed the fire in Forsky's eyes as the detective said, "Herschel, we're going to overlook this only because we don't want to compromise the whole operation at this late stage. But, if you even consider pulling another fast one on us, not only will you be looking at pen time, I'll personally contact some of the inmates and make sure you get to be the dayroom bitch!"

Mr. Foul was in tears as he pleaded, "Please, please, it won't happen again. I'm so sorry. What am I going to tell the courier? He'll be expecting his money."

Forsky said, "Tell him to bite your butt, tell him it's against your ethical standards, tell him whatever you like. But if you give him a thousand dollars, it comes out of your pocket, not ours."

"I guess this is my problem and no one else's," Herschel said.

Thompson told Herschel, "Let's go meet the undercover man you'll work with."

As Thompson and the snitch got up to leave the room, both detectives could not help but notice Herschel's knees were weak and he was unsteady on his feet for a moment. He would be all right soon enough, however.

Thompson and Forsky lurked in a crowded parking lot adjacent to where Herschel and the vice cop would meet the courier. They were fifteen minutes early and had a clear view of the meeting location. Shortly after their arrival, Herschel and the undercover man drove into position. Promptly at 3:00 P.M., a familiar silver Lexus with Rufus Mathison behind the wheel pulled up.

"Damn, Wade, that's that old has-been gangster again, Rufus," Forsky remarked.

Thompson replied, "At least we won't have to have him ID'd this time. We have a case on him, too. He took the money out of the envelope, looks like he's counting it. What do you want to bet he's fixing to have a conference with Herschel?" At that instant, Herschel and the old criminal got out of the cars and walked to the rear of Mathison's Lexus. Herschel stared at the ground like a puppy caught peeing on his master's carpet. Rufus was severely rebuking the informant. He finger-poked Herschel in the chest twice, using enough force that the frightened man backed up with each poke. Herschel knew better than to stiff someone as treacherous as Mathison. Finally, each got into his respective vehicle. Mathison was furious and smoked his tires as he left in a big hurry, almost colliding with a van as he entered a freeway service road.

Within thirty minutes, everyone returned to the office. Herschel was still shaken from his encounter with Rufus.

Forsky asked Herschel, "Well, what did Rufus have to say?"

"He's a bit upset. He gave me a week to come up with the money. He didn't threaten me but just being around that guy when he's mad is threatening enough," Herschel said, his voice cracking.

Thompson replied, "I'd stiff him, Herschel. He won't kill you over a thousand dollars, but he might make your life miserable for a while."

"Easy for you to say...I'd like to go home now, I don't feel well at all," Herschel remarked.

Thompson said, "Go ahead, Herschel. We'll talk to you before the party."

Herschel Fowler was miserable and scared as he left the Vice office. Thompson couldn't tell him that he had nothing to worry about from Mathison. The gangster would be in jail in a few days. He would have no bond or at least a very high one that he could not make, as Rufus would be a definite flight risk.

On the twenty-first, Thompson and Forsky both came to

work at 4:00 P.M. instead of six. Last minute details had to be completed. The coordination of efforts between the three cities was not crucial to the overall success of the joint venture, but was, nevertheless, of some importance. In addition, the traffic officers had to be given the basics of making prostitution cases.

Thompson called Houston PD Vice; Forsky did the same with the San Antonio group. All was set. Four Houston detectives were stationed at different hotels and would begin calling the service at 5:00 P.M. Five San Antonio vice cops would do the same in their city beginning at 6:30 P.M. The two contact officers, Witkowski in Houston and Perez in San Antonio, would always have a phone handy even though each was participating in the actual undercover work.

Traffic officers began showing up at the Vice office around 5:30 P.M. Most of them were well dressed and there was not a leisure suit in the group! Not one of them looked like a cop. Everyone was present by ten minutes of six. Forsky put on a brief training session regarding what can and can't be said by an officer in making a prostitution case. This was critical. State law was considerably relaxed in comparison to the guidelines required by the Vice division. Consequently, losing a prostitution case in court was a rare occurrence.

The traffic cops were attentive. While Forsky was prepared for him, the only time officer Dickhead spoke was to ask an intelligent question. He continued, "Okay, now if everyone understands what it takes to make a case, we'll move on to other things that need mentioning. Don't take firearms into the hotel room. Some of the vice officers will have access to weaponry should it be needed. It's too easy for a girl to feel or brush up against a gun if you have one on your person. No individual handcuffs. We'll have a box full of cuffs in the room that we use for such occasions as tonight. Carry your badges and ID's if you wish. These women have been instructed not to individually ask for any form of ID. You have all been 'pre-approved', so to speak. Use your real name. We have some professionally printed nametags with a company logo and all on them. You all work for the same computer business and tonight is supposed to be a business meeting and dinner. The undercover men will get with you in a minute. They will have some sort of signal that everyone will be familiar with when it's time to make arrests. Make as many cases on as many women as you feel comfortable with, just remember who said what to whom and the time. If that's too much to remember, then take it easy. For the arrest reports, you have to be sure of everything you put in there. We all know that. These are only misdemeanor cases. Let the whore walk rather than make a bad or a shaky case. If you've made a case and you're not sure it's a good one, we'll talk about it. If we need to release someone, let's do it before we get to the jailhouse. In a little while, we'll go in a group to the hotel. We'll have a catered Mexican food dinner and the girls will show up between 8:30 and 9:00. We have a bar and a bartender in the room. Have a drink or two if you wish, just don't get carried away," Forsky remarked exhaustedly.

The undercover officers spoke to the traffic men for all of three minutes. Everyone adjourned to the hotel. Thompson and Forsky had never used a hotel as elegant as this one. While Forsky's catering arrangements wreaked of low-rent sleaziness, the Mexican food was excellent and the price could not have been better.

By 7:30, everyone was through with dinner. Thompson and Forsky would have to leave soon and hole up in the basement security office until the arrests were made. Both were saddened that they would not be able to participate in the event they had spent so much time and effort planning. Being true to their ritualistic ways prevented one from discussing personal feelings with the other.

"Wade, have you noticed how quiet and somber the traffic guys are?" Forsky asked.

"Yeah, it's sort of reached a peak that's been building since they got to the office. They're nervous, but they'll do all right."

"Well, let's put the bartender to work mixing a few drinks," Forsky said.

Forsky instructed the young undercover officer to open the bar. Perhaps some drinks would loosen the traffic cops up a bit. The group was far more sedate than if it had been composed entirely of vice cops. The library atmosphere caused Thompson some concern, but then, he had to have something to worry about on every such operation.

Arlie Holland cornered Thompson. Grinning, he remarked, "These guys are much better behaved than vice people. I kind of like it."

Thompson did not smile as he replied, "Sort of like being at a funeral."

Forsky said to the captain, "Arlie, we're going downstairs, it's almost eight. I hope we're leaving this whole affair in competent hands. Don't screw anything up."

"You need to have a little faith in your captain. You might show him a little respect occasionally, too," Captain Holland replied.

Herschel Fowler had kept to himself the entire time. He was uncomfortable being around so many policemen. He ate nothing and did not want a drink. He approached Forsky as the detective and his partner were leaving the room.

"Mr. Forsky, I know you both are very concerned about my presence here. I assure you I'll be on my best behavior and you needn't worry about me trying anything with the women," Herschel said.

Forksy replied, "Herschel, I know you'll be on your best behavior. However, should temptation strike, give serious thought to your role as the dayroom bitch. That'll bring you to your senses."

Herschel nodded in affirmation but said nothing. He was very aware of the seriousness of Forsky's remark.

Thompson and Forsky adjourned to the vacant security office. The hotel's night security man was an off-duty DPD officer. He gave them free run of the place while he made his rounds. He furnished them with a walkie-talkie radio should they need to contact him. Otherwise, he would be back at the office in an hour.

CHAPTER 29

Competent hotel security personnel have a watchful eye for hookers on the property. Ninety percent of prostitutes are easy to recognize. The other ten percent could not be picked out by the most jaded and streetwise vice cop. It was Thompson's guess that a fair number of the women coming to the suite might be in the latter category. The whores had to have at least a basic awareness of hotel security. That dictated they would not meet in the parking lot and come into the hotel as a group. One or two together, trickling in from different entrances at different times meant that few of them would be observed by the only security man on duty. Of course, the hotel security guard had already been asked by Thompson and Forsky not to confront or follow any of the women that might be suspect.

Thompson sat at the large security console in the office, afraid for a moment to touch anything. There were four TV screen monitors for every floor and additional monitors for all doors leading outside the hotel. Other screens covered the entrances to the bar, kitchen, offices, and the parking lots. Thompson thought it would seldom be necessary to leave the security office unless an apprehension was necessary.

Clearly intimidated by all the electronic gadgetry, Thompson worked up the nerve to hit a few buttons. The security man had given the detectives some very basic instructions, but Thompson was overwhelmed and had no real understanding how the system operated. He developed a false confidence after he worked the console for a few minutes. Then, all of a sudden, every screen went blank.

Forsky was sitting in a corner reading a magazine.

"John, get over here and look at this!" Thompson exclaimed.

As if speaking to a small child, Forsky remarked, "What did you do, tear it up?"

"I don't know. See what you can do," Thompson replied with despair.

"Move over, Lo-Tech, let an expert have a look," Forsky said.

Many of Thompson's co-workers occasionally called him Lo-Tech, and for good reason.

Forsky played with the buttons and switches for several minutes. The monitors regained their images.

Forsky looked at a relieved Thompson and said, "I'll be in charge of this gizmo for the evening, Wade, so don't touch a thing!"

"Gladly," Thompson said.

Forsky zoomed in with the camera covering the elevator door area on the floor where the suite in question was located. With another camera, he got a close-up of the door to the suite. Both depictions were shown in amazing clarity on adjacent monitors. There were eighty monitors, with all but six on the far right connected to functional cameras.

At twenty minutes after eight, Forsky observed two women approaching the hotel's main entrance. Both were in their early thirties. Neither appeared to be a prostitute. They were well dressed in conservative office attire. It was later discovered they had legitimate day jobs.

Thompson called Captain Holland and said, "Got two on the way, Arlie."

"Fine, these guys are about to go to sleep," Holland said.

Officer Maynard Tompkins sat on a couch away from most

of the group. He was consuming his first bourbon and water of the evening. Maynard hardly spoke to anyone, ever. Sixty-four years old, the traffic cop had been on the department for thirty-nine years. Only two other officers out of almost three thousand had seniority on Maynard Tompkins.

He had not had an alcoholic beverage of any kind for at least five years and for good reason. Maynard had a minor heart ailment for which he took medication. He was not supposed to drink at all, but he thought one or two drinks on this one occasion could not possibly hurt anything.

After his first drink, and just before he started on the second, Maynard became quite talkative. Every one of his co-workers noticed. He did not appear intoxicated to anyone and perhaps he was not. He just acted very strange for quiet Maynard. He joined the group for a few minutes, talked to several officers, then returned to the couch where he had been sitting alone, adjacent to the hot tub.

Forsky was learning his way around the security camera console as he told Thompson, "Looks like we have one coming in a side door and another single through the main lobby."

"Good, good," Thompson said, as he began to experience some exhilaration, though not nearly as much as if he was involved in the undercover work.

By 8:40 P.M., twenty girls had arrived. Only four of the women were even close to having a hard and whorey look about them. Even those few would have escaped detection by an untrained eye. Three women appeared to be forty years of age or older. Hookers in this age group were making far more frequent appearances for reasons unknown to Thompson and Forsky. Just a few years before, these "old" whores were rare indeed. When they did surface on an escort service date or elsewhere, such women looked twenty years older than they were.

Everything appeared to be under control even as the large suite became quite noisy. About half of the women smoked and several of the traffic men puffed on foul-smelling fat cigars. Captain Holland decided to open the French doors that led to the balcony to allow fresh air to enter the suite. As he walked past the darkened area where the hot tub was located, he noticed a naked Maynard Tompkins in the hot tub with a similarly-revealed hooker. Each had their arms around one another's shoulders and they shared the same drink.

"Hey, Arlie, come on in! The water's fine!" Maynard said in a slur to the Captain.

The hooker echoed Maynard with, "Yeah, Arlie, shed those clothes and get in! I'll take care of you both!"

Captain Holland was momentarily baffled. In all his years of supervising cops, he had never been confronted with a situation even close to this one. Maynard Tompkins was out of his head. Holland not only had to prevent the old cop from having sex with the whore, he had to do it in a way that would not compromise the undercover investigation.

Like a cat, the young hooker began pawing Holland's crotch area. It seemed she was losing interest in old Maynard.

"Come on, Arlie, get in!" she kept saying.

Holland leaned over and the girl put her arm around the captain's neck. Arlie Holland whispered in her ear, "Be careful around Maynard. He's a good guy and all, but Maynard's had a social disease for years. If you'll look, he's got some nasty looking runny sores that just don't ever heal."

Captain Holland hadn't quite finished the sentence when the naked prostitute sprang to her feet, almost vaulting out of the hot tub. Dripping water on the marble floor, she grabbed a towel and wrapped it around her.

Holland told the woman, "You might spread the word about Maynard so nobody else gets in the tub with him."

"Believe me, I will! That's so gross!"

Now Arlie Holland's only concern was to keep Maynard Tompkins from drowning. It was apparent Maynard would never extricate himself from the hot tub under his own power. Moreover, Holland could see no reason for poor, naked Maynard to get out of the tub anyway, at least not while the suite was full of people. Holland would have to stay with him.

By 9:30 P.M., prostitution cases had been made against all the women. The traffic cops did very well for a first-time endeavor. One of the old-timers, who was very nervous and had been talking incessantly with practically all the hookers, could not remember which girls he had made cases on. He could not remember a single case. He cornered one of the vice detectives twice and tried to discuss the dilemma with him. Each time, the detective told the officer they would talk about it later. The old guy finally stopped worrying about his memory problem and decided to enjoy himself for the remainder of the evening. It made no discernible difference, however, since cases had been made against all the prostitutes.

According to policy, each harlot would only be charged with one case of prostitution despite the fact that multiple cases may have been made on her. Should the matter ever be taken to court, it certainly did not hurt the state's position that one woman agreed to fill dates of prostitution with six different undercover officers.

The arrests went without incident. Herschel Fowler, though visibly saddened by the event, behaved in an admirable manner throughout the entire episode. Of course, his days of using the 800 service were over. Few persons besides Herschel had experienced the feeling of being viewed as a traitor by a bunch of whores and whore service operators. This was an awful, almost unbearable feeling for the informant. However, it was deadened somewhat by the thought of no longer having to worry about being the dayroom bitch for a bunch of fellow inmates.

Captain Holland was still babysitting Maynard Tompkins as he called Thompson and Forsky. They could not get to the room fast enough to suit themselves. Since arrests had been made and this phase of the assignment was over, most of the traffic cops were excited about the successful completion of their undercover task. As Thompson looked around the room in hopes of recognizing some of the women, one of the traffic men was telling two of his mesmerized co-workers how difficult it was to make a case on a particular girl. Thompson stopped and listened to the exaggerated tale for a moment. One of the undercover detectives stood behind the storyteller, shaking his head in a negative gesture as the narration progressed.

Suddenly one of the listeners came to his senses and with a booming voice said, "Foster, all you did was make a simple whore case, not buy heroin from the Mafia!" A round of laughter quickly ended the embellished account.

Thompson and Forsky could barely make out Arlie Holland in the distance. He was still seated in a chair next to the dimly lit hot tub that contained the semi-conscious carcass of Maynard Tompkins.

"What's going on here, Arlie?" Thompson asked. Forsky was silent as he stared at Maynard.

"Wade, everything's fine and this won't be brought up again. Okay?" Captain Holland said.

"Okay with me," Thompson said. There was no curiosity. He did not want to know what happened.

Thompson and Forsky recognized none of the arrestees. This surprised Thompson. He had felt certain there would be at least a couple of familiar faces in the crowd. After purses were searched and proper identification was made on all the prisoners, they were transported to the office where Thompson, Forsky, or Sgt. Sanderson would interview every prostitute.

As a group, the women were typical opportunists. The cheapest date agreed upon was a straight date for two-fifty. One requested an outlandish one thousand dollars for a half-and-half adventure. The traffic cop had no trouble agreeing, but remarked to the young lady that he had just put a new floor in his kitchen for quite a bit less money.

    A sullen Herschel Fowler stayed behind as the women were taken down the hall to the elevator. Forsky approached him and asked, "Herschel, are you alright?"

    "No, I'm not. An anxiety attack has triggered a severe case of diarrhea. I would like to go home now," Herschel said.

    Forsky replied, "Go ahead."

    A sad, dejected, and now sick Herschel Fowler left the scene of the biggest and last whore party he would ever attend.

    Forsky and Thompson left for the office. They had heard nothing from Houston or San Antonio. In fact, neither detective had given much thought for the past two hours to the cooperative efforts of the other cities' police departments. Now, and with expected urgency, Thompson and Forsky wanted to find out what had transpired a couple of hundred miles or so south of Dallas.

    There was a message from Bert Perez at the office that read, "Got four at this time and one more is supposed to show at 9:30, will call after that." The message had been received at 8:00 P.M. Bert should call any time. It was ten o'clock.

    Not a word from Houston. Thompson called Ed Witkowski.

    "Ed, Wade Thompson, had any luck yet?"

    "Sort of, Wade. The first girl out recognized our undercover man right away. Of course, she took off. Then we made three girls in a row, three officers, different hotels, different times. We have one man now at an airport hotel. He's waiting on one. I think they're hurting for girls, Wade. She's not supposed to show up until eleven. I was going to call it off since it would be so late and the Dallas and San Antonio deals would probably be over with," Witkowski related.

    Thompson replied, "It won't hurt anything to wait on her, but the word may be out by now. The worst that can happen is that your undercover man will get stood up."

"Yeah, that's what I was thinking. How did everyone do?" Witkowski asked.

Thompson was proud to respond to a question that he could not wait to answer. He said, "San Antonio has four confirmed, maybe five by now, and we got twenty."

"You really got twenty to show up at your slut party? That's great, so collectively we've made almost thirty whores," Witkowski exclaimed.

"That's right. It turned out to be a pretty good night. Ed, I have to go. The girls will be here any minute and we have to interview them. I'll be in the office the rest of the night. Call when you get word on your last man."

"Will do. Our three are being interviewed right now," Witkowski said.

As everyone was leaving the suite, Maynard Tompkins was coming to his senses. He was finally able to get out of the tub, dry off, and get dressed.

"Captain, I'm sorry. I really don't know what happened awhile ago, but if I'm getting dressed now, I know I must have been naked and that's not good. I only had one drink and part of another, but I'm not supposed to drink at all. What happened and what's going to happen to me?" an ashamed Maynard Tompkins asked.

"I think everything'll be okay. Just don't mention this to anyone. As far as I know, the people in the room weren't aware of anything out of the ordinary. Let's leave it at that, Maynard ."

"Okay. But you didn't tell me what happened," the officer said.

"Let's leave it at that, Maynard," Captain Holland said with added emphasis.

Captain Holland and Maynard followed two traffic officers and two prostitutes into the Vice office. The Captain walked past the group just inside the reception area. He found Thompson and Forsky in the squad room.

"There are two women seated in the reception area. From watching them once they got to the room, I'd say they were in charge of the whole group. Whenever one of the girls had a question about something, they went to one of these two. A couple of times, I saw each of these women whisper something to other girls. It just looked to me like they were directing the whole affair. Some of the other guys may have noticed it, too," Holland said.

"Okay, thanks Arlie," Forsky said as the Captain left the room.

"John, take your pick," Thompson said.

Forsky replied, "Okay. This office is going to be packed in the next few minutes. We need to make sure no one uses the phone until we're through interviewing everyone."

"Yeah, we do, but that may take two hours and we'll probably have some lawyers here before then. I guess they'll just have to wait until everyone's booked," Thompson said.

Forsky added, "I think our biggest problem is finding the space to keep the girls separated until we can talk to them."

Tal Sanderson approached Thompson and Forsky and asked, "Where do you want me to start?"

The detectives told him about the alleged ringleaders that they would interview. They also mentioned the logistical problem of adequate space and keeping everyone apart.

Sanderson said, "I'll work something out on that. Both of you get started on the main players now. Any suggestions as to whom I should speak with first when I begin my interviews?"

"The choice is yours, Tal," Thompson said. "We don't know any of these women."

CHAPTER 30

Thompson and Forsky approached the two women. They were seated apart from one another in the same row of worn out upholstered chairs where prospective licensees sat when they applied for various city permits to operate bars, adult theaters, and adult bookstores. At first glance, both women were attractive.

Other officers and prisoners could be heard in the distance. They had just stepped off the elevator and would be in the vice office in less than a minute. The place would become noisy and crowded in short order. Thompson had to find the officer who had arrested the woman he was to interview. He would feel more comfortable if he had at least a tiny bit of information about the circumstances of the arrest. Thompson located the traffic officer just as he began to prepare the arrest report. He was one of four who had made a prostitution case on the woman.

As Forsky asked the thirty-five year old dark-haired woman to follow him in his search for a suitable vacant office in which to interview her, Thompson took the older blond into an unoccupied sergeant's office. The woman was very much at ease. Too much at ease, Thompson thought.

He asked her, "Is Katrina your true name?"

"My name is Roxanne Sachs," the woman said, emotionless. Like some escort service whores, she left her purse and identification in her car before going to the hotel room.

Thompson said, "I've been told you were given your rights and that you understand what your rights are. Is that correct?"

"Yeah. When can I use the phone?" the impatient woman

inquired.

Thompson answered, "It'll be a while. We've got arrest reports and booking paperwork to do before you will have access to a phone."

"It appears to me that you're doing neither and I do have a right to make a call," Roxanne Sachs stated.

Thompson answered, "No one will deny you access to a phone. The officer who arrested you is preparing your paperwork at this moment. By the way, you had four cases made against you this evening."

"Maybe so, but you'll only file one. The DA's office won't allow multiple cases like that and you know it, detective," she said with stone confidence.

Thompson thought to himself for a moment how few prostitutes would be armed with such procedural knowledge.

"You've been in this predicament before, if you're privy to details like that. I won't waste your time or mine. I'd like to ask you a few things about this escort service you work for. If you choose not to talk about it, that's certainly your privilege, but you're being given an opportunity to help yourself as far as your whore case goes. If you choose not to help yourself and you have a prior conviction for prostitution, we'll ask the DA's office to push for maximum jail time on this case," Thompson said, using a standard yet often effective line.

Roxanne Sachs, not budging in her defiance, said, "Even with a prior conviction, this case would still be a misdemeanor."

Thompson replied, "You're right, Roxanne. But a Class 'A' enhanced case could get you up to a year in the county jail. If we thoroughly investigate this and discover we can file a promotion case on you, we'll do just that. The whole works will be taken to another level then, in other words, a felony and possible pen time."

Thompson paused. The prostitute said nothing, staring into space instead.

"I'll take you to the officer who has your paperwork," Thompson told the woman.

Roxanne Sachs stood. Her initial attractiveness began a quick fade. Boob job, salon tan, capped teeth, and grossly long fake nails belied any real beauty. She would be a far better looking forty-three year old woman without the counterfeit amenities, Thompson thought.

As the detective gathered up some papers that he had brought with him, the woman asked him in an angry tone, "What exactly is it that you want from me?"

"Information about the people you work for, that's all," Thompson replied, somewhat oversimplifying the request.

The woman began to open up and said, "Look, I'm raising two children alone. I've held the same job for fifteen years. I've done this on the side for five. My kids and I need the extra money. I can't go to jail in my situation and you know that."

Roxanne Sachs sat down again. Thompson felt like he might be getting somewhere at last.

"Were you in charge of this group tonight?" Thompson asked.

Roxanne replied, "Sort of. With big parties like this, the service will give me a hundred dollars to oversee the other girls and make sure everything goes okay. The girl your buddy is talking to is Connie Stearman. She was doing the same thing. We've worked parties together before, but never with twenty women."

Thompson was trying to ask the most important questions he could think of, just in case Roxanne decided to stop talking.

"Who do you work for? By that, I mean the actual person or persons who run this service," Thompson asked.

With her pensive stare at the wall, the woman hoped to avoid a direct answer. With what seemed to be regret, she said, "Oh why did you have to ask me that? Besides, I'm not sure I even know who really runs the service. I can get in some big trouble, and I'm sure I've already lost my job."

As she made an unsuccessful attempt at being evasive by changing the subject, Thompson was curious why the woman was so sure she had lost her job.

"Why did you say you lost your job? How could you know that?" Thompson inquired.

"Because I didn't check out the men at the party. I knew Herschel. Everybody knows Herschel. I took his word for it these men were okay and not cops. Connie will get fired, too, and this was her only job. Who would have thought Herschel would be working for the cops?" she said in anger.

Thompson asked, "One more time, Roxanne, who runs the show?"

"I'll have to think about that for a while. I'm scared, do you understand that?" she asked.

Thompson answered, "Yeah, I suppose I do. Are these unnamed persons going to make your bond or send a lawyer?"

"Oh, not them. I'm on my own."

Thompson replied, "These people have fired you and they aren't going to get you out of jail. I'm not quite sure I understand that degree of loyalty here."

"They might send a lawyer, but only to make sure we don't talk. Their lawyer wouldn't really represent any of us," the woman said. "If I give you the information you want, would you get this case dismissed?"

Thompson responded, "The DA's office can do it based on our recommendation. We make no promises, but your case would likely be dismissed if you cooperate."

"I'll still have to think about it," the prostitute said.

Hoping she would talk tonight, Thompson told her, "That's fine, Roxanne. But your friend, Connie Stearman may be writing an affidavit at this very moment telling all she knows. If it's enough to suit our purpose, then your knowledge of the operation and your testimony may become less valuable as far as we're concerned. You need to consider that."

"I understand what you're saying and I appreciate the opportunity. Connie can help you, but not nearly as much as I can. I'll let you know something tomorrow," Roxanne said.

For some reason, Thompson knew that Roxanne Sachs would not have much concern over Connie Stearman writing an affidavit. He had no idea if the other woman was even cooperating at all. Roxanne Sachs' knowledge of the escort business would provide far more prosecution evidence than that of anyone they had confronted up to this point. Roxanne knew that better than Thompson or anyone else.

Thompson handed the woman a business card and said, "Call me at six tomorrow evening. If I don't hear from you by then I'll file the case and you can take your chances."

Roxanne Sachs glared at the card before putting it in her pocket. She had nothing to say as Thompson led her to the officer who was preparing her arrest report. Prisoners and cops were everywhere throughout the office. It had been a long time since Thompson had seen such a crowd in the Vice office. He searched for Forsky and Connie Stearman and found them in a conference room across the hall from vice. As he quietly opened the door, he observed the prostitute writing an affidavit. She had not noticed him, but Forsky did. Thompson remained in the hallway, but motioned for his partner to come to the door.

"Is she going to be of any help, John?" Thompson asked.

"She'd like to, but I don't believe she knows all that much. She did snitch off your girl, Roxanne, though."

Thompson asked, "What do you mean?"

"Roxanne has worked for this group a long time. According to my girl, Roxanne used to go with the owner. Is she going to do an affidavit?" Forsky inquired.

"I don't know, John. If she does, it won't be tonight. I've already turned her over to the officer doing her paperwork. She implied that she could be very helpful, but she's scared. I haven't checked yet, but I'm pretty sure she has a conviction. She has two kids and can't do jail time, so she may not have much choice. I told her I would file the case if she doesn't call by tomorrow evening," Thompson said.

"We sure need her affidavit. Connie Stearman knows Herschel and that flunkie gangster and not a whole lot more. She's had a DWI, but no whore cases," Forsky said.

It was no secret among police officers that once a suspect left a police facility, chances of that suspect returning to provide information diminished by a considerable degree. If a lawyer for the escort service got to Roxanne Sachs, he or she would be obligated to do the utmost to convince the woman that talking to the cops was a very poor idea. She would only hurt herself and her "innocent" employer by pulling such a stupid stunt. The lawyer was not being paid for his righteousness; he was being paid to protect whoever signed the check. That is what lawyers are supposed to do.

Connie Stearman finished her affidavit and was returned to the arresting officer for processing. Tal Sanderson had interviewed several women, all with negative results. Thompson and Forsky began working on the remainder. By 3:00 A.M. they were through and had nothing to show for their efforts but exhaustion. A few of the women would have written affidavits but their knowledge of the business was minimal, far less than even Connie Stearman's.

As Thompson drove home, he realized that the night had gone rather well, despite the limited success with the interviews. He still breathed the fumes of exhilaration, but they would soon evaporate. It was not the same feeling one experiences with true success. The faulty inner-workings of his own mind would prevent that from ever occurring. Twenty prostitution cases were made. While most vice detectives would see that as a noteworthy achievement, Thompson now asked himself why he had not had the foresight to request thirty. For him, such reasoning had nothing to do with greed. It was instead fueled by an unrealistic concept of efficiency.

When Thompson got home, he slept soundly for eight hours, something he seldom did.

At work that evening, Thompson hastily looked at his phone messages. Bert Perez and Ed Witkowski had both called. He had almost forgotten about them. Three lawyers had also called.

"Wade, do you have any messages from attorneys?" Forsky asked.

"Three. San Antonio and Houston called, too. I guess I had better call those guys right now. You want to call the lawyers?"

"I'm busy. I'm filing the case on Rufus Mathison. They'll call back if it's important," Forsky said.

Thompson called the San Antonio Vice office. At 6:30 P.M., he was reasonably certain Bert Perez was gone for the day.

"Detective Perez speaking," he said.

A surprised Thompson remarked, "Bert, what are you doing at work this late in the day?"

"Sir, I'm glad you called," Perez said, "We didn't make the last case; she never showed."

Thompson replied, "That's okay, Bert, just fax copies of the arrest reports when you get a chance."

"Already done, sir. Look by your fax machine. The reason I'm still in the office is because one of the women we arrested is writing an affidavit this minute. She's been here since 4:30. She is a registered nurse and has worked for the service off and on for two years. She's never been arrested."

"We really need affidavits, Bert," Thompson said with encouragement.

"I'll fax it when she's through and you can determine whether or not the information is useful. Sir, I must tell you this is the first affidavit I've ever taken. If you have any advice, I'm open to suggestions."

Thompson concluded, "Bert, as far as affidavits go, you're doing at least as well as we are for the time being. I'm going to call Houston now, but I should be in the office most of the night if you need anything."

"Okay, goodbye, sir," Perez said.

Thompson called the Houston PD. Ed Witkowski was off duty, but he always had a department cell phone within reach.

"Witkowski," he answered.

"Ed, I'm sorry to bother you when you're off, but I wanted to ask how things ended last night."

"We struck out on the last one, she never came out. The ones we got were all inexperienced. There were no previous prostitution arrests. Uh, no affidavits. Two of the girls had regular, full-time jobs. The paperwork is on my desk. If you want, I'll call and get one of the night detectives to fax it to you guys," Witkowski said.

"Please do, Ed, we could use the information," Thompson replied.

Forsky had gleaned bits and pieces from Thompson's phone conversations. He asked, "Well, what's the deal?"

Thompson explained and Forsky remarked, "We shook the hell out of the tree. Let's stand back and see what falls. Almost thirty whores arrested in one night is going to be cause for concern for someone."

"Officer Thompson," the familiar voice on the phone said, "this is Roxanne Sachs. Is the deal still on?"

With too much eagerness, Thompson replied, "Yes, when can you be here?"

"I'm terrified to cooperate in all this, but you people don't give me a lot of choices. You want me to come to your office tonight?"

Thompson replied, "Just as soon as you can get here."

"Give me an hour," the woman said with some

reluctance.

"Okay, you've got an hour."

"I'll be there," she said, now irritated.

Roxanne Sachs stopped at the threshold to the Vice office. It was as if there was a barrier in front of her that only she was aware of, but the barrier seemed real to the woman. She looked much rougher than she did the night before. She appeared to have had little or no sleep. Her clothes were disheveled and makeup was almost non-existent. Appearances aside, Roxanne Sachs showed up and that was all Thompson cared about.

He met her at the door. She tried to fake a smile as Thompson said, "Come on in, Roxanne. Let's find an office where we can talk."

In silence, she followed Thompson into the captain's office. Before he shut the door, he signaled for Forsky to join them. Forsky introduced himself to Roxanne.

"I'd like to say I'm glad to meet you but honestly, I don't care to be around cops any more than you want to be around me," she said in a matter-of-fact manner.

Forsky smiled and replied, "Your honesty is appreciated, Roxanne."

The woman looked at Thompson and asked, "Okay, what is it I have to do to keep out of jail?"

"First, tell us about the agency, then put it in writing. Just be truthful, that's the main requirement. Alright?" Thompson said, hoping she was in a talkative mood and not so defensive.

"You already know it's the biggest service there is anywhere. They have girls all over the country. The office where the calls are handled is in San Antonio. One of the owners, or maybe the only owner, lives in either Houston or San Antonio. I met him on an escort service date, before he ever went in business for himself. I worked for an agency here in Dallas then. For about a year, every time he came to town he would call the agency and request me. I guess I dated him four or five times. He was strange, and I don't just mean sexually weird, even though he's that, too. He always wanted to talk about the escort business, how many girls we had, how many phone lines, overhead, advertising, that sort of thing. I couldn't even answer most of his questions. The service I worked for then was 'Dallas Diamonds and Delights'. It was a tiny, fly-by-night shoestring operation if there ever was one. The greasy-haired pimp that ran it had maybe four girls at the most and one of them was his fat-assed ugly wife."

"Roxanne, let me interrupt you for just a second," Thompson said as she began to ramble, "What's the name of this man who owns the 800 number service?"

"Charlie, Charles Western. He's really an accountant," she said as Thompson and Forsky exchanged glances and faint smiles.

Roxanne caught the expressions on their faces and asked, "Do you all know Charlie?"

"Not really," Thompson remarked, "Let's say we've heard of him."

The woman continued, "Charlie's a wormy kind of guy, not exactly boyfriend material, but he's real smart. He's the type who would call an escort service on a regular basis. On a social and romantic scale, Charlie's a loser, but I'm afraid of him just the same."

"Why are you afraid of him?" Forsky asked.

"I'm not sure, I can't put my finger on it. He just gives me the creeps. As far as I know, he's never beaten any of the girls or even lost his temper. I would never date him again, though."

In a gradual way, Roxanne Sachs was becoming relaxed in the company of the detectives. It was apparent she wanted to talk about the service.

"How many women work for the agency in Dallas?" Thompson inquired.

For a second, she drew a blank, then said, "I'm not sure, but I would guess there are fifteen or twenty full-time girls, and at least that many part-timers. Of all those, there are three or four specialists, like me."

"What does a specialist do? What's your specialty?" Thompson asked.

She replied, "We cater to the weird folks, men and women, but mostly men. You have the fetish crowd. For years, this niche in the market was ignored by the escort services. Charlie Western used his smarts and has made a lot of money hiring girls that do specialty jobs. As far as I know, this is the only service that offers it. I'm a disciplinarian.

I tie people up, spank them, make them behave. We charge at least twice as much for a specialty date. The agency fee alone is three hundred dollars, but you can't just call the service and request a girl to come out and whip your butt with a riding crop. A customer has to do a regular date first. That's how you're checked out. Don't get me wrong, now, I do regular dates, too. Most women won't do specialty work, but they're instructed by the service to let them know about customers that request that stuff. They'll even give the girl a finder's fee after the customer's first specialty date."

Thompson thought for a minute. As perverse as all this was, this service was successful not only because it offered a bill of fare unmatched in this illicit industry, but because it was run like a business by a businessman. Charlie Western may have been quite odd and was probably a loser in many ways. However, it could not be denied that his enterprising acumen went far beyond that of the typical escort service operator.

"Tell us about, Charlie, Roxanne. How's he weird?" Forsky asked.

"Well, as strange people go, I guess he's really not all that weird. He likes to be scolded and told he's been naughty. He'd get down on all fours and have you spank him with a belt. Sometimes he didn't even take off his clothes. Or, he might put on a dog collar and I'd walk him around the room on a leash. If he didn't obey my commands, I'd kick him in the butt with pointed, high heeled shoes. He might bark and whine a little."

Roxanne smiled for the first time, then actually laughed. It also sparked laughter from Thompson and Forsky.

"Okay, Roxanne, we might be getting off the subject. I'm not sure I want to know anything else about Charlie Western's personal life," Thompson said, still laughing.

The woman said, "What I've told you is just about everything I know about the man. There's a rumor that's been going around the agency for a long time that Charlie and I used to be serious and that we lived together for a while. That's not true and I don't know how it got started. I think Charlie was married years ago. He's incredibly cheap but he's got to be worth millions. Very few of the prostitutes that work for Charlie know anything about him, if they know him at all. He hasn't called me in a long time. Charlie's probably found someone who spanks him a lot harder than I did."

Forsky asked Roxanne, "What do you know about the office in San Antonio?"

"They answer phones there and that's about it. I've been there with Charlie. It's a twenty-four hour a day business. They'll have four people there during the peak hours, five in the afternoon until two in the morning. Even during the slow times, like 7:00 A.M., two people will work the phones. Charlie is in the office two or three times a week. He has to have total control of everything, but he tries to be real sly about it. The employees there probably don't know he's the owner. They think he's an office manager or some flunkie hired by the owner. He likes it that way. Charlie wants to make sure no one takes a twenty-minute break when they're only supposed to take fifteen. He turns off the lights when no one is in a room, things like that. Maybe that's why he's rich and the rest of us aren't," Roxanne said.

Thompson had heard enough for the time being. He told the woman, "Here are some affidavit forms. Write your story.

Explain how you know Charlie and how he owns this huge escort service. Mention specialty work, agency fees, whore fees, everything. If you want to mention spanking Charlie and the dog collar, fine, just don't get carried away. Be truthful and if you're not sure of something, say you're unsure or leave it out altogether. If you don't remember dates and times, use words like 'about' or 'around'. Make yourself comfortable. I'll be outside this door if you have any questions."

Thompson left the door to the captain's office open. Not that it would necessarily happen, but he preferred that a prostitute not snoop around the boss's office. Had the boss known, he would have been in total agreement with Thompson on the matter. Thompson felt uneasiness about Roxanne Sachs's unpredictable disposition. She would smile and be quite cheerful, then alternate to a mood of uncertainty as if she had no idea whether she was doing the right thing or not. Forsky also sensed the wavering, but saw no need for concern, attributing the whole thing to anxiety and nervousness. Both detectives hoped that what Roxanne was composing at the captain's conference table would prove to be the master treatise on weird Charlie's whore agency.

"John, I'm going to check how our prisoners were released. You want to call Houston and San Antonio?" Thompson asked.

"I'll do it."

Thompson sat at the computer terminal with the complete list of Dallas defendants. Four of the twenty prostitutes used the services of one local attorney, Harry Neiman. Roxanne Sachs was one of the four.

None of the women had been permitted to use a phone until they were booked into jail. Jail personnel maintained a computerized time log. According to the log, Harry Neiman had been completing release paperwork in the jail office before the women were there. Several of the other prostitutes had called attorneys, but no two used the same one. Others simply waited until bonds were set and either posted their own cash bond or called a bondsman to do the same.

Thompson knew of Harry Neiman. He had a fine reputation not only among criminal defense attorneys, but also around the courthouse. Since Neiman had only dealt with four of the twenty, these must have been the four that someone believed had the most potential for providing damaging testimony against the agency. The woman Forsky had taken the affidavit from, Connie Stearman, was one of them. Roxanne Sachs was still the most important. The other two women were given the opportunity to talk, but refused. There was no point in re-contacting either of them. Thompson was certain their testimony could not top that of Roxanne. However, why had Roxanne not mentioned Harry Neiman to Thompson and Forsky? There was no doubt Neiman had given her the standard line about company loyalty and not trusting the cops. Perhaps that was at least part of the explanation for her moodiness.

Thompson entered the captain's office. Roxanne Sachs never looked up. She continued writing.

"Roxanne, pardon the interruption, but I need to ask you one question," Thompson said.

Irritated, she looked at him and said, "Okay, what is it?"

"Harry Neiman got you out of jail. Why didn't you mention that earlier?"

In anger, the woman replied, "I'm doing this for me, not for Harry Neiman or the agency. He told me it would be unwise to talk to you, but Harry Neiman's not the one that'll serve jail time if you file a case on me. I don't think he would take care of my kids, either. I don't owe that man or the agency a thing."

"That's all I needed to know," Thompson said as he left the room.

As Thompson walked from the captain's office, Forsky approached him and remarked, "I suppose it's not real critical now that we get the Oldsmobile driver identified, although it wouldn't hurt anything if Bert could catch Charlie Western at the

San Antonio office."

"John, to me it's kind of critical. I'd still like to physically link him to that office."

Forsky replied, "I know what you're saying, but what I meant was that we can make the case without it."

"Agreed," Thompson said, obvious that something else was on his mind. "John, there are a couple things that bother me about Roxanne and what she's saying."

"Like what?" Forsky asked.

"The information's not as current as we need it to be. On the other hand, she seems to be rather up to date on the habits and practices of someone she hasn't been around in a long time. She has a good general knowledge of the business, too," Thompson said.

"I think you're reading something into this that's not there, Wade. There's no reason why Western would do things any different now than when Roxanne spanked his naughty butt on a regular basis. Granted, we're going to have to look closely and do some checking to put ample credence in her testimony, but that's pretty much standard anyway," Forsky replied.

"You're probably right, but just the same, I don't feel real comfortable with her," Thompson concluded.

Forsky said, "Oh, about Houston and San Antonio, one girl in Houston used an attorney. I have his name. Ed Witkowski said he's a stretcher chaser, advertises on TV and billboards, and has a general reputation as being a horrible lawyer. I don't think this agency would use someone like him. One of the San Antonio whores used a lawyer. Bert said he's young, worked for the DA's office for about a year after law school, and just went into private practice. I don't believe there is anything there worth looking at, Wade."

Thompson replied, "There's not. The affidavit Bert sent was excellent from the perspective of an English teacher. For our purposes, it's about worthless. The girl just didn't know anything."

"In that case, what do you think about trying to make another whore or two from the agency just to see what happens?" Forsky suggested.

"We can give it a try, but we're about to run out of undercover people. We can't do it and we can't use any of the guys from last night."

"What about Bullethead Bentley and J.C. Cook?" Forsky said. "They hardly ever work outcalls."

Thompson replied, "That's because they hate to work them, but I guess we could ask."

Forsky paged them. Neither was crazy about the idea, but they agreed to set up in a hotel the next night. Bentley and Cook were experienced undercover detectives. They hadn't worked an outcall service in more than a year.

Bert Perez called just minutes after Thompson arrived at the office the next evening. "Sir, I have some important information for you."

"What's that, Bert?"

"I drove by the phone center at four this afternoon. The Oldsmobile was on the parking lot. I sat and waited to see who was driving it. About 5:30, Charles Western came out, got in the car, and drove to the freeway. He went south and I followed him, but only for about a mile. I lost him in heavy traffic. It was Western, no doubt about it. Before he left the parking lot, he sat in his car for a few minutes. He put three stacks of papers on the dash and sorted through them. I drove right past him to get a good look. He never saw me, but he looked just like the DL photograph."

"That's what we needed, Bert, thank you. There's no need to watch that place anymore on a regular basis, but if you've got nothing to do, you might drive by once in a while," Thompson said, glad Bert had found Charlie Western at the office.

"Okay sir. What did you think of the affidavit? Have you

read it?"

With reluctance, Thompson replied, "Bert, the affidavit itself was well done, but the girl just didn't know enough to help us out. We can't use it. It was worth a try, though. I wouldn't say you wasted your time."

"It sucked! I knew it sucked, I just couldn't admit it to myself."

Thompson said with encouragement, "Don't worry about it, Bert. The effort was appreciated. And thanks again for finding Charlie Western."

Bentley and Cook were situated in their hotel suite by 7:30 P.M. Despite the fact the pair was using a several hundred dollar per night accommodation, they had stopped at a South Dallas eatery on the way. They picked up a 'to go' order of their favorite vittles: barbecued pork rib sandwiches, deep fried sweet potatoes, spicy coleslaw, fried okra, and cherry fried pies. Bullethead dripped grease on a couch cushion as J.C. sipped highly sweetened iced tea. They discussed the game plan for the evening as they finished off their heart-attack-in-a-sack. It was decided that Bullethead would place the call to the agency and J.C. would cover his partner from the adjoining room.

Meanwhile, Thompson received a call from the attorney, Harry Neiman.

"Mr. Thompson, if this is a convenient time, I would like to discuss some issues with you," the lawyer said.

"Mr. Neiman, I can't discuss an ongoing investigation. I figured you were aware of that."

"Oh, I am, but it does no harm to ask," Neiman said with a slight chuckle.

Thompson responded, "Well, I guess that means our conversation will be a short one."

"I'll ask no questions, but there is a noteworthy point

I wish to bring to your attention regarding your investigation, something I'll throw out for you and your superiors to consider," Neiman said.

With a touch of impatience, Thompson replied, "I'm listening."

"The ownership of the escort service you and your cohorts targeted last night is in no way involved in the business of prostitution. I've been told they instruct their employees not to engage in any type of sexual conduct with clients or even discuss such topics with them. Employees are, in fact, required to end a session if a client persists in wanting to engage in an illegal act. If the women participate in acts of prostitution, it is done without the consent or knowledge of the ownership," Neiman said, "and, of course, 'knowledge' is a key element in proving up an aggravated promotion of prostitution case."

Thompson was disappointed that the famous Harry Neiman was unable to come up with nothing better than the trite, standard defense ploy for pimping.

Thompson replied, "You're right, knowledge must be proven. That's easy to do. Also, Mr. Neiman, if the ownership told you what you say they did, they lied to you. You had better be careful dealing with them. Just thought I'd throw that out as something for you to consider."

The lawyer said, "Thank you for your time, officer. I'm sure we'll talk again."

"John, that was Harry Neiman," Thompson said.

"Usual lawyer talk, innocent client and all that?" Forsky said.

"Yeah," Thompson remarked, "bet he's on the phone this minute with Charlie Western."

Forsky said, "Bullethead and J.C. called while you were talking to Neiman. Bullet asked for two fat girls wearing nurse outfits. It took them a while to find the girls, but they called back and said they'd be there at ten."

"I sort of had doubts they would send anyone out after last night. They probably think Bullet's just another weirdo," Thompson remarked, grinning.

Forsky replied, "Well, Bullet is a little strange, but I'll bet he'll make the cases."

Thompson asked, "Were the fat girls in nurse uniforms your idea?"

"How dare you think such a thought. No, that's pure Bullet," Forsky said.

Thompson went into the captain's office to check on Roxanne Sachs's progress. He picked up eight pages that were to her right. She had worked on the statement non-stop for two hours. He gave little more than a cursory glance at the material, but it appeared to be well written. He was anxious to study the completed version.

Roxanne put down her pen, looked at Thompson, and said, " I'll be through in another fifteen minutes. Is it too long?"

"Oh, no. I'll read the whole thing when you're finished," Thompson said as he put the papers down and walked out. He wanted to avoid making the woman feel rushed, but his impatience and eagerness were difficult to hide.

CHAPTER 31

"Wade, Bullethead and J.C. are on their way in with two; real prizes according to J.C.," Forsky said.

Somewhat preoccupied, Thompson replied, "Couple of steamers, I imagine."

Several minutes later, Thompson, Forsky, and just about everyone else in the building could hear a shrill female voice yelling and cussing, and occasionally crying. Forsky looked down the hallway and saw Bullethead, J.C., and the two "nurses" standing outside the elevator. The officers were attempting to calm one of the women who had been less than a good sport following her arrest. Lucky for everyone she was handcuffed. The woman was Bullet's size, about five-ten and two-fifty. In fact, except for Bullet's lack of hair, the two rather resembled one another. The detectives decided to give up on the amelioration effort and marched the mouthy whore toward the Vice office. She continued her tirade along the route.

"I did nothing wrong. I demand an attorney, now!" she screamed as the entourage entered the office. Bullet placed her in a soundproofed interrogation room, but the irritating voice penetrated the walls and was muffled little. The other prostitute handled the situation much better, but it was apparent she had been crying.

J.C. Cook seated his prisoner next to a desk. He approached Forsky and said in a low voice, "This girl will write an affidavit, I think. She works for three or four services. I don't really know just how much she can do. You want to talk to her?"

"Sure do," Forsky replied. "I'm going to put her in the other interrogation room. We've got one writing in the Captain's office now, and I'd just as soon the two didn't see each other."

Thompson overheard the conversation. He also wanted to hear what the portly prostitute had to say, but Roxanne Sachs was his major concern for the time being.

Forsky introduced himself to the woman and asked her name as he motioned her to follow him.

"I'm Claudia Madsen," she replied.

As Forsky drew the blinds on the window of the interrogation room door, he said, "J.C. told me he explained the procedure to you regarding helping yourself out of this predicament. Do you understand the process?"

The woman was around thirty. Despite being fifty pounds overweight, she had an attractive face. She did not look whorey, either.

"Look, officer Forsky, I've been in the pen. You'll find that out, I'm sure, that's why I'm telling you now. I'm no longer on parole and I haven't been in any trouble since I was released. I've done clerical work for an insurance company for three years," the woman said.

Forsky asked, "Why were you in the pen?"

"Forgery," she began. "I was mixed up with some rotten people and their dope. I served eighteen months on a five-year sentence. I've been out four years."

"How did you get involved in the escort business?" Forsky inquired, "J.C. said you work for several."

Claudia Madsen replied, "I needed the money. Look at me, I know what you're thinking, just like all men think: not bad for a fat girl. Some men prefer big women and those are the only calls I get, so I've signed up with several agencies. I only do five or six dates a month and most of those come from this service."

"Did you answer one of their ads?" Forsky asked.

The woman replied, "Yeah, but not the kind you're talking

about."

"What do you mean?"

"I'm from Alamo Heights; San Antonio if you're not familiar with the area. When I was paroled, I needed a job bad. I answered a newspaper ad for telephone work. Well, I ended up going to work at the phone office for this escort agency. Charlie Western hired me. I knew what I was getting into, but it was easy work and it paid better than some minimum wage job. I worked there for a year. I'd probably still be there if my boyfriend hadn't been transferred to Dallas. We broke up and he left not long after we moved here, but I was already working for the insurance company, so I stayed. After about six months, Charlie called one day and asked if I'd like to do some specialty work once in a while. I think you know the rest," Claudia said.

Forsky replied, "No, I don't, Claudia. Did Charlie Western ever discuss the business with you? Did he tell you what to charge for dates, for instance? Things like that. Did he mention details like checking out customers to make sure they weren't cops?"

"Sure, maybe not in those words, but yeah, we talked about those things. You would never catch Charlie talking about those things now, though. He became real suspicious for some reason. I never dated Charlie or did anything with him, but he always liked me.

Sometimes, when he'd come to Dallas, he would call and we would go out to eat or I would meet him in a bar at the airport. In fact, we went to dinner together a couple of months ago. I think Charlie's a very lonesome guy," Claudia said.

Roxanne Sachs was finished with her affidavit. Thompson, seated behind the Captain's desk, waited as she read each page, making corrections here and there. Once she was satisfied with her work, she handed the completed version to Thompson.

Thompson began reading. The affidavit was quite lengthy and was well written. It contained a great deal of information, including names, approximate dates, and details regarding the operation of the service. Despite this, what kept jumping out at Thompson from the pages he held was the fact that the information was not as current as it should be for filing a criminal case. That was Thompson's interpretation, anyway. Nevertheless, the woman had provided much useful material. Also, the detectives now knew enough about the service to verify some of what Roxanne Sachs had mentioned in her narrative.

"Roxanne, it's fine," Thompson told the woman. "Let's go down the hall to the homicide office and get this notarized. You can go home after that."

With no emotion, she replied, "That took what little energy I had. I'm ready to go home."

After Roxanne Sachs left, Thompson returned to the Vice office. As he stood at the copy machine with the affidavit in hand, Lt. Pricklee approached him.

"Detective Thompson, I need to see you in my office," Pricklee said, grim seriousness in his voice.

Thompson replied, "Give me a second, Lieutenant, and I'll be right there."

"No, it can't wait. This won't take long. It has to do with what you're working on," Pricklee said.

Lt. Pricklee walked toward his office and looked back to make certain Thompson was following. He was, though with reluctance from the obvious look of displeasure on his face. The supervisor sat behind his desk as Thompson stood in front of it.

"Sit if you'd like," Pricklee said, almost as it if was an order.

Thompson replied, "I'll stand. You indicated this wouldn't take long and I'm busy."

"Very well," Pricklee said. "I was contacted by Harry Neiman, the attorney representing the escort service you and John Forsky are working on. He's mentioned unethical practices that you have engaged in and he is very much opposed to the continuation of this investigation. Mr. Neiman is very insistent that his client has no knowledge of prostitution activity occurring within the agency. He told me this entire episode has been nothing short of an aggravating annoyance for him and his client."

Thompson, finding it most difficult to believe that Lt. Pricklee wanted to call off an investigation based on the unsubstantiated word of a defense attorney, replied, "Lieutenant, have Harry Neiman provide just one factual example of unethical behavior we have engaged in during this investigation. If he can do that, I'll voluntarily put a halt to the whole thing. That man is taking the word of his client. Harry Neiman has a fine reputation as a good person and a good lawyer. I can't imagine him believing what his client is telling him. On the other hand, I suppose Neiman's just doing what he's supposed to do."

"Regardless, I'm considering the termination of the investigation," Pricklee said.

Thompson was furious and remarked, "It's as if you didn't hear a thing I said. We've done nothing wrong. I would appreciate your taking our word for something here. You can stop the investigation and I don't question that you have such authority. But to do it based on limited and erroneous information would be a big mistake. My sergeant, the captain, our deputy chief, and anyone else with good sense will agree with me. And believe me, I'll be going through the proper chain of command writing letters to all those people if you pull the idiotic stunt you have in mind. That would be dereliction of duty on your part. Now, I've got work to do."

Thompson left the room. He was not concerned about retribution by Pricklee. He knew the man would be entirely wrong if he called off the investigation. Thompson felt certain Pricklee would come to the same conclusion after he gave it some consideration. Thompson was reminded of a Thompson theory. In short, it stated that this was the sort of problem that arises when a supervisor with no working knowledge of law enforcement interfered in a well-conducted investigation.

Thompson made copies of Roxanne Sachs' affidavit, then went into the interrogation room where Forsky was talking with Claudia Madsen.

Forsky asked the woman, "Claudia, would you be willing to write a statement based on those things you just mentioned? Stick with the business, your personal knowledge of it, things he told you about it, and so forth."

"Sure, if I can keep myself from getting a prostitution conviction," she said with eagerness.

Thompson said, "I'll get some forms."

Thompson and Forsky stayed in the interrogation room with Claudia until she had completed her first page. She had to ask a number of questions and it took her a while to organize her thoughts and put them on paper. Thompson read the first paragraph from a few feet away. That was no great feat as her handwriting was huge, larger even than Thompson's, and he wrote big. While Claudia was no journalistic genius, she had a distinct knack for saying a lot by using only a few words. This was a talent Thompson admired, but had never become proficient at.

Once Claudia Madsen was comfortable with her narrative, Forsky and Thompson left her alone. Thompson was tired. The confrontation with Lt. Pricklee seemed to expend all his energy. He sat at a desk and stared into space for a while. He clutched Roxanne Sachs' affidavit and the copies.

Forsky came over, sat on the desk top, and asked, "Roxanne's affidavit any good?"

"Very good," Thompson said. "But I think a lot of the information is too old to be of much use to us." Thompson handed the original affidavit to Forsky for his review.

Forsky replied, "Well, as usual, you need a second opinion, an unbiased one."

"I hope you see something I missed," Thompson said, almost in desperation.

Thompson waited impatiently as Forsky spent more than twenty minutes reading the affidavit.

When he finished, Forsky looked at Thompson and said, "Granted, there's a lot of dated information here, but there's also enough current stuff to file a case, in my opinion. It's a minimal amount, true, but it's sufficient and that's what is important."

Forsky's opinion was comforting, but Thompson was far from convinced. Thompson said, "John, do you still have court in the morning?"

"I know, I know, have one of the experienced assistant DA's look at it while I'm at the courthouse. Okay, if it'll make you feel better, I will," Forsky replied.

Claudia Madsen had been writing for over an hour. Neither detective wanted to interrupt her, but Thompson was most anxious to see the finished product. The urge to compare it with Roxanne Sachs' affidavit had become overwhelming.

When Thompson could not stand it any longer, he opened the door to the interrogation room. Trying hard not to appear eager and failing miserably at it, he asked in a low voice, "How is it going, Claudia? Any problems?"

"Fine, thank you. I'm on the second to last page now," she said.

As big as Claudia wrote, that meant three or four more sentences.

As Thompson began to close the door, he said, "No rush, just let us know when you're finished."

He sat at the desk nearest the room and waited. In less than five minutes, Claudia Madsen opened the door and announced that she had completed the affidavit.

Thompson extended his hand even before he stood up. The woman put a thick stack of papers in it. He had expected quite a few pages, but the bulk surprised him.

Claudia remarked, "That's twenty nine pages, but I make large letters."

"While we go over this, we'll let Bullet process you. Then we'll go up to the jail where you can sign it and we'll have it notarized," Thompson said.

In reading the first three pages, Thompson knew they had a winner. Claudia was not strong with dates and times, but she remembered names, places, procedures, tactics, and conversations well. Much of what Claudia Madsen mentioned was a continuation of the old information that Roxanne Sachs had discussed. Overall, Charlie Western's whore business had changed little over the course of several years. Claudia had done more out-of-town dates than Roxanne Sachs, though both had been to cities as far away as Seattle and Boston.

Thompson was elated. He handed the affidavit to Forsky and said, "John, this is a good one. While you're reading it, I'm going to start filing the aggravated promotion case on Charles Western."

Forsky said, "Relax, Wade, it's after midnight. Why not get a fresh start tomorrow evening?"

"Just think of it as going out to 'snag one more'," Thompson said as he looked through desk drawers for blank prosecution report forms.

Forsky remarked, "That's a dandy way to look at it. Say, we're at the point now where we need to get the FBI involved. You want to call Joe Burrell?"

"Yeah, I've already given that some thought, I just haven't gotten around to doing it. I'll call him in the morning. Maybe he can meet us tomorrow night."

CHAPTER 32

Joe Burrell was an FBI agent the detectives had worked with on a number of occasions during the years he had been assigned to the Dallas Field Office. With the Bureau's vast resources at his disposal, Joe could put his finger on information, services, money, and equipment that the vice detectives would never have access to otherwise.

FBI agents were largely despised by local law enforcement and had been for decades. The agency with the uncaring attitude had developed a reputation for unrivaled arrogance over the course of many years. At times, the reputation was well deserved. However, in many instances, it was not. Most agents were decent people, but there were just enough that were a bit too big for their britches to perpetuate the image that FBI agents were a bunch of pricks.

Joe Burrell was one of the good guys. He had no aversion to hard work and it did not bother him in the least for a police agency other than his own to receive well-deserved credit. If a federal bureaucratic impediment forbade local law enforcement from knowing, reading, copying, or otherwise gaining access to certain FBI information that would be helpful in an investigation, Joe would put his "practical plan" into action. He would walk in the Vice office and place copies of relevant material in an obvious location. Joe would then announce he would be in the men's room for a while. Upon his return, all paperwork would be neat and in place, organized just as Joe had left it. In short, Burrell shared the same philosophy about police work that Thompson and Forsky did: work together and get the job done.

Thompson prepared a rough draft of a prosecution report that night. At Forsky's pleading, it was much shorter than Thompson wanted to make it. Nevertheless, the report contained the essentials. They went home at 3:00 A.M.

Thompson was up by nine. He wanted to catch Joe Burrell while the agent was still in the office.

"Joe, could you come by the office around six? We have an escort service that's operating all over the country. You need to have a look at this," Thompson said, knowing it would pique the interest of the agent.

Joe Burrell replied, "Okay. I'm doing an interview at five. I'll stop by after that."

"Thanks, Joe. We won't keep you more than an hour. At least tonight we won't," Thompson said.

That evening, Forsky said, "Wade, I had two organized crime prosecutors go over both affidavits this morning. They see no problem if they're used in conjunction with one another. As they put it, the first one, Roxanne's, is of a historical nature, but that doesn't mean it's of limited usefulness. The second one, Claudia's, reinforces the first and describes a continuing criminal enterprise. In other words, the DA's didn't see the imaginary problems that you envisioned."

"Glad to hear it," Thompson said. "By the way, Joe Burrell should be here around six."

Forsky replied, "How do you want to work this? We should be ready to arrest Charlie Western soon. I don't know whether or not Joe Burrell's involvement will change things."

"That's why we need to talk to him. For the time being, we'll probably do what we've been doing. Look, we have Weird Charlie linked to the phone center. We hit that place with a search warrant and get his computer equipment, business records, what have you. We do the same at his home and his private office at the

CWA accounting firm. We get one for his car, too. We do all four warrants simultaneously. Western should be at one of the three locations, so whoever finds him can arrest him. What do you think so far?" Thompson asked.

"That's all fine, but what about Rufus Mathison? His paperwork's ready right now, I've just been sitting on it. I'm sure we can get no bond on him and we need to do the same with Western. Both would be flight risks."

Thompson replied, "Let's arrest them at the same time. Too much of a chance one will vanish if he finds out the other got snagged."

"Probably. You know, Rufus may just want to talk. A three-time loser at his age won't take kindly to the possibility of another pen trip."

"Something to keep in mind," Thompson said.

A strong New Jersey accent penetrated the office as a grinning Joe Burrell stood in the doorway to the squad room and said, "Okay, what kind of sham hooker operation did you guys get me down here for?"

The detectives had not seen or talked to Joe Burrell in several months. Joe was a diminutive man, five-feet-eight, and one hundred forty pounds, and in his late forties. He had worked organized crime from the Newark Field Office for nine years before his transfer to Texas. When he was brand new in Dallas, he strolled into the vice office one day and introduced himself to Thompson and Forsky. Joe was personable and offered assistance on any cases where he could be of use. This seemed odd to both detectives and quite out-of-character for an FBI agent. Neither had dealt much with the FBI before Joe arrived on the scene. While earlier encounters with the agency had not been unpleasant, they were not particularly successful ones either. Without fail, it had been a one-way street with agents always wanting information, never providing any. With Joe Burrell, that changed, as everyone worked together and a friendship was formed that had lasted ten years.

Thompson and Forsky spent the better part of an hour detailing Charles Western's operation to Burrell. As usual, Forsky did most of the explaining so that it could be better understood. He omitted all the intricacies that would cloud the important aspects of the case. Thompson would have been compelled to include many such insignificant factors had he done the narration.

"Alright, if I understand all this, I'll make some suggestions," Joe Burrell said. "Go with the state case of aggravated promotion of prostitution for the time being. You won't have to even concern yourself with anything outside of Texas for now. Get the guy in jail, maybe you can get him held without bond. We can work on the federal part in the meantime. The IRS will be involved in this, too. Big involvement," Joe Burrell said.

"What else, Joe?" Thompson asked.

"For the immediate future, that's about it. Do you have any idea how many prostitutes this service might employ?"

Thompson replied, "No, but our best guess is at least several hundred scattered all over the country. Right now, we have no lists or anything else that would give us an accurate indication."

Forsky said, "We're going to proceed with our plans, Joe. Charles Western and Rufus Mathison will be arrested within the next week. We'll do the search warrants and find out a lot more about everything, we hope. Then you can do your thing."

"That sounds good," Burrell said, "but don't even mention that the FBI, IRS, or any other agency will be looking at this. Everyone will assume it and rightfully so, but don't confirm it for them, at least not right now."

"Fair enough," Thompson replied, "and we'll let you know when we're ready to make arrests and do search warrants."

As Joe Burrell got up to leave, he told the detectives, "I'm anxious to rush home now and eat a cold dinner, courtesy of you guys. I'll talk to you later. And thanks for calling me."

"Thanks for coming by Joe," Forsky said.

The agent just smiled as he hurried toward the hallway.

CHAPTER 33

Anticipating a frenzied and exciting work pace, Thompson said, "Let's do at least a rough draft of the search warrants now. We can get a detailed physical description of the layouts from the Houston and San Antonio people. I guess we'll need to have one search warrant signed by a Bexar County judge and three done in Harris County."

Forsky asked, "Now, the big question. Do you want to do Houston or San Antonio?"

"Well, John, you know how my decision-making is slow and deliberate, too slow and too deliberate for you and most others. So, help me out here. You choose."

Forsky did not hesitate as he said, "I'll do Houston, then."

"Alright, you have Houston."

Forsky suggested, "What do you think about having Bullethead and J.C. stake out Rufus Mathison? They can snag him whenever we find Charles Western."

"Yeah, we really need to cut them in on this if they want it. Okay, let's do that," Thompson replied, thankful that Forsky's mind was working in its efficient, streamlined manner.

Within a few days, all paperwork was completed. Everything was planned. Paperwork and plans were checked and double-checked. To further satisfy Thompson, whose behavior had always bordered on being obsessive-compulsive when he became excited or nervous, the detectives continued to make random checks.

Thompson and Sgt. Sanderson would drive to San Antonio the next day. Forsky would fly to Houston. Through surveillances, Bullethead Bentley and J.C. Cook had become familiar with Rufus Mathison's routine. His factoring business had been very slow for a couple of weeks and he had been doing no traveling. Everyone counted on Mathison being at his condo at 8:00 P.M. Wednesday, the time when everything was set to take place.

Thompson was experiencing that wonderful, indescribable sense of elation again - that pleasant accompaniment to the unique work he did. A good feeling, always a good feeling, one that made life so bright, vivid, and concentrated that it was difficult to look at except for brief intervals. Was this perception real? It made no difference to Thompson. In his private world, perception and reality, his thoughts and outlook versus fact sometimes blended to the point where there was no separation. It was not lying, it was not a misrepresentation. It was his way of looking at life. With that as a backdrop, his perception was accurate and it was real.

Criminals are often characterized as being smart. Even Thompson sometimes described them using the erroneous term. They may be clever, shrewd, streetwise, and innovative, but never smart. However, 'outsmarting' the best of the criminals was a feat of no small proportion. Thompson knew this as well as anyone in law enforcement. But success never felt like it was supposed to, at least to Thompson.

At noon on Wednesday, Forsky drove the Pontiac to Love Field for his 1:00 P.M. flight to Houston. Thompson and Tal Sanderson had already been on the road two hours, headed in the direction of San Antonio. Both were talkative in an abnormal way during the four-hour drive, perhaps due to nervousness. No one knew exactly what to anticipate in the hours that lay ahead. All three vice cops had participated in enough similar ventures to be comfortable with this one. They were all but assured of reasonable success. They were not "comfortable" in the most basic meaning of the word. They never were. That was probably normal. If it was not normal, that is the way it always was. From an analytical standpoint, a slight bit of the nervousness could be attributed to the sheer size of the present undertaking. "Big" is a relative term and its very nature as such indicates only a sense of vagueness.

    Mid-afternoon found Forsky seated on a rickety, cheap black vinyl love seat in Ed Witkowski's office. He was reviewing search warrants that the Houston detective had secured in Harris County. The Houston Vice squad had more than fifty detectives and had outgrown its facilities within the Police Building. The City of Houston owned an ancient condemned building down the street that had once been a large grocery store. It had been hurriedly gutted and remodeled on a most marginal basis and now housed all vice personnel. Every detective could say he had his own office. Each room did have four walls and a door. Each office was the size of an interrogation room. The walls were so thin that a conversation could be conducted with someone in an adjoining office without the raising of voices. Ceiling tiles fluttered whenever a door was open or closed. Over the love seat was a black fish net arranged in a meaningless design that was tacked to the wall. Witkowski's metal desk was missing a front leg. A red clay brick, however, was just the right thickness to keep everything stable and almost level. One file cabinet drawer had an improvised handle fashioned from a coat hanger. A thick layer of dust coated everything in the room. Forsky concluded that vice facilities everywhere were just meant to be nasty. It was almost a fact of life.

    Ed Witkoski, accompanied by his partner, their sergeant, and a couple of patrol officers would hit Charles Western's personal office in the CWA office building. They would be in position, with a view of the structure no later than 7:30 P.M. Witkowski had done some checking and found that the alarm company that had the service on the CWA building had keys to the main door. Getting into an inner office, however, might be a different matter.

Witkowski put Forsky with a senior vice detective and his supervisor. The trio, with assistance from two patrol officers, would effect the search warrant on Charles Western's condominium. By 7:30, the group would be positioned in a city park a couple of blocks away and have an unobstructed view of the residence.

In San Antonio, Bert Perez asked Thompson, "Sir, what time do you want to be in position?"

"I'd like to be on the parking lot in front of the phone center by 7:00 P.M. We're going to be on the phone quite a bit coordinating everything between here, Dallas, and Houston. Might as well do it from there as anywhere else," Thompson replied.

"That's fine, sir," Perez said. "I'll need to advise our uniformed officers that will be with us. If it's okay with you, sir, I'll have them stand by out of sight in a parking garage two blocks away."

Thompson, comforted by the young detective's meticulous preparation, replied, "Perfect, Bert."

Bullethead Bentley and J.C. Cook had been watching Rufus Mathison's condo since 5 P.M. The silver Lexus was in the driveway. They had observed Rufus carry trash to a curbside receptacle. Should Mathison go anywhere before 8 P.M., the detectives were to arrest him. It was important that he be kept from using a telephone until Charles Western had also been taken into custody. If Mathison was at his residence at eight, Bentley, Cook, a vice supervisor, and patrol officers would serve the arrest warrant there.

As a last minute gesture the day before, Thompson

and Forsky had secured two search warrants regarding Rufus Mathison. They needed paperwork, notes, or any sort of records dealing with the credit card factoring Mathison had been doing for the escort service. One warrant was for the condo, the other for the Lexus.

The time for things to start happening was near. Everyone involved was as prepared as they would ever be. Seldom does everything go one hundred percent as planned in an operation of this sort. That worried Wade Thompson. It always had and always would.

"What better place to get good Mexican food than San Antonio," Tal Sanderson remarked as he, Thompson, and Bert Perez were stepping into an elevator just outside Perez' vice office.

Perez raised his hand as if he was a third-grader asking permission to speak in class and said, "May I recommend the best Mexican food in town? It's not a tourist eating place, but the Anglos call it Greasy Joe's."

"Greasy Joe's it is, then. That okay with you, Wade?" Sanderson asked.

In a less-than-convincing manner, Thompson replied, "Yeah, that sounds good."

Wade Thompson was much too anxious, excited, and worried to be hungry. He knew if he did not eat, however, he would have a massive headache by midnight. So, yeah, Greasy Joe's was as good a place as any.

At six-thirty, Bullethead and J.C. stared through the windshield in different directions. They had long since run out of things to talk about, which was typical for the pair. They were like an old married couple who got along with everyone except each other. They fought, bitched, and argued, but neither detective would ever consider working with a different partner.

Rufus Mathison came out the front door of the condo and

walked toward his car at a brisk pace.

"Bullet, he's leaving!" J.C. said, surprised.

Bullethead started the car and prepared to follow the old criminal. He told J.C., "See if you can get hold of a squad, we need to get him stopped."

J.C. Cook frantically attempted to call any patrol officer in the vicinity on his walkie-talkie. The nearest one was about two miles away, but was already headed in the direction of the vice detectives. Mathison was dressed in shorts, a T-shirt, and sandals when he emerged from his residence, so perhaps he was not going very far. Bullethead and J.C. followed him onto a nearby freeway. On an intermittent basis, J.C. gave the patrol officer information regarding the suspect's location. After four or five miles, the uniformed officer overtook the vice cops and stopped Mathison who was conveniently speeding.

The patrolman had Mathison out of the Lexus and spread-eagle before the detectives could exit their vehicle. Even at a distance, Mathison's facial expressions indicated he was not handling the situation well. J.C. quickly approached the gangster and handcuffed him. Searching Rufus took all of about two seconds since he was wearing so little.

The shoulder emergency lane of a busy freeway was no place to interrogate a prisoner or even attempt to conduct anything more than the briefest of conversations. Aside from being a dangerous location, the incessant roar of traffic was deafening.

"You bastards are making a big mistake!" seemed to be all Mathison could say as he repeated it several times. His anger was quite apparent in his reddened face and he sweated profusely.

The man was downright scary, Bullet thought. It brought back a childhood memory of capturing a live copperhead snake. He was not sure why he had done it, but that reason was secondary. The immediate concern was what to do with it now that it was in captivity. Like the copperhead, Rufus would require close observation until he was in a secure holding facility.

As he waited on a wrecker to haul the Lexus to the police impoundment lot, the patrol officer began a cursory inventory of the car's contents. Bullethead Bentley was attempting to enter a freeway lane when the patrol officer waved, then physically stood in their approach, and frantically signaled for them to stop. He held a leather-bound briefcase in one hand.

The excited patrolman ran up to the car and said to the detectives, "You'll be interested in what I found!"

The officer handed the briefcase to Bullet. The detective opened it. J.C. Cook was seated directly behind Bullet and leaned forward enough to peer over his partner's shoulder. Rufus Mathison gazed out the window, ignoring the whole incident in hopes that the briefcase would simply vanish.

On top of much paperwork was a loaded .45 automatic pistol. Hammer back, safety on, ready to go, the serious mode for carrying such a pistol. Five extra loaded magazines were loose in the briefcase. The pistol and ammunition shared space in what turned out to be Rufus Mathison's miniature office- his most recent factoring business records, unkempt as they were, rested under the weaponry.

Rufus turned his head. He and the two vice detectives all stared at the open briefcase, but Rufus was not smiling with the officers.

Mathison remarked, "I guess you jerks are going to charge me with carrying a pistol, too!"

"You guessed right, Rufus, unless you can produce your concealed carry permit," J.C. said in a calm voice. At that moment, he caught sight of Mathison's sandal-clad feet. His toenails were neatly manicured and painted with red nail polish. "Whoa!...nice toenails, Rufus!" J.C. said, unable to maintain control of his laughter brought on by the hideous sight.

Bullethead turned and leaned to his right as he tried to see the prisoner's feet which were by then well-hidden under the back of the front seat. It was understating the fact by a considerable degree to say Mathison was embarrassed. The redness in his face turned to a whitish gray in a split second. The detectives welcomed the prisoner's momentary speechlessness. Oh, how Rufus wished he had worn socks and shoes!

Somewhat regaining composure, J.C. said to Mathison, "I'll bet you made someone a honey of a wife in the joint, Rufus!"

"I wasn't nobody's bitch!" Mathison said "Besides, it's none of your business! When can I use the phone?"

J. C. told him, "It'll be a while, Rufus. We'll have to do your paperwork when we get to the office. Then you'll be booked. After that you'll be allowed to use the phone."

"What's the bond on this, anyway?" the indignant prisoner asked.

J. C. replied, "No bond on the aggravated promotion of prostitution warrant. You'll probably have a bond set later tonight on the gun charge."

"So what you jokers are telling me is that I ain't getting out of jail, right?"

J.C. gladly confirmed the gangster's analysis of the situation as he said, "Yep, that's right."

"You know I'm on lifetime parole, you know I'm sixty-three years old, and you know I'm going back to the joint for whatever life I've got left," Mathison said.

J.C. made no response. Instead, as they were within blocks of the police building, he dialed Sgt. Sanderson's cell phone number.

Thompson answered it on the first ring, "Thompson."

J.C. said, "Rufus is in custody."

"Okay, is he with you at the moment?" Thompson asked.

"Yeah."

"I'll talk to you later, then. Just make sure he doesn't use the phone until after eight. If things change, I'll let you know right away," Thompson said, "Thanks, J.C."

"You bet, bye."

Thompson called Forsky to advise him of Rufus Mathison's arrest.

Bert Perez, Tal Sanderson, and Thompson neared the service's phone center parking lot. When they entered, Sanderson parked within a cluster of a half-dozen dirty and derelict vehicles, all with for sale signs on the windshields. Few other cars were on the lot. Three were close to the building and likely belonged to persons working the telephones at the service.

It was five minutes of eight. Forsky and his Houston PD cohorts were leaving their city park surveillance post for Charles Western's condo. Ed Witkowski and his group stopped in the parking lot of CWA, Inc.

Bullethead Bentley and J.C. Cook still had the search warrant for Rufus Mathison's condo and his car. The car was on the way to the pound. It could be looked at anytime. They would go to the condo after Rufus was booked, but before he was allowed to use the phone.

Ed Witkowski had no problem gaining access to Charles Western's personal office at CWA, Inc. Two energetic young accountants were still working in an outer office when the policemen entered the reception area of the business. While the door to Western's private office was secured somewhat, the lock was a flimsy device, easily opened with a credit card. For the wealthy owner of a successful business, it appeared odd at first that the office was small and the furnishings cheap. However, this was not out of character for Charlie Western and his obsession with frugality. It was apparent the man did not spend much time in this office. Everything was dirty and dusty as if the custodial people were denied access. From the overall look of the office and its contents, there was little indication that Western was even in the accounting business. Assorted papers and notes regarding the escort service were found in two file cabinet drawers, but the material was old and of little use.

Thompson, Sanderson, and Perez interrupted the normal activity at the phone center. Three women in their twenties were working the lines. Perez was thrilled when Thompson asked if he would like to answer the phones during the time they would be at the business. After interviewing the women, Thompson and Sanderson were convinced they would be of little help in the investigation. They were sent on their ways.

"Wade, they have a fairly sophisticated computer system here. I suppose you want to seize all the equipment, right?" Sanderson asked.

Thompson replied, "By all means, we'll take everything." Thompson could not tell a sophisticated computer system from a 1952 jukebox. Sanderson could, however. He liked computers and knew about them.

"One of the girls gave me the passwords. It should be no problem to retrieve what we need. One of the file cabinets must have a thousand disks in it," Sanderson said. He was eager to play with the machines once everything was back in Dallas.

Thompson longed to find notebooks, index file cards, ledgers, or anything else produced with pen and paper. No such records existed. During the intensity of the search, Thompson felt the return of that all-too familiar feeling where he knew he had worked vice too long. Modern technology, in all its blatant rudeness, had stolen the moment from the detective.

Nevertheless, for case-making purposes, the seized computer system would likely be overkill. Sanderson had tinkered with it enough already to know there was a tremendous volume of files available, far more than what anyone had anticipated.

Forsky saw the Oldsmobile in Charles Western's garage before he and the other officers got to the front door of the condominium. Western answered the door. He was wearing a

1970's model, worn, stained, and once-white, terrycloth bathrobe. His home looked like his office. It was dingy, dirty, and had a foul smell about it. As Forsky searched Charles Western, he reached in a pocket of the robe and felt something strange. His hand came out holding Charlie's false teeth. It was as if the startled detective had grabbed a snake. He dropped the fake choppers on the floor.

Western had said not one word at this point. He did not seem surprised by the arrest, but there was no way he could have known it would happen when it did. He made no response when Forsky told him he would be held without bond. Perhaps he was a person who did not get upset about anything. The condo was so nasty that no one wanted to search it, but the officers did go through the motions, at least. Forsky seized a briefcase from the Olds that contained a few papers relating to the escort service along with almost a hundred thousand dollars worth of credit card invoices.

When Forsky asked Western about the whore agency, the owner replied, "I'll converse with you about anything except the escort service. And I'd prefer that you did not call it a whore agency."

Forsky called Thompson after he retrieved the briefcase. They compared notes for a moment. Things had gone well overall and they were ahead of schedule. Western would be jailed in Houston, Harris County. Forsky would spend the night in Houston. Thompson and Sanderson would remain over in San Antonio. All would meet in Dallas the next evening.

CHAPTER 34

Thompson received an urgent page to call Jan Doxee. He was much too busy; it would have to wait. His mind was moving in strange directions right now. He first saw the page as nothing more than an irritation, but what if the woman had some sort of relapse? What if she was drunk? She picked a great time to start having problems again. How inconsiderate could a person be? After all, Thompson had important things to do and none of them involved counseling an old alcoholic whore. He became more upset by the moment, but he would put everything on hold until he found out what Jan wanted and why it could not wait.

Tal Sanderson had all the enthusiasm of a little kid on Christmas morning as he played with the agency's computer. He was oblivious to Thompson's presence. Thompson walked outside into the fresh air and sat on a bench near the front door of the office complex. He dialed Jan's number.

The phone rang four times before she answered. She would never let it ring that many times if she was sober, Thompson thought.

"Hello," she said in a clear and pleasant voice. She had not been drinking. Thompson should have experienced a feeling of relief, but now he was not only irritated, he was puzzled as well.

Thompson asked, "Jan, what's the problem? I'm extremely busy."

"And you just let me know in no uncertain terms that I'm bothering the hell out of you. Right?" she said with justified indignance.

"I apologize. I am very busy and very tired."

"Well then, you need to take a break and rest if you're tired. You're disposition will be far more pleasant," she said. "There's something you need to be aware of. It has to do with your investigation and the reason you are in San Antonio."

Shocked by Jan's knowledge of his whereabouts, Thompson asked, "What investigation? And, how did you know where I am?"

"Settle down, my dear. There's no need to be so defensive. You're still at the phone center, are you not?"

Following a long pause, Thompson inquired, "Alright, what's going on here, Jan?"

"Wade, we will never get anywhere if we dodge answering a question by asking another one, so I'll take the lead in getting us out of this rut."

"Please do, I'm listening," Thompson said, now more frustrated than ever. He was not sure if he liked the sober Jan any more than he liked the drunken one. The sober one's mind was sharper which made her more difficult to stay ahead of. Thompson only kidded himself-he couldn't keep up with her clever ways even during her lush days.

"I've known what you and John have been doing since the mass arrests of the girls from the agency. I just didn't know how to approach the subject with you. You tend to jump to conclusions. As a result, I procrastinated," Jan said.

With growing impatience, Thompson replied, "Jan, I said I was listening, so please tell me what's going on."

"I'm the co-owner of the agency you hit. Charles Western is my partner. I assume you have him arrested by now. If you don't, he's on his way to who-knows-where and you will never find him," she said.

Wade Thompson was speechless. Jan knew he would be, and gave him the pause he needed. She could not believe what she had just told him. She was fearful he and Forsky had been closing in on her, but he really did not know. He had no idea. Jan had given the long-time vice cops more credit than she should have. Given enough time, would they have found out her involvement? Perhaps, perhaps not. There was no reason for Charlie Western to snitch on Jan. Her embarrassment of Wade Thompson was not intentional, but it happened. Maybe it was Thompson's fault for not being a more competent detective. The same could be said for Forsky.

Thompson replied at last, "Jan, I don't know what to say. I guess I should ask you some questions, but I'm a bit overwhelmed right now."

"Wade, I know what you want to ask. I'm thinking quite logically so how about if I provide the answers? You can worry about the questions later. Now isn't that total cooperation from a suspect?"

Thompson replied, "I'm still not sure all this is happening. I feel like I'm on drugs. But, alright, tell me all about it."

"Charles Western is an old whore groupie. He's strange, he's repulsive, he likes to be spanked, and he's very wealthy. He needed a 'consultant', so to speak, to get his agency going and that's where Jan the Drunk entered the picture. A mutual bookie friend introduced us. That was five years ago. No, in answer to the question you have in your mind now, or will soon enough, I've never dated Charles Western. I hope you know my standards are higher than that."

"Don't stop now, Jan," Thompson said. He had overcome his hateful attitude and irritability. It might take a while for the embarrassment to subside, however.

"The business was successful from the very beginning. In fact, it became far, far more successful than we ever imagined. After some haggling, I wound up with a twenty percent share in the entire operation, the only stipulation being that I would continue in my consulting capacity. I had not one dime invested in the business. We do 'specialty' work. I guess you know about that. It's very profitable and hardly anyone else does it. As far as regular girls go, we've got more than five hundred across the country. It's the biggest service in the country. No one else even comes close. It's made me wealthy, Wade. I own some valuable real estate in some neat places and I have a little cash as well. That's all I can think of right now, but that's an accurate rough sketch."

"Jan, I'm sure I'll have about a million questions for you later, but I can only think of one right now," Thompson said.

"And what's that, sweetie? I'd be glad to answer it," she said.

"How did you know I was at the phone center in San Antonio right now?"

She replied, "One of the girls you just ran off called Roxanne Sachs. Roxanne called me. You remember Roxanne, don't you, Wade?"

Glad Jan could not see the grin on his face, Thompson replied, "Yeah, I remember Roxanne."

"Now Roxanne didn't lie to you, Wade. She just didn't tell you everything she knew. No snitch ever will tell all, and you should know that better than anyone else," Jan said.

Thompson replied, "Jan, you're so calm as you tell me all this. How can that be? Aren't you worried about us filing the same case on you that we filed on Charles Western?"

"No, I guess I'm not," she said. Thompson sensed she was going to say something else, but decided against it.

Thompson said, "I've got to get busy here, Jan. John and I need to meet with you tomorrow evening when we get back. You're not planning any trips in the meantime, are you?"

"How dare you ask that in a most distrusting tone. No, I'm not taking any trips. Call me when you get back. I'll even come to your office if you'd like."

Thompson felt strange. He was not sure the conversation

he just had really took place. He did not feel like doing any more work. He walked in the foyer and opened the door to the office where he had left Tal Sanderson. The sergeant was still entertaining himself with the agency's computer. Bert Perez had been on the phone non-stop since they arrived and seemed to be enjoying every minute of it. There was no telling how many customers he had spoken with and Thompson did not care. Thompson went outside and sat on the bench again. He had to tell Sanderson and Forsky about Jan Doxee tonight. He had to talk to his FBI contact, Joe Burrell, first thing in the morning. With their three good minds, plus his own of questionable worth, they could devise an effective plan as far as how to proceed with the investigation.

"John, are you about through for the night?" Thompson asked his partner on the phone.

Forsky replied, "We are through. Charlie's in jail, we've inventoried what little evidence there was, and we're fixing to go out and have a beverage or two. Have you all finished yet?"

"Tal's playing on the computer and Bert's been answering the phones constantly since we've been here. They're both having so much fun I hate to interrupt them. According to Tal, we have a ton of information in their computer system. The records and other information are very complete. Got something else to tell you, John."

Forsky replied, "Wade, you sound like someone who was just told he had a week to live. What's wrong?"

"Jan paged me about an hour ago. I called her. She told me she's Charles Western's partner and has been since the agency was started five years ago."

Forsky responded with humorous cynicism, "Then there really was something to that information her mother gave us."

"There was something there all right, but that stuff we had was worthless as far as this agency goes. You know that. As I look back on it, the whole thing was mostly a coincidence. That old drunk knew nothing about what we've become involved in. I wanted to let you know about this tonight. I haven't told Tal about it yet, but I'm going to in a minute. Jan said she'd meet us in the office tomorrow night. I'll call Joe Burrell in the morning," Thompson said.

Forsky attempted to console Thompson and said, "Don't worry about it tonight, Wade. It's not exactly like we've been drinkin' malts during the course of this investigation."

The expression, 'drinkin' malts', was a Forsky-coined term describing the activity, or perhaps inactivity, of lethargic, lazy cops.

Thompson went inside and found Sanderson boxing up computer equipment. The new must have worn off the toys. Thompson broke the news to Sanderson. Like Forsky, he took it calmly.

"What's the next step?" Sanderson asked.

"I don't know, Tal. Me, you, Forsky and Joe Burrell are going to meet tomorrow evening at the office. Jan has agreed to come in."

"We'll get it worked out," Sanderson commented. "We're all tired, and there's nothing that can be done about it now, anyway."

At nine the next morning, Thompson called Joe Burrell. He did not go into detail. Burrell would meet them at six that evening in the vice office.

On the long drive back to Dallas, Thompson's mind raced with what seemed like a thousand thoughts regarding the significant change of events in the investigation. He had one idea that he gave only brief passing thought to at first, but then it would resurface periodically. He was not sure it was workable or ethical. He wanted to give it adequate development and consideration before he mentioned it to anyone else. Sanderson did not want to confront the issue at all until they got home. Maybe he hoped it would all go away by then so there would be nothing to confront.

Joe Burrell, Tal Sanderson, Thompson, and Forsky were huddled around Captain Holland's conference table right at six o'clock. Burrell had brought a close friend, Oscar Rayburn, who just happened to work criminal investigations for the Internal Revenue Service.

Thompson addressed the group, "We all know that this has turned into a successful investigation. The Captain held a news conference, so word of this will get the department some favorable press. However, Jan Doxee's situation, which is new to us all, remains. I'm not asking for any favors. She has to be treated like any other suspect, but we make deals with suspects all the time. I'll present my plan for your consideration. Now, I've given this a good bit of thought, but if you people think it's not right or you can come up with a better idea, I'll not argue with you. By her admission, Jan owns twenty percent of the escort service. Charlie Western has the other eighty. Jan's become wealthy from the proceeds of this service. Charlie's become much wealthier. What better witness would we have against Charles Western than Jan Doxee?"

Forsky and Sanderson both nodded in affirmation. They realized Thompson had made a good point. Jan was the ultimate witness against Western. Also, it was the most practical plan to implement, as it would require the least amount of work.

Joe Burrell was not as comfortable with the idea. He twisted in his chair as he collected his thoughts. Oscar Rayburn's expressionless face gave no hint as to what he was thinking or whose side he was on.

Burrell said, "Wade, I can go with her snitching Charlie Western off for state or future federal prosecution, but she's as involved as he is, even if she's made a lot less money. We can't just let her go simply for informing on her partner."

"That's not what I had in mind, Joe. Let me explain. She's acquired some real estate that's become pretty valuable. She also has some cash. She told me this on the phone last night, but I haven't verified anything yet. Keep that in mind. For now, let's assume it's all true. Why can't the IRS seize her holdings and levy some huge cash fine against her? We all know that will happen to Western, too. How about it, Oscar? I know you guys have a way of figuring how much money criminals make over a period of time. And then you send 'em a bill, right?"

Thompson had put Oscar Rayburn on the spot, but the IRS agent was not at all on the defensive. He replied, "Your description of the process is a bit crude and oversimplified, but, yeah, that's basically what we do. Her biggest problem would be after we seized real estate holdings. If she was assessed a cash fine of, say for instance, two million dollars and couldn't come up with the funds, she might be looking at some healthy federal jail time."

Thompson looked at Burrell and said, "What do you think now, Joe?"

"Okay, she turns on her partner, tells all, forfeits substantial real estate holdings, and pays a big fine. What about other witnesses against Western?"

Thompson replied, "We have some affidavits, two good ones in particular, but neither are nearly as incriminating against Western as Jan could be. She can make the entire case alone. Her testimony would be the most damaging. She's waiting for the word right now to come to this office and talk about everything. She might clam up if she sees you guys here at this point, though. Let John and I run this by her tonight, then I'll call and let you know something in the morning. How's that?"

Joe Burrell said, "I'm in agreement for the time being, but I'll have to talk to the bosses about this."

Oscar Rayburn smiled and asked, "You sure Jan's not on a plane to New Zealand right now with a suitcase full of cash?"

Forsky grinned and said, "No, she's at home. We know her pretty well."

Rayburn remarked, "Talk to her. No promises, but if she

gives an indication that she would be willing to go for something like what we've talked about, then we need to move fast. Me, Joe, and my supervisor need to sit down with the woman and get started. I can't emphasize enough that it needs to done as soon as possible."

"We'll do it," Thompson said as the two agents got up to leave.

Thompson sat at the Captain's desk and called Jan Doxee. "Jan, can you come to the office now?"

"I'll be there in twenty minutes."

Forsky asked Thompson, "Will she go for the deal? Sounds pretty generous to me, IF she has the cash."

"What choice does she have? But, yeah, the cash may be the big issue. No telling what they'll assess on her or what she has," Thompson replied, clearly in the dark as to Jan's financial assets.

When Jan Doxee walked into the vice office, Forsky was at the far end of the room. She did not see him. He realized that he had not laid eyes on the woman in a couple of months, maybe longer. It had only been a few weeks since she had come home after her stay in the psychiatric treatment center. He was amazed at her stunning appearance. Laying off the vodka and cigarettes, sleeping at night and eating food had done wonders for Jan.

"Wade, how are you? You look very tired," she said.

He replied, "I am very tired. Are you ready to go over this, Jan?"

"You're just not one for small talk, are you, Wade?"

Forsky came to his partner's rescue when he approached her and said, "HI, Jan. I must say you look very nice. Must have something to do with your new lifestyle."

"Thank you, John. I don't want to sound vain, but I've also noticed some improvement. Yes, I owe it all to the healthy and righteous way I live my life now," she said with a grin, as

Thompson directed Jan and Forsky into the Captain's office.

"Jan, we just met with the FBI and IRS. We only hit the high points. Everyone's going to have to get approval to do what we discussed. And we may not be able, for one reason or another, to do the things we discussed. There are no promises, and you need to understand that now. There is also the possibility you'll face jail time. So what I'm going to mention right now is a very rough version of what we hope takes place. Everything hinges on your complete cooperation, of course," Thompson said.

"Wade, I appreciate your explaining everything, but I would appreciate it more if you would just get to the point."

Thompson continued, "That's where I'm headed, Jan. If you choose to cooperate, you will have to meet with the federal folks very soon. They will fill you in on the details. There will be some federal charges filed against Charles Western, and in all likelihood, against you. You would be THE witness against Charlie. If you and he were fifty-fifty partners, the feds, or us for that matter, probably wouldn't even consider this. No one would care what you had to say. Since you were a twenty percent partner, I think we're all willing to make a concession. However, there are some other significant considerations here, if you're to avoid jail."

"And just what might those considerations be?"

Thompson replied, "Of course, it goes without saying that you're finished in the prostitution business."

"I'm through with that. It's part of my therapy. There's no need for concern there."

"Good. Now the FBI and IRS are going to do their own investigation and we may assist them. Somehow it will be determined how much of your personal fortune was acquired with the ill-gotten gains from the agency and maybe from any separate prostitution work you did. We didn't discuss the latter, that's just supposition on my part," Thompson said.

Jan interrupted, "You may not believe this, but there hasn't been what you refer to as 'separate work' in years. When I tried to go to work for that flea-bitten escort service I called you about several months ago, that was the first time in a long time that I had even considered such a stunt. I had hit rock bottom at that point in my life. Depression, a yearning for youth, or just being a drunk - I don't know. I think I was losing my mind at that point."

Thompson again realized how little he knew about the woman whose every move he thought he was aware of. He thought she was still servicing old, rich guys. The truth be known, they were probably all dead or at least incapacitated to the point where sex was not a factor in what was left of their lives.

"Good. I'm glad you cleared that up. Jan, they will seize property, bank accounts, cash, and perhaps other assets. The IRS will also bill you for back taxes owed and I'm guessing you will have to pay that in cash right away or maybe face the jail time; I don't have any idea what that might be. As you can tell, I'm really not familiar with their procedures and fine details, but that should give you a general idea," Thompson related.

"I understand. Now, what do you all suggest I do?" she asked, unwavering in the calm and positive attitude of the new Jan Doxee.

Forsky said, "If I were you, I would call Joe Burrell first thing in the morning and arrange for a meeting. And I wouldn't make any large withdrawals from bank accounts for the time being. It would surprise me if the IRS doesn't put some sort of holds on your accounts very soon, but you can ask them about that."

"And don't talk to Charlie Western, his lawyer, or anyone else associated with the agency. In fact, have your phone number changed tomorrow," Thompson said.

Jan replied, "I've already thought about the phone, I'll do it. Write down the name and number of this FBI agent I'm to call. It may be understating things a little, but I would like to get this resolved as soon as possible."

Thompson wrote Joe Burrell's name and number on the back of a business card and handed it to Jan as she stood, preparing to leave.

With sudden tears in her eyes, she said to the detectives, "Thank you both so much. I'm not sure if I'm getting preferential treatment or not, but I appreciate your efforts regardless. I apologize for any embarrassment I may have caused. I assure you it wasn't intentional."

"Be sure and call Joe first thing tomorrow. He's sometimes hard to catch in the office after nine," Thompson said.

Jan's tear flow increased as she left the vice office.

"You think she has any money, Wade?" Forsky asked.

"I think she's got quite a bit, at least, to me it would be quite a bit. I'm not sure the IRS would call it that, though. We'll see soon enough."

Forsky said, "For now I guess we need to concentrate on the computer equipment and see what's there."

"Speaking of that, Talbert played with it last night before we unplugged everything. He said there were at least ten thousand clients in the files, and about ten percent of those are 'specialty' nuts. Everything is very organized and cataloged," Thompson replied.

"Great, I'm curious to look at it," Forsky said eagerly.

"Don't spend too much time looking at a computer screen, John. It'll make you think illogically," Thompson warned, dead serious, even though Forsky could never tell for sure.

"Sounds like another Thompson theory of questionable worth if you ask me. To change the subject, do you realize tomorrow's the first? This month has really flown by," Forsky remarked.

Thompson experienced exhaustion as he never had before. He did not know whether to sit and cry or take a nap. He wondered if either would make him feel any better.

Thompson replied, "John, I haven't mentioned this to anyone else, but this whole thing has been a bittersweet success at best. I went into that office in San Antonio last night with some very unrealistic expectations. I wanted to seize boxes of paperwork, ledgers, and note card files, just like we used to do. Instead, we get nothing produced with pen and ink on paper. What a letdown to load up a bunch of computer equipment and their magical plastic disks. How dull can things get? Right after that, Jan drops her bombshell on my bald noggin. It was too much. I can't do this anymore. I'm just no longer suited for the work. Things are changing with this new chief and a lot of the changes are not for the better, they're for the sake of change alone. Police work is becoming a secondary issue with the department. Oh, it will probably get back to normal after the citizens become vocal because the crime rate has skyrocketed. The chief will be replaced, but by then no one will know how to do real police work because the concept hasn't been practiced in so long."

"For someone as optimistic as you've been forever, I can't believe I'm hearing this," Forsky said.

Thompson remarked, "I'm going to retire in the next month or two. I'm selling my house and moving to one of the Rocky Mountain states; I'll go into the guide and outfitting business. I'm so tired of this work, I'm not sure I'll be able to continue with this investigation. I feel like drinkin' malts until I leave."

"Wade, that's kind of a bombshell in itself. Don't worry about the investigation, we're ninety-nine percent through with it. I can take care of what's left. If you want to drink malts for the next month or so, be my guest! I hate to say this, but I think you might deserve it," Forsky said.

"Well, John, you may think I'm losing my mind, but I appreciate you listening to my tale of woe. There's one other thing…," Thompson said.

Forsky said, "I already know what it is: 'Don't mention this to anyone.' You're going to do a retirement letter at the last minute, no party, no happy hour, and most importantly, no farewell. You'll just leave work one day, never to return. Wade, it's not right to treat people you've known for thirty years like that, but that's your business."

Thompson dragged himself to the office at ten A.M. the next day. He was still tired and wondered if he would ever again feel rested. Forsky was reading a newspaper. As usual, he looked as if he had had twelve hours sleep.

"Wade, the IRS man called a few minutes ago. Jan called Joe Burrell at eight and he got in touch with Oscar Rayburn. Anyway, she's been at Oscar's office since nine. Neither one of these guys has had a chance to talk with their supervisors, but they both figured if she's willing to talk, they could get with their bosses later," Forsky said.

"I've never seen the federal government move at such lightning speed, but that's good," Thompson replied.

Forsky continued, "Oscar Rayburn and a helper or two need to go through all those computer disks. To avoid chain of custody problems, they're not going to take anything out of the property room. They'll go through everything there and copy the disks, too. One of us will have to be there with them when they do it. It may take a couple of weeks. Right now the FBI and IRS will be interviewing Jan in the mornings, then work at the property room in the afternoons."

Thompson replied, "That's fine. If you want to finish the investigation, I'll be happy to sit at the property room with them. I can catch up on some reading."

"That's what I was thinking. I figured you'd like that idea. They intend to start after lunch today, or as soon as they finish the interview with Jan. Why don't you call Oscar Rayburn?" Forsky suggested.

Thompson replied, "I'll do that now."

"Could you meet us at one-thirty at your property room?"

the eager IRS agent asked Thompson.

"Yeah, be glad to. Oscar, have you already gotten an okay from your boss on this?" Thompson asked.

"Sort of. Everything has happened so fast. We took a break during the interview and I gave my boss a thumbnail sketch. He's mulling it over, but he'll go for it," Rayburn said with confidence.

Thompson replied, "My boss, Tal Sanderson, is at the property room now looking through that stuff. He may be able to save you all a lot of time. He's become pretty familiar with everything."

Thompson's spirit was livening up some. He needed to make a quick stop at his home to pick up reading material. It would keep him occupied while everyone else poured over the mystical disks.

CHAPTER 35

Thompson had requested and received information on a couple of guide and outfitting schools several months previous as a matter of curiosity. They were expensive, month-long schools, but were a shortcut approach to learning the business. At one time, Thompson had considered not retiring and just using thirty days of his accumulated vacation leave to attend a school.

The big drawback to learning anything in this manner, at least for Thompson, was that these were schools and he preferred a less formal atmosphere for learning. If the material could not be self-taught, the method Thompson most favored, then on-the-job training would be the next best way. As an Eagle Scout, he was already well versed in much of the curriculum. Thompson had hunted and spent a lot of time in the outdoors since his early teens. Few could match his skill at outdoor lore, but his weaknesses were in horsemanship and business acumen. Still, he needed to look over the literature before making any important decisions.

Thompson was the last of the group to arrive at the property room. The IRS personnel were well armed with laptop computer rigs, portable printers, and all the necessary debris that accompanies such contrivances. Tal Sanderson had been there since early morning and had taken one quick break to pick up a sandwich for lunch. As it turned out, Sanderson's efforts did save the IRS at least a couple of days' work. He had printed close to two hundred pages of pertinent material.

Even experienced vice cops could not venture a guess as to what the client list of this, the largest escort service in existence, would be worth to others in the business. That's not even to mention the separate listing of 'specialty' clients that would indeed be priceless. For contemporary gangsters, wannabe mobsters, and anyone else in the blackmail and shakedown business the list would be the same as ready cash. Over the course of the next two weeks, Thompson would take breaks from his reading and go through the files that had been printed. Politicians, ministers, educators, physicians, attorneys, police officials, actors, celebrities, prominent businessmen, and foreign dignitaries were all represented in the files. And these were just the names that Thompson, who was not particularly up on current events, recognized.

"Oscar, how did Jan do this morning? She was helpful, right?" Thompson asked.

The IRS agent replied, "Very helpful. I think she'd like to wrap this up quicker than we would. She gave us quite a few pointers to save time when we get into the computer, but we still have to look at everything."

"How long will your part of the investigation take?" Thompson inquired.

"Joe Burrell and I talked about that this morning. With Jan's continued cooperation, we're figuring on no more than thirty days. Then we'll put our cases and paperwork together. And, of course, it's aside from the investigation itself, but I explained to Jan she would have to testify against Western if this goes to trial. She understands."

"Wade, from what I can tell, every dollar Charlie Western and Jan made in the last five years is accounted for in these computer files. All overhead expenses like rent, advertising, salaries, phone bills, are listed. It looks to me like Western actually entered most, if not all, of that information himself. No one tried to hide anything," Sanderson said.

"Good work," Thompson said with some difficulty. His boss deserved praise for his efforts, but he detested having to give credit to the efficiency of a machine in the same breath. In effect, the sincerity that he wanted to depict was not there. During the days when they seized real paperwork, it was never organized to perfection as this material was. In fact, Thompson was unable to recall making a seizure of records that was ever in anything more than a remote semblance of order. Something was always missing. If the material was presented as evidence in a formal courtroom setting, it was often a mess. Fortunately, convictions in these cases were easily obtained and not often dependent on seized records. Perhaps there was something to this dull world of computer technology after all, he thought.

Joe Burrell arrived at the property room. He pulled a chair alongside Tal Sanderson and began looking through a stack of papers the sergeant had printed. After a minute, Burrell said, "Wade, Charlie Western's attorney, a fellow named Harry Neiman, called earlier. He's pretty upset because the Harris County judge won't back down on Western being held without bond. I told him it's still a state case at this time and we had no jurisdiction, so he'll be calling you guys soon. Reading between the lines, they're going to plead. He all but said Western couldn't handle a trial. I really think Neiman would like to dump this case."

Thompson replied, "I've talked to Neiman once, and I'll talk to him again if he calls, but I can't help the man."

Thompson located a phone that was away from the group so he could call Jan Doxee. He was curious about her impression of Oscar Rayburn.

"Jan, I understand you were at the IRS this morning. How did everything go?"

"Very well, thank you. I will be meeting with Oscar Rayburn and/or Joe Burrell every morning for the next few weeks. Oscar is pleasant to work with. Wade, I've become quite concerned about my assets. Also, there's something I mentioned to Oscar today that I've never told you about. It's not something I've hidden, there was just never a reason to bring it up. Twenty years ago, I received an inheritance from my grandmother's estate. The grandkids were left with several hundred acres of rural property. When it sold, we each netted about $110,000. A little of mine went into a savings account. On my father's advice, I bought a piece of commercial property with the remainder. Presently, I own a number of parcels of commercial property. They have all appreciated in value a considerable amount. It's true most everything was purchased with income from the escort service. I hope the government can separate things for their purpose. I still have that first property I bought with the inheritance," Jan said.

Thompson replied, "I wouldn't be too concerned with that. Oscar can come up with an accurate accounting. Have you been paying income tax at all?"

"You think I'm a criminal? Sure, I've paid income tax, at least some of it. I've listed my occupation as investor for years. I'll have you know I declared an income of $150,000 last year and paid taxes on that amount. Granted, my income was somewhat greater than that, but I'm not exactly a deadbeat," she remarked.

"Okay, just curious. I've got to go now," Thompson said.

Jan replied, "You always, do. Bye."

The days passed at a speedy pace as Thompson enjoyed his new routine. Every day after lunch, he met with the federal agents at the police property room. They knew what they were doing and seemed to be very good at it. No real effort was required on his part. Thompson had contacted several realtors regarding the sale of his home. He finally hired one. The asking price was seven times what he and his wife had paid for the house. Of course, half would go to his wife when the house sold, but each of them would realize a nice profit.

Thompson also made a decision on the guide and outfitting project. Fall hunting season would begin in the next couple of months. He would place a 'job wanted' advertisement in the classified section of a number of newspapers that had distribution near prime hunting areas in the Rocky Mountain states. He would be willing to work the entire season for no pay, if necessary, just to become familiar with the business. For the long and hard hours involved, such businesses did not pay much anyway and Thompson did not need the pittance of an income. He reasoned that any reputable outfitter would be glad to have a solid, dependable worker like him in their employ, even if he did not know the business. The future was beginning to look bright for the worn-out vice detective.

One morning at the office, Thompson told Forsky about placing his home on the market and advertising for work.

Forsky looked at his partner in amazement and said, "You're really serious about all this, aren't you? I suppose this is classified information like your impending retirement, right?

"Definitely, John. It's not for broadcast."

"Well, let me tell you something. I don't intend to try and adjust to the quirks and eccentricities of a new partner. You're forcing me to retire as well. Oh, I'll stick around three or four months, then I'm moving to east Texas to start a fishing guide service. I'll be in business by next spring. I'll do as much tournament fishing as I can, too. I know you can't tell a bass from a carp, but I'll take you on a first-class fishing trip if you ever come back to Texas. In return, I expect a free occasional elk hunt in the mountains, all amenities included, of course, and I don't tip," Forsky said.

Thompson was enjoying the conversation and asked, "I presume this is all confidential?"

"You presume wrong. Tell anyone you like. I'm even going to take time to say goodbye to my friends and have a real retirement party, unlike some anti-social character," Forsky replied, a ringing phone interrupted the partners' conversation.

"Vice, Thompson."

Jan Doxee said, "Wade, I've been threatened."

"Who threatened you?" he asked, not surprised.

She replied, "That old bastard, Rufus Mathison; in fact, the creep's called twice."

"I thought you were getting a new phone number," Thompson said, wondering why she had not already taken care of it.

Jan replied, "I am, but they won't be out until late this afternoon. I'm at the FBI office. Joe Burrell suggested I let you know about Rufus. I've known him a long time, Wade. The guy's got quite a past and I think he could be dangerous."

"What did Rufus say, Jan?"

She replied, "He told me if I didn't hire a real good attorney for him that I would have some serious regrets. The next time he called he said the same thing and added that he had plenty of rough friends that weren't in jail and I needed to remember that."

"There's no way Rufus can get out of jail and I doubt he's got one friend, let alone plenty of them. But, let's not take any chances. Is there someplace you can stay for a while?" Thompson asked.

She replied, "I still have two weeks or so of these daily interviews. I could stay in downtown hotels that long. You want to come and protect me? I'm really very, very frightened, Wade," she said in an obvious jesting tone, hoping he would give in.

"No, I don't want to protect you and you don't sound frightened. Jan, you've lived in that apartment a long time. Have you considered a permanent move? If you plan to stay in Dallas, move to another part of town," Thompson suggested.

"After Rufus called the first time, I thought about moving. However, I decided that if I move at all, I'll leave Dallas. You wouldn't want to go with me, would you?"

"No, Jan, I wouldn't."

She said, "Just thought I would ask. Now, it's my turn to say I'm busy and I have to go. These men are waiting on me.

Goodbye."

"Wade, we've come up with some dollar figures here that you might find of interest," Oscar Rayburn said as Thompson arrived at the property room for the afternoon session.

The IRS agent and Joe Burrell had computer printouts covering every square inch of a twelve-foot-long folding table.

As he pointed to a figure in large and bold print, Rayburn told Thompson, "This is the agency's gross income for the sixty-two months it was in business."

As Thompson fumbled in an attempt to put on his store-bought reading glasses, Rayburn remarked, "We'll round it to an even fifty-four million for our purpose today."

"Fifty-four million dollars! Are you sure?" Thompson gasped in disbelief.

"It's at least that. In theory, some income could have been omitted from the records. I doubt that happened, though. This was all professionally prepared, probably by Western himself," Oscar said.

Thompson replied, "I knew they did rather well, but I had no idea they did that well. I have to call Forsky and tell him. He won't believe this."

"Before you do that, you need to look at these other figures," Joe Burrell said.

Rayburn interjected, "We have everything broken down by year and we'll make copies of everything for you. For now, though, let's hit the high points. Of the fifty-four million total, almost twelve million was expended on overhead. In the business world, that's not much. It's indicative of competent, cost-conscious management, that sort of thing. It's also apparent that Jan Doxee took Charlie Western's word for everything and never questioned his bookkeeping."

"Why do you say that?" Thompson asked.

Rayburn continued, "Because the so-called eighty-twenty

split was actually ninety-ten from the very beginning, in Charlie's favor, of course. It was intentional and to the penny, not just a little fudging here and there. She never knew."

"Okay, and I'm not about to mention that to her and I would suggest no one else does unless she makes an inquiry," Thompson recommended.

"Alright. Wade, look at this," Joe Burrell said as he pointed with a pencil to the bottom of a page. "After expenses, net income of the business was $42,000,000. Western pocketed $37.8 million. Jan wound up with $4.2 million. As you can see in the yearly breakdown, their income grew dramatically after the first two years."

"Does Jan know what her income has been since she's been in cahoots with Western?" Thompson asked.

Rayburn answered, "Not at all."

"What will she owe?" Thompson inquired.

Rayburn replied, "That's a little more complicated. It will be a week or so before we know for sure. With penalties, accrued interest, and so forth, it's going to be a quite a bit."

Thompson was uncomfortable with the vagueness of relative terms. 'Quite a bit' meant nothing to him; he much preferred real numbers. It would have to do for the time being, however. Had Oscar had any idea as to an approximate figure, he would have told the detective.

Joe Burrell said, "In addition, the government will seize several parcels of commercial real estate, nine, I believe, located across the country. Jan said she wouldn't contest anything, so it will make our job easier. There are three properties she will maintain ownership of, unless she has difficulty coming up with the IRS settlement. If that happens, those three will be subject to forfeiture."

"What about Western?" Thompson asked.

Rayburn smiled and said, "That's a different story. Jan is a pauper in comparison to Charles Western. He owns dozens of very expensive properties, many of them in Houston and New Orleans. The real estate holdings alone are probably worth more than $125 million. He has numerous other investments and I'm sure we haven't uncovered everything at this point. For now, let's just say his situation is far more complicated than Jan's."

    Thompson was out of reading material for the afternoon property room session. This would be the day to research the placement of ads for guide and outfitting work. It was after four when the feds left the property room. Thompson had enough time to go by a large downtown newsstand and purchase papers from Denver, Cheyenne, Albuquerque, and Salt Lake City. After that, he returned to the office and made a list of more than twenty smaller cities that were large enough to have at least a weekly newspaper. He would send letters to the chambers of commerce in these towns and request complimentary brochures, then prepare ads to place in these small publications as well as the big-city editions. That would take up all of the next afternoon.

CHAPTER 36

Thompson could do no police work. He still wondered whether this syndrome was a result of fatigue, burnout, laziness, a combination of the three, or something else altogether. Every time he gave the matter some thought, he always came to the same conclusion. The cause did not matter. He just knew he had to get out of police work for the condition to subside. The few minutes he had spent with Oscar Rayburn and Joe Burrell as they went over earning figures of the escort service had left Thompson exhausted.

The next morning, during a break in her daily routine with the federal agents, Jan Doxee called Thompson. He was at the office.

"Wade, I called to inform you of an important and difficult decision I made last night," she said.

Thompson felt another bout of exhaustion overpowering him as he asked, "What decision?"

"I'll be through with this morning ritual in about a week. You know I've been staying in a hotel. This afternoon, I'm going to call about having my furnishings and belongings put in storage for awhile. I'll be going home for a few days. After that, I can't tell you where I'm going because I don't know right now," she said.

Thompson replied, "Jan, that's probably a very good idea, but we're going to have to be able to get in touch with you. Have you talked to Joe Burrell and Oscar Rayburn about this? I'm not so sure they'll allow it."

"They will, but let me explain something to you. I'm

sure you will get a more detailed and perhaps more accurate explanation from them, however. Anyway, they are going to be filing some sort of charges or cases or something against me in the next few days. It's a formality, as I understand it, but everything will be fine as long as I agree to cooperate as a witness against Charlie Western, just as I've been doing. In addition, I've got to pay the back taxes and interest and penalties and give up the real estate and cash. Then, when I'm a poor person, living on the street and peeing in the gutter, the charges against me will be dropped. Oh yeah, you won't believe this, Wade, but I got a cell phone yesterday. I guess I'm in step with the modern world. I'll give you the number, but I'll have to look in my purse."

"I'll see Oscar and Joe this afternoon. I'll talk to them about it. I hope you're still doing alright. Let me know if you need anything," Thompson said.

"I'm not craving a double vodka, if that's your implication," she said with that Thompson-induced note of irritation in her voice. "I'm fine, Wade please believe that. If I'm not fine, I'll let you know right away. Okay?"

"Okay," Thompson said, embarrassed.

In a sense, Thompson was glad Jan was leaving. He worried about her, however. Perhaps her mental health and well being were not nearly as fragile as Thompson had thought. Would she be okay? He wanted to think so. He knew he would miss Jan, but he could never tell her that.

Over the years, a strong, although unusual, relationship had developed between the two. She needed his stable influence; he needed her logical mind. Ultimate happiness for either seemed impossible. When such a thought crossed Thompson's mind, however, he attempted to quickly dismiss it. He felt Jan had resigned herself to the fact that he would remain relentless in his perpetual distance from her. Now, unbeknownst to the woman, Thompson was beginning to see her in a different light. Jan was more attractive than ever. She was sober. She was no longer whoring. She had always been intelligent. For Thompson to reveal these thoughts to Jan or anyone else was unthinkable. He knew better than to dwell on them. Like everything else in his life, he was convinced that if he ignored the situation long enough, it would vanish altogether. At least, that is what he told himself. His flawed thinking process was acting up again.

Forsky said, "Wade, while you were on the phone your realtor called. You need to call him right away."

"Thanks, John. Did he sell my house?" Thompson asked.

Forsky replied, "None of my business. I didn't ask. But, I think he might have gotten a good offer. He's real excited."

The realtor said, "Mr. Thompson, thanks for calling back so soon. I know this is short notice, but is there anyway you can meet me at your home in the next half-hour?"

"I suppose I could if it's urgent. Did someone make a decent offer?"

The young agent, barely able to control his enthusiasm said, "Yes, within $2500.00 of the asking price, a cash deal. They would like possession within two weeks, pending an inspection. I'm at your house and they are in the back yard, but they will be leaving soon."

"Whoa! Two weeks? Why so soon?" Thompson inquired.

The youngster replied, "Both husband and wife work for the same company. They are being transferred to Dallas and don't want to rent a place now and then have to move again when they buy a house."

"I suppose that makes sense. I'll be there in fifteen minutes," Thompson said.

Forsky asked, "Was I right?"

"I hope so, John. I have to meet the kid now. See you tomorrow."

Thompson's house had been on the market for two weeks. Maybe a dozen people had looked at it, but not one had been interested to the point of making an offer. When Thompson got home, the realtor had forms spread out on the living room coffee table.

"What's all this?" Thompson asked the young man who might have been twenty-five.

He answered, "These require your signature if you wish to accept the offer and the terms as outlined on page one."

"Well, I'm not going to read all that, but I'll accept the offer," Thompson said.

As he put his signature on a myriad of forms, Thompson thought about how a simple matter like accepting an offer had been transformed into an incredibly complicated affair, and a needless one at that. Sort of like a title company, he reasoned. What function do they perform that people really need or can't do for themselves? Thompson knew the answer, but he also knew folks had been led to believe their questionable services were indispensable. He quickly turned away from such practical thoughts when he realized they were stirring around in his head. They only upset him. He signed all the papers and handed them to the realtor.

The agent said, "Thank you, Mr. Thompson. I'll be meeting with the client tonight. They will also have to sign some forms and put earnest money in an escrow account. It will be up to them to have the house inspected, probably within five working days."

Thompson had quickly grown weary of the house sale rigmarole. He told the agent, "I'd like to say call me when you have my check ready, but I know that's not in keeping with the perpetuated complex spirit of the game."

He smiled and told Thompson, "I never said this would be a painless experience. I have to call your wife now and get her okay on this. You'll hear from me in the next day or so."

"Okay, thanks," Thompson said, glad this phase was over. The episode had been about as pleasant as hemorrhoid surgery.

The next several days at the property room passed quietly. Joe Burrell and Oscar Rayburn and his assistants were still immersed in their work with the computer disks and the numbers. Thompson answered an occasional question, but for the most part, he read.

The final day at the property room came. Joe and Oscar, less the assistants, met Thompson and said they would be finished within a couple of hours. Tomorrow would be their final interview with Jan Doxee, at least for the near future.

Thompson thought about the many things that were coming to a sudden close. The 'sudden' was not in the literal sense but 'sudden' in that it was all happening much too quickly for Thompson's comfort. His career, Forsky's career, even Jan's career, were to be no more as they had been. The case was over, or at least the ride was, and the ride had always been the most enjoyable part of any investigation. Thompson's house was probably sold and he would soon be homeless. His wife was gone. Changes, many changes. All were pleasure-coupled-with-pain experiences.

"One more thing, Wade. We have the final figures for Jan Doxee and Charles Western. You'll be interested in this," Oscar Rayburn said as he handed Thompson a manila folder containing page after page of figures.

Thompson thumbed through the material, wanting to display an interest that was just not there. Oscar sensed the disinterest and said, "Don't worry about all that stuff in front, go to the last two pages."

Thompson took the advice and found the only numbers that mattered to him. Charles Western would forfeit twenty-two pieces of commercial real estate valued at more than $70,000,000. In addition, he owed the IRS almost $18,000,000. Should he be unable to pay his bill, other properties owned by Western could be seized. While CWA, Inc. would likely go untouched, the government placed a value of twenty million on it. This included the business and the real estate.

Jan Doxee would forfeit nine commercial properties worth close to six million. In addition, she would owe the IRS 1.4 million or they would seize her remaining pieces of property valued at about the amount owed.

"Does Jan have that kind of cash? Does anyone have that much cash?" Thompson asked Rayburn.

The IRS agent replied, "You'd be surprised, Wade. As for Jan, though, she told us this morning that she didn't know if she could pay the assessment. She'll have thirty days to come up with the funds. After that, we begin our forfeiture paperwork."

"Well, that's her problem, not mine. I suppose I shouldn't concern myself with it," Thompson said in an attempt to convince himself.

CHAPTER 37

Thompson returned to the office to find that Captain Arlie Holland had been transferred, compliments of the new chief. Arlie had been given an obscure assignment that entailed few duties. It was a shameful act, since no other captain in the department could handle the vice job as well as Holland had. In a twist of irony, Lt. Pricklee was named as Holland' replacement. Pricklee may have lacked competence and knowledge of police work, but he was friendly with the chief and a 'yes' man. With the new command staff, such traits were recognized as important assets. Something else had just ended, Thompson thought.

Jan Doxee would be gone in the next few days. Thompson's house passed inspection and he would have to begin packing soon. His wife, Rose, took almost nothing when she left. Thompson would have to hire someone to move and store all the furniture and large items. When the time came for him to leave, he would need little until he settled somewhere. He was anxious for that moment to come. He wanted to leave, but he knew it would be difficult.

Forsky cornered Thompson in Arlie Holland's vacant office and said, "I don't mean to interfere with your plans, but retirement red tape isn't geared for someone with your simplistic ways. Have you given any thought to turning in your equipment, the personnel interview, pension board, and other prerequisites? Wade, you can't come in one morning, expect to get all that done by noon, then leave forever. Some of these things need to be done two weeks in advance."

"I think I'll leave next Friday. That'll give me seven working days which should be plenty of time, don't you think?"

Forsky replied, "Well, you better get on it right away. You're going to have to tell someone whether you want to or not."

"Okay. Today I'll call the pension office, personnel, tell Tal Sanderson, and go to the quartermaster and turn in my stuff," Thompson said as he left the captain's office and approached his locker. Thompson had little in the way of department-issued property to turn in. His pistol belonged to him. Handcuffs, several uniforms, a bulletproof vest, a raincoat, and a nightstick did not.

Oh, that nightstick. He never did learn the proper textbook method for using that excuse for a weapon. He thought about how he always dreaded the periodic training session on the use of the stick. The department instructors gave trainees enough instruction in the use of the club to be confusing and little else, Thompson had always thought. He knew if he ever had to depend on nothing but a wooden club for defensive purposes, he could probably handle himself at least as well as anyone who could use the contraption gracefully.

He smiled at the irony as he placed everything in an empty box once containing a half-dozen life-sized, inflatable rubber women seized at an adult bookstore.

When he arrived at the quartermaster unit, the clerk refused to deal with Thompson because he had not made an appointment. Thompson was not going to make another trip, however. He taped up the box containing the police department belongings. He wrote his name on it and sat it behind the counter.

The clerk looked at Thompson with disbelief and said with an air of authority, "I can't accept that."

"Maybe not, but perhaps someone else around here can. You all can mail me a receipt if you don't want to write one up now. I trust you," Thompson said.

As Thompson started to walk out the door, the irritated clerk said, "Wait a minute."

Thompson stopped and turned to observe the clerk huff as he retrieved the detective's city-issued equipment file. Within seconds, he gave Thompson an illegible receipt. The retirement process had to be at least somewhat agonizing, rather like life in general. There was always someone around to guarantee that, but Thompson encountered no more resistance during the rest of the day.

CHAPTER 38

He returned to the office just before quitting time. Sgt. Tal Sanderson was at his desk reading the paper, his closed briefcase on top of the desk. He was ready to leave for the day as Thompson stuck his head in the door.

"Talbert, got a minute?"

"Sure, come on in, Wade."

"I want to let you know I'm retiring next Friday," Thompson said, wondering how his boss would react.

Sanderson replied, "I kind of figured you were. I just didn't know the exact date."

"How did you know?" Thompson asked.

The sergeant said, "You've been a million miles away since the night we hit the phone center in San Antonio. I saw that was some sort of turning point for you. Believe me when I say I understand. I know you're ready. I think we all arrive at some juncture where we just can't do this anymore. When it ceases to be enjoyable, that's the time to get out."

"Tal, I guess I should have said something sooner. You'll have to get a replacement and all," Thompson said.

Sanderson replied, "Don't let that worry you. It's not your problem. To bare my soul a bit, I've given retirement some very serious thought myself during the past two weeks. Too many changes around this place lately, and I'm not sure any of them are for the better."

"It's after six, let's go home. We can talk about this on the way to the parking lot," Thompson suggested.

As they walked out of the building, Sanderson said, "Let me guess. You've told no one about this except John Forsky and you swore him to secrecy. You wouldn't think of having a retirement party. You'll just leave work next Friday and never return. Am I right?"

"You know me pretty well, Tal," Thompson said, grinning.

Sanderson replied, "After twenty years in vice together, I hope I know you pretty well. See you tomorrow."

Sanderson drove away. Thompson sat in his own car, but did not start the engine right away. Instead, he listened to a Mills' Brothers tape and thought about Sanderson leaving, too. Something else would end. Or would it? They had been very good friends for many years. There was no reason why that had to change.

CHAPTER 39

Next day, Thompson found Forsky wrapping up the final details of the investigation. Soon, Joe Burrell would be filing federally on Charlie Western, Jan Doxee, and Rufus Mathison. Since the escort service had operated on a nationwide basis, several federal statutes had been violated. Joe would give the cases to an Assistant United States Attorney for prosecution.

Harry Neiman, Charlie Western's lawyer, had already indicated his client would plead guilty in exchange for a lesser sentence than what he would receive if he was tried and found guilty. He was still facing several years in jail, not to mention forfeiting much of his real estate holdings and paying the huge IRS assessment and penalties for back taxes.

Federal penalties were generally much harsher than state chastiscments. Jan's federal cases would ultimately be dismissed due to her cooperation and testimony against Western. However, she still had the IRS assessment and penalties to contend with and the loss of almost all her property and cash. Rufus Mathison's violation of his lifetime parole would keep him incarcerated for the rest of his natural life, painted toenails and all.

Harry Neiman would do anything in his power to rush Western's guilty plea. He was most anxious to be finished with this client.

No part of the investigation, its aftermath, or the outcome held any interest for Thompson now. He was not even sure if he saw the conclusion of the initial investigation as an accomplishment. It was more like a game won, as in a sporting event. With his disinterest in organized sports, he questioned the real worth of any athletic victory. He always concluded that it is only a game and nothing of any great significance.

"Mr. Thompson," the creaky male voice said, "this is Trotter Langley in Salmon, Idaho. I read you ad. You still looking for work?"

An excited Thompson replied, "Yes sir, I am. Do you have something for me?"

"I just might. I have four good guides that have been with me for a while, but I'd like to hire one more. My fellows could train a new man this season and he could be pretty much on his own by next year," Trotter Langley said.

At first, Thompson was unsure how to respond. The call had taken him by surprise, but he responded, "That sounds good, Mr. Langley. When would you need someone? I'll be available next week."

"We're leaving in the morning for the mountains. We'll be setting up camps for about two weeks, then we'll come back to Salmon, load up supplies, and be off again. It'll be about three weeks before I can use you," the old man said.

Thompson replied, "Good, that gives me some time for thought. I appreciate you calling me, but I can't make a decision right this minute. I hope you understand."

"Sure, sure, I understand. I'll give you my home number. You just leave a message with my wife. I check in with her every day. I have a cell phone, but I don't turn it on except for an hour or two a day when I'm in the mountains," Langley said.

It was difficult for Thompson to picture the old man on horseback in a remote part of the country, yet equipped with the latest in modern communication technology. He had to give this offer much serious thought. What about others who may call? He realized now that he was not sure how to evaluate these potential employers based on a phone call. He would be much more comfortable with a face-to-face interview. It was a unique predicament to be in while searching for employment. In one sense, Thompson would be conducting the interview.

"Well, you got a job?" Forsky asked in his Forsky way.

"Got an offer, at least...in Salmon, Idaho."

"Don't be like a street whore and accept the first offer," Forsky suggested as he looked down toward his paperwork.

Thompson was preoccupied and paid no attention to Forsky's remark as he said, "John, I've got some things to do, but I'll be back here by five."

"Fine," Forsky said without looking up or missing a stroke with his pen.

When Thompson returned to the office, Forsky waved a small piece of paper and said, "Come here, Wade."

Thompson approached his partner, extended his hand, and said, "A message?"

Forsky handed it to him and replied, "This guy's from Wardlaw, Wyoming. I'll bet I know why he called."

"Bob Tucker, may I help you?" the voice answered.

"Wade Thompson, Bob, returning your call."

"Wade, if you're still looking for work, I may be able to help you out," Tucker said in a voice clear and distinct, like a news commentator.

Trying to sound self-assured, Thompson replied, "Yes, but I'm already considering an offer."

"Can you fax or mail a resume to me? I'll look it over and we'll go from there," Tucker said, ignoring Thompson's comment about the first job offer.

Thompson said, "Give me your fax number, Bob. I'll send my resume in the next few minutes."

"Okay. I'll call after I review it. Will you be at your home number tonight?" Bob Tucker asked.

"Yes, I'm usually home by six-thirty."

Bob Tucker called Thompson's home before seven and

said, "Wade, your resume is fine. Can you be here next week? We need to sit and discuss this," Tucker said.

Thompson replied, "Bob, you do realize I have no experience, it's just something I've wanted to do for a long time."

"I've been in the guide and outfitting business off and on for thirty years and I've hired and fired lots of folks. You're work record and stability are more important to me than experience. I can teach you everything you need to know about the business if you're willing to learn. My guess is that you want to learn. Come up next week. I promise you won't regret making the trip," Tucker said.

Thompson replied, "I don't think you'd take no for an answer, so I'll say okay. I'm closing on a house sale on Monday. I could leave Tuesday."

"You can fly from Dallas to Cheyenne. There is one commuter flight daily from Cheyenne to several places, including Wardlaw. Unless they've changed schedule, the commuter plane leaves Cheyenne around noon, our time. After you've made your arrangements, call me and I'll pick you up at the Wardlaw airport," Tucker said.

With some hesitation, Thompson said, "Alright, I'll get on it and let you know something."

Once again, things were moving much too fast for Thompson's comfort with decision making. He made the necessary calls. He would leave Dallas / Fort Worth International Airport at 8:00 A.M. Tuesday. He would arrive in Cheyenne with adequate time to catch the commuter flight to Wardlaw at 11:50 A.M. Bob Tucker would meet him at the small airport at 1:30 P.M.

Friday was Thompson's last day at work. It began quietly and ended that way, predictably, as Thompson preferred. For the last time in his law enforcement career, Thompson had lunch with Sanderson and Forsky.

As they finished their meal, Tal Sanderson remarked, "You won't find good Tex-Mex like this where you're going, Wade. You do realize that, don't you?"

Before Thompson could reply, Forsky commented, "That's right. Those people up there eat dull food like fried otter and boiled potatoes. The strongest seasonings they use are salt and black pepper, and very light on the pepper."

"I can make do and I'll come back here on occasion anyway," Thompson said, enjoying their company.

Sanderson asked, "When will you be back from your trip? We can get together for some drinks and celebrate your new career."

"I'll be back late next week. I'll call you," Thompson said.

Forsky replied, "No, we'll call you. Plan on Friday night. Have you used your new cell phone yet?"

"No, but I do turn it on sometimes," Thompson said.

Forsky remarked, "You're the only customer they've got on the ten-minute-per-month plan and you'll never use all those minutes."

Thompson had purchased the phone a week earlier. With his soon-to-be homelessness and roaming through the Rockies, he gave in to the technology temptation. He was still unconvinced the purchase was a wise decision, despite Forsky's urging.

Thompson said, "I've endured all the personal affronts I can stand for one day. I think I'll leave work a little early today if it's okay with you, Tal."

"I wasn't planning on giving you any assignments this afternoon," Sanderson replied, grinning.

Thompson stood up and said, "I enjoyed the lunch, thank you both. I'll see you guys next week." He knew they were not ready to leave. He could walk out alone. He was not sure why he had to have it that way, but he knew he did. Forsky and Sanderson would understand.

CHAPTER 40

At ten Monday morning, Thompson arrived at the title company office for the closing formalities on the sale of his home. Everyone, the lawyer representing Rose Thompson, the boy real estate agent, and the title company woman in charge of the shakedown were seated around a conference table staring at one another and waiting on him. The proceedings lasted all of fifteen minutes. When everything was completed, customary fake pleasantries and insincere handshakes were exchanged. The group left, except for Thompson. He had been too embarrassed to ask in front of the others, but he wanted to know where his check was.

The title company woman was almost out the door when she noticed Thompson, still seated.

"Mr. Thompson, is there something else?" the woman said, her voice exuding arrogance to the point it filled the room and oozed out the door.

"Yes, I was wondering about my check."

"No check. The money will be deposited in your account within twenty-four hours. I thought you were aware of that," she remarked as if Thompson were a complete dunce and she had no time to deal with stupid people.

He replied, "I had no idea. No one mentioned that to me. I'll be out of town tomorrow and I'd like to have the check today."

He realized he did not really have to have the check today, and had the woman been pleasant he would have left it at that. She was so obnoxious, however, he felt not just a desire, but a duty to become a huge thorn in her side. She reminded him of a certain type of person a cop might occasionally stop for a traffic violation. The officer's intention is to release the driver with only a verbal reminder, too mild to be referred to as even a warning or reprimand. The violator, however, had an unbridled compulsion to display such a high level of despicability that it became apparent to the officer that the person was actually crying out in a loud voice for one or more traffic tickets. Consequently, the police officer was always very obliging to the needs of the person.

"We're not set up to handle things as you wish," the pudgy title company lady remarked.

Not believing this was happening, Thompson said, "Someone owes me $125,000. At this point, I'm not really sure who that someone is, but I think you can find out. I'll leave when you present me with a check."

Realizing her rotten disposition would be ineffective in this instance, the woman only huffed and disappeared into a hallway. Within thirty minutes, she returned to the reception area and handed Thompson a check. She had nothing to say, only a hateful look on that chubby little face.

Thompson had nothing to say to her, either. As he left the title company, he wondered why there are so many people in the world who feel an undying obligation to make things unpleasant and difficult for others. To make things worse, he realized that for a moment he had become one of them.

CHAPTER 41

The turbo-prop commuter plane descended from the high clouds toward the tiny airport at Wardlaw, Wyoming. Thompson was amazed at how short the strip was in comparison to the one he had left in Dallas a few hours earlier. When the aircraft touched down, the sensation of slowing to a stop was vivid in Thompson's imagination. He pictured the pilot standing frantically with both feet on the brakes, the nose of the plane slightly abrading the runway's concrete due to the tremendous compression of the landing gear.

There was a sort of terminal, or at least a building just off the runway, some seventy-five yards from the nearest wingtip of the plane. A welded tubular steel staircase in bad need of a paint job was mounted on the bed of an old Ford pickup that had a smoky exhaust. The driver of the truck pulled alongside the aircraft. A third of the twenty-odd passengers departed. Thompson found the crudeness of the setting very much offset by its refreshing simplicity and ease of access.

Those persons picking up passengers had parked their vehicles on the edge of the airstrip, between the building and the plane. Airport security wasn't a big issue at the Wardlaw Municipal, nor did it need to be, another reinvigorating indication that life was a little different here than in the big city.

Thompson had no difficulty spotting Bob Tucker. About fifty-five, balding, stocky, and powerfully-built, Tucker wore khaki shirt and trousers and work boots. With patience and calm, he leaned on the hood of a new, somewhat banged up, Suburban the four-wheel-drive variety that were so common in the Rocky Mountain states. Tucker smiled and extended his hand as Thompson approached.

"Hi, Wade, Bob Tucker, very glad to make your acquaintance," he said with a simultaneous mighty handshake. Thompson compared his genuine sincerity with that of people who hung out at title company offices.

Thompson replied, "Thank you, Bob. I'm very glad to be here." He was. The air smelled clean and the sky was a sharp blue, not hazy blue from too many exhaust fumes.

Bob Tucker took Thompson's single piece of baggage and placed it on the folded rear seat that comprised the cargo area of the Suburban. It was littered with a couple of empty feed sacks, a partial roll of barbed wire, a saddle and other tack, and an abused, or at least well-used, Winchester lever-action carbine.

"So you've been a policeman for thirty years?" Bob Tucker asked in a way that indicated he had an interest in Thompson's past rather than making meaningless small talk.

Thompson smiled and replied, "Yeah, but it sounds as if you want to know more than that."

"I do. You spent most of your career working on the vice squad. You've probably seen things that regular people could never even imagine and I'm not just making reference to sex deviates and weirdoes. I'm talking about some of the world's most unfortunate and miserable people. That must have a terrific effect on you or anyone else who does that sort of work on a regular basis. Just something I pondered after I read your resume. I'm not trying to put you on the spot. If you care to comment, fine, if you don't, that's okay, too."

Virtually everyone who inquires about vice work wants to talk about their own self-perceived idea of a filthy job, one that requires dealing with perverts and otherwise crazy depraved souls on a daily basis. That is one depiction of vice work, and not an inaccurate one. Some people who have a curiosity about the work also have a prurient engrossment with the subject matter. It took Thompson a while to figure this out, but when he did, he had no interest in discussing vice work with them. Bob Tucker was one of the few who ever inquired about the work from a humanitarian standpoint.

Thompson replied, "You're not really putting me on the spot, Bob. Everyone else wants to know about the really foul stuff. People who have never been involved in law enforcement work may not realize this, but minus the oddities, vice work is police work. Period. In answer to what I guess was a question, yeah, it's affected me. It's affected everyone in the business of police work. What I don't know exactly is what those effects have been. We're venturing into some pretty deep philosophical territory here and I'm not sure I'm intelligent enough to continue," Thompson confessed.

"You've answered my question even if you feel you haven't," Tucker said, "and I thank you for that."

Thompson was glad that part of the conversation was over and asked, "How far to your place?"

"Oh, maybe three more miles. Our place is twelve miles from the Wardlaw airport. For some reason, everyone thinks we're much farther out in the wilderness," Tucker remarked.

What Thompson observed when Tucker stopped was not at all what he expected. In front of him was what he assumed was Bob Tucker's small home and / or office. To the rear of the structure was a barn and corral where several horses were penned. There were a number of other buildings on the property, including six large guest cabins. Apart from it all, perhaps a city block distant, was a huge restaurant. Another building joined the restaurant, but was only about half the size. Everything was constructed of logs. Thompson guessed the complex had been built in the 'fifties and professionally refurbished in the last few years. This place was not as Thompson had envisioned. It was not located on some desolate washboard gravel road that would make for hazardous wintertime travel. Instead, the entire complex, or what Thompson had seen of it, was on a paved state highway, and a heavily traveled one at that. Surely, Thompson thought, Bob Tucker did not maintain something like this with earnings from a hunting guide service.

"Wade, come on in and relax a bit," Tucker said as he opened his door on the Suburban, "and leave your bag for now, I'm not sure which room you'll be staying in."

Thompson became more impressed with the setup by the minute as he entered the two-story log building. The entire lower floor was a large open office area. Just to the right of the door was a rustic log staircase. In the very back was what appeared to be a small kitchen or break room. A substantial freestanding rock fireplace occupied the space in the very center of the office. A half-dozen heavy wooden captain's chairs were situated around the fireplace with small end tables separating the chairs. A very cozy office, Thompson thought.

Bob Tucker said, "Wade, make yourself at home. There's refreshments and snacks in the kitchen. I'm going to find the boss and we'll all hunker down and discuss your situation. Excuse me for a few minutes."

Thompson helped himself to a cold drink. He would have preferred a beer after the long trip but there were none in the refrigerator. He sat on a couch and picked up a magazine from the coffee table. Within moments, he was asleep. He had been sleeping fifteen minutes when someone nudged his shoulder several times. He was not fully awake and his eyes remained closed when he heard what he thought was a familiar voice but decided he was dreaming.

"Wade, Wade, time to wake up. I didn't go through this elaborate scheme getting you up here to watch you sleep," Jan Doxee said.

Thompson's level of consciousness reached the point where he became aware this was no dream. He knew Jan was standing next to him, but before he opened his eyes, he was realized how confused he was and wondered what she was doing in this part of the world.

Jan mildly punched Thompson in the shoulder with a clenched fist and said with impatience and a half-smile, "Wade, you can sleep tonight. Right now, we're going to talk."

Jan had an ear-to-ear grin as Thompson opened his eyes wide and asked, "Would someone kindly explain what is happening here?" Thompson said as he tried to refrain from smiling, but could not hide his feelings about being so pleasantly surprised.

Thompson noticed Bob Tucker standing a few feet behind Jan. The one-man audience was enjoying the scene unfolding before him. Then, Jan and Bob sat in chairs on the other side of the coffee table facing Thompson, who had remained seated through it all.

"Okay," Jan said, followed by a pause that indicated a momentary loss for words. She grasped for a place to start and said, "You weren't really brought here under false pretenses as you probably think. However, there were a few things you were not told and for good reason."

Thompson interrupted, "Jan, just spit it out, you've said nothing so far."

"Well, there's a lot to say and I don't want to leave anything out. It's important to me that you get a clear picture," she said.

In this instance, the woman was explaining in a manner no better than what he would do. It was irritating.

"This is my place. I bought it with my inheritance for practically nothing a long time ago. I've remodeled and restored, the restaurant does a tremendous business, and I have a small facility for meetings and seminars. I can keep the cabins rented year 'round if I want to. We're very close to major ski areas and we do a lot of tourist business most of the year. I hired Bob as a sort of general manager, my assistant. This is just too much for one person to handle. The place used to have a guide and hunting service and Bob worked here back then. We're going to start that up again, but only if you'll stay. I don't know the first thing about it, but I've got the money to put in it to make it a first-class operation, better than any in the area. Bob's already lined up a couple of large private ranches within thirty miles of here that I can lease for our clients' exclusive hunting rights. If you want to help out, I'll call the property owners today and pay the lease fee. We're running out of time, so I need your decision soon," Jan said.

"Talk about being put on the spot! I feel like I'd like to stay, but there are some things I have to know first."

Jan Doxee replied with an obvious note of seriousness, "I know there are and I'm prepared to explain to your satisfaction. I'm also going to tell you things that perhaps haven't crossed your mind yet. They will, however. I hope I can put you at ease regarding this place and what's going on here now as well as what happened here in the past."

Bob Tucker began to feel uncomfortable with the direction the conversation was headed and excused himself, saying he had work to do. He did have work, but neither Thompson nor Jan would have minded had he preferred to stay.

"Wade, the government just about cleaned me out. It surprised me that I had the cash to pay the IRS. Kind of funny in a way, kind of sad in a way, but I had more than forty bank accounts, all over. Some of them I must have opened when I was really smashed. I had cash in boxes in closets. There was almost a hundred thousand in a suitcase in a storage building. I had no recollection of putting it there. I can't believe I lived that way for such a long time. The government seized all those properties, some of them very valuable. Now, I have this place and two small strip shopping centers, across the street from one another, in a run-down part of Denver. I have less than $300,000 in cash. This business makes good money, so I'm not concerned where my next meal will come from. Even if I have to put a good bit of what's left of my cash into this hunting thing and it loses money for a year or two, that's okay if you'll stay," Jan said.

"Jan, I'm very interested in what you're telling me and I want you to continue. But on a lighter note, and to get off the subject for just a minute, my curiosity is getting the better of me. How did you pull off this scheme to get me here? Forsky had to be involved."

"I met him for lunch two weeks ago. He told me you were retiring and keeping it a big secret. He said you were selling your house, your soon-to-be-ex-wife had moved across the country, and he mentioned your plans for the future. I already had 'your' perfect place. I was homeless at the moment, like you are now, and it all just sort of came together. The hardest part was watching for your ad," she explained. "Bob Tucker really helped me out there. He'd probably be a good undercover man, don't you agree?"

"Yeah. Now go on with your story," Thompson said, smiling. The woman had duped him again, but he was not embarrassed this time.

"This place was a part, a very small part of the escort business. I had a lady who lived in and worked out of one of the cabins. On occasion we would send other girls here when businesses would have seminars and so forth and make a request. We had no need to solicit business. I was going to have to get rid of Lilly LaMarque anyway after you all hit the service. Lilly was stealing from me and had been for quite a while. I had already shut down the agency part before I hired Bob. Lilly had sporadically helped with running the restaurant, coordinating seminar bookings, the whole works. She had uncontrolled access to too much of the business. Bob and I went through the books after he got here and there were discrepancies amounting to more than seventy-five thousand dollars in the last two years. Maybe that's not a huge amount, but I couldn't keep a thief on the payroll," Jan remarked as she paused. She wanted him to say something.

"Okay, anything else?" Thompson asked.

"Yes. I want to emphasize that this entire operation is one hundred percent legitimate. Even when prostitution occurred here, profits from that were entirely separate from the righteous business that took place here. Wade, it's important to me that you understand this business was not financed or supported, even in part, from the proceeds of a prostitution enterprise. You can ask your federal friends if you like. They know more about this place than I do now."

"That was a big concern of mine and I appreciate you addressing the issue," Thompson said, quite satisfied with her explanation. Had he just spent a few minutes going over the paperwork provided to him by Oscar Rayburn and Joe Burrell, he would have known all about the restaurant, the cabins, and the mountain whorehouse. He never looked at it. Sensing his lack of interest in the entire affair, the federal agents had never mentioned it to him.

Jan smiled and asked, "Now, do you want to stay or not?"

"Give me a little time to think about it. What I'm not sure about is our relationship. It might be a bit awkward."

Jan replied, "It's always been awkward. You won't allow anyone to get close to you and that goes double for me since I'm a tainted lady. You know I haven't done any of that in years. I'm sober, I'm not depressed, and I'm a very different person than the one you knew for so long. I'm also a very attractive, intelligent, sensitive, and interesting woman. Some day, maybe you'll see that instead of trying to hang on to the past like you do. The past is not there, Wade. Someday you will realize that. If I'm still around when that happens, we'll go from there."

Thompson did not know how to respond, so he said nothing. He realized, however, that Jan Doxee's talent for explaining things in a clear manner had improved remarkably in the past few minutes. He knew where he stood in her plans for the future.

His silence signaled his agreement to Jan, and she said,

"Okay, then I'd like to start on this project right away. With all that's going on here, we are going to be very busy."

Thompson smiled.

∧∧∧∧∧∧∧∧∧∧∧